Praise for *The Vision of Emma Blau*

"Smoothly written . . . rife with life and death and magic realism in the sweeping-saga tradition of Gabriel García Márquez."
—Linton Weeks, *The Washington Post Book World*

"[Hegi] creates such a complex world around each of her characters that you can't help but admire her generosity toward them and wonder how so much could come from one writer's imagination. . . . A story told with great ambition."
—Anne Stephenson, *USA Today*

"There are deft, vigorous portraits in *The Vision of Emma Blau* and beautifully drawn moments of individual revelation."
—Marcie Hershman, *The Boston Globe*

"Hegi has a canny eye for the lingering effects of a German background on manners, furniture, and food, and also for the subtle resentments created by the family's cross-cultural heritage. This is a novel of wide range, richly interesting in both character and episode."
—Phoebe-Lou Adams, *The Atlantic Monthly*

"Absorbing . . . Hegi chronicles the course of this family with a compassion that's full to bursting and with a lyricism that's often achingly beautiful. . . . Vivid and startling."
—Susan C. Hegger, *St. Louis Post-Dispatch*

"Hegi is an old-fashioned storyteller, and her characters are deeply engaging."
—Ann Patchett, *Chicago Tribune*

"[Hegi] is a born storyteller. . . . The gradual assimilation into the melting pot of a family with roots in another country is a story that has been told many times before, but rarely with such distinction."
—Lorna Williams, *The Washington Times*

P9-DBY-405

OTHER BOOKS BY URSULA HEGI

———————■———————

TEARING THE SILENCE

SALT DANCERS

STONES FROM THE RIVER

FLOATING IN MY MOTHER'S PALM

UNEARNED PLEASURES AND OTHER STORIES

INTRUSIONS

The Vision
of
Emma Blau

———|———

Ursula Hegi

SCRIBNER PAPERBACK FICTION
PUBLISHED BY SIMON & SCHUSTER

New York London Toronto Sydney Singapore

SCRIBNER PAPERBACK FICTION
Simon & Schuster, Inc.
Rockefeller Center
1230 Avenue of the Americas
New York, NY 10020

Copyright © 2000 by Ursula Hegi

First Scribner Paperback Fiction edition 2001
Originally published in Canada in 2000 by HarperCollins Publishers Ltd.
SCRIBNER PAPERBACK FICTION and design are trademarks of Macmillan Library Reference
USA, Inc., used under license by Simon & Schuster, the publisher of this work.

Designed by Deborah Kerner

Manufactured in the United States of America

3   5   7   9   10   8   6   4   2

The Library of Congress has cataloged the Simon & Schuster edition as follows:
Hegi, Ursula.
The vision of Emma Blau / Ursula Hegi.
p. cm.
1. German Americans—New Hampshire—Fiction. 2. Immigrants— New Hampshire—
Fiction. 3. Women—New Hampshire—Fiction. I. Title.
PR9110.9.H43 V57 2000
823—dc21   99-056392

ISBN 0-684-82997-5
0-684-87273-0 (Pbk)

A C K N O W L E D G M E N T S

For their valuable insights and suggestions I thank Olivia Caulliez, Martha Copithorne, Gordon Gagliano, Mark Gompertz, Deb Harper, Gail Hochman, Kathryn Hunt, Lesa Luders, Marianne Merola, Carl Phillips, Rod Stackelberg, Sally Winkle, and Barbara Wright. I thank Eastern Washington University for grant support. In my research, I learned much from the works of Frederick Lewis Allen and Adair D. Mulligan.

For my grandmother
Gertrud Maas

The Vision of Emma Blau

CHAPTER ONE

1894–1909

It didn't look like the kind of house that would carry a curse. Built by a German immigrant of brick and dark timber, the *Wasserburg* was six stories tall with six apartments on each floor. In the small New Hampshire town that carried the name of the lake it bordered, the U-shaped building took up an entire block and stood high above the clapboard houses and the shoreline. It was the kind of structure you might expect to see in New York—with marble bathrooms and stained-glass inserts in the tall windows—and it was too flamboyant, the townspeople said, too conspicuous for this part of New England where dusk set early upon the vast lake that was flecked with hundreds of islands and that the Indians had named Winnipesaukee—Smile of the Great Spirit.

When Emma Blau was a child, her grandfather's *Wasserburg*—water fortress—was still splendid with carpet runners in the hallways, the design and colors of peacock feathers. Often Emma would pretend she walked on the tail feathers of an immense peacock *who sweeps himself with her into the air. She soars above the sand-colored trim at the roofline and the glazed blue tiles set into the facade; above the courtyard with its brick walks and the birdbath fountain; above the elevated garden with its swing set and flower beds where her German grandmother Helene is planting snapdragons and geraniums and camomile and pansies*—Stiefmütterchen—*an affectionate term for little stepmother, a role Helene had taken on for the children of her husband's dead wives.*

Ever since Emma's grandfather had brought her to the secret place where the house breathed, Emma had returned there alone, though it was a forbidden place where children might fall and get mangled by the green machines and wires that spun dust motes in the half-light. She'd steal the key to the roof door from behind the pewter cups in her grandparents' china cabinet, ride the elevator to the top floor, and slip into the brick structure that sat like an immense smokestack on the flat roof. As she'd climb the wooden ladder to the platform above the elevator, the breath of the house would raise the fine hairs on her arms with a *whoosh,* and she'd laugh with delight. Steady puffs of warm breath emanated from a wheel that turned to the left. Wound around this wheel was a chain—similar to the one on Emma's bicycle—that ran up to an oval loop and connected to moving rods that clicked and hummed in an always changing song. Whenever the elevator stopped, she'd feel a shudder rise from the shaft as if the building were stirring itself awake.

Emma knew the house from within and from above: she had crawled into its guts, played behind the boiler in the vaulted furnace room, climbed out of the second-floor window onto the curved balcony above the entrance, and balanced on the edge of the roof far above the town. Sometimes she felt she *was* the center of the house, breathing its breath-song, while other times the house was at the center of her like a pulse that warmed her as she held it safe within her body.

∽

Her grandfather, Stefan Blau, was only thirteen when he ran away from his hometown in Germany one rainy November night in 1894. Convinced he lived in the most fascinating time possible—an age of transformation and discovery—he'd felt restless in Burgdorf. Too many traditions. Too many restrictions. America, he believed, was the country where people brought about changes instead of resisting them. But his parents didn't want to listen when he read to them about immigrants earning fortunes, about inventions, about gold in the hills; they didn't know that America had grafted itself to his mind so tenaciously that he had dreams of it every single night, dreams of an odd and magnificent landscape that fused what he had culled from various books, a landscape inhabited by buffaloes and by buildings so tall they pierced the clouds.

When Stefan bought an English dictionary and memorized forty new words each day, his parents shook their heads and told him they were not about to leave Germany, and when he suggested he'd make the passage alone and send for them and his sister once he'd made his fortune, they smiled. "What a child he still is," they said to each other.

They were asleep when he left.

Although short for his age, he was sturdy and talked his way into work on a coal barge that floated north on the Rhein past Oberhausen and Xanten into Holland, where the river split into two tributaries that swirled into the North Sea. The language of the Dutch—even more guttural than his native German—sounded harsh to Stefan. When he reached Rotterdam and was unable to trade labor for passage to America, he started toward Amsterdam and walked through cold nights and days, resting in barns or churches only when he was too chilled and exhausted to keep moving. But he never lost his enthusiasm because with each step— so he reminded himself—he was getting closer to America. Besides, people helped him along the way as if to make certain that he'd really get there: a bald priest gave him woolen earmuffs that some other boy had forgotten in the confessional, and a farm woman fed him *Schwarzbrot* with *Blutwurst*—black bread with blood sausage—and packed him enough for a second meal to take along in his wooden toolbox that already contained his clothes and books.

It was sleeting the afternoon he got to Amsterdam, but he felt lucky because before nightfall he was hired as a kitchen hand on a passenger ship bound for New York. So what if he wasn't sixteen as he had claimed to be? What if he hadn't worked on river barges for two years? Things only became a lie if you couldn't follow them through. Someday he would be sixteen, and as long as he could do the work he was hired to do—and do it well—it was his to decide what he told others about himself. Besides, he could pass for sixteen. He had more hair on his body than most sixteen year olds. Especially on his back. Black and soft and curly like the hair on his

father's back. Though not as thick. Not yet. "You can recognize a
Blau by his back," his father liked to say. "Regular pelts. If you line
up a hundred men, their backs to me, I'll pick out the one who's a
Blau anytime." His father's hair covered his back and shoulders
and ran down his arms to his knuckles like sleeves that were too
long. "All Blau men shave before they're fourteen," he had told
Stefan when he was just three, making him look forward to that
day when he, too, would lather his face and scrape off the foam
with a *Rasiermesser.*

One dawn at sea Stefan awoke early and couldn't get back to
sleep because he started thinking about the good jacket his father
had sewn for him in his tailor shop, and how it must have hurt his
parents that he hadn't taken it along. He worried more about that
jacket than about the note he'd left for his parents, telling them he
was going to America, and it wouldn't be until he was a father and
his own son, Tobias, would run from him in anger, that he'd begin
to understand how his leaving must have devastated his parents.

Once he thought about the jacket, he remembered other items
he'd left behind, especially the telescope his mother had given him
for his seventh birthday. She'd set it up for him by the kitchen window next to the larger telescope that used to belong to her grandfather whose name had also been Stefan. His mother knew
everything about stars and planets because her grandfather had
shown her how to draw star charts when she was a girl. "You can
inherit interests the same way you inherit money," she'd told Stefan
and his sister, Margret, and she'd taught them about the stars long
before they'd learned the alphabet. Stefan had understood quickly
that each star rose and set four minutes earlier every night. In one
month that made a two-hour difference, and in a year it came to
twenty-four hours. Lying in the grass behind their house, his
mother would rest her head on the broad flank of their dog, Spitz,
and point toward the sky, the white of her arm linking earth and
the stars in one luminous arc. Sometimes he'd have to stare hard
because all he'd see were the brightest stars, and it would take minutes for the others to emerge, although—so his mother assured
him—they'd been there all along.

Whenever she talked about stars, she got so excited that she seemed more like a sister to him than the mother who powdered her face and made the crispiest *Reibekuchen*—potato pancakes—in Burgdorf. Eyes flickering with anticipation, she would unroll her linen star charts or sketch a swift pattern of chalk stars on Margret's blackboard, urging both children to guess which constellations they formed. At first they made mistakes, connecting the wrong stars or leaving out lines that should have been there. Soon Margret became bored, but Stefan was determined to get it right, and by the time he was nine, he knew how to figure out which stars were in the sky any night of the year. "Well done," his mother would say. Stefan was glad he didn't have an old mother: she was younger than the other mothers in town—only fifteen when his sister was born, barely seventeen at his own birth. That meant she would live for a long time. He'd remind himself of that whenever he became afraid of her dying before him, leaving him.

And now she doesn't even know where I am.

To escape his uneasiness and the stale air of the sailors' quarters, Stefan climbed the stairs to the promenade deck, bracing against the icy fog. All sky was as gray as the sea, blurring the horizon. In the last few days he'd seen whales and flying fish, waves as tall as his parents' house, but now the gray made everything seem flat, though he could feel the ship heaving in the waves. There was not a single star. No moon—not even an orange sliver of moon—and yet it came to him, then, *that orange moon in a sky so clear you can make out even the faintest stars. The air is still warm—tinged with the scent of the last lilacs. High above stands Vega, bluish-white, part of the Lyra constellation. It's easier to connect imaginary lines to her stars than to Hercules' whose stars don't shine as much and spread over a larger area. His mother reaches toward the sky, snags it with her right forefinger that's been crooked since birth, and pulls the sky down, down till he can touch it too. Velvet and night. All his and smooth. "Can you see Pegasus?" his mother asks. When he says, "yes," she tells him and Margret the story of the winged horse that carried Perseus and Andromeda to safety. From the taller grass by the brook comes the croaking of frogs—*

Not frogs. No. A different sound. Thin and long. Then silence again. Stefan glanced around. There, next to the stack of canvas chairs lay a seagull. It looked dead, one eye clouded over; but when he picked it up by one leg to fling it overboard, it flapped its wings and he could see that much of its back had been torn out. Stunned by the sudden awareness that it was dying alone—*now, as one day I too will have to die alone*—Stefan supported the bird with both hands, trying to make it more comfortable. It let out a frail screech. Then another. He lowered it to the planks. Backed away, knowing it would be best to kill it. *Kill it swiftly. Now. Release it from its suffering.* If he tossed it into the sea, he wouldn't have to look at it, wouldn't have to think about it. But he couldn't. Knew that he couldn't. He winced at the thought of crushing its head with his foot. Yet to let it live would be even more cruel. *A slab of wood. Lay it on top of the bird. Step on it. Step on it hard.* He ran off to find something. In the passenger lounge five chessboards were stacked on a shelf. He took one. Started for the door. But then sat down instead and rubbed his palms across the smooth-grained wood. *Who wins?* He thought of not going back. Of letting someone else find the bird. *Because it isn't me who's done it, the hurting. And so it isn't mine to decide what to do about it and then live with that. With that.* Yet already he was out there again in the fog, ready to lower the chessboard on the seagull and step on it.

But it had died.

Had died without him, and he felt weak with relief. Sorrow.

∽

In lower Manhattan, he found work in an elegant French restaurant, where he peeled vegetables and washed dishes with the same eagerness that he would, years later, bring to his own restaurant. Only the owner was French; the rest of the staff were foreigners from other parts of Europe, who gesticulated and shouted scraps of Italian, Yiddish, Hungarian, German, and fractured English across the three long stoves in the center of the well-stocked kitchen. Not all had come to America as willingly as Stefan: some had fled from religion; others from family or war; but what kept each of them here was hope.

Being part of his new country would never be quite as total for Stefan as when he first arrived and wanted to be American in every way possible. How he loved the lack of convention, the instant familiarity. Here, respect had nothing to do with age but was earned with success. Class differences—that complicated ladder of human worth he'd grown up with—did not exist in America, he believed, and it would take him years to grasp the many subtle shadings of prejudice.

One day as he walked to work along West Street past vendors' carts and people on bicycles and horses pulling delivery wagons, he felt protected from the raw wind in his American coat and bowler hat, and it struck him that no one could tell he was a foreigner. As long as he did not speak and reveal his accent, he blended in like everyone else. He breathed it in, that certainty of belonging, held it in his body with deep exhilaration.

From the head chef, Tibor Szilagi, a Hungarian with a slight limp and a contagious laugh, Stefan learned about passion for food and its preparation. He enjoyed the work, the effort of it, the results. Liked the scents of grilled meats and sautéed vegetables. His eagerness soon earned him the job of kitchen assistant, as well as an invitation to the poker games that the Hungarian organized in his apartment on Gansevoort Street in the early morning hours. Curtains drawn, a group of tired men—policemen just off duty and others from the restaurant business—would gather around the table that was covered with one of the embroidered linen cloths the Hungarian's maiden aunts sent him for his birthdays. To revive his guests, Tibor would serve thick coffee with whiskey in porcelain cups, and when he'd push Stefan's winnings toward him, he'd accuse him of being far too lucky.

"It's because you don't have the fever of gambling in your soul yet," he told him one morning and winked at him.

"Not now. Not ever."

"It's a fine lover."

"Not for me."

"Always hot and never gets enough of you." Tibor Szilagi crushed half a cinnamon stick, mixed the tiny splinters into a handful of tobacco, and began to roll his special cigarettes. "It'll get you too."

Stefan smiled and shook his head.

"At least use your money. Travel. There's a lake you would like, I swear. I've only seen it once, but it reminded me of Germany.

Trees and mountains and so much water that you can never see all of the lake at one time."

"Where is it?"

"New Hampshire. I took the train there my second summer in America. To a town with the same name as the lake. Winnipesaukee."

But Stefan didn't have time to travel. And he was far more interested in studying French recipes and checking the newspaper for yet another success story of immigrants. His new language was filling in around him, and he liked being able to read some sentences without looking up one single word.

"You should get some reporter to write up your story," he told Tibor one evening in the kitchen. "It's better than most I see in the paper."

"And who would wish to know about me, please?"

"Lots of people." Stefan liked hearing the story of how the Hungarian had come to America. Lame with polio since he was eight, he'd been unable to help on the family farm. His parents approved when he worked in the kitchens of married women, but when he was hired as cook in a bordello, his mother and her three unmarried sisters conspired to save his soul by hauling him to the priest for absolution and then bribing him with passage to America. After Tibor said farewell to his father, his mother and the aunts traveled with him on the train to Rijeka, where they hired a carriage and took him to the ship that would carry him south around the heel of Italy, west through the Strait of Gibraltar where monkeys lived in the crevices of high rocks, and then further west toward America.

"Lots of people would want to read about your miraculous recovery," Stefan said. "How you hobbled up that gangway. And how, when you got here, you stepped off with just a shadow of a limp. And how it has been like that ever since."

"And how this and how that . . ." Tibor Szilagi's laugh got two of the waiters laughing.

"But it is true," Stefan insisted.

The Hungarian removed a speck of cinnamon from his front teeth, inspected it, and flicked it off his thumb. "The limp might have gotten better anyhow."

"No. It's coming to America that did it."

"Some fellows have to see meaning in everything."

"Because there is."

"Ah, Stefan . . ."

From the Hungarian, Stefan learned to decode their employer's moods as well as his favorite sayings. The Frenchman considered English a crude language and spoke it as seldom as possible, antagonizing the delivery men by pretending to understand less than he could. *"C'est comme pisser dans un violon"*—"It's like pissing into a violin"—meant that whatever you were about to do would make no difference. Though extravagant by nature, the Frenchman would occasionally search for evidence of waste, stalking through the kitchen with its copper pots and painted serving platters, through the dining room with its marble fireplaces and stained-glass windows; yet, that same evening he might send you home with half a bottle of wine or a ticket to the opera. He'd urge you to buy American stocks—railroad and mining and telephone—while warning you not to make big plans based on shaky optimism: *"Ne batissez pas des châteaux en Suede"*—"Don't go building castles in Sweden."

He liked to remind Stefan that he could afford to rent a better place, but Stefan was content in his room on Cornelia Street. It was small and on the top floor of the same boarding house where—during his first few months in the city—he had paid fifty-five cents a week to sleep on the chairs and sofas in the parlor with three men from Italy. At least this room was his alone, even if the windows were painted shut and he had to share the water closet down the hall with the Austrian family who lived in the room next to his. The building was better maintained than most on the block that had paint peeling from their doors and water standing in their cellars.

By keeping his rent low, he could invest most of his wages and poker winnings, except for the money he used to send presents to his family. He also mailed letters to his sister's best friend, Helene Montag, who lived next door to his family and had started to write to him. Occasionally their letters crossed, a current of words—more than they had ever spoken to one another. While his family wrote to him about events that happened in Burgdorf—weddings and births and funerals—Helene's letters kept the texture of his hometown alive for him: high-water marks that the Rhein left on the inner slope of the dike; early frost that turned the hill by the chapel silver gray; willows arching with the weight of first leaves.

As Stefan worked next to the chefs at the wooden counters, he volunteered for chores that carried greater responsibility. He began to smoke. Grew a mustache that met his thick sideburns and made him look more like a man. He had enormous energy. Thrived on hard work. By the time the new century began, he was nineteen and wore one of the starched white jackets that set the chefs apart. It was what he had wanted, and he felt as proud of his achievement as he did of the wanting. Because it was the wanting, he knew, that had brought him across the ocean. To this city. To being a chef. Pastries were his specialty: delicate concoctions of layered dough with creams and fruits and chocolate curls. Though his German accent would always tinge his English, he developed a flawless pronunciation of French words that related to food.

One July evening, as the Hungarian poured cognac over medallions of veal, a slender flame licked his wrist. *"Az istenit,"* he cursed and dropped the bottle on the stove where it shattered. The cognac ignited as it raced across the hot surface into a pan of sizzling beignets and from there through a basket with stained aprons and towels. After the fire leapt up the exhaust shaft, it twined itself through the dining room and an adjoining store, killing five women and four men, among them Tibor Szilagi who died while Stefan carried him into the street. Stefan knew the moment of his friend's death because the body felt suddenly limp and heavier. It seemed that without breath—breath that usually smelled of cinnamon and tobacco—Tibor's flesh could no longer sustain itself. The smell of burned hair and of burned flesh blotted out all else, blotted out all cinnamon, all tobacco, blotted out the starch-smell of table linen and flowers and cognac and freshly ground pepper; and what was most horrid about that smell of fire and flesh was how familiar it was, evoking the smell of chicken being grilled—*or pork rather? don't think about it don't*—just when the heat gets high enough to release its smell.

The clamor of fire bells burst through the smell, the screams, through night that was brighter and hotter than noon as horse-drawn fire engines pulled up, brakes screeching. When Stefan hoisted the Hungarian's weight higher, rocking him up, up in his arms, he felt Tibor's face dry and hot against the side of his neck, felt it slide and, for the instant of that motion, let himself hope his friend was still alive, though he knew it was Tibor's skin coming off against his neck.

After the flames had been extinguished and the bodies taken away, Stefan peeled off what was left of his white jacket and staggered home. His hands were blistered, and all hair was gone from his arms. Though his room was warm and stuffy, he was shivering as he crawled between the sheets in his scorched clothes. He slept, only to wake sobbing from dreams in which he was enveloped by fire and the familiar stench of burning flesh, dreams that got jumbled with memories of being small and soiling the kitchen floor with cow manure he'd dragged home on the bottom of his shoes, and his father—"How often do I have to tell you to wipe your feet?"—carrying him to the barrel of rainwater out back and then being inside that barrel—*headfirst and cold and not breathing because how could you?*—and afterwards the fever, hands like wicks of candles and yearning to cool them in the barrel that's no longer there.

When Stefan finally got up, a sticky, clear-yellow fluid was seeping from his arms and hands. It hurt to wash himself, to chew a piece of rye bread, to think of the Hungarian on whose sofa he'd often dozed after a poker game. He wished he could open his window. As he stared at the ashen wall of cinder blocks across the alley, even the light that leaked into the alley was ashen. *Ash. Used up by fire.* All at once Stefan was taken by such a powerful longing that his throat felt raw, a longing for air and clear light and his parents and the Hungarian's laugh and his hometown and family's dog, Spitz, and the French restaurant—but most of all for himself as a boy. And it was then that he remembered Tibor Szilagi telling him about the lake that reminded him of Germany.

∞

The smooth skin on Stefan's arms felt stretched as he rowed a wooden boat out on Lake Winnipesaukee, and as the oars spooned the water and left swirls that trailed behind him, he thought of the whirlpools in the Rhein where it flowed past the meadows of Burgdorf. From the boat, the stone gables of the church looked like St. Martin's where he'd gone to mass every Sunday as a boy, but beyond the outline of this town rose mountains, unfamiliar and stark. Tibor had been right: this lake was too large to see all at once. Wherever Stefan looked, his eyes came up against land: peninsulas and islands and the curving shoreline—the promise of water around each turn.

He glanced back toward the dock where he'd rented his boat and toward the vacant clapboard house next to it. On the other side of the dock grew a cornfield, and all at once, within the shimmer of summer air, he saw the farm where he'd played as a boy, the *Sternburg*—star fortress—a castle for centuries until it was turned into a farm. With his friends Michel Abramowitz and Kurt Heidenreich he'd swung from the chains beneath its drawbridge, played hiding games in the stone tower. In that instant, as the water between him and the shore became the moat of his childhood, he saw the house he would build in the cornfield, *a tall apartment house with pillars and a flat roof . . . a substantial but graceful building with a courtyard . . . rooms with high ceilings . . . windows that gleamed in the light. . . .* He could even see the reflection of his house and understood how water retains the memory of all that is reflected in its surface, takes it and holds it in its depth, and that the deeper the water, the more it can retain, including your vision, and mirror it back to you. *Wasserburg,* he decided to call the house. Water fortress. And he would build it with bricks the way they built houses in Germany, not of wood like so many American buildings. Deep within his chest something settled—solid and calm—and he knew he would not return to New York.

As he rowed back toward shore, he could already see *marble fireplaces as wide as the ones in the Frenchman's restaurant, fulllength beveled mirrors, a carpeted elevator with a brass gate that pulls apart like an accordion. . . .* Raising his face into the moist wind, he felt the breath of the lake on his skin as it rushed past him like fire. *Not here, fire. Fire wouldn't live this close to water.* He shook himself. *Saw wrought-iron wall sconces in the hallways of his house, tiled windowsills wide enough for flowerpots.* It didn't occur to him to wonder where the money would come from—all he felt was a wild confidence that, in time, he would build this house just as he saw it now. Because he wanted it. Had he known how the *Wasserburg* would seduce and corrupt him and his family, Stefan Blau would have taken the train back to New York that day, but to detect rot is often impossible in its early stages: it starts beneath lush surfaces, spreading its sweet-nasty pulp, tainting memories and convictions. It entangles. Justifies. But what Stefan saw that summer afternoon was only the splendor of the *Wasserburg* as it would be the day he would finish its construction.

And he saw more—*a small, stocky girl in a black dress whirling through the courtyard as if she were dancing or, perhaps, throwing a tantrum. Her skirt fans around her, and as her arms move in a windmill pattern, white-blonde hair flies around her face and shoulders. Graceful and robust, she spins around a fountain, face bursting through her hair only for flashes as if she were sculpting her own features that moment.* The boat swayed as Stefan stood up, one hand raised toward the shore to touch this child. He would search for her face in his daughters, but it wouldn't be until his granddaughter Emma was born that he would recognize the girl he had seen from the boat.

∽

With his poker money he rented the clapboard house by the lake and installed a used stove in the kitchen. In one of the upstairs rooms he set up a cot and a dresser for himself. He sold his stocks to buy good china and tablecloths, but saved on pots and other items that his customers wouldn't see by bidding for them at auctions. After he built tile counters, he hired a waiter and opened a small restaurant, a French restaurant of course, much appreciated by the French-Canadians in Winnipesaukee. But most of the towns-people asked him why he wasn't running a German restaurant. And the name, they said, was hard to remember—*Cadeau du Lac*—even after he told them it meant Gift of the Lake. Why couldn't he just call it that? Besides, it was too fancy, they complained, too expensive. They'd speculate about where he got his money because he used it so easily—his own as well as theirs—yet, they'd arrive in their Sunday clothes to test the food at the *Cadeau du Lac,* and they'd go home with tales of Stefan's oyster *soufflé,* his *cassoulet,* his *crêpes au chocolat.*

Still, they didn't think his restaurant would last. After all, ordinary people didn't spend their money eating out. Yet, they'd return with their friends, with relatives. It turned out that the tourists were his best customers, already in the mood to spend from the moment they arrived on the Boston and Maine Railroad in their city clothes and loaded their fishing rods and beach umbrellas and sand pails and dogs and croquet sets into the horse-drawn cabs that would take them from the station to the hotels, the small cottages along the lake, or to the marina from where they could get a boat to the islands. Though most of the cottages were small, others were more substantial with lawns and porches and docks. A few even had boathouses or floating gazebos.

New Hampshire was not at all the way Stefan had imagined America back in Germany. No tall buildings like those in New York. No buffaloes. It reminded him much more of Germany with its small towns, except that forests here were denser, mountains higher, and the lake larger than any he'd seen before. Stone walls, flecked with lichen and moss, fenced in cattle and sheep. Some of the farmers in town liked to say their land grew rocks. After clearing their fields and meadows, they could always expect to find more rocks in the spring when the ground, upon thawing, heaved them to the surface as if giving birth to them. Early crop, the farmers called these rocks, and they'd pile them on the low stone walls that marked their boundaries. Building these walls continued every year and was hard work, as hard as bringing ice in from the lake. His first winter in Winnipesaukee, Stefan learned to cut slabs of ice from the lake, drag them to shore on a sled, and store them beneath layers of sawdust in the icehouse that was built into the earth against the side of the foundation.

By April, the hair on his arms finally began to grow again, though not black and curly as it had been, but reddish as though it held the memory of fire, and it would never grow beyond a stubble that felt coarse to the touch. In May he offered to buy the building from its owner, a widow in her eighties who still had all her teeth, and when she refused to sell, he purchased a porcelain statue of St. Joseph, about a foot tall with a brown porcelain coat and a patient smile that suggested eternal waiting. It was night when Stefan dug a hole into the hard earth next to the front steps of his restaurant, lowered the saint headfirst into the ground, and packed the hole with dirt. That's how the nuns back home had come to own the land for their convent.

"Nuns can get any land they want," his mother had told him when he was a small boy. "All they do is bury St. Joseph upside down."

"Why?" Sitting on the edge of the table, he watched her as she kneaded dough, her forehead moist with sweat, a smudge of flour on her chin. She believed things were safest in the earth. She even had a burying box for her silverware—tin lined with wood—that she'd dig up for special occasions and then bury again behind their house as though it might grow roots and flourish. Multiply. But he'd never seen nuns bury anything. "Why?" he asked again.

"Because St. Joseph is known for his patience," his mother said.

"But why upside down?"

"Because then the saint is uncomfortable and wants to work his way out." As she leaned into the dough, her fists sank into the pale mound, folding it over, punching it down. "Once the nuns have their land, they make sure to dig St. Joseph back up again. Because he keeps working as long as he's in the ground. You see, if you forget to take St. Joseph out, the land keeps going to new owners."

His mother was more superstitious than anyone Stefan knew: scratches stopped hurting if you blew on them and then sang, "*Heile heile Segen, morgen gibt es Regen . . .*"—"Heal heal, blessings, tomorrow there'll be rain . . ."; white spots beneath your fingernails revealed how many mortal sins you had committed; the small crab inside her amber necklace protected her from spider bites; and her favorite saying, "*wer sich das Zeug am Leibe flickt, der hat den ganzen Tag nicht Glück,*" meant that if you darned your clothes while you still wore them, you wouldn't have luck that entire day.

Small towns fostered superstitions. And yet, ironically, after crossing an ocean, Stefan had ended up in another small town with its own superstitions: if a bridegroom dropped the ring, it meant bad luck; if you had a cold, you should rub your feet with butter; if you bit your baby's fingernails, it wouldn't become a thief.

But it felt familiar to live in a town where, soon, he knew almost everyone: Frank Weber who owned the hardware store; Father Albin who placed the communion wafer on his tongue every Sunday; Clem Weeks who had his cigar stand on Main Street; Lucie Magill who'd just opened a store called Magill's Fine Clothing; Jules Margaux, the lamplighter, who came down Main Street at dusk with his ladder to turn on the gas streetlights. Stefan wrote to Helene that he enjoyed walking through town and having people greet him by name, enjoyed welcoming them into his restaurant, which was already known for the finest meals around the lake.

Within a year, he dug up his St. Joseph and rinsed him off in soapy water because his landlady was moving to Boston to marry a coffin maker young enough to be her grandson, and she was eager to sell her building, along with the cornfield, for a price Stefan could afford. Some days he worked sixteen hours. He expanded his kitchen. Hired two more waiters. An assistant cook. A kitchen helper. By adding an enclosed porch that overhung the water, he doubled his seating capacity and gave his guests the illusion of floating above the lake. He liked to make decisions on his hunch of things to come. That was the American way, he explained to Helene Montag in a letter, to plan beyond the obvious. He wrote to her about becoming an American citizen. About the satisfaction of accomplishing something that you first just see in your mind and then make real by doing it.

To honor the porcelain saint, Stefan built him a shelf in the lobby, and when he climbed on the old piano bench he'd set beneath it and positioned the statue on the shelf so that St. Joseph could see everyone who entered the restaurant, he thought he heard the voice of the Hungarian. *"You're far too lucky."* Stefan spun toward the door. But he was alone, except for a hint of cinnamon and tobacco in the air and the Hungarian's infectious laugh. *". . . far too lucky."*

The winter he was twenty-four, he married his first wife, Elizabeth Flynn, a flutist with delicate wrists whose pale hair covered her entire pillow at night. Though she'd never kissed a man before him, her fingernails were speckled with mortal sins and were so thin that they seemed transparent.

Stefan adored her small, bony face. Adored her extreme shyness that kept her from talking to people. Even adored the tenacity that replaced the shyness once she knew you well. When he built a fire escape and tiled the upstairs floors to block any flames that might start in the restaurant, Elizabeth decided she'd learn how to paper their walls. Though her parents objected, she stripped the bedroom walls by herself, covering them with bottle-green paper that was scattered with white roses—the same pattern she'd had in her childhood room. Since her fingernails kept breaking as she worked, she trimmed them close to the tips of her fingers. In the evenings guests in the restaurant would hear the haunting sound of her flute above them.

What Stefan did not adore about her was her mischievousness. She liked to hide things when he wasn't looking: his toothbrush or his coffee cup or his slippers. She'd laugh, make him search, even though he'd grow irritated. "It's childish," he'd tell her and stalk off to his restaurant. Only to come home and find that she'd knotted the bottoms of his pajamas.

They used some of her dowry to order a birch armoire, bed, and two nighttables from a South German carpenter in Wolfeboro on the other side of the lake. Most afternoons Stefan would slip from the kitchen for a while, and they'd tumble onto their mattress and sink into the feather quilt, laughing as he'd peel her out of her petticoat and corset cover. Still, even here, he would stay aware of what needed to be done next in his restaurant—*dice carrots, marinate veal, sauté mushrooms, order sugar and olives*—while below them in the kitchen, his assistant cook and kitchen helper would stare at the ceiling, placing bets on how long the thudding of the bed would last.

"I'm so glad we met here in America," he told her one evening.

In the light from the oil lamp, she ran one thumb around his ears, down the frown lines between his thick eyebrows. "Tell me why."

"Because in Germany the president of a bank would never allow his daughter to marry the son of a tailor."

"Fuck him then."

"Don't say that."

But she liked to shock him by talking dirty, and it astounded him when she told him she'd gotten that way in college. "Women alone, locked away in a school . . . you'd be surprised what we talk about."

That lewd side of hers made him feel he was guarding a secret whenever they were in public, and he'd wish for her shyness to come back. Still, knowing what she might say was exciting. Troubling. Certainly her parents didn't know that side of her. They were polite. Formal. Sitting across from Elizabeth at her parents' cherrywood dining table, Stefan would compliment her mother on how she'd decorated the ceiling fan with silk flowers, say, or with vines, while all along he'd be afraid his wife would say something vulgar, and that her parents would blame his influence on her.

He knew it meant entirely too much to him to be accepted by a wealthy family like hers, and that embarrassed him because it was so . . . German. He was in America now. Where everyone was equal. What embarrassed him too was that he couldn't stop feeling proud when on Sundays after church, his in-laws would stroll with him and Elizabeth along the lake, his wife's shoulders at the same height as his, her gloved hand floating in the bend of his arm, her Persian lamb coat with its seal collar shielding her from the cold. And if he sometimes felt irritated because Elizabeth would correct his pronunciation, even in bed, he would tell himself that it was to his advantage to shed his accent and sound like an educated man.

∞

As soon as Elizabeth discovered she was pregnant, she urged Stefan to borrow money from her father's bank to build his apartment house in the cornfield.

But Stefan was reluctant. "I figured on waiting until I'd saved enough from the restaurant."

"That could take ten years," she persisted.

Every evening she talked about it.

Every morning.

"That's what banks are for," she'd remind him.

It was her father who summoned Stefan to his bank and took him into his office, a suite of three rooms divided by velvet drapes that were tied open with silk tassels. "Sit," Hardy Flynn said, "sit," his voice high and impatient as he pointed Stefan toward an overstuffed leather chair, smooth and golden-brown.

The color of wealth. Stefan sat down, knowing that one day he would buy a leather chair for himself in that color.

Hardy Flynn remained standing. His gray beard looked out of place in his pink, unlined face. "Take one of these." He extended a silver box with cigars, lit one for himself, then Stefan's. "A personal loan. That's how I want to do it. Without interest, of course."

"That wouldn't be right."

"What's not right about me helping my daughter get ahead?" The banker stroked the forked ends of his beard. "What's not right about you wanting the same for her?"

"I—"

"Elizabeth should not have to fill the lamps. She should not have to live in rooms full of cooking smells from your restaurant."

"I didn't know that bothered her."

The banker crossed his arms in front of his wide chest. "Elizabeth is used to certain . . . comforts in her life."

"Which I will provide for her." The moment Stefan said it, he could see his wife's broken fingernails and felt ashamed. Felt a sudden rage at the banker for knowing about the broken fingernails *and* his shame.

"Let me explain something to you. Money I give to the church has nothing to do with the church."

"I don't understand."

"It has everything to do with what my wife needs. Lelia enjoys visiting with the priest—investigating her soul, Father Albin calls it—and he is generous with his time when it comes to the wealthy wives of this town."

The back of Stefan's neck felt itchy, his starched collar too tight. There was too much of everything in the banker's office, the banker's house. It all only emphasized the gap between Elizabeth and himself.

"With a loan from me, you can provide what my daughter needs much sooner than you can on your own. I want you to think about my offer. Both your names on the deeds—for the house and the restaurant. With right of survivorship."

To get away, Stefan promised, "I will think about it. A very generous offer," he added on his way to the door.

But when he told Elizabeth, she misunderstood and assumed he had already accepted. She was so delighted that he felt miserable telling her about his misgivings.

"Misgivings?" She stared at him. "About what?"

"About borrowing money from your father."

"But he offered."

"I know. And it makes me feel selfish, expecting you to live above the restaurant. Especially now that you'll have a child."

"It should make you feel selfish . . . damn selfish."

"I feel pushed. By you and your father."

"You are."

"I think of you wallpapering by yourself and—"

"I wasn't pregnant then." She grasped him by the arms. "Can't we just celebrate? The loan and the baby?"

When he finally agreed, she bought him a present, a green rowboat. He found reasons not to use it: he was too busy; he was tired; the weather was not right. But by summer—the only summer the two of them would have together—she was taking him for moonlight outings on the lake. She'd line the bottom of the boat with pillows and bring a thermos filled with hot chocolate. As he'd point out the pattern of stars for her, they'd sit with their backs against one ːdˑ of the boat, feet dangling across the other side.

Now tʰ² an architect was drawing up blueprints of the building with its thirty-six apartments, Stefan was glad he didn't have to wait any longer, and it gave him pleasure to listen to his wife plan their own apartment on the sixth floor. The largest in the house, it was to take up one entire side of the U-shaped structure, with the living room and kitchen facing the lake. Elizabeth knew exactly what she was going to buy and described everything to him in vivid detail as if she were already living in those rooms with velvet sofas and chairs, white china with a border of golden leaves, painted wicker baskets with asparagus ferns. But while the windows in her parents' house were covered with lace curtains and brocade drapes, she planned to keep hers bare, their only backdrop the sky and mountains.

Those nights on the lake had a timelessness about them, infusing Stefan with a feeling of being totally at home, more certain than ever that he'd been meant to leave Burgdorf and come to this very place, and when he would remember those nights as an old man, they would seem to fill years of his life.

By November, when the workmen had erected the massive foundation, Elizabeth lay in a hard-breathing labor that took hold of her for forty-one hours and seized her life as her child pushed through her flesh. While the midwife, Mrs. West, pried the infant's head and shoulders from its cooling grave, Stefan shook Elizabeth's arm and cried out her name as though he believed he could jolt her back into life.

"Like a crazy man," the midwife told Mr. Heflin when she bought salt and molasses from him the day before Elizabeth's burial. "Stefan Blau shoved me from the room as soon as his wife was dead. Told me to never come back."

"Like a crazy man," Mr. Heflin told his sister-in-law who, in turn, repeated those words to others who climbed the path to the cemetery where Stefan stood with the infant pressed against his chest, though several of the women would have liked to relieve him of that burden.

The cemetery lay right at the edge of town on a plateau from where you could see most of the houses and, beyond them, the lake and white-capped mountains. A path with deep ruts—the outer ones from carriage wheels, the center rut from hooves—stopped about five hundred feet from the cemetery. There, you would leave your carriages and carry the coffins the final stretch, which was so steep that the old people of Winnipesaukee quite often didn't make it up here for funerals of their family and friends. It was said that once you were very old, the one way to get up to the cemetery was if you were to die and get carried.

Between and around the graves, a lot of the pines and birches had been cleared, and those that were left had moss hanging from their lower branches as if they were weeping. From a distance, these long, greenish strands looked airy and soft and swayed with the slightest wind; but if you happened to walk into one, it would feel coarse against your face, and you'd notice bits of bark woven into the moss along with specks of dust that looked like fleas.

Since winters were so cold that you couldn't bury the bodies deeply enough in the frozen ground, all of the graves had stones piled on them to prevent animals from digging. Come spring, white flowers would sprout from between those stones, but at Elizabeth Blau's funeral the only flowers were wooden tulips, three yellow and three red, that stuck in the mound of stones on the Heflins' family plot. These stones had partly sunk into the earth, the smaller ones in the middle and the larger ones around the outside.

As Elizabeth's mother stepped up against the edge of the cemetery, her heart went still because all she heard was the noise of the brook that came off the mountain behind the cemetery at a steep angle and tumbled in swirls of white toward the lake. She knew if she were to take a single step on the other path behind that plateau that brought you down to the brook, her skin would feel cooler as a hush of cold blossomed around her, drawing her downward toward its source. But she knew not to go there. Not now. And not for at least a year. People in town called it Brook-that-finishes-grieving because mourners had thrown themselves into its white fall after the loss of someone they had loved. They fretted especially about their children who were old enough but not wise enough to love, and who climbed down to hidden pockets of forest along the brook to do their loving in secrecy. It was a hazardous path. A path that some—who now lay beneath the earth—had returned to after their love had ended.

Elizabeth's mother turned back to the grave of her daughter and circled her son-in-law's wrist with her thin fingers. "Promise you won't go near that brook," she said.

The townspeople would look upon him with mercy, this foreigner who had become a widower after not even a full year of marriage, and they would pray for him and for Elizabeth's parents who had brought up their one child with the best of everything they

could give her, only to lose her twice—first to marriage and now to
death—the interval between those two passages so fleeting that
they would fuse into one for the townspeople in the decades when
the newborn girl would grow into a woman far older than her
mother had ever been.

Elizabeth's parents, who expected Stefan to turn from the child
in his pain, offered to raise her in their house, but he thanked them
and promised to bring their granddaughter for a visit every Sunday.
When she was christened the week after her mother's burial, he de-
liberated on names that were common in America and Germany,
and he chose his sister's name, Margret, but called his daughter
Greta. Clearly, she was not the child he had envisioned dancing
around the fountain. She was of delicate build like her mother, and
her downy hair was the color of the stubble on his arms as though
she had sprung from fire.

⚭

He hired a nurse for Greta, but in the late evenings he'd rock her on
his knees, stunned by the absence of his wife's current of words. It
made him mute, that longing for her voice, and he found it unbearable to speak to his daughter in her mother's language. But it eased
him to talk to Greta in his native language that he'd rarely spoken
in years, cradling her in one arm while she sucked on her bottle, her
clear eyes on his face as if she could understand every word.

"*Fröschken,*" he called her. Little frog.

And he pointed to himself. "*Vati,*" he said. Daddy.

When she was teething, he rubbed her gums with whiskey, and
when that didn't help, he climbed into the icehouse, where he
scraped the sawdust from the top layer of ice, carried a large chunk
with tongs to his kitchen, and chipped off long splinters for Greta
to suck on. That summer she learned to swim before she could
walk. With the lake right there, Stefan believed in preparing her for
water so that it would never become a danger to her. As a boy, he'd
swum in the Rhein with his father, and he took Greta into the water, one hand beneath her, the other holding her head above the
shallow waves, keeping her safe the way his father had kept him
safe, the way he would teach each of his children and grandchildren to swim.

35

After the year of mourning had passed, he began his careful search for a suitable mother for Greta. He noticed Sara Penn who worked behind the counter of her family's bakery. The firstborn of eight children, Sara had looked after her sisters and brothers since she'd been tall enough to fry an egg without burning herself. She had what the people in Stefan's hometown would have called *Schlafzimmeraugen*—bedroom eyes—with smooth, long eyelids that seemed always half closed. Although five years younger than Elizabeth, she seemed more like a woman while Elizabeth had remained a girl.

The summer of 1908 he began to invite her for walks with him and Greta, who'd toddle between them, gripping one of their fingers in each pudgy hand and linking them in that manner, breathing in the smells that identified them for her: tobacco and melted butter for her father; warm bread and rose water for Sara who wore dresses in shades of blue, ranging from indigo to pale blue, who had a long, easy stride and a dark braid that swung across one shoulder, who would hoist Greta on her hip as though she belonged there and carry her without effort, singing in her low voice.

Sara had firm hands that touched Stefan's temples if his head ached and held on to his broad shoulders when he bent above her in his struggle to erase the features of Elizabeth which, too often, superimposed themselves upon Sara's face.

Sara's favorite possession was a lined notebook she'd filled as a schoolgirl with legends she'd heard, and Greta loved hearing about the first white settlers and the Winnipesaukee Indians, especially the one about the Indian princess, Ellacoya. As she'd listen to Sara's words, pictures would shape inside her mind, pictures of Kona, the young chieftain who crossed the lake to court Ellacoya, pictures of Ellacoya's father, the warrior Ahanton who said no to anyone who wanted to marry his daughter. Greta saw him attack Kona, saw the princess step between them. After the wedding Kona returned across the lake with his bride, and a storm nearly overturned the canoes. But all at once sun split the clouds, showing the way to safety. Ahanton called this the Smile of the Great Spirit—Winnipesaukee.

"That's how our lake got its name," Sara told Greta.

A gatherer by nature, she took Stefan and Greta to a slope on Belknap Mountain where blueberries grew in rich and deep-blue patches and showed them how, from up here, you could see the entire town the way it lay around the curved shoreline of the lake like the arm of a woman, hugging it closely. Its houses—some brick, but most white or gray clapboard—clustered around the three churches: Congregationalist, Baptist, and Catholic.

One afternoon, while Sara and Stefan made love, rain pelted his bedroom window, and after the rain stopped, they woke Greta from her nap and took her for a walk. At the edge of the school-yard, they came across Elizabeth's mother, breaking a white rose from one of the bushes that she and her husband had planted here where their daughter had gone to school—one bush for each year of her life. Though Father Albin—whose guidance Lelia Flynn sought out far too often, the townspeople said—had cautioned the Flynns that roses did not always survive the harsh New Hampshire winters, they'd still planted them because Elizabeth used to love white roses; and they had done so without the help of their gardener or even the principal who had offered to assist them when he'd seen them out there in their expensive clothes, wielding shovels, awkward and determined. Despite the priest's warning, the tender shrubs had already made it through their first winter and were thriving, forming what was to become a lush hedge between the playground and the lumberyard across the street.

When Mrs. Flynn noticed Sara with Stefan, she stood with the stem in her fingers as if she'd been caught taking something that didn't belong to her. "Stefan," she said. "Stefan?" Her eyelashes fluttered for an instant. "Greta."

The air was still so moist that Sara felt it wet against her face, her neck, between her thighs that still held the memory of Stefan's body. And what had felt right when she'd lain with him, felt like sin now that she was standing in front of his dead wife's mother. "Let me wrap your flower," she offered and unfolded her handkerchief, dipped it into a shallow puddle. "It'll be fresh when you get it home."

Lelia Flynn glanced at Stefan, then at Greta who clutched a blue fold of Sara's skirt.

"It's clean, the handkerchief," Sara said.

"Oh—it's not that." Lelia Flynn extended her rose.

When Stefan tried to introduce the two women to each other, Sara said quietly, "Mrs. Flynn knows me from the bakery." Carefully she wound her wet handkerchief around the stem.

"Thank you. I will have this washed so I can give it back to you next Sunday."

"Sunday?"

"When my son-in-law brings you to my house."

Sara frowned.

"I did not intend to imply that you should feel honored to be—" Lelia Flynn sounded flustered.

Stefan watched Sara, impressed that she was *not* impressed at being invited by the banker's wife.

Lelia shook her head. "What I wanted to say was that I would be honored if you came to my house. Father Albin will be there too."

From then on Sara was invited along every Sunday and sat at the table that Lelia would decorate with settings of varied height, three-tiered silver trays with petit fours, glass bowls spilling grapes and plums and bananas, strawberries scattered in deliberate disorder on the tablecloth between the candlesticks and bud vases. By the time Sara married Stefan—almost exactly two years after Elizabeth's death—Lelia had grown so fond of her that she gave her an exquisite set of Italian silver trays. At the reception that was held at Stefan's restaurant, Sara propped Greta on the table next to the wedding cake and fed her icing right from her thumb.

While working in the restaurant kitchen, Sara often balanced the child on one hip while she measured ingredients. Though Stefan still arranged the final garnishes on his pastries, she prepared the crusts and fillings. He was careful not to mention his first wife in front of Sara, but he was constantly reminded of Elizabeth because her features were growing more pronounced in his daughter, whose gray eyes would settle themselves upon others, absorbing, memorizing. Most people felt uncomfortable and glanced away, but Sara laughed and swung Greta around in her arms, telling her not to be so serious, unaware that the child was aching with the knowledge of Sara's death.

She gave Greta crayons and sheets of butcher paper and hung up the stick figures the child drew for her. Two weeks before Sara became pregnant, Greta's drawings took on pear-like curves that softened the silhouettes of her stick figures and contained another, smaller shape curled within the curve. Sometimes there'd be two shapes, not touching, one far tinier than the other as though it needed time to bring it to fruition.

∽

When Sara hadn't bled for two entire months, she took Greta to her parents' bakery and left her with one of her sisters, while she walked along the lake by herself, the collar of her coat turned up. The water was choppy, and crests of foam bobbed above its lead-colored surface. The only boat out was the mail boat, its long, knotted ropes hanging from its hull. Wind snatched at the white haze that rose from the smokestack, and the sun bounced off the windows of the pilot house, brief flashes of light, as if a child were playing with a pocket mirror. There'd always been children to care for in her life . . . her siblings, and now Greta. Children she loved. But she couldn't imagine herself with a child of her own.

She returned for a walk the following day and the days after that, returned till she was used to the idea of herself being a mother. And only then did she tell Stefan.

He stood in front of her like an awkward boy. "Are you happy then, are you?" Pressing her hands between his, he asked, "Are you?"

He took his best suit from the hanger and told her he'd be back soon; but instead of stopping at the construction site to supervise, he headed for the Catholic church, careful to avoid the deep mud. While the lower regions of the mountains had been turning green, their summits were still capped with snow, and spring thaw had left the roads of the town so spongy that carriages and delivery wagons had been getting stuck all week. Pete Morrell and some of the other farmers were earning extra money by keeping their teams of oxen ready for towing.

As Stefan approached the churchyard, a flock of swallows rose from a puddle, forming a cone that spun upward and was sucked into the mild, damp wind. On the church steps, he scraped the wet earth from his shoes before he entered. The oxblood-colored curtain of the confessional enveloped him like an embrace of shame, and after Father Albin's raspy voice absolved him from years of sins—pride and greed among them—Stefan knelt by the side altar, where the statue of the Virgin cradled the waxen corpse of Christ. There, as he remembered the banker's words—*money I give to the church has nothing to do with the church*—he proposed his own deal to God: he would attend church every Sunday, sing in the choir, and contribute ten percent of his income *if* Sara and the child survived.

"And future children," he made sure to remind God.

The construction of the *Wasserburg* was progressing, and the town had become accustomed to the sight of Stefan's short, solid body—always in a dark suit and crisp white shirt—as he strode among the workmen with blueprints from the linen originals, issuing orders in an accent that sounded both stern and melodious to the townspeople, who still whispered about him as much as the day he'd arrived: that he had a way with money; that he looked like a Frenchman—not a German—with those black curls and fierce green eyes; that the bathrooms in his apartment house would be divided—toilet and a sink in one room, tub and sink in another. At a town meeting some complained that his building blocked their view of the lake, while others speculated that it was too big to ever fill with tenants.

But what they talked about most was that the fire inspector had said it was ten times as safe as any other structure in town. "Goddamn thing's so heavy," he'd muttered, "it's anchored right to the middle of the earth."

Between each floor were ten inches of cement, ten inches of sand, and another ten inches of cement—an impenetrable fire barrier. The outer walls were built of brick and heavy timber, while the inside walls had masonry between layers of plaster.

Sara preferred their rooms above the restaurant and felt uneasy with the growing debt. "A banker's taste," she called the *Wasser-*

burg late one evening when she and Stefan were sharing a custard tart from the restaurant as they often did before they went to bed.

"And what would you want?" he challenged her. "A baker's taste?"

She took a small bite, set the tart back on the plate between them, and chewed slowly before answering him. "Tell me then— what is wrong with a baker's taste?"

"I'm sorry."

Both elbows on the tablecloth, she leaned toward him. "I like the baker's taste."

"I said I'm sorry." He dabbed one finger against the side of her mouth. Smiled at her. "You got custard on your face," he said and licked off his finger.

"And the farmer's taste. And the chimney sweep's taste. This entire town is built in that kind of taste. It suits me. The house you're building does not fit into this town."

"It's the most beautiful house I've ever seen."

"Oh, Stefan. Of course it's beautiful. But it's so large that it changes the way the other houses look . . . so large that I get embarrassed."

"Embarrassed?"

"It's like . . . bragging, a house like that."

"Not to me. And you knew. . . . You knew from the beginning that I was building it."

"But I didn't know how much it lived inside you. With something that big there isn't much room left. And what's left is still taken up by her."

"So that's what all this is about? About Elizabeth?"

She looked straight at him. "It's her name that's still on the deeds."

"I told you I would change them over to you. I just haven't had time." *Marjoram,* he reminded himself. *I'm also running low on pepper. Plenty of paprika left, though, and salt.*

"And you did nothing to stop her mother when she ordered me to visit."

"I thought you like visiting there."

"I go because of Greta and you. But when I'm there, I still feel like someone who stole you from their daughter."

"Elizabeth was dead before you and I—" He stopped. Be patient, he reminded himself. Patient. He kissed her forehead. "The Flynns are always kind to you."

"They are. The way they would be to a servant. Because I'm from trade."

To agree with her would mean admitting that equality was not as total in America as he had figured it was, and letting in the uneasy certainty that Elizabeth's parents had never really accepted him either. "No. It's because they're both generous people."

"The kind of generosity that comes with conditions."

"They've never pushed me for the loan."

"Because you're the father of their grandchild."

"I don't understand you," he said, feeling this one chafing hurt between them that he'd sensed before, though it had never risen like this in words. To reassure Sara, he added, "It's you I'm married with." Right away he knew he should have said married *to*. Elizabeth would have mentioned his mistake. But Sara didn't even know enough to notice.

∽

The morning he felt movement beneath the swelling of her belly, he went to mass though it wasn't a Sunday, and when Father Albin's wide, pink hand floated up to bless the congregation, Stefan felt a deep conviction that God would keep Sara alive. Still, the evening her labor began, he was snagged right back to the night of his first wife's death. Sara's screams were ripping through him, and when he tried to get into the room where her mother and Dr. Miles bent over her in the wide birch bed, they kept him from her and sent him to look after Greta who was alone in her room.

When he opened her door, his daughter was crouching against the wall in the far corner of her bed, legs drawn to her chest. *"Fröschken,"* he whispered. *"Fröschken?"*

A gingham pillow was crammed in the tight space between her knees and stomach as though she, too, were giving birth. When he picked her up, she was shivering so hard that he knew those final

42

screams of her mother had survived in her memory. Touching his lips to Greta's forehead, he wished he could reassure her that Sara would soon be well again, but since he didn't know how to ease his own fears, he was silent as he guided her arms into the sleeves of her checkered coat and tied the ribbon of her matching hat beneath her chin. After he buttoned her shoes, he lifted her on his shoulders, and as he walked along the dark lake with her, she linked her fingers across his forehead, preserving the heat of his skin in her palms. Autumn wind molded the trees to the shoreline, their branches reaching for the restless surface of the lake with the promise of a diviner's rod.

"Look, *Vati*," Greta said and pointed to the reflection of the half moon that swayed on the water like a slab of frost. It was an image that would come to her in later years—the moon, just like that, on the water—usually before she perceived something about people that most others could not see, and it was like that now though she was too young to frame it with words.

1 9 0 9 – 1 9 1 1

Stefan's second daughter was born in the early morning hours. When he knelt next to Sara's bed, her eyes were tranquil, and he knew God had honored his bargain. Sara agreed to call the child Agnes, another name that was the same in German as in English, though she told him it made her wonder if, eventually, he wanted to return to Germany.

"Only for a visit." He pressed his lips to her wrist, and as he tasted the cooled sweat of her labor, he felt her waiting for him to see the uniqueness of their daughter; but to him Agnes looked like a tiny, old woman. Black tufts of hair like spider silk. Face heart shaped—wide temples, pointy chin. A band of freckles across the bridge of her nose like a minus sign. When he picked her up she began to cry, and he quickly handed her back to Sara. "A visit with you and our daughters," he said.

"That's good." Her long eyelids closed. "*Our* daughters . . ."

On the wall behind the bed was the pattern of roses his first wife had chosen, and as he watched Sara sleep, he felt unfaithful because he saw Elizabeth's fingers flattening the paper against the wall, saw translucent fingernails so short that her hands looked like those of a child.

At church his tenor climbed above the other voices, and if you listened closely, you could make out his lavish accent in the higher notes. He relinquished ten percent of his income to the priest though it slowed the completion of the *Wasserburg* and meant delaying the installation of the elevator and the arrival of the South German carpenter from Wolfeboro, who would set up his workshop in the basement of the restaurant and carve arched doors for each apartment. Instead of ordering new fire escapes from Boston, Stefan bought used ones when the local hospital was renovated. His workmen attached the sets of metal steps to each end of his building, where they hung ten feet above the sidewalk and sank down only if weight was applied from above.

His contributions to the church also postponed the return of the loan to Elizabeth's parents; but they urged him not to worry whenever he brought it up—not just once, but on three separate occasions, so he would remind himself in later years—when he arrived at their house on Sundays with Sara and his daughters. Though Lelia and Hardy Flynn made a fuss over Agnes and welcomed Sara, it was evident that their real delight was in Greta. Sara could understand that: after all, her own parents were closer to Agnes than to Greta, and that was only natural—the ancient tug of blood—while she, however, felt linked equally to both children because Greta had been in her life longer than the daughter who'd grown from within her own body.

But what troubled her was that Stefan did not seem interested in Agnes. One morning while she was nursing the baby, she said to him, "Maybe you're not close to Agnes because she never shared your evenings. The way you did with Greta."

He closed his starched collar, put on his cuff links. "What do you mean?" he asked and reached for his waistcoat, ready to take the stairs down to his restaurant. In his mind he was already measuring ingredients for the *potage à l'oignon gratiné*—onion soup—and the *rognons à la dijonnaise*—veal kidneys—he would serve tonight.

Sara bent across Agnes and adjusted the white-and-yellow blanket that Stefan's mother had knitted for the baby in Germany. "Maybe it's because the two of you lived alone."

When he looked at her, her lips were pressed together, her *Schlafzimmeraugen* anxious as if it were crucial that he find the reason that very moment, find it and remedy it and move on from there. And because he felt a sudden tenderness and pity for her, he did not contradict her. One of the baby's feet, impossibly tiny, poked from the blanket. Squatting by Sara's chair, he laid one side of his face against her belly—already pushing at him with a new child—and rubbed one thumb across his daughter's velvety arch. "Agnes is still so . . . young," he said carefully. "Once we get used to each other . . . You'll see." It was kinder than telling Sara how Greta still evoked Elizabeth for him. Simpler than telling her how he had somehow expected this second daughter to be the girl he had seen from the boat. It made him uneasy, this vision of a time he hadn't lived, and he never invoked and nurtured it; yet, it rooted itself in his mind as potent as memory, influencing his decisions, shaping his future.

∽

It pleased Sara when—that June as soon as the lake began to warm—Stefan taught Agnes to swim. From the dock she watched as he walked into the water with their daughter, grimacing and shivering before he carefully lowered her. Agnes took to the lake instantly, kicking her legs and arms, cooing and laughing.

He held on to her. "This one will never be afraid of water," he called out to Sara, but what he really thought was: *This one won't drown.* In the cemetery on the hill were already too many graves of children who had drowned. Wedged between rocks on the Robichauds' family plot was a glass case containing a white-and-pink china doll that used to belong to a daughter who'd fallen into the lake when she'd scrambled down the bank to get some flowers. *Not my daughter.*

But even though Agnes learned to swim quickly, she never got old enough to walk. And it was not the lake that claimed her that November, when her mother was in her last month of pregnancy. For over an hour that afternoon Sara had been expecting her daughter to wake crying, wanting to be picked up and fed as Agnes did after every nap, anxious to have it all that very instant she opened her eyes—the holding and the feeding—as if she already sensed that there would never be enough for her. And what Sara would not forgive herself later was how she had savored that quiet time, how she had wanted it to last—*though not a lifetime, not that*—while she'd sat by the window. She had pulled a chair into the path of the low November sun, letting it warm her breasts and shoulders. Stefan was downstairs in the restaurant, Greta with her Grandmother Flynn shopping for Christmas presents in Concord, and for these few rare hours the apartment was Sara's alone. Twice, she raised herself up, awkward with the bulk of the new child, and wandered down the hall to the open door of the girls' bedroom, smiling as she watched Agnes sleeping on her belly as usual, one side of her tiny face pressed against the crib sheet, lips puckered as if in anticipation of being fed. Like a young, hungry bird. *Little bird.* It made her think of how Stefan called Greta his little frog—*Fröschken*—and she reminded herself to ask him what little bird meant in German. *Little frog and little bird.* Humming to herself, she returned to her chair and closed her eyes, letting the sunlight paint the insides of her eyelids the color of pumpkins. It was the third time Sara stood in the doorway of the bedroom that she knew—knew all at once and with undeniable conviction—that her daughter was dead, had been dead each time she had checked in on her in the hope she'd stay silent a bit longer, and she didn't have to step into the room because she could feel the death—*beaks and claws and feathers*—pecking at her womb where the new child shifted with sudden violence to remind her of its claim on her.

Dr. Miles could give her no reasons. Not even after he had taken the small body to the hospital for an autopsy. When he released Agnes to be buried, he tried to comfort Sara by telling her of other infants who'd suddenly stopped breathing without anything obstructing the passage of their breath.

"Your wife did nothing wrong," he assured Stefan.

Sara's parents arranged the details of the funeral while Stefan stayed with Sara day and night, feeling inarticulate because his own grief felt paltry in the face of her magnificent despair. The day of the service, Lelia Flynn made sure Greta was dressed properly in black, her face clean. "Don't cry," she said. While Hardy Flynn reminded Greta to mind her manners, to say hello and thank you, the girl kept her lips closed and stretched her tongue into the high curve of her mouth, trapping the sad words and tears.

At the cemetery a hole had been hacked into the frozen earth next to Elizabeth, and earth-covered rocks were piled up next to the gravestone. Along the sides of some older graves, mounds of rocks were overgrown with lichen as if, when the grave diggers had opened the earth for death, they'd only returned the soil once the coffin was inside, and what had stayed outside were the leftover rocks, looking almost like another grave, though less orderly.

As Sara felt Greta's hand slip into hers, she envied Elizabeth who would get to lie with Agnes beneath the earth as though they had traded children—*the wrong mother with the wrong child.* Shadows of clouds raced across the granite stone, across the graves and the plateau, toward the islands where the crowns of trees blurred as if painted onto one huge, multicolored surface, while—in the lower rows—their trunks stood separate. Straight and separate. And recognizable. *The wrong mother with the wrong child.* Sara tightened her fingers around Greta's. *Look after Agnes,* she implored Elizabeth. *Guide her through wherever she needs to go . . . I'll do the same for your child. In life.*

Wind ruffled the blond fuzz on Father Albin's pink cheeks. After he raised his strong arms to make the final sign of the cross over the coffin, he turned to Stefan and Sara. "It is God's will to have little Agnes with him and the angels."

"God's will?" Sara whispered, her lips gray. She felt her mother's touch on her shoulder, felt her sisters and brothers right behind her.

"You are more blessed than other women," the priest said, "because you have been graced with another child ready to come into God's world." Though the priest's hoarse words carried the proper sum of compassion, it was still the voice of a man who had not lost a child, a man who could not possibly grasp that kind of loss.

Blessed— The word filled Sara's head—*blessed blessed*—made it hard to breathe, made her drop Greta's hand and glance around wildly for a paring knife, a scythe even—*blessed blessed blessed*— anything she could use to slash the priest's fleshy throat, his pious throat, before he could say more, but then Lelia Flynn's slender shadow darkened the priest's chest as she stepped between him and Sara, who felt the pulse of her words though she could not hear them because her head was swarming with the *blessed blessed bless*—

The townswomen worried that Sara Blau's grief would mar the soon-to-be-born child. Once it lived outside her body, they could help care for it, of course, wean it from the poison of sorrow that now was its sole sustenance. Till then they did what they could to pull Sara's will back to the living by bringing her their pies and their gossip; by stitching the softest clothes for her new child; by praying their efforts would lessen Sara's pain, although—from their own sorrows—they knew only time could diminish them, and even then never fully.

∞

The morning Sara's belly rose and hardened, Stefan held her, kissing her forehead again and again until Sara's mother and Dr. Miles sent him away; and when he stood waiting outside the bedroom door, her mother called out to him to take Greta for a walk to the bakery. After he pulled Greta's moccasin boots over her ribbed wool stockings, he walked with her along the icy path by the lake to the bakery, where his father-in-law, a slight-shouldered man with broad hips—body shaped like a pine tree, Sara was fond of saying—fed them gingerbread cookies, hot from the oven, and wrapped a loaf of rye for them to take home. On the way they stopped at St. Paul's where Stefan lit a dozen candles by the side altar.

For three days after Tobias' birth, Sara looked radiant, smiling when she held him up and watched his legs uncurl like petals of a tropical plant. The boy had been born with his knees tucked up high, but with every day the muscles in his legs seemed to ease more, and it looked to Stefan as if his son were growing rapidly while he watched him.

As long as Sara held him, Tobias seemed content; but if Stefan touched him, his bright, curious eyes became guarded and his scrawny body grew rigid. With his wisps of black hair and heart-shaped face he could have been Agnes' twin: all that stood between those two was time—fourteen months since Agnes had left the shelter of Sara's womb; fourteen months during which Agnes had lived and died and been buried and Tobias had been born. He even had that same line of copper freckles high across his nose, and by the time he would be a young man, these freckles would have darkened so much that he'd look as if his eyebrows were touching, but once he was in his seventies—when his niece, Emma, would beg him to lift the curse that encumbered the house and their family—his freckles would have paled and merged into a smudge that would make some people want to step up to him and wipe it off with spit the way their grandmother, say, or a favorite aunt might have done.

On the fourth day of Tobias' life, a sudden fever pushed Sara into the pillows that turned damp as she pitched her body from side to side. Dreams of birds fell at her, *tiny and naked birds that drop from their nests and crash to the ground, bone-white and flat, so flat and still in their human nakedness against the brown earth, half-formed and cold so cold*—"I'm not letting you die." Stefan, it was Stefan's voice, pulling at her, pulling her back from where Agnes waited while he sponged her body with melted snow. Cold. So. Cold *and those beaks, those shallow beaks like baby-girl features, while others fall into her dream naked and cold so*— And then he was carrying her. Carrying her to the window. Telling her about the journey they'd take to Germany come May. *May? How can it be May?* The roofs of her town were white with new snow *but the birds are of all colors now, not naked but huge with feathers of all colors all colors and cries as extravagant as their feathers.*

"Now they have feathers," she said slowly, "feathers . . ."

But her husband was crying.

She pressed one palm against the side of his face till he stopped. "How do you say bird in German?"

"*Vogel.* Why?"

"And little bird?"

"*Vögelchen.*"

She raised her other hand toward the ice flowers that bloomed on the glass panes; and while Stefan told her about the barges that hauled cargo up and down the Rhein, she climbed into his voice, *bringing with her the naked birds and also the birds with feathers,* while he drew word-pictures for her of chestnut trees with candle blossoms, of an ancient town he called Kaiserswerth across the river from his hometown.

As he stroked Sara's arms, her flushed face, Stefan suddenly could no longer recall the features of his first wife; there was only Sara now, and he wondered how he could have ever *not* recognized her fully. For the two hours before her death she was lucid, and he tried to explain to her that he would take Elizabeth's name off the deeds and put hers on instead, but all Sara wanted from him was to circle back with her over Agnes' brief life—that inquisitive way she had of raising her head; how she loved to swim; the way her hair clung to her temples when she slept; the surprised look she got when waking up as if she'd expected to find herself somewhere else. . . . It moved Sara how much Stefan had noticed about their daughter, and as they circled over every movement and sound of hers they could recall, their words became more hurried, while— outside their locked bedroom door—Greta was pressing herself against the painted wood, absorbing those words into her memory, shivering because she could feel the shape of the something she'd known about long before her sister's birth, the something that al- ready had taken Agnes and was now here for Sara. Even her father wasn't powerful enough to stall it any longer.

∞

In the months after Sara's burial, Stefan would hike up to the ceme- tery early every morning while Greta and Tobias and their new nursemaid were still asleep. Standing in front of the grave, he would try to keep his gaze above ground, to not let himself imagine his two wives lying on their backs the way they had in their coffins, side by side with Agnes between them. Because if he let himself see them like that, *Sara and Elizabeth turn to each other, murmur across the child beneath the dark earth, there, palms touching palms as if they were lovers.*

Sometimes the people of Winnipesaukee would raise their faces toward the hill because they'd hear Stefan, even from that distance. They'd never heard a man howl like that—a sound not quite hu- man, they said. Some whispered that it was his howl that made the pines in the cemetery shed their needles that winter because his was too formidable a grief to let anything living adhere to where it belonged. In their empathy for him and in their fretting that he might throw himself into the Brook-that-finishes-grieving, they grew closer to one another, closer yet than they had been in this village by the great lake; and oddly it all tied in with his tall, new house that became more theirs, now, as they talked about Stefan Blau more than ever before. About how, instead of statues, he'd placed fire extinguishers into the alcoves of the hallways as if to protect what was left of his family. About how he'd stopped giving Father Albin money. About how every dollar of profit from his restaurant went into his apartment building—the best of everything: Italian marble and Dutch tiles; stenciled beams and oriental rugs; German carvings and crystal chandeliers; balconies with flower boxes atop the ornate railings; a stone fountain with two tiers like something you might see in picture books of Venice.

He immersed himself in his restaurant, trying variations of his ratatouille and *salade niçoise,* testing new recipes like *poires au vin rouge*—pears in red wine. Sometimes his work could blunt his sorrow for a few hours, but then it would raise itself again, a savage beast that tore at his memories, a beast he could cage until late at night after he'd close the restaurant, a beast he'd take with him into the green boat and row far out on the lake to drown it. As the bow crushed flimsy layers of ice, sweat coated his chest, and he knew he would freeze to death if his boat were to tip over. Stripping off his clothes, he felt the cold, black air against his slick skin, but he kept rowing toward the faraway center of the vast lake and the dim mounds of the islands whose legends Sara used to collect. To row to the far end of the lake would take days, maybe even a week. He longed for the ache in his arms and shoulders to expand till it blotted out all else, longed to shatter and disperse into fragments no larger than those specks of stars above him, longed to get sucked into the sky and vanish—but whenever he'd look toward shore, the massive shape of the *Wasserburg* would summon him.

∾

Though his rents were far more expensive than others in town, Stefan already had a waiting list of prospective tenants that spring of

1911 when he moved with Greta and Tobias into their seven rooms on the top floor of the *Wasserburg,* where high ceilings met the walls in graceful curves and the windows framed the lake and mountains. It all looked the way he and Elizabeth had planned it— only now it no longer meant anything to him. Since she had taken such delight in describing each detail to him when she'd been pregnant with Greta, he still thought of the apartment as hers and furnished it with the tufted sofas and painted fern baskets she'd wanted, left the windows without drapes. The birch furniture in the bedroom he kept, and he ordered a leather chair like the one he'd seen in the office of Elizabeth's father.

Greta, who had been listless since Sara's death, started humming and smiling in the new apartment. Fascinated by the haze of unfamiliar smells, she'd bring her nose against the cool tiles, dry plaster, and gleaming woodwork, inhaling deeply as those odors revealed the house to her. Often her face would be smudged, and it wouldn't be until she was five and Dr. Miles would prescribe glasses for her, that she would discover colors beyond those that now made up her surroundings; but by then the habit of sniffing would be so ingrained that she'd continue to form many of her first impressions by scent.

Like the scent of her brother.

Who smelled like Agnes.

Powder and diapers and tears.

And who lived with knowing about Agnes long before anyone would tell him about her. Because Greta had taken the white-and-yellow blanket that used to belong to Agnes. Had plopped it into her brother's crib. And as Tobias slept within its folds, *sleeps and dreams, dreams and turns, he is living for himself and for Agnes. Someone like me; almost like me. Dreams and turns within the folds of the blanket. Dreams and cries. And remembers what he cannot possibly remember from his own experience but what, nevertheless, is imprinting itself on his soul. Deeper with each day. More permanent with each day: someone like me; almost like me.* So much like Agnes that even his father, when bending over his crib, would feel momentarily confused, thinking he was seeing

Agnes—*those tufts of hair, that minus sign of freckles, that urgent grasp, too urgent*—and then realize it was Tobias. *Me. Someone like me.*

∽

The first tenant to move in was Miss Garland, just retired from the shoe factory that had calloused her hands and curved her spindly back slightly to the left. It was where work had been available the year she'd graduated from school, and she'd started there, certain she'd find something more interesting in six months. A year at most. But she hadn't left. Not for half a century.

From the kitchen window of her old apartment, she had witnessed every step of the construction as the *Wasserburg* had grown to obstruct her view and the view of everyone else who lived in the clapboard houses behind it. While others had grumbled, she'd been mesmerized. Five years it had taken the house from start to finish, five years for her to imagine what it would be like to make her first withdrawal ever from her bank account that had grown astonishingly over decades of living frugally while making scant, weekly deposits from her pay. She hadn't known what she was saving for until the *Wasserburg* had begun to rise outside her window like the manifestation of desires too glorious to admit to anyone. But then she had understood. And had gone to see Stefan Blau, shy around him—*because how could you have known so precisely what I want?*—as he wrote her name on the first line of a list that would grow during the years of construction.

When it was time, he came to her door and did what he had promised her, though she had not believed him, offer her the choice of any apartment—*any, except his own*—in his *Wasserburg*, though it must have been obvious to him that she could only afford the least expensive one. Still, he led her through every single room in his vast building, adjusting his pace to hers—*I notice that, things like that*—his widower's face almost pleased when she told him how splendid it all was. Imagine, a button inside each apartment to let people in from the outside. And another button recessed in the parquet floor where her table would stand so that with the touch of one foot, one toe even, she could summon a maid. Imagine. Her own flush toilet instead of a privy behind the house. Ceiling lamps that could be turned on with one switch.

On the day she moved into her small apartment on the main floor across from the brass mailboxes and the elevator, Stefan Blau told her, *"Willkommen,"* and explained it was a German word to greet esteemed guests. What Miss Garland had always liked was to watch others, and her apartment was ideal for that because her windows opened to the courtyard and street. And to think that the street view was less expensive than the water view, that she was saving money by choosing what she preferred.

Inside her linen closet, she stashed her canning jars with cloudy contents, sacks of flour, and bottles of maple syrup she'd been hoarding for years in anticipation of emergencies. For her living room she ordered the most luxurious furniture you could buy in Winnipesaukee; but in the bedroom she kept her sagging bed and scuffed dresser, concealed behind the door along with her shame at having earned her money by working. All her life, Miss Garland had yearned to be married, supported by a husband who worshiped her, and after moving into Stefan Blau's *Wasserburg,* she began to invent her past as though she had settled in a different country where no one knew her history. She would hint at an inheritance, at a young fiancé who had died tragically four decades ago. And because she cherished the idea of herself living in a building this magnificent, she rarely left it, except to watch it from outside while she sat on the bench that the German carpenter had bolted to the end of the dock, her back to the lake and the tourist cottages on the islands and the lower slopes of the mountains.

Harsh work had catapulted her from being a girl of fifteen to being a woman of sixty-five—nothing in between for her—but now that she had leisure for the first time in half a century, she could feel herself growing younger as if her life had opted to reverse itself. Without checking in mirrors, she could tell her body was getting nimbler. She read articles in *Ladies' Home Journal* on how to decorate elegantly on a small budget, scanned the advertisements in *The Saturday Evening Post,* already knowing she wouldn't buy any of those wares. Some days she took three baths. After a lifetime of carrying a pitcher of water to her bedroom and washing herself from a basin or, occasionally, crouched in a metal tub, she loved turning on the faucet and watching an entire white bathtub fill up, a bathtub so long that even when she lay stretched in it, her toes could not touch its other end. And when she was clean, she could let it all run down the sink instead of pouring out slop water. Already, her hands were softer, and the yellow cracks beneath her feet had healed. To make sure her feet would stay like that, she sewed three pairs of soft black felt slippers and embroidered them with hummingbirds.

Inventing a fiancé wasn't all that different from what she had done since childhood—make up what she longed for—and as her history as a woman who had almost married grew into a lavish tapestry, it covered the worn cloth of her past, except for moments when strands of light dropped through the gaps between the stitches and illuminated fragments of her barren years. She'd been raised in a small, remote house where her mother bred and sold cocker spaniels, and her father left every morning on his bicycle to work at the shoe factory. Sometimes he talked about looking for other work, but since the tools he worked with at the factory didn't belong to him, he didn't think he could afford to leave there. Besides, he hadn't been trained for any other work. "Make sure you get skills and tools of your own," he'd tell his small daughter, who would not play with other children until she'd started school. The few visitors who came to the house were customers who fussed over her mother's puppies. How she wished they'd buy every single one of those dogs that followed her all day. If she ran from them, they'd chase her, brown-and-white ears flopping, tiny needle teeth nipping at her ankles. "Scram," she would holler, "scram scram scram," flailing at them with her pinafore. One day behind the house she kicked one of them away, and when it didn't move, she nudged it behind the lilac bush by the back steps and ran inside. For several days she didn't use the back steps, and when she finally looked behind the lilacs, the puppy was still lying there. "Here, puppy, puppy. . . ." She bent to pick it up. "Wake up, puppy. Wake up." In her hands it felt light, curiously light, and when she turned it around, it had a hole in its white-and-brown belly that was filled with white rice. *Rice?* And then the rice moved.

∾

Feet smooth in her felt slippers, Miss Garland would sit by her window, her good suit jacket over a housedress, not ashamed to be noticed by people who passed by the *Wasserburg,* and if she kept her door half open, she could also see everyone who came to the mailboxes. She was intrigued and appalled by Nate Bloom, the most dazzling of the tenants, who had a telephone and was divorced. His mustache was so thin it looked painted on. As president of the local factory that built railroad cars, he had his own railroad car that he could hook to the Boston and Maine Railroad. Though Miss Garland had only seen it from outside, she'd heard it had red velvet seats and mahogany tables bolted down to the floor, mahogany trim around the windows, and a separate compartment with a large bed. The railroad car was stocked with the best liquors, and Mr. Bloom gave extravagant parties while the train traveled from one place to another. Sometimes he'd order as many as fifty dinners from Stefan Blau's restaurant, and Miss Garland would see waiters in tuxedos leave the *Cadeau du Lac* to deliver their covered trays to the railroad station. From one of the waiters she knew that Nate Bloom particularly liked Stefan's *rognons,* prepared in a wine-and-mustard sauce, and the *filet de sole* served with wine-soaked prunes.

Though Nate Bloom invited Stefan Blau on several of his journeys, Stefan declined, just as he declined all invitations, except those from his dead wives' parents. He was grateful to them for all they did for Greta and Tobias, but even with the help of a nursemaid, he knew that wasn't enough. Eventually, he would need to find a mother for them. But he postponed thinking about that by working late every evening. Besides, the people of Winnipesaukee—though they praised his devotion to his children—kept their daughters of marriageable age away from him. Often he'd roam the hallways of his apartment house after the restaurant closed, and he'd touch the brass crowns of the fire extinguishers in the alcoves, the wrought-iron sconces—much in the way his granddaughter, Emma, would touch them many years later.

Nate Bloom was persistent—not just with his invitations, but even more so in wanting to rent the largest apartment in the building, the one where Stefan lived with his children. Though Stefan was clear in his refusal, Nate Bloom would approach him about it every time he saw him in the elevator until Stefan offered to rent him two apartments on the fifth floor and combine them by breaking through the connecting wall with an arch.

He hired Homer and Irene Wilson, a married couple who used to manage a building in Florida and came with the best of references. Though Homer Wilson was easygoing and only in his thirties, his tanned skin was already creased across his neck and forehead. His wife had the flat build of a boy, and her mouth was set in an eager but dissatisfied expression as if she worried that whatever she did was not enough. Her first day on the job, she caught Stefan by the front door and confided that she and her husband had moved to Winnipesaukee to live close to the child they were about to inherit.

"You see, my Homer's sister, she's been ill with lung problems ever since she left Orlando with some fellow and took Danny along, that's her son, and we're first in line to adopt him since he's got no father, never had, at least not one who'd stay long enough to give him his name on a certificate, so Danny's last name is already Wilson which means he won't even have to change his name once he's ours, once his mother dies, that is just so you know he'll be living with us."

Stefan blinked. "Of course."

She laid one hand on his sleeve. "You of all people know what a tragedy that is for a child, Mr. Blau, losing a mother and—"

"I need to get to my restaurant."

"He's eleven, our Danny is, born a month after our girl, but she only lived five hours, that's all, and it broke my heart all over again when Danny's mother took off with him like that two years ago, and for what, I ask you, to come north and end up working at a factory that makes hosiery, dragging all of us up north, never mind that Homer has a hard time getting used to the cold, and the time, I tell you the time it took us to look for work that's right for both of us, that's why we're so glad you hired us, well, at least Homer's sister did that much for us, wrote to us about your building when it was going up so that we—"

"I'm sorry about your daughter."

"Homer and me, we can't have no more."

As religious as her husband was irreverent, Mrs. Wilson wavered between praying for her sister-in-law's recovery and her swift death. The boy would visit on weekends, lanky and sullen, and Mrs. Wilson would cry Sunday evenings when she'd surrender him to his rightful mother.

From her apartment in the basement, she supervised four maids who lived in a suite across the hall from her, ready to be summoned by the tenants. All four were young, local girls who moved about the house in crisp, gray dresses and white aprons that never seemed to get soiled, and who rotated their one day off so that there always would be at least three of them. They liked Miss Garland because she never talked down to them and did her own housework, and they looked forward to being called to her apartment because it meant a rest. Unlike some tenants, Miss Garland remembered their names, and after urging Birdie or Heather or Gladys or Stella to sit, she'd brew a pot of strong tea, knowing exactly how much sugar, milk, or lemon each of them liked. Along with her tea she'd offer stories about her dead fiancé and delicious peanut brittle that she made every Saturday. In return, the maids brought her gossip from other apartments: Mr. Bloom, so wasteful with his money, saved slivers of old soap in a canning jar by his bathroom sink; Mr. Blau—God bless him—had not been with a woman since his last wife died; Mrs. Wilson kept a chart in her closet and marked down her sister-in-law's visits to the hospital; and Mr. Bell, that retired lawyer from New York, cooked on a hot plate that sat on top of his four-burner stove.

If the maids visited for too long, Mrs. Wilson would come looking for them. She worked much harder than Stefan expected her to: not only did she keep the hallways clean, but she even scrubbed the floors of the incinerator rooms; and she demanded that same kind of exertion from the maids and her husband, who'd shrug and let her do most of the talking. Usually she'd find him puttering around the garage that was separated from the basement by a fire door. His jobs included stoking the furnace and washing the tenants' cars. He also had a knack for fixing them. Though only a few had automobiles, Stefan figured most would within a few years, and he had planned the garage large enough for twenty stalls. Already, over half a million people in America owned cars—powered by steam, gasoline, or electricity—and that number would likely triple in another decade.

Each time he thought of making a payment to Elizabeth's parents, he reasoned with himself that the loan could wait till everything was completed. He expanded his restaurant to include the second floor where he used to live. From Boston, he brought in a designer of gardens and, on the flat roof of the *Wasserburg*'s garage, had him lay out a long, symmetrical space with lawns and hedges, flower beds and a stone bench, a swing set and a sandbox where his and the tenants' children could play.

Once, in the bleak morning hours, after Stefan had paced through the house, he entered the rooms of his children, and when he found them both asleep as of course they would be at that time, it struck him as such incredible faith—sleeping here like that—faith in him, that he was overwhelmed by the sum of their future needs. He felt as though he were the only person awake in the town, perhaps even the world, and he suddenly knew his next wife would be here entirely for his children's sake—not his; that he would not kill another woman with his seed.

And that's when he thought of Helene Montag.

 ♪

Two grades ahead of Stefan in school, Helene Montag would have been mortified had the other kids discovered she loved him. That in itself would have been bad enough; but to be taunted about a boy two years younger than you, a boy nearly a head shorter than you, would have been excruciating. She tried to stop that passion which confused her, but it remained part of her—gaudy and persistent— concealed even from her best friend, Margret, Stefan's sister, with whom she had shared every secret since kindergarten.

The window of Margret's room above the tailor shop next door was so close to Helene's bedroom window that the girls could lean out and pass messages to one another across the span between the stucco houses. Both would have liked to have more glamorous names—Carmen, perhaps, or Odelia, or Isabella—like the heroines in the books that Helene's parents lent out in their pay-library. Since their own names struck them as the kind other people's great aunts had—names that suggested varicose veins and inherited fox stoles with beady eyeballs—the girls would call each other by new names; but soon they'd forget or discover even better ones that they'd test on Margret's mother while she'd fry *Reibekuchen* for the girls or let them help her bake bread.

Helene's mother was always reading or sewing or writing in her diary, and any preparation of food seemed an inconvenience to her. Quite often, meals would be overcooked until most color had leached from them. But her soups were rather good. She only made them in winter, and they were different each time since she was too impatient around the kitchen to follow a recipe and would just leave the soup kettle on the stove for days, adding ingredients as the level went down. She would urge her children to read Annette von Droste-Hülshoff and Theodor Storm. "Minds like yours need substance," she would remind Helene and her little brother Leo. They were not allowed to read anything from the pay-library. "*Schmutz*—filth," their parents called those romances, mysteries, and war novels that embarrassed them, yet provided an income for the family.

Some evenings their father would sit at the piano in their living room, shirt collar unbuttoned, his pale, thick fingers stubborn—so stubborn—in pursuing harmony with this instrument that had resisted him since he was a boy. It baffled Helene that a man as quiet as her father would want to make sounds this loud. If she stood next to him at the piano, she could smell his sweat. Those were the only times she could smell it. Nowhere else. Not even when he raked the earth behind the house. Only at the piano. Sweat strong enough to mute the scents of tobacco and mothballs.

Usually her mother would pull her and Leo into the kitchen where the noise wouldn't be so hard on their ears. "When your fa-

ther was a boy," she told them one spring day while he was prac-
ticing Easter hymns with dreary devotion, "he dreamed of being a
musician. It's the saddest thing, wanting something so much and
finding out it's not in you. That's why you must always love him
hard." She would slice apples for them and recite lines of poetry
that were filled with colors and sounds and smells they recognized,
with the cries of roosters at dawn and the whisper of bushes in the
dark, with bees that hung from twigs and white kittens born in
May. Poems, she told them, could take them to places they'd never
been to and make them familiar: islands in the ocean; a gray city in
the mist; a balcony in a tower. "If you have books in your life," she
told them often, "you're never alone."

Helene read every book her mother gave her, but since she'd
fought the habit of obedience ever since she was a small girl, she
also smuggled romance novels from the pay-library into Margret's
room where, fascinated by the forbidden, the two girls would read
love scenes aloud to each other. They'd practice dancing with each
other. Practice passion by kissing each other's forearms until their
lips would leave prickly red circles that would take days to fade.

Inspired by the romance novels as well as stories of their own
families, they'd make up plays and bully their brothers into being
their audience in the dusty, half-dark attic of the pay-library. Stefan—just two years younger than the girls and unwilling to mind
them—would get away from them to run around with his dog,
Spitz, or his noisy friends, Michel Abramowitz and Kurt Heidenreich. In that group of three, Kurt was the only follower, while Stefan and Michel were usually fighting for leadership. Both knew
what they wanted, though they went about getting it in different
ways—Stefan by simply doing it without thinking of what it might
mean to others, and Michel by striving for agreement. Not that it
was all negative. Quite often what they wanted had to do with ex-
celling at school or collecting money for the poor at Michel's synagogue or Stefan's church.

But Leo always listened to what his big sister and Margret told
him to do. For hours he'd sit on an apple crate, skinny elbows
propped on his knees, watching the two girls with such rapture that

they'd feel real as ballerinas and pirates and heiresses. Already, his eyes had the look that would eventually mesmerize most women who came close to him. Here, in the attic, with Leo as their witness, Helene and Margret became anyone they wanted to be; anything they wished could happen because he would make it so. Born when both girls were six years old, he had become their favorite toy— much better than a doll. For hours they'd played family with him, taking turns being mother or father. On him they'd practiced diapering a baby, feeding a baby, burping a baby; and he, of course, worshiped them. For a few years they'd lost interest in Leo, but now he was their best audience: he frequently applauded, and he only got up if they needed him to play a minor part or fetch some prop.

Next to the attic was the room where Frau Montag sewed at night after the pay-library closed, but during the day the third floor belonged to Leo and the girls. Draped in a torn lace curtain or wearing huge boots and a top hat, Helene and Margret would perform for him in front of their stage curtain, a gray blanket they fastened between the window and the closest rafter. They had splendid props: false teeth inside a leather pouch; a porcelain clock that forever showed ten to five; two trunks with ancient clothes; a frayed hammock; white gloves with an oval red stain; a brown sofa with its stuffing poking through; a walking stick with a silver grip; rusted ice skates; a broken shovel; a wooden chair with a missing leg; a blue hat with a veil.

Helene would wear that blue hat and her mother's high-heeled shoes and a goose pillow under the front of one of the old-fashioned dresses she chose from the trunks when she played Lieselotte Montag in "Ja, Manfred," a play about her grandparents. When Lieselotte was a young woman, Manfred got flustered whenever he noticed that his wife was pregnant once again. From what Helene had overheard from her parents, Lieselotte would try to hide her condition by wearing shawls and loose dresses, but inevitably her husband would catch her one morning as she strained to close a button over her belly or her breast, and he'd ask: "Lieselotte?" Margret, who wore a captain's hat and jacket for the part of Manfred, had his voice just right—stern and blaming and just a bit tremulous. "Lieselotte?!" she would ask, and Helene, who had turned from the accusing gaze, would glance at Margret over her shoulder, letting her body follow the motion of her neck as she raised the veil of her hat and admitted, "*Ja,* Manfred."

While Leo applauded, out flew the pillow, and he got to catch it and hold the baby in his arms while Lieselotte and Manfred sat down to eat pretend food from real chipped plates. As soon as they lay down on their hammock-bed, Manfred began to snore with his mouth open, and Leo got to pass the baby to Lieselotte, who yanked it beneath the sheet. By the time she arose, it was back in place, a good-sized pregnancy. As Lieselotte fussed with her buttons and shawl, Manfred sat up in the hammock, yawned twice, then stared at her in disbelief and bellowed, "Lieselotte?!" Since the real Lieselotte had given birth to eleven children, "*Ja,* Manfred" was a long, long play.

At fourteen, Helene was brilliant, clumsy, shy, and far more flamboyant within her fantasies than in a reality where she frequently blushed. Just worrying about blushing would make her feel hot: the humiliating rose color would splash from her chest to her hairline, causing others to stare at her as though the blushing had something to do with them, while she'd shrink further into the curve of her shoulders and try to avoid occasions where she might blush.

Once, when Stefan passed her on the stairs to his sister's room, Helene got so hot and embarrassed that she spent an entire afternoon in the library of St. Martin's church, searching through medical reference books for remedies that would terminate the blushing forever. When Kurt Heidenreich's sister, Anita, said that her grandmother used to blush too until she'd stopped it forever by drinking vinegar, Helene forced down two cupfuls of vinegar, but she only gagged. Nothing else changed. She didn't even feel light-headed, though Anita had warned her that drinking vinegar could leave you so pale that you'd faint. Finally, Helene went to the pharmacy and asked Herr Volkenstein if he sold any medicines that cured blushing. At first he didn't understand what she meant, and as she repeated it, she loathed herself for turning red, while he consoled her, "It's becoming for a young girl to blush."

That's what her mother's friend, Frau Buttgereit, had told Helene too, but Frau Buttgereit couldn't even see, had been blind all her life, though it wasn't her fault. Everyone in Burgdorf knew the ill-fated story of how her blindness had come about the night of her birth in the convent hospital, when her mother had raised herself on her elbows and demanded the nuns take the crucifix from the wall. "I don't want my child to see that Jew when it opens its eyes." No one in town had been surprised when the child had been born unseeing. *God's punishment.* Helene's Catholic youth group had adopted the blind woman for their purgatory project, and the girls took turns reading to her in the evenings. There were two benefits to that: the immediate one was the pleasure Frau Buttgereit found in those readings; but the more significant one was the reduced time in purgatory the girls were accumulating for her.

Their group leader, Ingeborg Weinhart, had taught them that although you couldn't diminish your own purgatory ahead of time, you could do it for others through good deeds and prayers. How you prayed made all the difference. For example, if you made the sign of the cross with holy water *before* you said a prayer, it counted for three and a half prayers. That meant ten prayers with holy water added up to thirty-five prayers. A hundred prayers became three hundred and fifty. And consider a thousand!

For confirmation, the youth group leader had given all the girls glass vials filled with their personal holy water. Helene and Margret hoped that they, too, would find people to donate purgatory reduction to them once they were old, and they made a pact to pray for the other if she died first; but in the meantime they cleansed their souls every Saturday in the confessional. While Margret was constantly confessing to Herr Pastor Schüler about being greedy and vain—something that likely would get worse with age unless she changed quickly, so the priest warned her—Helene worried about her temper but even more so about impure thoughts.

The temper had to do with being a biter, her mother had told her. As a two year old, Helene had bitten several children in the neighborhood, and one afternoon her mother had cured her by biting her right back. Carefully, she had taken Helene's arm into her mouth and clamped her uneven teeth shut, leaving deep marks and smudged lipstick. Then she had cried, harder even than Helene, and had rocked her in her firm arms until they'd both stopped sobbing. "This will teach you not to bite," she had whispered. And it had. Except the rage then found its way out in other ways, in feet-stomping and ugly words, and her mother would remind her that the biter still lived within her.

But impure thoughts were even uglier than rage. At school, the nuns warned the girls about impure thoughts and urged them to avoid near occasions of sin. Dancing with a boy could be a near occasion of sin. That's why it was so important to always leave space for the Holy Ghost while dancing with a boy. So far, Helene had never danced with a boy—only with Margret and that didn't count—but she'd had lots of impure thoughts. She was convinced her blushing would go away if only she could stop those impure thoughts. Because surely that's what they had to be, those pictures that stirred her when her room was dark at night. The ones that agitated her the most were about the girl ready to be married. *Her fiancé's parents insist on sending her to the priest—always a faceless priest—to insure she is pure for their son and sometimes the priest comes to the girl's room but usually the girl has to go to the sacristy where the priest takes the crucifix from his neck touches it against her breasts in a blessing and tells the girl to hold it and lie down and open her legs and the girl obeys has to obey of course because the priest tells her to—you have to he says it's all part of pronouncing you pure—and then Helene is the girl almost pure almost and afraid not knowing why this is happening no no and ashamed because she feels herself getting wet there as he presses one hand against the girl there and searches her there and maybe he will scold her for getting wet against his fingers—not clean he will say—and the girl wants him to stop to go away to stop now now oh don't don't and the edges of the crucifix cut into her palms and a sweetness steals into her belly now a sweetness that makes her warm dizzy as it kneads itself into the panic and her heart is pounding and she feels warm so warm hot and wet and doesn't want it to stop no don't but she can't say it of course doesn't say it hears her breath only and then the priest has his mouth against her down there oh God oh down there and whispers into her do you want me to stop do you do you and she doesn't say anything doesn't because any word of hers will stop the sweetness down there and if she doesn't speak it is all the priest's doing who keeps his lips there in the name of the father and the son heavenly scepters of fire and the holy spirit as he whispers deeper into her in the name of the father burning her up with his prayer and the son and the holy spirit and the holy spirit oh God absolving her because she doesn't choose this doesn't tell him to go on as he whispers his prayer into her hard now his prayer so hard whispers do you want me to stop do you want me to stop do you do you and she crushes herself against his words around his words silent so silent and her fear so sweet against his prayer his hard whispered prayer—*

∽

One spring afternoon, when Helene balanced across the brook behind her house on a felled birch that Leo had dragged across the water, she felt graceful as she spread her arms and sang. She was Carmen, the tightrope walker from Brazil, Carmen in her silver dress right from the book jacket of *Splendor in Rio de Janeiro,* Carmen who sang the ballad of the famous matador as she raised her face to the sun and—

Above her, in the branches of the willow, sat Stefan and Michel and Kurt. Heat climbed from her chest, painting her neck and cheeks. She missed her step. Swayed. Fell. And though the brook was cold, she was still burning, burning up, and wishing she'd drown. Afterwards she didn't know if it was Stefan or one of the other boys who helped her—she was too embarrassed to glance beyond the smudged hands that reached for her—and it wouldn't be until Stefan was an old man and asleep next to her one Sunday morning that she would look at the knobs of his wrists on the quilt and recognize the hands that had reclaimed her from the water, and as she'd see herself as that long-ago girl, it would be as though all she had done in those years was blush and fall. She would smile and, her left thigh touching Stefan's, close her eyes with the tempered pain of the awkward girl.

It was Margret who showed her the note Stefan left when he ran away from home. For over a year he had pushed at his parents to let him go to America. Frustrated by their repeated "you are too young," he finally disappeared one night after his family was asleep.

His parents looked dazed and brittle whenever Helene saw them. Stefan's father had to close his tailor shop for a week because he punctured his right thumb at the sewing machine, and his entire hand swelled up red. Stefan's mother who prided herself on her clean house and her Dutch ancestry, and who'd offended some in the neighborhood by insisting, "the Dutch are so much cleaner than Germans," now sat at her kitchen table in a soiled dress, staring at the open star charts she'd pinned down with her elbows, her bent finger roaming the dense pattern of constellations as though she might locate her son there.

Although the people of Burgdorf presumed Stefan dead, they tried to comfort his parents: "Some boys just need to see the world. . . ."

"You'll hear from Stefan. Soon . . ."

"No boy could have asked for better parents. . . ."

But Helene was certain that Stefan had reached America and that, someday, he would come back for her. By then, of course, she would have outgrown the blushing, the way your body outgrows a church dress that never was right for you. *His arm around her, they walk through the meadow behind their houses toward the fairgrounds, and where the brook is at its widest, they stop as he pulls her toward him in a kiss.*

She wasn't at all surprised when, three months after Stefan had vanished, Margret came running into her house, waving an envelope with foreign stamps that had just arrived and proved that Stefan was, indeed, in America. That night Helene stayed up late. Her feather pillow bunched up behind her in bed, she sat and composed a note to him. While her movements around him had been ungainly, her words on the page took on a grace that compelled Stefan to answer her with a postcard, and when she wrote him another letter, he began to see this newfound grace in the neighbor girl until he believed it had always been there and that he simply hadn't noticed it.

He started addressing her as Lenchen, the affectionate form for Helene. *Liebes Lenchen,* he would start his letters as they became lengthier. When the Hungarian died in the fire, she grieved with him, and when he first thought of opening his restaurant in New Hampshire, she encouraged him and dared to imagine herself there with him. She liked to write to him late at night, making her letters last several weeks, continuing them the way she might a diary. Usually she'd start a new one as soon as she'd send the last, but then she'd hold on to it and date it after she'd get his answer because she didn't want to overwhelm him. She wrote him about her studies to become a teacher; cried as she wrote him about her parents' sudden death from influenza; sent him details of her visits with his sister who now had a husband. . . . And all along she related the stories of his American life to the people of Burgdorf until, gradually, she knew far more about him than his family did, and they came to her with questions about him.

When he married Elizabeth Flynn, Helene felt cut off from the possibility of her life changing; and she was still sick with a jealousy she believed she had no right to when Elizabeth died. He kept writing to her: when the walls of the *Wasserburg* were up halfway; when Greta learned to walk; when he married once again. She swore to herself that she wouldn't let him block off any part of her life. Reminded herself that she had her friendships and the satisfaction that came from them. The satisfaction she found in her work.

Yet, while she taught children born to other women how to form their numbers and letters, she sometimes felt a sharp envy of her married friends, wishing poverty and illness on them. *The biter in me.* She'd feel mortified. And it was not even that she wanted any of their men. True, no one had actually asked her to be his wife, not even the biology teacher Axel Lambert who walked her home after school once or twice a week. A shy man, a decent man who did not excite her, he sometimes reached for her hand with such hesitancy that she knew it must have taken him planning and courage, and after she'd briefly squeeze his fingers in hers before withdrawing her hand, he would not touch her like that for months to come. He was a good teacher, liked by the children in his classes, yet stiff with adults, a loner who didn't like to be around his family but preferred evenings alone in his apartment next to the synagogue, writing crossword puzzles for the newspaper.

While one after another of her classmates got married, she still slept in her childhood room in the house she shared with her brother, who had taken over their parents' pay-library. The six-year span between them had seemed vast when they were children, but now it no longer mattered, and she savored those evenings when Leo was not at the gymnast's club or the chess club or out dancing, because then he'd sit with her in the living room, reading or talking. He was a considerate brother, a kind brother she could trust, but she pitied the women who were drawn to him because his very kindness was dangerous to them. She'd seen it happen again and again, the way he held himself apart from women by adoring them without giving much of himself—not because he was stingy, but rather because he was so accepting of them that he didn't yearn to bridge the distance between himself and these women. And always he was bewildered by the pain he caused them. But inevitably there were new admirers because Leo was considerate and polite, a good listener who was truly interested in what each woman told him. And he had such a fascinating face, they agreed, a bony face both delicate and strong.

The first few months of each new courtship would be pleasant because Leo enjoyed being adored as well as being the adorer, but as soon as a woman tried to cross that gap between them, he'd retreat. *Pope Leo,* some called him behind his back. *Holy man Leo.* In their attempts to hold him or take revenge for his aloofness, they'd confide in Helene, who knew more about her brother than she wanted to: that he simply did not like sex; that there was a fastidiousness about him, a shrinking back when it came to physical contact; that he was still a virgin.

Virgins, she thought. *A family trait. We'll both be ancient and alone.*

One of his earliest girlfriends, Ilse Korfmann, had cried when she'd told Helene, "He would make a great father if he ever went that far with a woman. But not a husband."

Leo didn't mind when women who once had loved him found other men, and when Ilse married Michel Abramowitz, Leo felt more comfortable around her because now he could adore her once again from a distance. He valued his friendships with women who'd once turned from him in hurt or anger.

"*Ein ewiger Junggeselle*—an eternal bachelor," people said about him.

The woman Helene felt most sorry for was Gertrud Hagen— wild and fragile—who believed Leo was the only one for her, had always been the only one for her even when they'd been school-children, sitting next to each other at their desks or catching tad-poles by the Rhein; Gertrud who was prepared to wait till he was free from his next new love because she knew that this new next love would try to seize more of him than he wanted to relinquish; Gertrud who was always willing to start over as his friend, start with that first sweet and hesitant grazing of hand against hand; Gertrud who took what she knew he was capable of giving—ten-der, brotherly affection—and learned to hold him by pretending contentment in that, by letting him detain her in that limbo of not touching, that limbo where other women had learned to leave.

But then she would forget.

Hold him too tightly.

Press her lips against his too fervently.

And watch him step from her arms.

Sometimes Helene was afraid for her, afraid her brother would push Gertrud deeper into the craziness that seemed to live just be-neath her jittery smile, once she understood that ultimately she would never reach Leo, and that a kiss on the forehead was just that—a kiss on the forehead—and not a prelude to greater passion.

Helene thought he was far more passionate about chess than she'd ever seen him about a woman. Usually he'd have a board set up on the counter of the pay-library next to the bins with tobacco for sale. While stacks of books waited to be shelved, he'd study his chess moves with unwavering intensity. It wasn't that he didn't like the bodies of women. Once, while cleaning beneath his bed, she'd seen two magazines with pictures of naked women and men. She was sure he'd gotten them from his friend, Emil Hesping. Though she found Emil intimidating in the way all handsome men intimidated her, she knew he tried to come across as more of a cad than he really was. Actually, he was quite generous. When she'd turned her mother's old sewing room into a study for herself, he'd helped Leo carry her rosewood desk up the stairs, and the two had built bookshelves for her and papered the walls with purple-and-yellow pansies.

Leo's friendships with Emil and other gymnasts and chess players were long lasting and far less complicated than his connections to women. As much as Helene enjoyed her brother's company, she also cherished her evenings alone in her study where she wrote some of her letters to Stefan, who by now knew every one of her students by name, knew of her concerns and hopes for them. But of course he had no idea that she compared every man to him and that, quite often, she imagined her wedding to him, *looking up into his eyes as they promise each other eternal devotion, walking on his arm from St. Martin's church into the bright-white sun while the townspeople congratulate them.* It was always summer in those picture-book fantasies that came complete with the texture and style of her dress, with a reception on the lawn behind the pay-library and tailor shop, with the smell of cut grass and of sun-warmed camomile and roses, with the taste of wedding cake and the delicacies that the women of Burgdorf brought to her celebration.

Stefan would never know that, more and more, he took the place of the priest at night, no longer faceless, though his features were still those of a boy because all Helene remembered was how Stefan had looked as a thirteen year old. And if the priest fantasy didn't take, she would shift to others, like that of the bride stolen by the ushers and the best man from her own wedding reception. Whenever Helene knelt in the confessional or parted her lips to receive communion, she'd feel guilty about that deep-hungry woman inside her, but that didn't stop her. *The best man is tall and looks like*

Stefan and he and the ushers take the bride to an attic and promise they won't do anything to her if she lets them make sure she is still intact and they open her salmon-colored corset to caress the pink marks the stays have left on her skin where no man has seen or touched her before—and never will, Helene thought to herself, touching the silk rosebud at the cleavage of her corset—*but now one of them touches her breasts and they all kiss her there and touch her between her legs and say do you want us to stop and the bride doesn't answer and they say we will stop if you tell us to and she is silent with her face turned away so they can't see how much she wants it as they take her each of them each of them and the heat comes into her and she wants it too only she doesn't let them see that she wants it wants each of them in her again and they never know they're doing it for her for her—*

CHAPTER THREE

1911

Stefan wrote to Helene when Agnes died, when Tobias was born, and a week later when Sara died, and then she didn't hear from him for over half a year—though she kept writing to him, worrying about him, hoping—until one July afternoon in 1911 when he knocked at her door, wearing the black suit of the widower. With both hands he reached for hers, making her feel mute and far too tall. He hadn't grown much in the seventeen years he'd been away, was shorter than in her fantasies and quite a bit hairier. His fingers were steady, dry, and she longed for the composure she'd felt while reading and rereading his letters.

Instead of looking up into his green eyes as she had imagined, she had to look down. "No one told me you were coming," she managed to say.

He didn't offer any reason why he hadn't answered her last letters but told her he'd just arrived in town. "My parents don't know yet that I'm here. I came to you first."

His voice sounded odd to her. *An accent. He has an accent in his own language.* He stood close enough for her to smell the man-scent of his skin—so different from Leo who was part of herself, a man too, but not unsettling like this. She couldn't help staring at Stefan while her nose and thighs felt larger, while sweat collected on her palms. Pulling her fingers from his, she dried them against the sides of her navy-and-white-striped dress. The air was hot, moist, and on the Abramowitzes' roof across the street, sparrows were fighting over some scrap of food.

"I walked here from the railroad station," he said.

She admonished herself for not inviting him in, for standing there so stiffly. He looked accustomed to sorrow—so serious, distracted even—and she was sure he had to be thinking about his dead wives. From the window of the pay-library came the voice of Frau Simon, the milliner, and the high laugh of Gertrud Hagen. Helene wanted to tell Stefan how her brother had surprised himself as much as everyone else in Burgdorf by getting engaged to Gertrud after breaking up with her at least once a year over the past decade; but considering how Stefan had buried two wives, any mention of marriage felt inappropriate. Or about the bride-to-be who was older than her brother. Even if just one day. Not two years, like the gap between Stefan and herself. Leo had told her it was Gertrud who'd proposed. "I've never heard of a woman asking a man first," he'd said, "but then I thought if I married—and I always figured I would, eventually—it would be good if it were to someone I've known since we were children, someone where everything won't be so new all the time."

In the street the Abramowitz children, Ruth and Albert, were skipping rope, counting aloud: "*. . . elf, zwölf, dreizehn, vierzehn, fünfzehn. . . .*" The girl's dress was as purple as the geraniums in her mother's window boxes.

"Michel and Ilse's children," Helene said.

"Ilse Korfmann?"

"I wrote you when she married Michel Abramowitz." *Is that all I can talk about? Marriage?* Quickly she added, "He's a lawyer now. I wrote—"

"You did. He must be good as a lawyer . . . the way he loved to talk, wearing us down with endless discussions. Still—those are old children."

"Not much older than your Greta. The girl is seven, the boy six. Ruth and Albert."

Stefan shook his head, slowly. "I guess whenever I think of people back home, they've stayed the same age."

As Helene tried to recall what she'd looked like at fifteen, her face turned hot. "Remember Gertrud Hagen?" she blurted. "She was in Leo's class."

"I got whipped by the priest because she confessed to helping me paint those rocks around St. Stefan's feet."

"I can still see Herr Pastor Schüler marching up your front steps, shouting this was going to be your last prank. Why did you do it?"

"Because that saint is my namesake. Because he was the first Christian martyr stoned to death. And because those rocks should not be sky blue. I thought rocks should be brown."

"The priest must have agreed. He never changed them back to blue."

"When I sneaked in there, I was sure the church was empty. I didn't see Gertrud because she was behind a pew. Kneeling on the floor because it was harder on her knees." He motioned toward Ruth Abramowitz. "She was only about her age. But that's the way she was."

"She still is."

It occurred to him how much easier it was for both of them to talk about others than about themselves. "Gertrud came up to me," he said, "and asked what I had in my bucket. When I said chocolate for the saint, she dipped her finger into the paint. I stopped her before she could lick it off, told her it was holy chocolate. 'Only for saints,' I told her. 'Wipe your finger on those rocks. If you promise to be quiet, I'll let you cover one rock with holy chocolate.' She promised and held out her hand for the brush. Then she painted a rock and watched me do the rest. Without one word."

"Leo—he got engaged to her."

"Little Leo."

She had to smile. "Well . . . he's actually taller than you."

Stefan grinned back. "It doesn't take much for that, does it?"

Just then, the cart of the ragman turned around the corner, and Ruth Abramowitz ran toward it, followed by Albert. Shaking his bell, the ragman called out, "*Lumpen, Eisen, Papier*—Rags, iron, paper." His shirt glinted white in the sun.

"She's a thin wire," Stefan said.

"Gertrud?"

He nodded.

"What's a thin wire?"

"Something my grandfather used to say about people who were stretched so tight they could snap any moment."

As I could too, Helene thought, wanting him to fit both palms beneath her breasts and rub his thumbs up her nipples. *As I could too.*

"I can't believe how much shorter the distances here are," he said. "I'd forgotten what it's like to walk through streets where the houses share connecting walls or are just a meter apart."

"It must feel foreign to you. After all these years."

"In the town where I live buildings are surrounded by open spaces."

She saw his American town, *hundreds of huge, ornate houses like the apartment house he'd described in his letters, each building set apart from the next by orderly squares of forests and meadows. There, wind and air move freely between the buildings, cooling her neck, her ankles. . . .* "Could you imagine yourself living here in Burgdorf again?" she asked.

"But I'm an American now," he said, tilting his face up to study her kind eyes, the high forehead, the firm curve of her chin. Yes, she would be good to his children. But she was so unlike the articulate woman he knew through her letters. She was stiff and awkward—the way he suddenly remembered her from his childhood—and he felt saddened, sensing that if she agreed to marry him, he would forfeit that part of her that had been linked to him all those years with written words. "How about you?" he asked gently. "Would you ever leave here?"

"Oh yes," she said before she could lose the boldness to give him the response she'd kept prepared for him since she was a girl. At twenty-nine, he was still a young man who could easily find himself a bride five or ten years younger, as was the tradition, while as a woman of thirty-one she was considered beyond the age of being asked to marry. And yet, by being here, Stefan made real her secret knowledge that one day he would return for her. She wanted him to go away, wanted him to press himself against her, back her into the hallway and against a wall.

He reached into the pocket of his jacket and took out an envelope with photos of his children. "They're with their American grandparents while I'm away. Tobias in the apartment above the bakery, Greta in the banker's house."

As Helene touched the photos, she surprised herself with an odd yearning for these children as if they were her own and had already been separated from her far too long, and by the end of that week, when she would wear the white lace gown that Stefan's father would sew for her in his tailor shop, she'd feel oddly removed from the festivities because she was already picturing herself with Stefan's children, far away in America.

Years later, whenever she would think about her wedding, she'd remember most of all her impatience to be done with it because she had already lived that day so many times in her fantasies. All the details matched—the groom, the sun on her veil, the scent of fresh grass, the tables with white cloths behind the pay-library. While Herr Pastor Schüler blessed her union with Stefan, and while Michel Abramowitz was taking the wedding photos, she saw the ritual as if set in a frame—already defined, already completed—hers to review from a distance of decades if she chose to.

Yet, as always, her good manners saw her through: she thanked Margret and her husband for setting up all the tables, and she comforted Stefan's mother who was irritated with Gertrud for taking apart her white-and-pink flower bouquets and mixing them with clumps of cornflowers and camomile she'd pulled from the Rhein meadow at dawn.

When Helene followed Gertrud to the pay-library, she found her crying behind the last shelf of romance novels. "Thank you for the wildflowers," she whispered to her. "I'm so glad you remembered how much I like them."

Gertrud hiccuped with tears and embraced Helene, face hot and damp. "I'm afraid of her."

"Frau Blau? It's just that she's fussed all day over those flowers. She's really quite friendly once you—"

"Not Frau Blau. This one here." Gertrud laid one palm against her flat belly. Her lips pulled away from her teeth. "The girl who's coming into me here."

"Are you— You and Leo?" Helene asked though she didn't think her brother and Gertrud had slept together.

"Not yet and it's your wedding and you have to dance." Gertrud laughed shrilly and pressed her index finger against Helene's lips.

All at once Helene felt afraid for her. Gertrud was so physical. So passionate. Not at all like Leo. She'd seen the way he held Gertrud, lightly. Had witnessed the faint brush of his lips against Gertrud's cheek. Some in town gossiped about Leo being more comfortable with the touch of men. They saw his easy camaraderie with men and didn't know him well enough to understand that this was not because he desired men, but rather because touching them in competition or play was less complicated than touching a woman who might then want more of him.

"You have to dance with every man," Gertrud sang out and bolted from the back door.

"Wait—"

But Gertrud was already flying toward the tables, black curls springing loose from her knot, the sleeves of her yellow dress flapping around her arms, the tips of her shoes leaving imprints in the fine, orderly ridges of earth that Leo had raked behind the pay-library. As Helene followed her, people kept stopping her to compliment her on her new husband, her new life in America, her new children. Even more people than in her wedding fantasies were here: neighbors, friends from church, colleagues from school— though not Axel Lambert—and several of her students. It was summer as in her fantasies, and though her gown wasn't as elaborate as the one she'd pictured herself in—not enough time to prepare, after all—it didn't matter to her.

Guests had arrived with gifts and with food: cream of leek soup and cucumber salad, sheets of plum cake and roasts with gravy, liver sausage and herring salad, pickled beets and sliced peaches. Three dogs were sniffing the grass around the tables, tails twitching as they waited for scraps. While Frau Buttgereit turned her sightless gaze toward the sun, her daughter-in-law, Ottilia—much beloved by the older woman because, ironically, she'd been named after the patron saint of the blind and therefore seemed to offer a direct link to the saint—was arranging white stalks of asparagus on a platter,

tender points meeting in the center, clouds of parsley in the gaps between them. Ottilia's husband stood too close to the baker's wife,
who used to be the second-most-beautiful girl in school. The first-
most-beautiful girl he had married eight years ago, never guessing
how drastically childbirth would transform her. Each child, four
living daughters and two stillborns so far, had either added to Ottilia Buttgereit's body or taken away from it, but all in the wrong
places—a rising of her belly so that she seemed perpetually pregnant; a drooping of her breasts and the corners of her mouth; a
waning of her neck until it looked stringy—while her husband,
with increasing fervor, sought to recapture her beauty in other
women. "This one for sure will be a boy," he would tell people
each time Ottilia was pregnant, not knowing that she would have
to give birth to nine daughters altogether before his one son would
be born, and that this son would not live for long.

Leo was halfway into a chess game with nine-year-old Günther
Stosick, a superb player despite his youth and shyness, who kept
his eyes on the board, elbows on the table, fingers in his dense hair
to keep himself from making rash moves. He seemed more grown
up than the rest of the children, who played hide-and-seek in the
dark space beneath the back of the pay-library, where massive
stones from the riverbed formed the foundation as for most houses
in Burgdorf. When the music started—one accordion and two
fiddles—Günther didn't even glance up, but the other children
came running, faces and clothes smudged, and danced with each
other.

Ruth Abramowitz's pinafore was silvery with spiderwebs, and
her father wiped them off with his handkerchief. "Hold still,
Schätzchen." When she darted from him, he laughed. "Always running, this one," he told Stefan. "Running and dancing."

"I saw her and your boy the day I arrived," Stefan said. "Skipping rope. Running. Just the way you say."

"Check." Günther advanced his white bishop.

"You're getting too good for me," Leo said, realizing he was
about to lose a rook.

The townspeople wanted Stefan to taste everything. "Strawberry tarts the way you used to like them as a boy." "I bet you don't get head cheese like this in America." "I made fresh blood sausage just for you." He and Helene both tasted. Tasted from silver forks that his mother had stored beneath the earth and dug up for this celebration. Tasted until all those flavors merged inside their mouths.

As they washed them down with Mosel wine, Helene felt as light and fast as the swirl of children; and in that moment of joy she wanted to pull Stefan into that dance where he, too, could be light and fast; but she didn't because there was something oddly formal about him, and when he finally asked her to dance, holding her in his arms for the first time ever, his body felt so unyielding that all lightness left her. Together, they were rigid and clumsy as they moved across the lawn to the music, and she felt relieved when Emil Hesping tugged at her sleeve and requested his dance with the bride. Then there were others, and gradually she felt it again, that lightness. "You have to dance with every man," Gertrud had told her. And she did, danced more than she had in five years, and it amused her that men who'd never flirted with her before now acted as though she were breaking their hearts by leaving the country.

"I know you'll recover," she told Emil, who had a reputation with women.

To Kurt Heidenreich, the taxidermist, she said, "You've hidden your feelings too well."

And she didn't even blush—not once—that's what she and Kurt's sister, Anita, laughed about most when they sat down together.

One of her former students, Agathe Lange, who was getting ready to enter the convent the following Monday, came to her table to give her a rosary carved by Trappist monks. "You are a brave woman, Fräulein Montag—I mean, Frau Blau. I would never get on a ship to go to America."

"Then how would you get there?" asked Frau Simon, who had recently scandalized the town by divorcing a perfectly decent husband. "Walk on water?" When she raised one elegant shoe—dyed robin's-egg blue to match her new hat and purse—as if she were about to step onto water, several men gaped at her strong, slender ankles.

"It is bad luck to make fun of religion."

"Oh, but I wasn't making fun. It was a practical suggestion. Considering . . ."

Agathe Lange studied the milliner with practiced patience, the kind that comes from many years of kneeling in hard pews. "Considering?"

Frau Simon laughed, eyes bright as always when she managed to draw someone into her banter. "Considering how in your religion things like that are done."

"One of many miracles." Agathe Lange turned to Helene. "I will pray for—"

"I saved you some of my asparagus." Ottilia Buttgereit extended her platter to Helene.

"That's very kind."

"I bet you don't get asparagus like mine in America. Mr. Buttgereit and I, we want to grow enough next year to start selling it. People keep asking us if they can buy any, and I think we're getting ready to do it."

"I will pray for you every morning." Agathe Lange finished her sentence and added, "Until you get there safely."

"Thank you."

"I'm so pleased it's your wedding. I never thought you—" She clasped her fingers across her mouth.

"Don't worry," Helene said. "You're not the only one."

The townspeople kept telling her how unlike her it was to make such a big decision in a hurry—insisting as if to convince her they were right about her and that, therefore, she must be acting against her own nature—and she smiled politely, feeling no need to explain herself to them.

But Stefan's father was eager to explain to everyone, "Of course there is a rush. There has to be a rush because my grandchildren are in America, and Stefan has to get back to them." His powerful upper body was stooped from decades of sewing. He fanned out the photos on the tablecloth between two ashtrays. "That's Tobias, the youngest, just seven months old. And Greta here—see?" He pointed to another picture, tufts of gray in the hollows between his knuckles. "She'll be five in November."

"Don't forget to tell them that Greta speaks German." Stefan's mother stubbed out her cigarette.

"Already, two languages." Stefan's father nodded.

"And she's just a bit of a girl," Ingeborg Weinhart said.

Stefan's mother motioned for Stefan to come closer. "Keep your eyes on that Gertrud Hagen. She's been messing up my flowers."

To Stefan it was shocking how his mother had aged. Though still in her forties, she looked far older—*her neck so thin now, her hair so sparse*—and what he kept coming back to was that now, a few months away from turning thirty, he was as old as she had been that day he'd left home. And he thought about being a parent and about loss and about grief. A few days ago, when he had first entered her kitchen and embraced her, she'd cried his name and begun to tremble till he was trembling too, and as they'd held on to each other, he'd felt as if he and his mother were the same age, and as if it were his duty to console her about the son who had only now run off to America. Time was letting him understand her in that grief as if it were happening now; and it was like that for her too: whenever she looked at him—there in her kitchen and now on his wedding day—her tears would well up as if that old sorrow were too immense to be contained within the body of one woman and she were passing it on to him. *I know,* he wanted to tell her, *I know.* He'd heard people say the worst loss you could suffer was that of a child. And perhaps that was so. Still, for him losing two wives had cut far deeper than losing Agnes.

∞

Helene felt the presence of those wives when Stefan followed her that night to her bedroom above the pay-library where she had imagined him countless times, and she wondered if he, too, sensed Elizabeth and Sara here with them. And then she knew that he did because he spoke about them and about some deeds he should have changed over to Sara's name from Elizabeth's, blamed himself for not doing it soon enough as if that delay had taken her life.

"The day we get back," he promised Helene, "I'll make sure your name will be on the deeds." He hung his suspenders over her chair. "I want the house and restaurant to be yours as much as mine." In the path of moon that slanted through her window, he unbuttoned his shirt. "If you like—" His voice was careful. Tender.

"Yes?"

"If you like, we can wait. With . . . with me approaching you as a husband. Until we know each other better."

"But I've known you all your life."

Still, as he came to her in this room of her childhood, just an arm's length from the house where he'd lived as a boy, the fantasies that had served her so well—*always happening to someone else to someone else*—no longer worked for her. They did not remove her, take her. Because this was *not* happening to someone she had made up inside her head. And, strangely, that's why it made this here—*thishere*—feel less real. Her fantasies she could split from her life; and they always lasted as long as she wanted them to. But *thishere* was not nearly as exciting as her own touch. *Thishere* was over in minutes, concluded before it was consummated as if Stefan didn't need her to be part of it. What he did was raise himself away from her before he gave himself fully to his lust, and as his breath reached its height without her, he spilled himself atop her belly, and she felt further from him than she had all those years he'd lived on another continent. Yet what could she possibly say to him? He was the one with the experience, a married man, twice married he was and now the third time, while she was new at *thishere*. And she could not even leave *thishere* behind, could not pretend *thishere* had happened to another woman in a church or an attic because morning did come, and the man next to her in the narrow bed—*your husband in the name of the Father and the Son and the Holy Spirit*—got up without acknowledging the skin between them, the night between them.

He poured water into the basin, washed his face, slipped the loops of his mustache trainer across his ears, and adjusted its mesh triangles to cover his mustache. While it dried, he got dressed. Then he went downstairs and waited for her to make his breakfast. He smiled at her as he ate and talked to her brother as though nothing had changed, *nothing*, while she kept her anger and confusion from him, kept her back to the table and busied herself by the stove, pouring more coffee for both men, getting up again to add water to the many vases with yesterday's flowers.

A few times Leo glanced at her, but he knew not to break through with words when she was separate and silent like that, and it made her even angrier that Stefan didn't know her well enough to notice that something was not right. The rest of that day she barely saw him. He was out, purchasing materials for a tile stove he planned to build in their apartment, while she and Stefan's sister took the train to the Mahler department store in Düsseldorf, where they bought toys and clothing for his children. When Helene tried on a green loden coat with leather buttons and asked Margret if she thought it was stylish enough for America, she wondered all at once how Margret's husband was with her at night and what Margret would think if she knew how it was between her and Stefan.

Though Stefan was attentive, he kept himself so busy in the following days that Helene wondered if he was avoiding her, but she told herself, *it's just for now, till we leave here. Once we're in America, it will be better.* Nights with him did nothing to make her feel more confident about being a wife, but at least she felt secure about becoming a mother to his children. She knew she was good with children, had years and years of proof of schoolchildren gravitating toward her, liking her, respecting her.

∽

On Helene's fourth day as a married woman, Stefan's mother led her through her house that was crammed full of belongings she should have thrown out decades ago. Yet everything was spotless because she cleaned each morning after mass.

"Whatever you like," she said, "you just pick it out."

Though Helene tried to object, Stefan's mother gathered lace doilies and tablecloths, pillowcases and scarves, a picture that Stefan had drawn as a boy of the family's dog, Spitz, long since dead. Helene was still trying to adjust to the changed relationship with this woman who'd always been her neighbor and now was family and expected her to call her *Mutter*—mother. Since they had only fifteen years between them, she used to think of Stefan's mother as belonging to her own generation, while her new father-in-law, though just nine years older than his wife, seemed an entire generation ahead.

In the attic Stefan's mother held up a carved dollhouse with tiny blue dishes. "My grandmother played with this as a girl in Holland. She gave it to me the day of my first communion. Now you take it for Greta."

"Don't you want to save it for Margret?"

"Five years married and no children yet? You tell me." Frau Blau raised a corner of her apron and dabbed at the sweat on her powdered face.

"There's still time," Helene said, though she knew Margret didn't want children and was afraid to tell her mother. Easier to pretend she couldn't have them and go to the midwife who knew how to keep you childless by fitting half an apricot pit deep inside you. If you came to her already pregnant, she'd boil shreds of birch bark with tea leaves, wrap the cooled concoction into cheesecloth, and pack that up inside you till you bled. But if you didn't bleed, your child would be liable to carry the sign of the tea leaves somewhere on its body—out of sight, if you were lucky—a birthmark in the shape of a few dark and tiny leaves, and then all you could do was pray that your child would never find out it was marked with the sign of the unwanted.

"Margret never cared for that dollhouse," Frau Blau was saying. "The one day I let her play with it, she broke two cups. You make sure now Greta doesn't break anything. And don't let the boy play with it. Do you like those lion chairs?" She pointed to the wall where two needlepoint chairs stood, their legs and armrests thick wooden spirals. "They're over a hundred years old."

Helene touched the upholstery, a dense pattern of greens and browns. As she bent closer, she saw vines and trees and orchids, and then, as if emerging step by step from this jungle, half-hidden animals: lions and elephants and giraffes. "They're beautiful."

"Sit down. Try one."

Each armrest ended in a small crouched lion, and as Helene closed her fingers around the lions' heads, she felt the carved strands of their manes.

"They're yours."

"I wish we could take them with us. But they're way too heavy."

"Not nearly as heavy as your desk or those tiles Stefan bought for his stove. I'll talk to him." Before she let Helene go, Frau Blau insisted she take some of her lentil soup along for Leo. She poured a generous amount into a large porcelain bowl, set it atop a dish-towel, and tied the four corners of the towel together so that Helene could carry it by the knot.

When Leo helped Helene with the crating of her belongings, he teased her about all the things her mother-in-law wanted her to take along. "Did you forget how to say no?"

"I can't with her. Because of her eyes. They're always so tragic."

"Ever since Stefan ran off."

"And now he's running off again. With me."

"After only a week," he teased her. "Disgraceful."

"After half a lifetime."

He looked at her, gravely, as if he'd understood all along how she'd waited for Stefan, but had been too considerate to tell her; and since it bothered her to think of her brother knowing, she stepped away from him to glance out of the window. That narrow border all at once seemed to define her hometown—what she could see and beyond: church and marketplace and meadows and river—containing it so that she could take it with her, small and manage-able, just one more thing to pack along with her mother-in-law's tablecloths and furniture and five bundles of Stefan's letters.

As she lowered the bundles into the crate, she said to Leo, "We'll write to each other."

"Often. To take the place of your letters to Stefan."

"That's true," she said slowly, thinking how much she would miss those late nights of writing to Stefan and imagining his reac-tion.

He pointed to one of Frau Blau's silk scarves, green with a yellow sailboat. "You really plan to wear this *Kitsch?*"

"No." She folded it into the crate. "But it gives her comfort to know we have some of her things. We've told her that we want them to visit, but I don't think they will."

"You know the Blaus. If they can't get there on their bicy-cles . . ."

Helene smiled. "I know, they won't go." Lots of the old people in Burgdorf were like that. They didn't even like to take the train to Düsseldorf for the day because anything unfamiliar felt dangerous. The older they got, the more modern the world around them became, tricking them, constricting them. While she was getting ready to travel to a different continent. "But you will visit," she said. "Real soon?"

"Gertrud and I."

"Of course," she said quickly, ashamed she hadn't included Gertrud in her invitation. How could she possibly tell her brother that she sensed something half-broken beneath Gertrud's loveliness, something that might eventually cause him more pain than joy? She laid her mother's black leather purse into a crate that was just about full. "Do you ever wonder—" She hesitated. Filled the rest of the crate with cardigans she'd knitted over the years.

"Wonder about what?"

"Oh . . . nothing. You're getting too thin."

"I've always been too thin." He pushed his pale curls from his bony forehead. "What is it really?"

"I shouldn't ask. I don't want to be the sister who holds on too long."

"Ask."

"If Gertrud is right for you. Do you ever wonder about that?"

"Do you?" He knelt down to nail the first crate shut. "About Stefan?"

She was startled. "No. I guess I've never wondered. And here I'm asking you. I'm sorry."

"I'm not even sure what that means . . . being right for someone. None of us can know for sure if someone is right for us. And maybe that's good. But what I do know is that Gertrud feels like a second sister to me."

Helene felt queasy. "A sister?"

"Not like you. But familiar in a way because we were children together."

Slowly, Helene wrapped the wax Madonna her students had given her last Christmas. "Of course you'll bring Gertrud to visit us."

"After we're married and have saved up." He packed her encyclopedia. "And you'll show us America."

"Listen to us." She forced a lightness into her voice. "I haven't even been there, and already I'm showing you all of America."

He laughed.

She spread her arms. "Well then—where would you like to go first?"

"To the town where you live, of course. Then New York. Then the highest mountain you can find in America. Then the Wild West and—"

"You have thought this out."

"I've had an entire week."

She rolled her great-grandmother's pewter cups into cloth napkins. "I haven't given you much time."

"Or yourself," he said softly.

∽

When she embraced her brother and Margret the morning of her departure, she knew she was following the myth she had created as much as she was following the man, but she was ready to begin the life she had staked out in her fantasies.

As she walked next to Stefan up the wide, curved steps in front of the *Wasserburg,* she recognized the building from the descriptions in his letters, but she was not prepared for the opulence when he set down his leather suitcase and unlocked the double oak door. From the paneled vestibule, they entered through a set of French doors with half-moons of stained glass above them. The marble-tiled lobby was larger than any hotel lobby Helene had ever seen: stenciled beams supported the high ceiling; brocade chairs and sofas were grouped around gleaming tables; an inlaid desk stood below one of the front windows. Two long mirrors enfolded her reflection as if to compare her to Stefan's previous wives, and she felt the urge to climb out of a window to escape that verdict, an urge she would forget until nearly forty years later when she would come across her grandchildren, Emma and Caleb, climbing on top of the desk and squirming out of the window as though compelled to give shape to their grandmother's long-ago impulse.

She had never ridden in an elevator, had never been inside a building this tall. When Stefan took her up to the sixth floor, her hands felt cold despite the summer heat, not because of the elevator—although that made her stomach leap to meet her heart—but because she was anxious about meeting Greta and Tobias. How she wanted to love his children for whom she'd longed from far away.

But they weren't there yet. Somehow she'd forgotten, though Stefan had told her that they were still with their grandparents. When he left to pick them up, she walked through the huge apartment, feeling unstable because the many curtainless windows let the outside in much more than she was accustomed to. The lake was speckled with islands and reflected the clouds, the mountains, and a sky so immense that Helene felt dizzy. Though no one could possibly look into these windows—after all, no other houses stood as tall as her husband's—she felt exposed and resolved to get drapes as soon as possible, and to replace the delicate chairs with something solid that would balance this feeling of being up here in a tree house.

When Stefan brought his children to her, she crouched to embrace Greta, who had something calm and mysterious about her that drew Helene to her instantly. As the girl's gray eyes took her in, squinting as if to see only her and no one but her, Helene kept her arms around her, their faces at the same level, until Greta smiled, relieved that this new mother would live to be an old woman. When Helene stood back up, she felt still, protected even. But the boy unsettled her: his eyes pulled at her for more affection than anyone could possibly give him; yet, when she lifted him up and kissed his cheek, he arched away from her and began to wail, resisting her tenderness, his body as unyielding as that of his father when he'd danced with her on their wedding day. She had wanted Stefan to see how natural it was for her to be a mother, and she could feel him watching, perhaps even judging, as she failed to soothe his son.

In the meantime, Greta was tugging at her skirt, and Helene ended up balancing her and Tobias in her arms. She braced her legs—not just to support the children's weight, but also because it felt unnaturally high up here on the sixth floor.

"Look . . . the mail boat." Stefan pointed to a large boat that was approaching one of the islands, leaving a triangle of light on the water.

"How beautiful." Her eyes followed the wake, triple lines that emerged from the stern and widened the further they were away from the boat.

"I'll take you for a tour on it," he said. "Soon. See that?" With his free hand he motioned to a bald spot high on a hill across from them. "I wish they wouldn't cut so many trees. Two centuries ago shipbuilders used to get their masts here . . . white pines that were over two hundred feet tall. They're all gone now."

She waited for him to take one of the children from her arms, but as soon as he offered to, she felt compelled to object, "No, it's not necessary. They're just getting used to me. Why don't you get their presents instead."

"Surprises from Germany," he announced. "And when the rest of our things arrive, there'll be more." He unwrapped Tobias' gifts, a cast-iron milk cart with a horse, and a play-circus with painted wooden animals. "You're next, *Fröschken*," he said to Greta.

"My dolls are careful. They don't break dishes."

"Have you already told her what's in there?" Helene asked.

He shook his head. "Sometimes she worries me when she gets like this."

For the town of Winnipesaukee, Helene's presence was a reminder that Stefan Blau did not trust the endurance of the women in his adopted country. The first time she went to mass at St. Paul's, the people looked solemn as if they saw the sign of death on her face.

". . . too soon, that marriage," they whispered.

". . . just a mother for his children."

". . . someone close to him at night."

They lit candles for her at the side altar where Stefan had once bartered with God. Some wondered if he still carried a spell on him that destroyed the women who bore his children, and most agreed that a man who grieved with such passion would need a woman far more exciting than Helene to make him forget his dead wives. After mass, when he stood waiting for her outside the church he had promised himself to never enter again, Helene linked her arm through his, only too aware that people were speculating why a handsome man like that would take such pleasure in walking home with her—a plain, large-boned woman who was older than he but still blushed like a schoolgirl. And yet it was obvious that he liked being with her. He was content. Took her to the fair. To a town meeting. Came home for early dinners with her and the children before he returned to his restaurant to work till late most nights.

By now, the crates they'd shipped from Burgdorf had been delivered, except for the one with Helene's cardigans and her mother's purse and the letters from Stefan she'd saved all those years. The cardigans she could replace. And she had other things that had come to her from her mother. But those letters . . . What made their loss even harder for her was finding out that Stefan hadn't kept any of hers. It was as if that part of their history had suddenly dissolved.

He tried to console her. "That crate may still arrive."

But she didn't believe it would. Because somehow it felt as though she'd traded his letters for the reality of being here. With him. As his wife.

Sometimes the townspeople would come upon the new Mrs. Blau by the lake where she'd be playing on the beach with the children or reading to them from a picture book in her own language. Greta, a dreamy expression on her face, would kneel in the sand and, with a twig, draw pictures into the dirt. She had an ability to see and appreciate details that others didn't stop to notice: the shadow of a leaf, the shape of a stone, the contrast of branches against a blue sky. Tobias would be propped up in his wicker carriage, chattering to himself in wordless sounds. If he banged his head against the backrest, steady and fast as he often did, his stepmother would cup the back of his head in one palm and whisper her soft and foreign phrases to him.

While Helene craved words that fit her thoughts, words that didn't feel so unfamiliar, the people of Winnipesaukee mistook her silence for snobbery; they saw her as a proud woman who kept herself apart from them; they didn't understand that she'd always seen herself as smart, capable, and now felt frustrated in her new language where she could barely make herself known; they had no idea how confused she was by their lack of formality. Americans told her, "I'll see you," and she wanted to ask, *"When?"* But then they didn't visit. Was it because she didn't respond properly?

Though she'd studied English in school, it was much harder speaking the language than reading or hearing it. Often she'd feel so slow that she'd stay silent rather than risk not being understood. "Huh?" people would ask, and if she'd repeat what she'd just said, they'd ask again, forcing her to repeat herself three or four times until she was whispering with embarrassment.

It made her feel different, made her think how—although everyone carried some difference just by the separation of skin from others—that became magnified when you were an immigrant, when there were more details to set you apart. Language, for one. And then of course the experience of having grown up a certain way. Here in America she felt more German than she had back home. Because here she stood out. She envied her husband who blended in because he'd come to this country as a boy.

At home, they only spoke German.

One afternoon when she took the children for their daily *Spaziergang*—walk—Tobias in his carriage with Greta holding on to the side as usual, she saw a group of small boys—all of them hunchbacked—chasing a ball around the playground of the granite school building. Their legs were knobby around the knees. Choked with pity, Helene stopped by the rose hedge. How could there be so many of them in one small town when all of Burgdorf had only one hunchbacked man? But at least the parents of these unfortunate boys had brought them together in a game where they were all alike and would not be teased by healthy children. It made her appreciate America, that magnitude of concern. Grateful that her stepchildren's bodies were not deformed, she bent to kiss the tops of their heads.

At the dinner table, she added a prayer for the hunchbacked boys and their parents.

"Hunchbacked boys?" Stefan spooned mashed potatoes onto Greta's plate.

"You must have seen them before. There were nine of them. Their legs were all swollen around the knees."

"Here in town? I haven't seen a single one."

"Their heads were covered with little helmets. To protect them, I guess. They were playing with a ball, kicking it and—"

Stefan started to laugh.

She stared at him. It was the first time she'd seen him laugh. She'd seen him smile through his grief—always through his grief— and she'd respected that; but now he was laughing. And about this? Someone else's misfortune? "I don't know you at all," she said.

"Lenchen. . . ." He wiped his eyes. "It's padding they put on. To play football. So they won't get hurt. It's a rough game."

"Of course," she said slowly, feeling drained by her worries about those children.

"Don't feel foolish. Everyone who comes here from another country has stories like that. Of not understanding. Hey . . ." He covered her hand with his. "It's funny."

But it was only when Greta said, "Fun-ny . . . fun-ny . . . ," slap- ping the back of her spoon into her mashed potatoes with each syl- lable, that Helene could join in the laughter.

❧

After that, laughter seemed to happen easier between her and Ste- fan. When Stefan gave a reception in the lobby of the *Wasserburg* to introduce her to his tenants, Nate Bloom arrived with four bot- tles of champagne and a young woman whose hat was decorated with silk peonies and the feathers of songbirds. "This here's Eileen," he said. "My girlfriend."

Stefan led them to the buffet table where two of his waiters were serving the food he'd prepared in his restaurant. Beeswax candles and tall vases with gladiolas were set up on either end of the long table.

Eileen's left hand shot out toward a tray with hors d'oeuvres, but instantly she pulled her thin fingers back as if against their will. "Do any of these have shrimps in them?"

"I do not know," Helene said.

Eileen frowned at her. "Huh?"

"My wife said she does not know," Stefan said, "but I can assure you that I didn't use any shrimps today."

Still, she hesitated. "But have there been shrimps on any of these serving plates before?"

For an instant he observed her without speaking, but then he said in his most polite voice, the one reserved for difficult guests, "I'm in the habit of using clean plates."

"I didn't question your habits."

"Honey . . ." Nate circled one arm around her shoulders. "Honey, why don't we just have a glass of champagne for now? We both know that agrees with you."

"Please. I'm trying to tell you that I even get a reaction if I eat from a plate that had shrimps on it hours before."

"What exactly happens?" Stefan encouraged her.

"My breathing passages close up. And I get hives all over."

"Is that so?"

"And I have been known to collapse."

"You mean you can't speak at all when that happens?" He managed to sound concerned.

But Helene could tell he was close to laughing. And so was she. Bringing her lips close to his ear, she whispered in German, "Let's feed her some shrimps then, quickly."

When Mr. Bell, the retired lawyer, started playing his violin, Nate led his girlfriend toward the double door in back of the lobby. "Let me show you the lake, honey."

As the party spilled out toward the dock, a few of the children got their swimsuits and ran into the water.

Mr. and Mrs. Evans from the fourth floor pulled Helene aside. "We brought you American pralines," Mr. Evans said and handed her a red velvet box much prettier than any box she'd seen in Germany.

But when she passed them around and tasted one herself, it was too sweet for her, too soft. Still, she managed to thank them without lying. "My first American pralines," she said in her halting English.

"I am so glad you like them." Mrs. Evans was leaning on a cane though she was barely forty.

"Some of the other girls from the building will join us in a while," her husband told Helene.

She was amazed when those girls turned out to be women older than she. One of them had a tiny face with fine, silky creases so stretched that her eyes protruded. That tautness was there in her movements too, as if her entire body had been compressed.

"Welcome to our building," she said as if she were one of its owners and presented Helene with a red cake tin that was filled with peanut brittle. "I'm Miss Garland, and I made this for you. For this occasion."

"Thank you," Helene said, trying to touch the back of her teeth with her tongue so that it wouldn't sound like *zank you*.

"You may keep the container."

"Thank you."

"Those wasps again," Mr. Evans said and swatted at the air.

"I've always been fond of Germany," Miss Garland said. "My fiancé traveled widely in Germany as a boy, and he said he'd like to take me there on our honeymoon."

Helene saw Miss Garland *arm in arm with a dapper, old man, standing by the railing of an excursion boat . . . eating dinner at a linen-covered table on the terrace of the Kaisershafen Gasthaus high above the Rhein, where he pours Mosel wine into her glass, leans toward her voice. . . .* How splendid, Helene thought, that here in America people can marry so late in life. It made her feel like a young bride. Through the open door, sun and the voices of children streamed into the lobby, and far out on the lake the striped sails of a boat filled up with light.

"I hope you will like it in Germany," Helene told Miss Garland.

"Oh, but you don't understand . . . The wedding, it was all set, but—"

"He departed," Mr. Evans said.

"Died," his wife corrected him. "Buried. Gone."

Stunned by the lack of compassion, Helene turned to Miss Garland. "I am very very sorry. And that it should happen now."

Miss Garland blinked. "Now?"

"When you go to your . . . how do you say? . . . weddingmoon."

"Honeymoon. Except that my fiancé died forty-four years ago."

"But—"

"He died young, and he died tragically. A riding accident. Some people—" She frowned at Mr. and Mrs. Evans. "—may think it foolish that there's not a day I don't think about him."

"Oh, but it is not foolish," Helene said fervently, wishing she could express herself better.

Miss Garland felt a satisfying moment of connection to the new Mrs. Blau because she could tell that Helene, too, had experienced the longing that was so familiar to her. "Tell me about him," she said.

"It is not like that," Helene said quickly. She didn't want to let Miss Garland or any of the other tenants see how confusing it felt to be the third wife of a man who still carried his other wives with him. For Stefan, she would have liked to be flamboyant and glamorous, the type of woman who'd capture his passion and make it equal to her own, who'd make him forget any other woman. Lying next to him at night, she'd curse her pride that made it unthinkable to reach for him first, to stroke his hairy chest and thighs and back and tell him of the love she had carried for him all those years. Marriage, she had believed, would make it possible to express that love. But Stefan never spoke of love. He'd signal what he wanted by laying one palm on her belly but then—determined to not lose her in childbirth—would separate himself from her all too soon, condemning her with that lightness, that absence of flesh that left her only with the weight of her love.

But at least I'm capable of that kind of love. It was a magnificent love, she knew, a stubborn love; and she would try to ease her pain by imagining herself decades away, an old woman who'd feel compassion for the husband who had shunned a love like that without understanding what he had forgone.

Many nights after he had escaped from her into sleep, leaving her with a loneliness greater than any she had known while lying alone in her bed in Burgdorf, she would slip from beneath the covers, fill the deep tub in the marble bathroom, and let the warm water surround her, permeate her the way her husband would not. Stretched to her full length, the back of her head resting against a folded towel, she'd read German novels that her eyes could follow without the barrier of translation. Sometimes, though, she'd simply lie there, tears blurring the outlines of the hexagonal tiles, and as the water around her cooled, she'd flip up the hot faucet with her toes, astonished by the luxury of it all. In Germany she used to stoke the tall stove next to the tub and wait for it to heat; but in her husband's house, she could take a bath any hour of the day. *Or night. And he won't even notice I'm gone.* As she'd step out of the tub, the amber lamp in the ceiling would cast her into a soothing halo, and in the mirror above the porcelain sink her face would look like that of a woman accustomed to being caressed. *The irony of it.*

Tell me about him, Miss Garland wanted to ask again; but she postponed her curiosity, filed it away for later. "I believe my fiancé must have known he wouldn't be here for long. You see—" Her voice receded.

When Helene leaned forward to hear better, she saw tears in Miss Garland's eyes.

"He wrote me into his will the morning of the accident. Just hours before he—"

"Do not make yourself sad by telling."

"He wanted me to have a certain life."

"He was a . . . how do you say? . . . considerate man."

"Most considerate."

"Dear? Dear, I believe you have other guests," Mrs. Evans reminded Helene.

"And he was very well to do." Miss Garland glared at Mrs. Evans. "Poor white trash," she whispered to Helene, "from Maine. Grew up in a one-room shack and figured she'd marry the most ambitious man she could find. You come to me if you ever have questions about the other tenants. Or about the building."

Late that evening, after their guests had left, Helene and Stefan walked to the end of the dock, untied their shoes, and let the black water slap against their bare feet. They were laughing as they outdid each other with ideas for shrimp recipes they could feed Nate Bloom's girlfriend.

"Shrimp Louis."

"Shrimp salad."

"Shrimp bisque." He leaned against her, and when she shifted, he surprised her by resting his head on her lap, right out in the open where anyone who walked along the lake could see them.

"We'll sauté shrimps for her in butter."

"We'll have to do it fast, though. Because Nate's ladies never last."

"What's Miss Garland's first name?"

"I don't know. Maybe nobody knows."

"She must have signed her lease with her full name."

"All she wrote is 'Miss Garland.' "

"She told me about her fiancé."

"If there was a fiancé . . ."

"But it sounded so true."

"It probably feels true to her."

"I believed her."

"People here say there's never been anyone for her, that she's worked all her life at the shoe factory."

"She made all this up?"

"I haven't lived here long enough to know for sure. But it's what they say about her. She likes to pretend the *Wasserburg* is hers."

"There's no harm in letting her pretend . . . nothing she can take away from you."

On his chest, he felt the hand of this third wife whose strong fingers he'd seen pluck wilted blossoms from their stems, smooth the earth around plants, brush the hair of another wife's child from a fevered forehead. "Lenchen?"

"*Ja.*"

He covered her hand with his and thought he felt his heart beat through both their hands, through sinews and bones and flesh. Ever since she'd arrived here, he'd had more memories of Burgdorf . . . memories of a forgotten side of himself. Coming to America had been so abrupt, and he'd wanted so much to fit in that he'd shed everything German. Now he was surprised how much of it was still there for him. *Because of her.*

"Thank you, Lenchen."

"*Warum*—why?" She gazed out over the lake. Moon had spilled itself across its black depth, and as the wind mottled the sheen, it looked as if a river of silver were flowing toward her.

"For coming here," he said.

In the dark she nodded.

"For marrying me," he said.

With her free hand she reached down into the moon and cooled her throat, her forehead.

CHAPTER FOUR

1911-1914

When Helene noticed that Greta was squinting a lot, she took her to Dr. Miles who prescribed glasses for her. The morning the optician fitted the glasses on Greta, shapes and colors hurled themselves at her from a world that had been blurry till now. It was a transformation that stunned her and filled her with reverence. Even just on the walk home with her stepmother, she saw the foam riding on the crests of waves where before there had just been gray and white, saw two chipmunks chasing along a fallen log that was covered with moss and dried leaves.

"We need to get home," her stepmother said.

But Greta squatted to pick up a black feather. The feather had one tiny speck of red, one speck so tiny and yet so brilliant that Greta thought she might need fewer words from now on.

At the apartment, her little brother was crying, although Gladys was pacing back and forth with him, trying to calm him. His temples were pale and bluish.

"Let me," Helene offered and took Tobias from the maid. "You go and get some lunch for Greta."

Greta slipped her hand into Gladys'. "I'll let you look through my glasses," she said.

As Helene rocked the scrawny boy in her arms, her chest damp from his snot and tears, she felt certain his skin had to remember the touch of his real mother, the only touch that could possibly console him. Filled with pity for him, she rested her lips against his left temple. After being so content with Greta, she felt an abundance of patience and love that she wanted to give to this boy who was breathing noisily through his mouth as if even something as simple as taking in air was burdensome for him. In between breaths, he wailed. She rubbed his hard belly, rocked him against her shoulder as she walked with him. From the living room into the kitchen into the dining room while he wailed, and then that same circle again while he continued to wail.

After years of enjoying her work as a teacher, she had not expected to feel so inadequate as a mother, at least with Tobias who'd either struggle away or cling to her. Sometimes Mrs. Wilson offered to help with the children. Although Helene appreciated her work in the building, she didn't trust her with the children because Mrs. Wilson envied her the children so obviously. Whenever Helene tried to turn Tobias over to one of the maids who came to the apartment every day for a few hours, the boy would cry even louder, except with Birdie, who had a special affection for him. The oldest of the maids at twenty-four, Birdie Robichaud had a new hair color every month and sang to the children in her nasal voice. But Birdie was not always available. And you couldn't ask Birdie to take the children to the beach—not even on the hottest day—because she refused to go near water, terrified to see one of the children go under and not come up again, the way she'd seen her sister drown after falling off the earth right next to her while reaching for a yellow flower.

Tobias was hiccuping in Helene's arms, and when she turned him over to pat his back, she heard a thud against one of the windows that faced the lake. A bird had flown into the bare glass, leaving specks of feather and blood before plummeting. Four other birds had died like that since Helene had arrived, and all because of Stefan's first wife whose idea it had been to let the light and sky in. Her light and sky were exactly what killed the birds because all they saw was their reflection. Birds didn't understand about barriers of glass that could kill them. No more, Helene resolved. Tomorrow she'd talk to the seamstress about covering the windows with sheer curtains and drapes. Mrs. Teichman worked for several families in the building. Skillful and energetic, she'd arrive at Helene's door every Wednesday morning with her flowered suitcase full of patterns, pins, threads, interfacing, buttons, fashion books, and a clean, folded bedsheet that she'd lay over the carpet in the dining room. Curtains would warn the birds. Curtains would make the apartment feel less drafty. Curtains would feel more like home.

Tobias' cries were not quite as loud as before. Helene hummed to him—"*Schlafe mein Prinzchen, schlaf ein . . .*"—hummed the German bedtime song her mother used to sing to her and Leo until Tobias was finally falling asleep, and as she tightened her arms around him to accommodate the weight of sleep, she wished she had another woman to talk to. *Someone like Margret.* But she couldn't imagine writing to Margret about her troubles with Tobias because that would mean admitting that not all was going well in her marriage. Better to send letters to her and to Leo about how the children were growing, about what they'd done together as a family—blueberry picking on Belknap Mountain; excursions on the mail boat that stopped at many of the islands; a train ride to Concord to buy furniture that replaced the wicker of the first wife.

∾

It felt odd to Helene to be an immigrant in this country where no one could see her otherness by looking at her. How she wished she had the physical signs to mark her as a foreigner before strangers spoke to her because that would take the surprise from their faces when she answered, would make them approach her with the expectation of that otherness. From Stefan she knew that the town wasn't much used to foreigners. Except for the Greek man who worked at the lumberyard and a group of Japanese laborers who stayed in apartments assigned to them by the hosiery factory, Winnipesaukee was made up of families who'd lived here for generations and hadn't traveled far beyond their hometown. Although there were quite a few French Canadians, including the lamplighter and the two barbers, Helene didn't think of them as being foreign since Canada was just a few hours away by train.

It was difficult for newcomers to fit in, though Stefan—despite the heartache he'd brought to the families of his dead wives—had been absorbed by the town, although his accent reminded all of them that he had come from a different place. About him they could speak with pride, point to the ornate building that elevated the town's reputation among neighboring communities. A building like that gave you cause and desire to look after your own property with even greater care than before; to replace your entrance door or shutters, say, with fancier versions of what you used to have; to paint your walls before they showed the slightest wear; to lay a path of bricks right to your front step to keep the mud off your floors.

For Helene, living in America was a constant shifting between discovery and loss. She liked how the houses were separated by gardens, not constructed side against side as in Germany. Liked the vastness of her new country, the dense forests, the mountaintops that held snow till late in the spring. But she didn't like the taste of lamb—a bit wild, she thought. American shoes were flimsy, she decided, and though the town's major industry was a shoe factory that shipped merchandise throughout the country, she ordered the shoes for her family from Germany, along with rosehip tea and delicacies like marzipan or the strawberry syrup she liked to pour over her puddings. Since American bread was fluffy and left your belly empty half an hour after eating, she baked her own solid-crust *Graubrot*. Through furniture, tablecloths, and paintings, she created Germany for herself in her husband's house.

She tried to substitute what she missed: walking along the lake and watching the reflections of the house and trees and islands would remind her of the Rhein and the meadows along its banks and made her miss the Rhein somewhat less. She'd swim in the lake. Read by its shore. Row the children out in the wooden boat. Upon waking, she'd always look out over the lake first and orient herself to the weather by its ever-changing colors that depended so much on the sky. Some mornings, both sky and lake would be gray until a few slices of light would fall from behind the mountains across the bay. That light—broken by the shadows of clouds— would lie on the surface of the lake, pointing directly at her window, and if she'd move from one side to the other, the light would follow her like the eyes of saints in some paintings.

She was always comparing things, weighing for herself if she liked them better here or in Germany, marveling at luxuries she hadn't experienced before, while missing the familiar. She might turn a corner of a street in Winnipesaukee, say, and find herself in front of a tree or a doorway that evoked Burgdorf for her. Just as she might watch her husband as he dressed by the mirror—those fierce green eyes in his agile face; the planes of his short, compact body; the V shape of his dense chest hair where it thickened downward—and recall the longing she used to feel for him in Germany.

And because she missed the written words that had formed the intimate connection between her and Stefan for seventeen years—so much more satisfying to be with him on the page than in person—she began to write to him again, fervent notes in German that she would hide and never show him, letters in which she didn't have to hold back with her love for him or with her anger, letters that—after her death—her granddaughter Emma would find in a red cake tin behind Helene's shoes in the armoire. Assuming her grandfather had received every one of these letters, Emma would construct a history of passion and understanding between her grandparents, and resolve that this was the kind of love she wanted for herself.

But her letters to Germany, Helene sent off, and Stefan enjoyed it when she read to him Leo's responses. It disappointed her that Margret only sent brief notes. But she'd known all along that Margret didn't much like to write. Increasingly, she missed Margret, wished she could see her laugh when she told her that in America a woman old enough to have grandchildren was still called a girl. When she'd written her about that, Margret hadn't even mentioned it in her short answer. Often Helene had dreams about her hometown right after getting mail, dreams that took her to the Rhein and Schreberstraße where she'd lived, dreams about Stefan's parents or about some of the nuns from the Theresienheim, and when she'd wake up, she'd feel it even stronger than usual, that seesaw existence of not belonging to either country, of living two fragmentary lives—that of Helene Blau married to Stefan in America and that of Helene Montag still waiting for Stefan in Germany.

Nothing has changed.

Everything has changed.

It did not take her long to become impatient with herself: she did not want to wrap her life around Stefan or his absences. Back at home she'd had her achievements as a teacher to balance that yearning for him; she'd had Leo and Margret and her neighbors and colleagues and friends; but here she only had his children who reminded her of him, and a language that got in the way of connecting to others. All her life she had thought of herself as intelligent, something that had been confirmed again and again by her parents, her teachers, and later her students; but in this new country she couldn't even work as a teacher—at least not until the language would become as familiar as the one she'd grown up with. In this country she only had things because her husband provided them for her. But she refused to settle for that. It was enough to feel lacking as a mother and wife. About the language she could do something. Although Stefan spoke English with ease, she didn't want him to become the voice to link her to his world. Determined to make this new language her own, she borrowed books from the library and struggled through them, even though she only absorbed every fourth or fifth word. But she finished them. For herself. And went back for others.

Sometimes, in public, she'd feel embarrassed by her accent and impatient with herself for not adapting faster, but Stefan would assure her that it would all come together in time. "It's gradual," he told her, "at least for me it was. It got easier once I started thinking in English. At first just a few sentences, maybe ten percent, then more, until it got to be forty percent, fifty, and then one day I realized I'd been thinking entirely in English for some time. Except for counting. I still do that in German. Sometimes I dream in German."

He gave her suggestions on how to speak better, reminded her when she forgot to push her tongue forward in the *th* sound and said *ze* instead of *the*. The *r* that he'd worked on so hard sounded like an *l* with her. And if she had a word that had both a *th* and an *r*, she sounded as though she'd just stepped off the boat. Like wanting to say *three* and having it come out as *zlee*.

Gradually, she recognized more words. During the day she spoke German to the children: it was easier than taking every thought, translating it into English inside her head, and then saying it aloud, a process that always meant one extra step between herself and the meaning. Greta already knew some German from the months she'd spent alone with her father, but Tobias resisted it. It occurred to Helene that the children's response to German was like their reaction to the milk she heated for them before bedtime—Greta drank it willingly, while Tobias loathed the skin that formed on top of it and pulled into wrinkles as the milk cooled.

∽

It pleased Stefan to hear Greta and Helene speak in the language of his childhood. Though he'd lived most of his life in America, he was drawn to the German side in Helene—her oldest identity—and he felt ready to reclaim some of the traditions, the customs, for himself as much as for his children. He told them about his hometown. Showed them the painted tiles for the stove he'd brought from there. Let them watch when, with the help of Homer Wilson, he cut an opening into the wall between the dining room and kitchen and installed the stove. Coal was sent up in the dumbwaiter and shoveled through the stove's iron door from the kitchen.

The wide bench that hugged the contours of the stove where it protruded into the dining room became one of Helene's favorite places. Facing the mountains across the lake, she'd sit there with a book, her back against the tiles that radiated a gentle heat.

She and Stefan agreed to celebrate Easter and Christmas the way they had in Burgdorf, and to adopt American holidays like the Fourth of July and Thanksgiving, which Stefan called the holiday of all immigrants. They talked about having a Christmas party for the tenants in the lobby and perhaps another party each summer. When Helene suggested a summer solstice party, Stefan liked that idea.

Her first Thanksgiving, Helene tasted squash and yams, and she liked both so much that she decided to prepare them from then on. That December, she bought a life-size nativity set: Mary with the infant in her arms, Joseph with his walking stick, an ox, and a donkey. They were white and glossy and unexpectedly light; and they barely stood out against the snow when Helene and Homer Wilson arranged them around the fountain in the courtyard.

"Will I ever get used to this cold weather?" she asked him.

"No." He wiped the snow from his face. "At least I haven't."

Two days before Christmas the nativity set was stolen, but the thieves abandoned the Madonna in the bushes a block away as if they'd found it too cumbersome to travel with an infant molded to his mother's chest. When Homer Wilson who referred to the Madonna as a BVM—Blessed Virgin Mary—cleaned off the mud, Greta noticed that one of the Madonna's cheeks was dented and that the infant's nose was chipped. Mrs. Wilson cried when she and Greta followed her husband who carried the BVM into the furnace room and stored her behind the colossal boiler that was wedged between two columns.

Afterwards Mrs. Wilson took Greta into her bedroom, where she knelt with her in front of her dresser and prayed for the evil souls of the thieves. "Redemption," she told Greta, "waits for even the most blasphemous sinners, even for sinners that the pope doubts can be saved, and that's why I always trust nuns more than priests when it comes to forgiveness because it's in the nature of women to redeem, you'll find that out once you are older and a woman yourself, because think, why else would God give the Angel of Mercy such an important place in heaven, so even he can learn from her about redemption and . . ."

Greta stretched her neck to see the top of Mrs. Wilson's dresser, where a three-dimensional Last Supper glittered in pretty shades of green and purple. On its left stood the white plaster angel with lipstick smudges all over. On its right a framed photograph of the Wilson baby who had died because she was so special that God wanted her back by his side. That's what Mrs. Wilson said. Fastened all around the frame with faded ribbons were baby toys—rattles and teething rings.

"I know about sin and about redemption because I have felt the wings of the Angel of Mercy in my blood." Mrs. Wilson crossed herself. "Many nights." She reached for the angel and kissed the side of her gown, adding to the residue of red. Then she kissed Greta's cheek. For some time now she'd been sure there was something holy in Greta, and she liked to ask her advice even if the child was daydreaming and didn't answer. "About Danny," Mrs. Wilson said, "when do you think he is going to move in with us?"

Greta hoped Danny's mother would stay alive for a long time. A pink-faced woman with large pores, she coughed when she came to fetch Danny after his weekend visits. Her lungs had holes in them. Danny said so. Being scared and waiting that long for someone to die could make you mean. Danny was mean. He'd pinched her when she'd spilled lemonade on his new shoes. Maybe if her own mother had taken that long to die, Greta would be mean too. But Danny hadn't liked it when she'd told him that.

Mrs. Wilson set her Angel of Mercy back on the dresser. "It'll be soon now," she said. "We both know that Danny will live here real soon, right?" Taking Greta's right hand, she guided it toward Greta's face, mumbling, "forehead, chest, left shoulder, right shoulder," as she dabbed against each in the sign of the cross. "Now you say Amen."

"Amen."

"Good. Amen." Mrs. Wilson stood up and showed Greta the fishing pole she would give Danny for Christmas. "Mr. Wilson promised me he'll build a bobhouse with Danny out on the bay once it's frozen thick and they can sit in there and fish through a hole in the ice, and just think Greta, once Danny's living with us every single day, he'll have a real family like you have a real family now, not just with a father but with a mother too, so lucky, she is, your stepmother, let me tell you, she knows what it means to get a child from another woman when you don't have one yourself. . . ."

❧

Helene found that German food did much more than feed her and her family: it connected her to Burgdorf and to her memories so that, when she shredded potatoes for *Reibekuchen,* she could see Frau Blau making them, see herself and Margret eating them, brown-crisp, as quickly as they came from the pan; *Erbsensuppe*—pea soup—meant first snow, which was when her mother used to start simmering her soups; *Erdbeertorte*—strawberry tart—conjured that picnic by the Rhein when she'd swum for the first time across the wide river with Leo and Emil Hesping. Food kept her linked to certain incidents. To seasons and traditions. While measuring ingredients for *Stollen,* it made her feel less isolated to think of women all over Burgdorf doing the same as they got ready for

Christmas. Margret's *Stollen* would have more raisins than Inge-borg Weinhart's, and Frau Buttgereit's would be sweeter than any-one else's because she measured her ingredients by touch and always used too much sugar. What Helene liked about her own *Stollen* was the grated lemon peel she mixed into her icing. Food, of course, was also a way to show her competence, her love. While Tobias was a fussy eater, Greta would snitch cookie batter by the fistful if Helene didn't set it high on a shelf. Twice now Greta burned her tongue by tasting vanilla pudding before it had cooled.

For meals in America, Helene learned, you served more meat than in Germany. Fewer potatoes. And the main meal was in the evening, not the middle of the day. But there she kept the German pattern because of Stefan's schedule. After serving lunch at his restaurant, he'd come home to eat with his family. By four he'd be gone again, which made for solitary evenings after the children were asleep. She looked forward to Christmas Eve when his restau-rant would be closed and he'd be home all day. He was planning to bake pheasants for her and the children. Though she enjoyed his elaborate meals on special occasions, she'd get annoyed if he went on about his recipes as if they were poems, while barely acknowl-edging the food she prepared for him.

When he carried the tray with two pheasants into the apartment and saw the tall Christmas pine decorated with dozens of burning wax candles, he suddenly smelled the scorched flesh of the Hun-garian.

Dropping the covered platter on the piano bench, he rushed at the candles with his breath, his hands. "Are you trying to destroy my house and every person in it?" he shouted at Helene.

Tobias started to cry.

Greta pressed herself against Helene's skirt.

"Do you understand the danger?"

Helene stroked Greta's hair and bent to pick up Tobias. "We al-ways have candles on the tree in Germany." She kept her voice steady for the children, though her body was shaking.

"Always doesn't count in America."

"There must be others in America who light Christmas candles."

"Yes, but they're not living in my house."

"Your parents have candles on their tree."

"We are *not* in my parents' house." He was circling the pine, kicking aside wrapped presents as he splattered wax and singed his fingertips. Helene's wax Madonna toppled from the crown of the tree and landed sideways on the floor, splitting her starched brocade gown.

"I don't know of a single house that has ever burned because of candles."

"And that's why you're trying to burn—"

"You're not being reasonable."

"You are the one who is not being reasonable."

"Stefan—"

"You know what it's like when a house burns? When people burn to death?"

"It was there in every one of your letters for over a year."

"It's still there."

"Candles on a tree are different from a restaurant fire."

"All fires start with one little flame."

"*Ja,* and not all flames turn into huge fires."

"But they can. One flame it takes. One flame is all. I forbid you to use candles on the tree again."

"Forbid?" She felt his fear as though it had a body of its own and was about to attack her. "Forbid?" She raised her chin toward the heavy, blue drapes and lace curtain that Mrs. Teichman had sewn to cover the bare windows his first wife had loved. He'd wanted to keep the windows exposed and have all that light move through the rooms, but she'd told him she couldn't bear to watch birds fly into the glass and die. And she'd made other changes. Without Stefan's permission. Had sent for Mr. Wilson to take the first wife's delicate, tufted sofa and wicker baskets to the storage area and had set up her mother-in-law's lion chairs, had bought a sturdy leather sofa to match Stefan's chair. "Forbid?" she asked once more as she led his children from the living room, leaving him there with the rest of the lit candles.

It was the only time Stefan would ever speak to her like that. In bed that night he said he was sorry, and as he talked to her about the Hungarian and the others who had died in the fire, she held him and reassured him she understood. Yet, she was still angry with him. What confused her was how grateful she felt to have him in her arms like this. She didn't want to be grateful to any husband for allowing her to touch him. It only made her angrier.

And that was good because anger was so much clearer. Anger kept her separate from him, gave her the sudden boldness to take him—roughly almost—using his shock to straddle him, cage him between her thighs, her arms.

"What is this?" he said and then laughed, flustered, and said her name as if to remind her who she was—"Lenchen," he said, "Helene"—but already he was raising his face toward hers as she weighed him down with her breasts and her belly, crushed herself against him till his body thrashed to meet hers, escape into her though he twisted away before she could fill herself with him.

She didn't trust herself to look at him the next morning while they got ready for the tenants' Christmas party in the lobby. And it wasn't just her face that was hot, but her entire body. The worst ever: endless waves of red waiting beneath her skin to betray her, to spill up across her chest, her arms, her neck. She busied herself with the children, making sure to have at least one of them with her at all times so that she and Stefan could not possibly talk. Relieved when he left to roast two dozen chickens in his restaurant oven, she fussed with her platters of German potato salad and cold cuts, garnishing them with radish crowns and slices of boiled eggs the way Frau Blau had taught her and Margret. She didn't see Stefan again until it was time to set everything up in the lobby, and then she kept her eyes on the white paper cuffs that he'd slipped around the ends of the crisp drumsticks.

As she moved about the linen-covered tables and made sure all the tenants had plenty of food, she felt the presence of the night between her and Stefan. No, she did not have a fever, she told several of the tenants who commented on her flushed cheeks, and she distracted them by asking about their families, their work. Most of them she knew quite well by now: they'd welcomed her last summer, and some liked to deliver their rent checks to her door instead of leaving them in the mailbox. Nate Bloom—as usual he'd brought champagne and his latest girlfriend—was talking to Mrs. Braddock from the second floor while Mr. Braddock was feeding a bottle to their daughter Fanny. With her slack features and placid eyes, the little girl always looked as if she were grinning. "Something's not right about her," the tenants would say. Fanny couldn't sit up yet by herself, although she was the same age as Tobias, who'd recently learned to walk and would fiercely attach himself to Helene's hand or whatever part of clothing he could get hold of—a little bur—and straggle along.

"Join us," the tenants told Helene. They whispered to each other how lively the third Mrs. Blau looked today, and how much easier the language seemed to come to her. "Join us and eat, please. Everything is so delicious."

But she kept flitting about, ladling two kinds of punch—spiked with rum for the grownups, plain for the children—and to keep from blushing, she tried to distract herself by fretting about candles and about how much she would miss real candles on the tree next year and in the years to come, because that's what she was used to as far back as she could remember, *candles, real candles, that's what I grew up with, real candles, lots of candles. . . .* From across the lobby she felt her husband watching her, felt her skin, her entire body flush blazing hot until she was the candle, the only candle allowed. *Allowed?* She moved away from his gaze, found Mr. Bell, urged him to play Christmas carols on his violin. "For the children," she said, "oh, please," and thought she heard Stefan cry out *please* in the dark, *please,* and then Mrs. Evans was slicing the fruitcake she'd brought, a moist loaf studded with fragments of red, *please,* while Miss Garland led the children in "Silent Night," a melody Helene knew well, and as she sang along the words she'd learned as a girl—"*Stille Nacht, Heilige Nacht . . .*"—another voice picked up those same words behind her, came closer, closer yet, but she didn't have to turn to know it belonged to her husband, *please oh please,* and as he held her there with his voice, held both of them, she let her voice fuse with his and felt the blushing surge downward, not up, down, down to her groin, *please,* hot and wicked and pleasurable all at once.

∽

After that, blushing was never quite the same again. Now that she knew how to take that panic—*I'm going to blush*—and redirect it to where it met her rapture, she could gather it at will—*now . . . down*—send it there. She began to think of her orgasms as blushing, began to welcome that hot rush that used to mortify her. Amazing how powerful it could make you feel. *And no one else knows. Or has to know.* All you had to do was think *no, I don't want to blush, no*—and that familiar heat would rise through you. After that, it was yours. To send where you wanted it. And you didn't even have to touch yourself.

It could happen at the grocery store. At the beach. In the laundry room. At Magill's Fine Clothing. In church even. Helene liked to play with how high she'd let the blush rise. If you sent it down too soon, its pulse faded quickly. The trick was to let it wash up beyond your waist, to trap it as it raced across your breasts red hot and then—before it spent itself on your neck and face—to force it down. *Yours. Alone.*

For this you did not need a husband.

Knowing this way to pleasure herself made it bearable for Helene when Stefan broke away so quickly after reaching for her at night. Though she longed for children of her own, she knew it was too soon. Being a mother to Stefan's children was the hardest work she had ever done. She used to feel far more competent teaching a class of twenty. Still, sometimes she would let herself fantasize about having babies, speculating in what ways they would resemble both her and Stefan. She could see parts of him in his children: Greta had his slender nose and could be quietly observant like he; Tobias had his black hair and tenacity.

But whenever she tried to talk to Stefan about having a child of her own, he'd grow quiet.

No need to rush him.

Or myself.

There will be time.

And till then she had plenty to do. Starting with manners. American table manners, she thought, were atrocious, and even Stefan, who'd learned the proper ways as a boy, had become careless. But already she'd noticed a change in him. He'd watched her teach Greta how to behave. To say *thank you.* "No elbows on the table," Helene would coach her. "Only your wrists." Though Greta was old enough to hold her knife in her right hand and her fork in her left, all this was too soon, of course, for Tobias. He wasn't even toilet trained yet. At home, Helene knew, she would have started him at six months, the way her mother and grandmother had done before her.

Often Helene felt tired at the thought of all the other work she had waiting for her, not only in the apartment, but also in the garden above the garage, where she trimmed bushes and planted camomile along with flowers that reminded her of home: tulips and geraniums, snapdragons and pansies. And this was how Emma would remember her grandmother many years later—kneeling in the rich dirt between the flower beds, half moons of earth under her fingernails. She would remember the clean scent of soap as her grandmother scrubbed her hands in the kitchen with a bristle brush, remember her Aunt Greta's stories of playing in the elevated garden with Uncle Tobias, gathering empty beechnuts that the squirrels left on the paths and heaping them into pyramids that they stabilized with earth and water.

∞

It was impossible to adore a wife whose shoulders stood a hand's width above yours, who looked down into your eyes instead of looking up at you, who had known you when your nose used to be runny, when you'd come home muddy after playing in the brook. But it was good to depend on her competence. To value her dignity. To admire her brilliant mind. The least he could do to protect her was curb his lust. And so he surrounded her with possessions instead—crystal bedroom lamps with candle-shaped lights, a set of the finest silver, Persian rugs—but Helene would have given up all that to be adored by him. He suspected that her love was larger than his, and he felt uneasy because his feelings were unequal to hers.

When the people of Winnipesaukee complimented him on his children's manners, he felt proud. Though he never went back to church, he approved that Helene took the children there, and he tolerated that she invited Father Albin to dinner once a month to please Lelia Flynn. Ever since Hardy Flynn had died from heart problems, Lelia had taken to arriving at the *Wasserburg* right after mass, and it cheered her to sit next to the priest whose heavy thighs strained against his cassock. She'd ask him how he'd come up with the thoughts for that morning's sermon, and they'd end up discussing his kidney stones and her arthritis. It gave Stefan a certain pleasure, the priest coming to his house like that. *The house of God. The house of Stefan. Blasphemy.*

About those nights she took him, he and Helene never spoke. Both acted as if those nights didn't happen between them. And yet they did—though not often. And never when they felt close to each other. The only times Helene could forget herself like this—forget everything she had been taught about marriage and manners—was when she got angry with him because he felt far away from her, say, or had waited too long to reach for her. And though it bewildered her—being this brazen and powerful woman, so unlike anyone she used to encounter in her fantasies—she felt exhilarated because this woman was someone she would have liked to be at times, this woman who didn't care about being proper, this woman who laughed with ease and took what she wanted.

Those nights—they shocked and aroused Stefan, made him feel oddly virile and yet helpless. Though he didn't understand what was happening—*a lady never indulges like that*—he did not want Helene to stop. Had Elizabeth or Sara chosen to force themselves upon him—*not that they would, not that they ever would*—he could have lifted them from him in one simple motion. But Helene was too strong, too heavy. Helene was broad in the hips and shoulders. Helene was agile. Dangerous perhaps.

At work while seasoning bouillabaisse or brushing raspberry glaze on his marzipan cake, he would catch himself wondering if he could win against her were she ever to wrestle him in earnest.

But of course that was an absurd thought.

Something to dismiss as soon as it stirred you.

Because what kind of husband would wrestle with his wife?

Those nights, they never happened when he reached for her, but if she turned from him silently—hurt or angry about one thing or

another again—he might awaken to discover her above him, blocking the moon as she crushed him into the mattress.

From there, of course, it became easy to figure out how to get her
there.

Because that's what he began to crave, really, secretly—to have
her take him. To have it happen and then not speak about it. And
he could prolong his excitement by watching her the following day,
and by letting her catch him watching her for signs of what had
gone on between them, while he'd wait for the familiar red to stain
her neck and face. But that flush of embarrassment occurred less
and less, and then only for an instant, while her eyes half closed
and her lips curved upward, mystifying him.

Some evenings after dinner Greta liked to seclude herself in the delivery box—a low compartment between the apartment and hallway
for the delivery of milk, groceries, and newspapers. Each tenant had
one, and its wooden doors could be unlatched from either the kitchen
or hallway. Too tight for anyone but a child to fit in, the dark box was
lined with metal and stayed cool even on the hottest of days. You frequently had to scour it to get rid of the sour smell that rose from
spilled drops of milk. Greta didn't mind the smell. Inside her cubicle,
with both doors shut, she liked to play her mother's flute, long notes
that sounded like the calls of large birds flying through the night and
made Helene wish she could follow her stepdaughter and shed the
absurd habit of walking on earth in sensible shoes.

Eyes wide open in the dark, Greta would see translucent clouds
against a silver sky, and her wooden flute would reel them in, those
clouds, sucking their luster into the cubicle till it glowed. When Helene called for her—time to get ready for bed—Greta reversed her
notes, releasing the clouds and the light to where they belonged,
and as she emerged, face radiant, her pupils black pinpricks behind
her glasses, Helene felt she had reclaimed her from a place far beyond the house. It made her want to treat Greta with special care—
reverence almost—and offer her lavish refreshments as you would
to an honored guest who has traveled a great distance and won't
stay for long.

A guest like Leo.

All that winter Helene looked forward to his visit, imagining the places she would show him and Gertrud. They were getting married the third Sunday of April, and for their wedding present Helene and Stefan had already sent them round-trip tickets to America on the *Kaiserin Auguste Victoria*, a German ocean liner with a winter garden and a grand staircase. But about a week before they were to start their trip, another ship sank on its first voyage to New York, and Leo sent a telegram, postponing the trip. "If it were just me, I would come anyhow, but Gertrud doesn't feel safe."

A letter followed. Gertrud, he wrote, had first wanted to go ahead with their trip even though some townspeople kept asking if she wasn't afraid to cross the ocean, considering how even the best of ships could sink. "Stefan and Helene got there safely," she told them. "I'm not worried."

But then Herr Pastor Schüler had given a sermon about five thousand millionaires who had drowned when their ship rammed into an iceberg. "There's a lesson in that for all of you," he declared, and while he proceeded to preach about greed and icebergs that really turned out to be the fire of hell, the altar boys went around with their shiny collection plates.

After mass, when Leo pointed out to him that not five thousand, but twenty-two hundred people had been aboard the *Titanic* and that seven hundred had survived, the priest pretended not to hear.

"Such hubris. And they said even God himself couldn't sink their ship," he announced in his sermon voice, the kind of voice that allowed for no doubt when he spoke about sin.

After listening to the priest, Gertrud realized she could not be on a ship. Any ship. At least not yet.

"But the one we're booked on is different," Leo told her. "Faster than other ocean liners." Still, he could not persuade her.

"The *Titanic* was supposed to be unsinkable," she told him. "God slaughters those who challenge him."

"I understand," Helene wrote back to her brother. "Maybe you'll be here in the summer. It's a better time to be here anyhow because you can swim in the lake and hike up Belknap Mountain with us." She described to him how much the beach was part of her daily life in the summer. Instead of walking to the Rhein and changing clothes behind some bushes as she had in Burgdorf, she now could wear a swimsuit beneath a bathrobe, take the elevator down to the lobby and walk out, down the grassy slope and across the sand to the dock. She ended her letter by telling him, "We'll have a wedding dinner for you in our lobby. . . ."

She sealed the envelope, returned her stationery and blue ink to her rosewood desk, and walked to the kitchen where Gladys was getting lunch ready for the children. When Tobias darted away from the maid and toward Helene, she dodged him and instantly felt like a bad mother, the most wicked of stepmothers right out of fairy tales. Then, of course, she had to make it up to Tobias, had to read to him, play with him, let him come along to do the laundry in the basement. In the drying room, where the air was so hazy and silver with steam that it would have been easy to lose a pillow case, say, or even a small child, she let Tobias hold the ends of wet sheets as she straightened them and draped them across the heating rods that were hooked up to the boiler.

Though it took twice as long than when she did them alone, she stayed patient; yet, as always, Tobias wanted more, and when Helene finally tried to pry herself away in the elevator and the boy still clung to her with those tiny claws, she felt a sudden rage. *The presence of the biter.* She had not asked Stefan to bring her here, even though it was what she had longed for. But she had *not* asked. And she had come to his children with her best, her very best, had come to them ready to love them. Yet it was only Greta who responded to her with affection. Whatever she did for the boy was not right. Sometimes he wanted more of her. Other times less of her. In any case—never what she was giving him.

He wants his real mother.

She felt her fury ebb and right away felt sorry for Tobias, who stood next to her in the elevator, mouth twitching, about to cry. "Come here." She picked him up. Carried him into the apartment. Made cinnamon toast for him. Washed his hands. His face. Sat with him by the kitchen window and promised herself to be even more patient. He pointed up to the fan that was set into a boxy recess in the wall next to the window, and though she had a dozen other things to do, she let him touch the metal pole with the hook that hung from the fan, helped him to open the top of the little trap door to let air in. She didn't much like those fans because wasps liked to nest in there, a nuisance Mr. Wilson took care of by cleaning the fans out.

Once she was doing better with Tobias, she'd have children of her own. To balance the two Stefan already had. She knew of other women over thirty who'd had babies. But what if it was her failure with Tobias that kept Stefan from being closer to her? Or maybe it was the other way around. Maybe if Stefan were closer to her, Tobias would be too. Maybe he felt his father's separateness from her.

As Tobias blew tiny spit bubbles and played with the buttons on her blouse, it occurred to her that if Stefan were to write home about the new stepmother, he'd probably describe her as an unnatural mother, impatient, frightened even. Sara had been a much better stepmother—she knew this from Stefan's letters, knew how gentle Sara used to be with Greta, how natural. But Sara had only inherited one child—the more likable of the two.

∽

Leo barely mentioned the trip in his reply but wrote instead about the tournament his chess club was organizing for its one-hundred-year anniversary. Twelve other clubs were traveling to Burgdorf, and all trophies would be engraved with the profile of its founder, Karl Tannenschneider. Helene shook her head. Like most of the women in Burgdorf, she had little regard for Herr Tannenschneider, while the men spoke of him with respect because his passion for chess had been so great that he'd forsaken his wife and children.

That Christmas, Helene sent travel presents to Leo and Gertrud: a small alarm clock; two collapsible cups; maps of New York City and New Hampshire; toothbrushes that folded to half their size.

"She just isn't ready yet," Leo wrote.

Helene's frustration with Gertrud left her in no mood to celebrate anyone's marriage, least of all that of Nate Bloom; but Stefan was curious about the cabaret singer Nate had just married after a two-day courtship. The instant Helene saw Pearl Bloom, she noticed two things about her: that she did not wear a corset like other women, and that she looked barely twenty—just about half the age of her husband who was telling everyone how he'd seen her in Boston at one of her performances and had invited her to have champagne and smoked salmon with him in his railroad car.

Small and feisty, Pearl Bloom fastened onto Helene as soon as they met, ignoring her other guests. "I was swept away by Nate." Her voice was deep. Dramatic. "Simply swept away. And by the time I noticed that the train was going, I wouldn't have stopped it for anything." Her bobbed hair fell back from her ears. "Hell, you must know how that is."

Helene had to laugh. "Don't we all?" She rather liked how that came out, the kind of response a woman far more experienced than she would have thought of.

Pearl looked at her closely. "Besides . . . it was snowing."

"What does snow have to do with it?"

Pearl lit a cigarette and held it between her thumb and forefinger as if she were a man. "My shoes—they're hardly made to walk in snow, Sweetie."

Helene motioned to Pearl's high-heeled sling backs. "You were wearing shoes like that?"

"Always."

"I'd break my neck. My stepdaughter, though—she'd love your shoes. She doesn't like to wear the ones I order from Germany."

Pearl contemplated Helene's feet: black solid leather laced to the ankles; chunky heels. "You are a very independent woman," she said.

When Pearl arrived in Helene's life like this—all at once, jostling past her shyness and reserve—Helene knew she was a manifestation of her yearning for a friend to take the place of Margret, who grew fainter with each of her brief, hasty notes. Pearl thought Helene was the most intelligent woman she'd ever known, and she flew at her with confidences and questions, with genuine admiration that astounded Helene who felt huge and slow in comparison. Still, she was so dazzled by Pearl that she dismissed the German custom of developing friendships slowly. Pearl was everything she was not—glamorous, vivacious, vain—and yet, with her she could talk in a way Stefan would not understand. Both were wives of men who had been married before. Both had been transplanted, leaving everyone they knew behind.

Within a week of meeting Pearl, Helene found herself telling her about all the years she had loved Stefan secretly, and she did not flinch when Pearl counted on her fingers the men she'd slept with before marrying Nate.

"If I hadn't married Nate, I'd be counting toes by now."

"Maybe that's what toes are for."

Being around Pearl made Helene funny and outrageous. It also made her aware of how she'd been raised to say and do what was proper, and how immensely bored she was with that. And Pearl, she felt dignified when she was with Helene, smart, valued for her thoughts. Men usually had preconceived notions about her, but with Helene she was someone she could have been all along.

Since Pearl had lived on both coasts and had even worked as an entertainer on ocean liners, she found the town of Winnipesaukee confining, but she provided for her own entertainment by giving parties every Saturday evening, some in Nate's railroad car, others in her music room that she decorated with peach-colored velour drapes and upholstery. Sometimes there'd be dancing. Leaning against the white piano Nate had ordered from New York, she'd sing for her guests in her low, low voice, one shoulder cocked above the other. Often she invited local musicians. Though most of them had not performed in public, she quickly found out who was talented—the old organist from the Lutheran church; the florist's sister-in-law who played the saxophone; Mr. Bell from the second floor with his violin—and for a few hours she would make them feel famous.

Pearl had no problem understanding Helene's accent, and she never asked her to repeat what she'd just said. For her, everything that came from Helene was profound. With Pearl here, the house felt different to Helene, fuller. Whenever the two women wanted to reach each other, they'd rap against the heating pipes, a signal that would carry to the other's apartment: *two raps—come to the window; one rap—open the dumbwaiter.* Helene would lean from her window or into the dumbwaiter to shout down that she was going for a walk or a swim, and Pearl would yell back that she'd meet her in the lobby. As their voices flickered up and down the dumbwaiter shaft, their echoes trembled into other regions of the building. Typically, Pearl would run out of pepper or butter or onions—never lipstick or shampoo—and if the dumbwaiter was in the basement and the item light enough, she'd span a silk scarf in the opening and catch whatever Helene dropped from above. "I'll get it back to you," she'd holler, but she never returned anything, and Helene—who would rather lend than borrow any day—did not remind her.

This woman with her raunchy laugh who cursed so elegantly, who mooched shamelessly but gave generously of herself, was Helene's only friend in America, and at first Helene worried that their friendship might end as abruptly as it had begun. But gradually she trusted that it would still be there the next day. The next year.

Once the evenings got milder in April, the two women would sit on the flat roof of the *Wasserburg* on folding chairs and talk. A vertigo tug at their stomachs, they'd rest their feet on the low brick wall that ran along the edge of the roof. Since this wall was only two feet high, and the ventilation pipes had pointed tops that could impale a running child, the roof was off-limits to children unless they were with an adult.

Far above the town and the spires of its three churches, the women would sip coffee or Pearl's favorite, peach brandy straight from snifters or mixed with champagne and ice cream in tall glasses. They'd lean back in their chairs and keep talking while in the houses below them lights multiplied and the green surface of the lake turned flat and fused with the dark shoreline. Each time the elevator was in service, they'd hear a buzz—not unlike that from a thousand bees. Looking forward to that ritual of evenings with Pearl often sustained Helene through days that belonged almost entirely to the children. Recently she'd been worrying about Greta who was not doing well in school. Her ability to appreciate details that others didn't stop to notice—the shadow of a leaf, the smell of a stone, the texture of a feather—made her forget where she was or what she'd been told to do.

Whenever Pearl visited at the apartment, Helene's days felt lighter, and even the caring for Tobias became less complicated because Pearl was intrigued by the small boy who attached himself to her with quick searching attention as if perhaps she was the one who would make everything right for him. Birdie, whose favorite he'd been at first, had shrunk from that intensity, but Pearl was accustomed to attention and enjoyed the child.

One afternoon, when Tobias' belly hurt because his Aunt Pearl was drinking tea with his mother again, he toddled away from them—*they don't see me they don't*—and into Greta's room where the dollhouse was set up on the table. His mother had said he wasn't allowed to play with it till he was older. He touched it with one finger. Climbed on a chair. Brought his face against the front of the house. Just when he was wondering how to get in there and sit on the tiny furniture, his arm swiped the house to the floor.

As Helene rushed in, her first worry was for Tobias' safety, her next worry how to explain the damage to Stefan's mother.

"You don't have to tell her anything," Pearl said as she rocked Tobias who was crying furious tears because the dollhouse hadn't let him inside and now it was broken. "Sshhh," Pearl sang out. "Sshhh . . . Things break. That's just the way it goes, Sweetie. No reason to cry." She glanced up at Helene. "All children break things. It's natural. Let me see . . . what did I break when I was your age? Dishes, I'm sure. Oh yes, my mother's necklace. Fake pearls, but still . . . I pulled at them when she wore them, and they scattered all over the floor."

"Stefan's mother told me to only let Greta play with it. She'll say it's my fault."

"Aren't you lucky then that you are an ocean away."

"I guess I am." Helene reached for Tobias. "Come here."

He hid his face against his Aunt Pearl's neck.

"Go to your mama." She positioned him in his mother's arms. "Here."

"I'm not angry with you." His mother rocked him on her hip, and he felt her breath skim over his hair while she talked to his Aunt Pearl. ". . . but I know she'll ask Leo and Gertrud about that dollhouse."

"If they ever get here."

"Don't say that. Leo promised. Maybe he'll come alone."

"You'd like that better anyhow. . . . He can tell your mother-in-law that the dollhouse is just lovely, that you've painted the roof and shutters—what? Orange? Green? And that your friend Pearl Bloom has it in her apartment right now because she is sewing tiny lace curtains for the windows."

"You don't even know how to sew."

"Exactly." Pearl nodded. "It's a beautiful story. Your mother-in-law will picture me with a tiny needle sewing tiny curtains. And you'll have your frigging peace." She reached out to tickle behind Tobias' knees. "That's the most ticklish place on my body. See, for you too. Now what do you think, Tobias? You want an orange roof? Or a green one?"

∞

Helene was sure her brother would like Pearl, and she looked forward to introducing them, but his visit kept getting delayed. At first it had to do with Gertrud's fear of the ship sinking, and when she finally agreed to make the voyage despite that fear, they had to delay it again because she was not well.

"She's not talking to anyone," Leo wrote. "She lies in bed all day."

"We'll have a bed for her here," Helene wrote.

"It's more serious than that," Leo wrote.

"She won't have to talk to any of us."

To Pearl she said, "I don't think they want to come here."

"Why don't you go then?"

But before Helene could decide, Austria-Hungary declared war on Serbia, and Germany followed by declaring war on Russia, France, and Belgium. Gertrud sent a jumbled letter about bloodying her knee and about Leo fighting Russians in Poland and about Emil Hesping's motorcycle. "It's my fault if Leo doesn't come back."

Helene could not picture her brother as a soldier: he was too gentle to be an effective fighter, too considerate. Every day as she read newspapers, she'd fight off images of Leo *dead, or about to die with blood on his throat and chest, or half-buried in a ditch as he claws at the dirt that fills his mouth and eyes. Leo*—and when she'd try to dislodge those pictures with memories of Leo, she'd find it impossible to evoke him as a man. Only as a boy: *age three, playing*

by the brook, hands muddy, face so sweaty that his pale curls stick
to his forehead as if painted on; age four, learning his chess moves
with such concentration that everyone calls him kleiner Professor;
age eleven, at the gymnast's competition, swinging from the trapeze
with such grace that he appears to be flying.

"He is stronger than he looks, your brother." Stefan would comfort her. "And he's smart. That counts for more than physical
strength when it comes to surviving." He didn't tell her how worried he was about Leo and several of his friends who were soldiers.
Though Emil Hesping had managed to stay out of combat, Michel
and Kurt were fighting, and Stefan had no idea what was happening to them.

Greta's grandmother asked about Leo every Sunday when she
came to the house with chocolate for the children. She'd tilt her
head to let Stefan kiss her cheek and offer a bouquet of flowers to
Helene. That November, when she arrived to celebrate Greta's
eighth birthday, Helene was crying as she opened the door for her.

"He's alive," she sobbed. "My brother . . . he's alive."

Carefully, Lelia Flynn placed both arms around this woman
she'd never embraced before, this woman who was taller and wider
than she. Taller and wider than her Elizabeth had been. "I'm so
glad about your brother. So very glad."

Helene disengaged herself, pulled a letter from the pocket of her
gray pleated skirt. "From Stefan's parents."

Lelia unfolded it. "I can't read that. It's not in English."

"I forgot." Helene laughed. Started crying all over again. "Here's
what they say." She translated: "Leo is injured, but only in one
knee. The left one. They operated on him in Poland and put in a
plate of steel where his kneecap used to be."

Lelia flinched. "That must be painful."

"I'm so grateful he's back home alive."

"So am I."

"That injury is saving his life. He has trouble walking and is useless now as a soldier."

Since it was an uncommonly warm afternoon, Helene and Lelia
took the children down to the lake, where they sat on striped canvas chairs, blankets spread across their legs, and talked while To-

bias and Greta played in the green rowboat that was tied to the side of the dock. Leaves were blowing across the boat, and while Greta tried to catch them, Tobias was building a tower from his alphabet blocks on the seat. When he was done, he rocked the boat, whinnying like a horse as the blocks tumbled down, and then stacked them up again.

"Look at those two," Helene said, "playing like that . . . So innocent."

"They're children. Of course they're innocent."

"I mean innocent of what's happening in Europe."

"We're lucky we're far away. And that we're neutral. President Wilson is going to keep it that way."

"I think of it a lot, the war over there, worry about it before I fall asleep, wake up worrying about people I know, their safety. . . ."

"Your brother, thank God, is back."

"Yes, but other men in our neighborhood are still gone, including Stefan's friends and Axel Lambert."

"Who is he?"

"The biology teacher from the school where I used to work."

Each time his building blocks collapsed, Tobias whinnied. He couldn't hear his sister above his noise because he was so totally enjoying the water and the wind, letting them fill his eyes, his ears, his entire head until there was only blue, a far-distant blue so all encompassing and familiar that he made whooping noises, rocking the boat back and forth.

To Helene his frolicking seemed disrespectful, considering the horrors in Europe. And yet she envied both children their carefreeness. "Tobias? Calm down."

He didn't even look toward her.

"Calm down!"

Lelia bent toward her. "May I ask you something?"

"Yes."

"This biology teacher—was he important to you in your life?"

"He was a friend. A colleague."

"The way you said his name . . . Ochsal . . . ?"

"Axel. It's pronounced Axel."

Satisfied, Lelia Flynn nodded. "Men like that . . . they may not be important to us when we are young, may be a bother even, but they're the men we remember when we're old because their fascination with us will forever stay the same. You see . . . it was never tested. Never had a chance to fade in marriage."

"I always thought of marriage as deepening that . . . fascination."

Lelia didn't respond. She was frowning at the solid and unbroken line of mountains in the distance where the sky was filling with puffy white clouds that looked as if something were bubbling up behind the mountains.

"Are you warm enough?" Helene asked.

Lelia nodded and rubbed her arms. "Did Stefan tell you that his second wife didn't like me?"

Helene shook her head.

"She never used the Venetian trays I gave her for when she married Elizabeth's husband. I—I'm sorry. Your husband. When she married your husband."

"I never knew Sara." Gently, Helene added, "Or your daughter."

Lelia raised her chin toward the clouds that were moving closer, flecking the dark surface of the lake wherever it held the pale reflections of the clouds' bellies.

"Maybe she used the trays on days you were not here," Helene suggested.

Lelia shook her head. "I would have known."

"But how?"

"I would have known. I gave them to her because I liked her. Not as much as you, though."

It seemed proper to say thank you, especially to a woman of her parents' generation. But Helene couldn't bring herself to do that. "Calm down," she called out to Tobias.

But he didn't hear her, didn't see her when she stood up and called out to him to stop rocking it and sit still, and it wasn't until Greta screamed that he quit shouting and froze, staring at where she was pointing, his arm, his right arm, wedged between boat and dock while the blue—a different and dangerous blue not at all like the far-distant blue inside his head—drained through his stomach, heavy and sick. He howled.

As Helene ran toward the dock, she felt guilty as though she had brought on his injury herself—*the biter in me*—by feeling jealous of his carefreeness. Before she and Lelia could reach the boat, Greta pulled her brother free. His breath struck her neck with each howl, and his hand felt cold to Greta. His arm was so limp inside the sleeve of his jacket that Greta gathered it against her chest. *Because touching is the other half of seeing. Touching enters through your fingertips and paints the image of what you touch inside your eyeballs.* All at once, she felt something shift within her brother's arm, and his howls ceased. Drawing in one startled sob, he leaned against Greta, feeling very tired.

After Helene carried Tobias to her chair, he lay curled in her lap like a much younger child, playing with the lace cuffs of her white blouse, absorbing the scent of her hands and her gray pleats, and as she stroked his fine, black hair, she found comfort in being able to soothe this odd little boy who so often spurned all tenderness, and she felt closer to him than ever before. She relished his silence, his yielding to the solace she could give him as she ran one finger along his temple and cheek, sticky from tears. If only she could give this kind of comfort to a child of her own. Her throat burned with abrupt yearning. *What if holding this boy is as close as I'll ever come to being a mother? Not enough. It's not enough. Never will be. And I'm getting older. Thirty-five last month. Where did the years of marriage go? Three and a half years. If I don't have a child soon, then when?* Even Margret who used to think she didn't want children now had twins. It struck Helene, the irony, that both she and Stefan were grieving—she for the child she would like to have, he still for the other wives.

Her eyes followed Greta and Lelia as they strolled along the beach where shallow waves had left a scalloped edge on the sand. Tobias was dozing, uncommonly quiet, and he didn't wake up until Stefan arrived to take them to Greta's birthday dinner at the *Cadeau du Lac.*

When she told him what had happened with Tobias' arm, he blew on it and sang, *"Heile heile Segen, morgen gibt es Regen . . ."*—"Heal heal, blessings, tomorrow there'll be rain. . . ."

Tobias pulled his arm away. "I don't want rain."

"It will make your arm better."

"My arm doesn't hurt."

In his restaurant, a table on the glass porch was set with white linen and red balloons. Greta's feet itched from sand that had gotten into her shoes and between her toes. Her face itched too whenever she glanced at her brother's arm. Her father had made her favorite food, flat noodles with white sauce and thin slices of veal, but Tobias wasn't eating. When her father glared at him, Tobias speared one noodle and sucked at one end of it until all of it had disappeared between his lips.

Stefan felt a familiar disappointment when Tobias chewed so reluctantly. There was something about the boy that didn't measure up—a softness . . . a shrillness. What bothered Stefan too was the head banging, something Tobias still did though Dr. Miles had said he was sure to outgrow it. But so far that hadn't happened, and usually the boy's fine hair was matted in back of his head.

As Tobias glanced up from his plate, he felt judged by the lack of faith in his father's eyes, and since he didn't know what it meant or what he could do to have his father regard him in a different way, he pulled the memory of his father's expression deep inside himself, nurtured it so that, oddly, in the years to come, it would give him a greater sense of what defined him, something that was in contrast to his father, something that was all his and that he could count on being.

Greta could feel him shrinking from their father, could feel her stepmother blaming herself for Tobias' injury, though Tobias was the one who'd caused it, could feel her father's concern for her grandmother whose face and body had become gaunt and whose skin had lost its pink ever since the death of Greta's grandfather.

"Here," her father was saying as he served her grandmother another slice of veal, though she'd barely touched the first.

"No, thank you."

"You have to eat more, Lelia," he said, but he was thinking about the loan. Whenever he saw Lelia, he thought about that loan. He still hadn't made any payments, though the apartment house was profitable. But it was essential to have some funds set aside in case the house needed repairs. And it was not as if Lelia needed the money—she was far wealthier than he. If he were to mention it, she'd only wave his words away with her beautiful hands—*so much like Elizabeth's hands*—and tell him she wasn't worried, that it would all belong to Greta some day anyhow.

Lelia pushed the veal aside with her fork. "I don't need much food."

Helene wondered if her husband and Lelia had been like that with each other when Elizabeth had still been alive. It occurred to her that, if she imagined herself out of this picture and placed Elizabeth here instead, they would be more like a family. Lelia was small boned like her daughter. As Helene saw the daughter in the features of the mother, she felt superfluous.

She saw herself lean toward Lelia. *"What was your daughter like?" she asks. The words come out in German, and oddly Lelia Flynn understands them and answers her in German.*

"Not at all like you," she tells Helene. "Elizabeth had more presence, more class. Charisma."

Stop it, Helene admonished herself, but the imaginary conversation continued while Stefan and the children seemed oblivious to it. *"It was better between Stefan and me from a distance,"* Helene *confides.*

"It always is," Lelia says.

"And I wish we could go back to that."

"I treasured Mr. Flynn most when he was at the bank and not right next to me. Maybe if you went back to Germany—"

"Then he'd be lost to me altogether."

"There'd be another wife soon . . . ja."

"You'd like that, wouldn't you, if I left?"

"It doesn't matter who the new wife is. You or someone else. What matters is that there is one at all. And that she is not Elizabeth."

"That I am not Elizabeth."

"If there had been only one wife," Lelia Flynn says, *"if he had lined up the three of you and chosen one . . . Do you really believe he would have chosen you? Or that Sara from the bakery?"*

"Yes," Helene lies. "I know he would have chosen me."

Late that evening when Tobias and Greta were asleep and Stefan was still at the restaurant, Helene opened his roll-top desk and stared at the two wedding portraits he kept in the small left drawer, at his posed smile as he turned to his previous wives—*he would have never chosen me*—and she felt heavy with the weight of her body and the weight of her duty toward the children of these women. But at least Elizabeth and Sara had not lived in these rooms. Though they had planned the *Wasserburg* with Stefan, she was the first of his wives to share it with him.

To replace them in his heart was impossible.

To feel their presence in these rooms would be unbearable.

As an old woman Helene would take out those photos again— sepia toned on stiff paper—and the other wives would seem identical in their naivete as they smiled without the knowledge that they already carried their deaths within themselves. She'd be seized by a great compassion for them, their youth, their lack of insight into Stefan. How could they have possibly understood him? She had aged with him while they had stayed the age they'd died: young, graceful . . . forever. And if she compared that to what she had been to him—companion, partner, confidante—she measured more. Far more.

⁓

She was still awake when he came to bed, and as his wide palm settled upon her belly, she lifted her silk nightgown for him and waited; but as she felt her body arching toward his in the sum of her yearning, she suddenly couldn't endure the thought of him removing himself from within her again, stealing the child that was meant to be hers, the child that should have been hers by now. In the flicker of the bedside candle, she dug her fingers into his buttocks and held him there, fused to her, though he struggled to tear himself from her. An uncommon heat between them, she followed him through the rise and the letting down and for a few moments— moments of incredible nearness she would still cherish decades later—he buried his face against her neck with words of tenderness unlike any he'd said to her before. His breath became faint as he pressed his lips against her skin; but then, as though he'd just returned to himself, he heaved himself from her and sat on the side of the bed.

"Don't you ever—" His voice sounded angry. Afraid. "Don't you ever do that again."

She felt his warmth damp between her thighs and, like a thief, tilted her hips upward to contain him within herself.

"I don't want to lose you too, Lenchen."

"You'll never lose me," she said urgently and believed it, too, though she knew how common it was for women to die that way, and how frightened her husband was of burying yet another wife. It struck her how sad it was: in other areas of his life he had succeeded, had become all he'd dreamed of being, and yet he lacked the power to keep those he loved alive. *Elizabeth. Sara. Agnes. But not me.* Taking his face between her palms, she forced him to look into her eyes. "You will never lose me," she repeated slowly.

"How can you know that?"

"I want children."

"No."

She pulled the sheet to her throat, felt its edge with the eyelet embroidery against her chin.

"No," he said again. "We already have two."

A deep sense of betrayal rooted itself within her. He had never wanted her for himself. Only for his children. Humiliated by the force of her love for him, she felt furious at herself for ever believing he could love her too. And it was at this moment that she stopped trying to love his children as if they were her own.

"Children that are mine," she whispered, her voice hoarse, rough. "Children that are ours." She thought of how she longed to be pregnant while other women she knew used means to prevent a baby. Like Pearl, who sprinkled peach brandy on a small rubber sponge she'd hollowed out on one side. To the other side she'd sewn a thin string so she could pull it back out.

"Lenchen . . . ," Stefan said gently. And reminded himself: *Make sure there's enough parsley. Lemon too.*

"You're making decisions that are mine to make too."

He touched her shoulder. "Lenchen—"

"No." She shifted her entire body from him.

His hand fell from her. "I couldn't bear to lose you, Lenchen."

Had she answered him, she could have told him there were ways other than death of losing someone.

CHAPTER FIVE

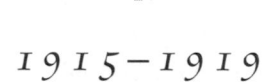

1915–1919

The morning she told him she was pregnant, he felt tricked. He stared into her joyous eyes, at the brave curve of her chin, and in one terrible moment her face was replaced by her death mask. Mute with grief, he saw himself *standing at her grave—a grave wide enough to hold an entire family and to contain her too, his third wife, whose boldness and tenderness have confused him. Prayers rise above the graves like wind, move through the moss that sways from the branches, brush its coarse strands against his face as he runs from the grave down the path toward the brook and its stillness, runs in the mist while listening so closely to that stillness that he hears birds, and as he looks toward the lake, all sky and all water are silver-gray, fused by the hazy mass of mountains.*

As he pulled Helene into his arms to keep her alive, she leaned into him, waiting for the words of love she imagined behind his urgent hold. But he pressed his forehead against her shoulder, making it impossible for her to see his expression.

"Tell me," she said, afraid that if he didn't speak she would retreat from him even further.

But he didn't trust himself to bring those images of her death into words, a death for which he alone carried blame—*as with Sara; with Elizabeth*—and in that moment he loved Helene so strongly that he wanted to undo his danger to her, undo his journey to bring her here from Germany, undo his marriage to her.

"Tell me," she said once more, already deciding that if his silence was all he could give her, she would find a way to live with that too. Already, she felt stronger. Strong enough to step away from him and walk to the window. It was snowing. Large weightless flakes dissolved as they grazed the lake. Melted before they could stick to the roofs and streets below.

But then he answered. "Lenchen, you—"And stopped.

"What?" she asked. "What is it?"

He knew he could not say aloud what he was thinking. "*You should have never married me, Lenchen.*" Instead, he told her, "You just take what you want," startled by the anger in his own voice.

She spun to face him. "And why not?" she challenged him.

How he loved her feistiness. But just as he was about to tell her that, she interrupted.

"If taking what I want means I'll have this child, then I'm glad I did."

"Even if it kills you?" And he was back in the cemetery again, *on his way to the Brook-that-finishes-grieving. A strong water smell comes at him, envelops him. It is a smell that, if you let it, will drown out everything inside your soul. And as that coolness spins around him, it clothes him. Pulls him toward the currents of the brook.*

"Don't worry so much."

"How can I not?"

"Because I'll be here," she said fiercely. "I promise you that."

"There is no way a woman can promise something like that. Any woman."

That afternoon, the snow grew heavier, and a loud wind rose up and tried to push you back into your house if you were foolish enough to leave it. Stefan insisted on making his way to his restaurant, though no one came to eat the food he prepared, not even his employees. For three days and nights the storm lasted: it destroyed several sheds and barns, tore shingles from some of the roofs, and swept over a hundred chickens into the grainy air, carrying them away as though they were dry leaves. Six feet of snow covered the town of Winnipesaukee, and the day it stopped snowing, icy rain glazed all surfaces. Under the weight of snow and ice, trees groaned: some split as if chosen by lightning or fell, smashing fences and windows; most yielded at least a branch, a crown. While Stefan's restaurant had four broken windows, his apartment building was one of the few houses that didn't suffer any damage. It didn't surprise the people of Winnipesaukee—it only made the *Wasserburg* stand out even more, overshadowing their town, its reflection biting into the lake further than anything they had built.

∾

During Helene's pregnancy Stefan was cautious with her, formal almost, and she'd find him looking at her as if bracing himself for her death. *I'll be here,* she reminded herself. Nights when he had trouble sleeping he'd watch her sleep. Whenever she rolled over, she'd automatically reach for her hair in back of her neck and—without waking herself—hold it in one hand until she'd settle herself back on the pillow.

Other nights it was Helene who would lie next to him long after he was asleep. She would hear his children's breathing like a heartbeat, waiting, tugging at her, invoking their mothers who had died giving birth, and felt a slow dread in her limbs. More than ever before she thought about Elizabeth and Sara. If she saw Miss Garland by the mailboxes or in the drying room, she kept her talking, hoping she'd start reminiscing about Stefan's first two wives. After all, Miss Garland had been a grown woman when Elizabeth and Sara were born: she'd seen them at mass every week; had watched them get married; had gone to their funerals.

Very quickly, Miss Garland grasped how she could befriend the third Mrs. Blau. Wishing she had observed Elizabeth and Sara closer, she sieved her memories, but what she recalled couldn't fill more than a few conversations. And so it was only natural to speculate: that woman by the lake with the red hat and the braid—she could have been Sara . . . quite likely had been Sara the first summer of her marriage to Stefan Blau. From there a tale would ripen about the summer Sara Blau had ordered that outrageous red hat from Concord. Images of Miss Garland's childhood would blend with glimpses she'd had of Elizabeth and Sara as girls: that infection in her leg from a dog bite now became Sara's; the teacher who'd ridiculed Miss Garland for not reading faster was reprimanded by Elizabeth's father; Miss Garland's yearning for friends was transformed into a large birthday celebration on Sara's fifth birthday . . . so that, gradually, Helene was left with an impression of her two predecessors that felt oddly out of focus as if they had lived decades before their time.

She tried not to worry when Leo wrote that Gertrud was pregnant too. He sounded so hopeful: "She is calmer now. Happier." His leg was healing. Slowly. "But at least I'll be able to walk without crutches once the baby is here. Otherwise it would be difficult to carry it." Their letters kept crossing, filled with anticipation of the babies—Gertrud's to be born in July, Helene's a month later—and with renewed plans for a visit. "Once the war is over."

Once the war is over . . .

Quite a few of their letters ended that way.

Already, she could picture the infants side by side, strong-jawed and fair-skinned, with the long legs and high span of forehead from the Montag side of their families. When she felt the first hesitant movements within her, she wanted to believe that—despite Stefan's resistance—the child would deepen her union with him. Everything around her pleased her: the echo of the tenants' voices in the lobby; the taste of maple syrup poured on snow; the scent of fresh pillowcases as she settled into sleep.

Maternity corsets were a discovery: they made it easier to breathe than regular corsets since they were only lightly boned. Letting out their stretchable lacers in front and back, Helene wore them as loosely as she could, just enough to define her, not hold her in. She bought yards of gray broadcloth, blue silk, white linen. Chose collars of batiste and lace. Hired Mrs. Teichman to come to the apartment twice a week, not just Wednesday but also on Friday, which was Pearl's regular day with the seamstress, to sew dresses with adjustable waists and longer belts, skirts with extra pleats held in place by snaps that Helene would gradually undo as the pregnancy progressed.

Evenings, when the bedsheet that Mrs. Teichman had spread on the floor was cluttered with scraps and pins, she'd scoop it up, tie the ends together, and carry it away. It would always mystify Tobias how, when Mrs. Teichman returned, that same sheet would be folded inside her flowered suitcase—small and tidy—as if it had shaken itself out while she slept. He liked the seamstress, not only because his family got to eat in the kitchen while she scattered patterns and fabrics and scissors and buttons all over the dining room, but also because meals were special on days she was there. Since she was in demand and enjoyed gossip as well as food, some of her customers in the *Wasserburg* competed with each other, courting her by offering her the best, hoping she'd tell their neighbors how well she'd been treated. It was known that Mrs. Evans served expensive food but only in small portions. And that Mrs. Clarke fed the seamstress' leftovers to her husband the following day.

What Tobias liked most about the seamstress was that she raised flesh-eating plants. But his stepmother didn't share his fascination for Mrs. Teichman's stories of feeding spiders and flies to her plants, and she got upset when the seamstress gave Tobias two of her plants. They were much smaller than both Helene and Tobias had imagined them, and it was their harmless size—rather than his insistence—that persuaded her to let him keep them.

Late one morning, while Helene was stirring a few grains of sugar and half a cup of white wine into the sour-sweet gravy for *Sauerbraten,* a dull ache pulled at her insides as if they'd suddenly liquified and were about to pour from her. With a cry, she sank to her knees, already grieving the loss of her child. Cold sweat slicked her back, her breasts. She shivered as darkness spun through her, around her. Held herself hard with her arms around her massive belly. And lived a lifetime of being a childless woman, *the four of them around the table . . . she and Stefan with Greta and Tobias . . . then the children growing . . . leaving her to stand next to Stefan at their weddings, a barren woman, useless to Stefan because the children he married her for no longer need her.* As darkness and pain coursed through her, she feared she didn't deserve a child because she hadn't loved the children of the dead mothers enough; and from that fear rose a sudden and vicious envy of Gertrud who would have a child despite her craziness. *No. I'd be the better mother. More stable and loving.* And it was then that she offered Gertrud's child up for hers—*take hers but let mine live*—an offering that came at her out of the darkness and thrust her from that darkness back into her kitchen where Greta crouched next to her on the floor, small face pressed against Helene's belly; and as Helene felt her stepdaughter's murmur pass through her flesh, the child within her solidified once more, took shape, and murmured back to Greta. Years later, when Helene would see the two children play together, she'd sometimes be reminded of the first moment they'd been linked like this, with her on the black-and-white tiled floor, a dusting of flour on her apron from the dumplings, enveloped by the sour yet sweet scent of the roast.

"What are we doing on the floor?" Trying to smile at Greta and feeling her lips tremble in that effort, she raised herself, one hand on her belly, which felt firm now.

Though she would not forget the pain, she would forget its severity until two months later when she'd be taken with a sequence of those very same spasms, leaving her chilled and sweaty— that too was familiar; that too—on the hottest day of July, no wind at all, the lake sullen beneath the blinding sky; and when Dr. Miles was called to the house—a month early for the baby to arrive—the people of Winnipesaukee lit candles for the third wife of Stefan Blau who, as she pushed her child into the world, suddenly wanted to hold back, keep it sheltered because she was terrified it would not be welcomed. Not by its father. Not by this country.

But the doctor's palms pressed down on her belly. "Don't stop now."

She set her teeth.

"You have to keep pushing, Mrs. Blau."

She had felt the townspeople's distrust ever since May when a German submarine had sunk the *Lusitania,* killing more than a thousand people. Stefan said she was too sensitive, but she could feel it like a shift in temperature. That sudden tightness in faces when she entered a store. Even in church. Maybe because to the townspeople she seemed more German than her husband, a more recent arrival with a stronger accent than his.

"Mrs. Blau? Do you hear me?"

Her child would never be as American as the children of Stefan's American wives who linked him to this town. Still, by birth her child would be American. A different nationality than hers. No—

"You must push."

For her child . . . for her child she would do it, become American. As soon as she could.

"Push. Now—"

Then, as all sky pressed down on the lake and squeezed the sun aside, squeezed it through the lace curtains Mrs. Teichman had sewn, squeezed it so hard that the sun turned transparent, Helene could no longer keep from bearing down, and he burst from her, the child, a boy, and as she touched him, cautiously at first and then ripping him into her arms, it was with the certainty that she and her son were alone in an inhospitable country.

Stefan came to her bed.

Bent to kiss her forehead.

Asked to hold the child.

"The child you didn't want?"

"Lenchen . . . don't say that."

"It's the truth." Without blinking, she looked at this man who had put her name on the deeds for his house and restaurant to force the heavens to keep her alive, to pacify her for not having a child. *Tokens of his belief. Trades I never wanted.* But she had her child now. Had it all—child and house and restaurant.

He reached for her son, and she let him. Watched him hold her son—awkward about it, so awkward—and found him useless. It was as though all the men of all her fantasies had fathered this child, had given her the brazenness to seize her husband, use him to get this child who was hers alone, thrust into life through her will.

∽

The same month Helene gave birth to Robert, Leo became the father of a girl, Trudi. When he sent a photo of Trudi with a letter that both she and Gertrud were doing well, the little girl's features looked so much like Robert's that they could have been twins.

"Except that her head seems a bit larger," Helene told Stefan.

He studied the picture. "Probably because of how the light fell when she was photographed in her cradle," he suggested.

"If we didn't have a child the same age, we wouldn't notice the difference."

To his father, Robert was merely one more child in the family, while Helene felt a bond to her son that stunned her, a bond that—in comparison—made marriage seem weak, her relationship with her brother insignificant. Robert absorbed her thoughts, her hours. Though she continued to take the best care of Stefan's American children, it was her son's quiet laugh that enchanted her, the tug of his hunger that filled her with awe as he drew his nourishment from her, his gaze focused on her. Only her.

After years of longing for Stefan, it amazed her to have her forceful love returned to her in every blink of her son's eyes, every movement. As her tenderness and passion shifted and settled on her son, Stefan felt no longer burdened by her unspoken love, and the marriage found a new symmetry in respect and shared accomplishments.

Her son was so much easier to raise than Tobias: content where Tobias had been fretful; affectionate where Tobias had been rigid.

Her son rarely cried and kept food down instead of spitting it up.

Her son let her calm him immediately with German words and songs if he was fussy.

Still, she felt overwhelmed by remorse that she never had enough time for him. Though one of the maids was usually available to help with housework, the American children wanted Helene to be the one who bathed them, fed them, pushed their swing. Again and again they pulled her away from Robert or interrupted the nursing by crowding into her lap. And because it made her feel stingy to be giving most of her love to her own son, she didn't let herself pick him up every time he cried, though she wanted to and ached with each unanswered scream. Besides, as a girl she'd been taught by her mother and neighbors that it was important to be strict with babies right from the beginning. As soon as he could sit, she began to toilet train him by propping him on the *Töpfchen*—potty—holding him like that on her lap while she nursed him, just as her mother had trained her and Leo. It wouldn't be until her grandchildren were born that she would regret all those times she hadn't soothed Robert—*such a waste, that insistence on strictness, a waste for her son and herself*—and she would become more spontaneous as a grandparent than she'd ever been as a mother.

If the Blaus had known how much of their private lives were absorbed into the town lore, they would have been mortified: the people of Winnipesaukee understood that Stefan loved the *Wasserburg* more than his third wife and his children; they felt uncomfortable with his Germanness whenever they read about the war, but they also noted how he helped the poor in town with baskets of food; they admired his wife's effort to be a mother to Greta and Tobias and forgave her for loving her own son best; but they did not approve of her friendship with Pearl Bloom, a woman who'd sung on ocean liners and still had a way of gazing past them as if seeking some foreign horizon.

∽

Helene didn't hear about the problems from Leo but from Stefan's mother, who confided that Gertrud was acting crazy around the baby. "She says something's not right with the child. She hasn't touched Trudi at all since she was born. If it weren't for neighbors like us, Trudi would have starved by now. Promise not to tell Leo that you know," she wrote. "He's doing what he can—given that he is a man. . . . Twice already he has found the child dirty and crying. While all Gertrud did was sit on the bed in her nightgown, hands over her ears." She wrote how Ilse Abramowitz had tacked up a list to the door of the Weilers' grocery store, and eleven women had signed up so far—women from the Catholic church and the Temple and the Protestant church who usually did not call on each other—to take Trudi home for a day or a few hours to tend to her along with their own children. With so many of the men still fighting in the war, the women had additional responsibilities; and still they found more time for each other because there were no men to feed, to clean for, to please. They would take turns sitting with Gertrud in her bedroom above the pay-library to make sure she didn't run away. Because that's what she'd started doing.

"And without her clothes," Stefan's mother wrote. "It's a disgrace."

"But what's wrong with the baby?" Helene wrote back. She wished she could ask Leo directly. Knowing more than he'd chosen to tell her made her letters to him awkward until, finally, he acknowledged what was happening with his wife.

"But it has nothing to do with Trudi," he insisted, "regardless of what others may have told you. There's always been something about Gertrud I haven't understood . . . something that gets twisted underneath her thinking . . . Maybe it's my fault that now it's out there, making her act like this. Some people say it's because of the baby. But Trudi is the most perfect child you've ever seen. I keep her with me in the library while I work. Her eyes, Helene, so intelligent, so wise. Like yours. And she has such strong hands. The way she grips my fingers . . . It's just that she won't be growing quite as much as other children."

"The girl is a *Zwerg*—dwarf," Stefan's mother wrote. "That's what Frau Doktor Rosen told Leo. But he doesn't want to hear."

Helene felt ashamed for being grateful that it was not her child who was marked like that. Guilty at having offered Gertrud's child up in turn for not miscarrying hers. But then there was Robert. And how could she ever regret having kept him alive? Still—it was because of her that Trudi was a *Zwerg*. Of that she felt certain.

In the meantime, Frau Weiler kept updating the volunteers' list, encouraging other customers to sign up if there ever was a lull. It gave some women in Burgdorf a chance to feel superior to Gertrud Montag. Virtuous. As tender as they were with the child, that scornful were they of a mother who didn't have it in her to touch her own daughter. Although they brought Gertrud soup and flowers, washed her linens and ironed her husband's shirts, fed Trudi and curled the ends of her fine hair around their fingers, they would never accept Gertrud back as being one of them because she had broken the natural law of being a mother, had challenged other mothers by magnifying that moment every one of them had felt, a moment when you're so depleted by a child's needs that you can't bear to go near it, a moment you forget instantly because it would shame you to remember; and you'll never understand that other mothers have felt it too because none of you will speak of it.

But Gertrud Montag embodied that aberration.

Gertrud Montag had become what you feared you might be capable of yourself.

"Leo looks sad and confused," Ilse Abramowitz wrote to Helene. "He's too thin. And he's losing customers because he has to lock up the library to find Gertrud whenever she runs off. Yesterday she was hiding in the cemetery. A few days ago by the river."

Even Margret sent more than her usual few lines: "If you were still here, Helene, you'd be such a support to your brother."

With strings of letters she formed a weave to her old neighborhood. With threads of worry and hope she nested herself in her brother's family. Sometimes she felt angry at her sister-in-law. But mostly she felt pity for her. *I warned him. At least I tried.* But Leo had reminded her, "None of us can know for sure if someone else is right for us." And then he'd said Gertrud felt like a sister to him. *Sister? Is that how you are with her at night? Is that what is taking Gertrud across the frail edge? Like a sister . . . It's the last thing I'd want from a husband. And yet how much better is it with me and Stefan?*

Trudi was so much a part of Helene's awareness that even Robert's steady growth served as a constant reproach that Trudi was growing too slowly. *My wickedness. My sin.*

Occasionally Leo's letters were hopeful. "Gertrud fed Trudi for the first time. . . . Yesterday she sang to her."

But the following letter showed how concerned he was about her. "She is getting too excitable again. Wants to carry Trudi around with her wherever she goes. I have to watch her constantly. She'd never want to hurt Trudi. Still . . ."

Helene spoke only German to Robert, taught him to call her *Mutti,* his father *Vati,* and as he learned both tongues as if they were one, he switched between them with ease depending on who was talking to him, and without awareness that he was even using two different languages.

"Gertrud gets impatient for Trudi to wake up because she wants to play with her," Leo wrote. "She cries when I lock her up in the sewing room. Calls me her jailer. God, how I hate to do that to her. But it's better to have her home than sending her to the asylum."

When he finally agreed with the doctor that it would be best to send his wife to the asylum in Grafenberg, it was with great reluctance. "Only for a few weeks. Frau Doktor Rosen says it will help her, settle her."

And then there were no more letters because Congress declared war against Germany, and Helene didn't even know if Gertrud was still in the asylum or back home, where her craziness might endanger her family as much as the craziness of war.

⁓

Tobias' friendship with the Wilsons' nephew puzzled the tenants because Danny was ten years older than Tobias. Tidy and strong with a small frame, Danny Wilson resembled his Aunt Irene as if, by all rights, he should have come from her side of the family instead of her husband's. Though Danny could be quite moody, rude even, he wasn't that way around Tobias, but rather patient despite the boy's incessant questions.

Tobias would follow Danny around whenever he visited his aunt and uncle. Though Danny would pretend to look pestered, Helene could tell he was pleased by Tobias' attention, and she figured he tolerated Tobias for the simple reason that the boy was so hard to like. Danny reminded Helene of young men she'd seen in Germany, hardworking young men who were fiercely handsome for a brief time, but whose jaws would settle and fall before they were forty, whose long, jaunty necks would turn stringy.

"You're the best friend I got in the building," Tobias told Danny the afternoon he moved in for good with his Aunt Irene and Uncle Homer.

After unpacking his boxes, Danny had come outside to sit on the front steps of the *Wasserburg*, where he was drawing circles and squares on the bottom step with a chunk of white he had in his fist.

"What's that?" Tobias asked.

"Chalk. My very own chalk, okay? And you should get friends your own age."

"Well, I don't, and that's that. It's because they're very, very immature."

"Is that so?" Danny sat hunched over, the collar of his black jacket drawn up.

Tobias nodded. He wished his hair were thick and short like Danny's, cropped close instead of his own fly-away strands. But even though he didn't like his hair, he liked being smart. Much smarter for sure than Greta who got bad grades in school because she daydreamed and now had a tutor twice a week. Smarter too than Robert. Twice as smart because of Agnes. *Even though he was only one. With Agnes he was half of one. Which meant two.* He'd known that for as long as he'd known anything—*someone like me; almost like me*—but it wasn't until one day in church that he'd understood what he already knew because the priest was talking about the animals on Noah's ark. *Two of one kind. Meaning each of them was half of that one.* The story of Noah had become Tobias' favorite because Noah had gathered two zebras and two chickens, two wolves and two elephants, two of each kind. That's how it was with him and Agnes. *Sleeps and dreams, dreams and turns, living for himself and for her.* His father said he couldn't possibly remember Agnes since she'd stopped living an entire month before he was born; but Tobias could feel her *living in his blood—a flash of movement, the sound of her voice, the crackle of her hair—Agnes, always one year older than he. Eight years old already.*

Tobias pulled on Danny's sleeve. "My mother is dead too."

But Danny didn't answer. He raised his face into the brisk wind that chased gray clouds across the faded sky. His cheeks were pink, the kind of pink you get when you're cold. But his lips were white.

"Like your mother."

"Hey, thanks for reminding me." Danny's arm slashed a white square around a circle. A circle around that square. Swift lines inward. *A collapsing sun.*

Tobias didn't dare tell him that his father didn't like people drawing on the steps or sidewalk. And even though it would wash away with the next rain, he'd tell the Wilsons to wash it off. But he could tell that Danny wasn't scared of his father. Because his sun was growing bigger. Growing lightning arrows. Growing clouds.

"She didn't even die the way she was supposed to," Danny said, teeth clenched. "You know what she did?"

Tobias nodded. He'd been home when Mrs. Wilson had run up the stairs to the sixth floor—not waiting for the elevator—with the news that Danny was hers now, finally, because his mother had died in a bicycle accident. A soft shoulder of road had given way during rain, and she'd fallen down an embankment, striking her head.

"Got on a stupid bicycle—" The chalk screeched across the step.

"Did you go to your mother's funeral? I did. I was just born. Actually, I was seven days old and . . ."

Danny groaned.

". . . and Greta's grandma says I had a tiny black coat. And tiny black shoes. Did you go to your mother's funeral?"

"You always ask that many questions?"

"Yes."

Danny flinched as the light in the stained-glass lanterns at the bottom of the front steps came on. "I went. All right? This morning."

"You get to stay here now."

"Till I find something better." Danny glanced up when he heard Tobias cry. "Stop it," he said as tears ran down the boy's heart-shaped face—*such an ugly child*—down the pointy chin, and into the collar of his little tweed jacket. "Hey now, what are you? Two years old?"

Tobias hiccuped and leaned against one of the cold, black railings that ran from the lanterns to the front door.

"I didn't hear your answer, Mr. Tobias Blau."

Tobias liked it when Danny called him that. "Seven. Okay? Seven."

"You got to act your age. Go away now. Hop hop." Danny leapt up and stalked past the fountain, around the corner of the house, and into the open garage.

But Tobias raced after him, eyes still blurry. Through the wide door. Beneath the boxy black heaters that hung suspended from the ceiling. *What if they fall and squash me?* Beneath the silver blades of exhaust fans that Mr. Wilson had installed up there for sucking car fumes from the garage. *Blades sharp enough to cut your head off.* Sniffling loudly, he tried to draw his tears back in.

"What are you snorting for?" Danny stopped in the last stall that was set up for washing automobiles. Its floor sloped in the shape of a V toward the drain. Hoses hung coiled next to the window, and a truck tire was fastened to the wall to protect the front fenders of cars while they were cleaned.

"I don't snort."

"I'll live here for a while. But only if you stop snorting."

"I told you I don't—"

"Forgive me, your highness. I'll stay then if my aunt doesn't try to bless me or pray over me while I'm sleeping." Danny broke the lump of chalk and passed the smaller part to Tobias. "Here."

It still felt warm from his palm. And it had a face, the tip of wings— "It's not chalk. It's Mrs. Wilson's Angel of Mercy!"

"*Half* of Mrs. Wilson's angel."

Tobias wiped his thumb across the rosy smudges from Mrs. Wilson's lipstick kisses. "She'll be mad."

"She wants to be my mommy. So she never gets mad at me. Because then I can say, 'I don't want you as my mommy.' Get it?"

"Do you hate her?"

Danny picked up a sponge, tossed it into an enamel basin. "This is how it is: she wants to be my mommy; he wants to go back to Florida. That's all they talk about . . . and fight about."

"I hate my new mother." But as soon as Tobias said it, it didn't feel true. Rather like something he wanted to impress Danny with.

"She's not new," Danny corrected him. "You've had her for years."

"But she's not my *real* mother. And that makes her new. Like my real mother is my old mother, and this mother here is—"

"Okay. Okay. You don't have to keep saying it over. You hate her all the time?"

Tobias thought for an instant. "When she makes me drink milk."

"And that must be about twenty-four hours a day."

"Danny?"

"What now?"

"Will you still be alive when I'm grown up?"

"Jesus—"

"Will you?"

"I guess so."

"I just want to make sure."

"You're a very strange child."

Danny taught him how to draw, first with the upper half of the Angel of Mercy, and later with oils he would buy from the salary he earned for assisting his uncle and aunt. In the garage, he'd save bugs for Tobias' flesh-eating plants and store them inside an old canning jar that he kept on the workbench. One Sunday afternoon in March, Danny showed Tobias how to build a miniature car from wooden matches. It quieted Tobias to set those matches together and glue them, to file down the points where they connected and make them smooth.

Usually words were his comfort, his weapon. If other children in the building excluded him from play, he'd call them bad names. Just as he was called bad names in school. "Hun." "Spy." His father had forbidden him to use those names because they were bad names for Germans. Now Tobias called the other kids "Stinky-face." "Stupid."

Often the front page of the newspaper had headlines about Germans, fighting dirty, gassing Americans in France—Americans like men of Winnipesaukee who were overseas to win this war so that there would be no other wars ever again. Though Tobias' step-mother wouldn't let him read those articles, he knew from other kids about Germans who set fires, Germans who hid time bombs in railroad stations. Worst of all were German spies because they put germs inside horses. Even inside houseflies. Those had to be real tiny germs, Tobias figured.

When he got German measles, Dr. Miles said they were called Liberty Measles now. Even though they were still the same measles. A week later, some girls smeared a rotten banana into Greta's hair, making her smell like glue. Tobias' father went to see the girls' parents and came home mad, saying they were not planning to do anything about it. His father was mad a lot. Because of money worries. "People don't like buying from Germans right now," Tobias' stepmother had said. "And some of your father's suppliers are not giving him the service they used to give him."

She was trying hard not to speak German at all, and though she sometimes forgot, she'd correct herself quickly. Whenever Tobias' little brother called her *"Mutti,"* she'd say to him, "Mother, Robert. Mother."

She refused to let Tobias go with Danny to see *The Kaiser, The Beast of Berlin* at the Royal Theater where the curtain and seats and carpet were all royal blue. The first moving picture Tobias had ever seen was *Romeo and Juliet,* and it remained his favorite because Francis X. Bushman who played Romeo had friendly eyes and the most beautiful smile Tobias had ever seen. A smile like Danny's. If you could make him smile.

One evening, after two of the older kids in the building teased Tobias into kissing a little American flag—"prove you're not a spy prove it prove it"—Tobias had the dream for the first time. He was surrounded by mist, a mist so hot and thick that everything was white except for the red hanging above him, a calf's head, severed, an ancient and mysterious image that bled down on him till he woke, hands against his mouth to keep from screaming. It was a dream that was to come back, but he never told anyone—not even Danny—because he was ashamed of it.

Besides, he knew how to quiet himself. He would spend hours alone in his room with matches, glue, paint, and sandpaper that he got from Danny, and he'd build miniature animals. *Always two of one kind. Meaning each of them was half of that one.* Dogs. Cows. Swallows. Horses. For his swallows he used only one third of a match for the wingspan, sanded the ends, glued on the red tip of a match for a beak, and painted them with Danny's smallest brush. To make sure each animal had another, he'd finish the second animal before he'd let himself start another kind. His own ark. Zebras. Goats. Ducks like the ones he watched down by the lake, their thick bodies a cluster of nine half matches.

∞

Robert was three when he found his own language in the piano. With a persistence that was rare for him, he badgered his parents for lessons, and whenever they'd tell him to wait until he was five, a quick rage would flare in him, a rage that he'd push right back because it was bad. Cookies smoothed it out, that rage. Pudding. Bread warm from the oven.

His pudgy fingers looked as though they couldn't possibly span the ivory keys, yet miraculously they did, leaping with a certainty that amazed Stefan and distressed Helene. To spare her son the discouragement that had bowed her father—*that sweat of despair*—she tried to distract him from the piano; but he returned to it every day, tapping at the white and black ivory keys while sitting atop the piano bench on four volumes of the German encyclopedia she'd brought from Burgdorf, and she usually had to lift him from there and carry him to his room for his nap.

No longer awkward or afraid of blushing, Helene moved through the rooms of her luxurious apartment, certain of herself in her role as Robert's mother. She liked to think of him as her summer child—warm and filled with light. The American children had been born in November and December. Robert had his father's nose and mouth, but he was fair-haired and his eyes were mild where Stefan's were determined. "A replica with weaker colors," Tobias would say many years later when Robert would enter veterinary college, but Helene thought Robert looked more and more like the boy who had grown up next door to her in Burgdorf, and she treated him as if he had the young Stefan's daring and exuberance—traits no one else saw in the patient and affectionate boy.

One morning when she really let herself listen to the sounds he evoked and found that they were delicate and powerful, she cried because she felt proud of him and sad for her father who'd never known what it was like to have that gift. Would he have treasured it in his grandson? Resented his grandson? From then on the organist from the Lutheran church came to the apartment on Tuesdays and Fridays. A slender man of seventy, Mr. Howard appeared old from the front, but his profile was young and didn't show his wrinkles.

Tobias said Mr. Howard looked like an angel because you could see the light coming through his sculpted white hair. He'd wait for him by the door and then sit on the floor next to the piano, watching him as he taught his little brother about music, asking him questions about the moving pictures Mr. Howard loved to go to at the Royal Theater. The latest movie he'd seen there was *Tarzan of the Apes.*

"I'm sure you'll like it," he told Tobias, "because it has lots of apes."

Now and then he saved his sweets for Mr. Howard, who accepted those gifts with a formal bow and the promise that he'd enjoy them for dessert that evening.

∞

The end of 1918, soon after the armistice was signed, letters from Burgdorf began to arrive once again. When Leo wrote that Gertrud was pregnant, Helene felt alarmed that he seemed so pleased: "a brother or sister for our Trudi. Gertrud has become more stable. Those stays in Grafenberg helped. . . ."

In a letter that arrived a scant week later, he was dismayed because Gertrud refused to speak to him or anyone else, and he blamed himself for burdening her with another pregnancy. "Because she's afraid the new child will be a *Zwerg* too . . . While I wouldn't mind raising half a dozen children like our Trudi."

But Stefan's mother wrote that the women of Burgdorf were not eager to raise another child for Gertrud Montag. Granted, with the first child she hadn't known how wretched she'd be as a mother, but to have another child meant relying on your neighbors too much. Not that they wouldn't be there for Gertrud's next child too. They would do their duty, just as they did their duty to God and to their government. But especially now—with their men back from the war or, worse yet, fallen and buried on foreign battlefields—they had no room in their lives for anyone beyond their own families.

Beneath Leo's signature on his next letter, Gertrud added five lines. Now she seemed excited about the pregnancy. She had her own logic why this baby would be all right: "It's God's way to make up to us for Trudi." Already she was planning how the new child, a boy of course with a normal-length body—"We'll name him Horst"—would safeguard the future of her *Zwerg* girl long after she and Leo would be buried.

There was a second postscript. Leo's. "I didn't contradict her. Still, I assured her our Trudi will safeguard her own future."

It would be Horst, born too soon to breathe for himself, who would be buried before any of them. His funeral was the week after Easter, the same week that Irene and Homer Wilson—following the proper interval of mourning for Danny's mother—gave an adoption party for Danny. After all the years of waiting to be his mother, Mrs. Wilson was not about to let herself be cheated out of a celebration, though most of the tenants thought it was foolish to adopt a man old enough to start a family of his own. Danny, who had grown up with her detailed plans for his adoption party—to be held in the lobby of the *Wasserburg* like the Blaus' parties, with so much food that every guest would have some to take home afterwards—didn't care enough to deny his aunt that ritual.

"Embarrassing," Mr. Clarke said to his wife, but they were both too curious to decline the invitation.

"I'll sing if you want me to," Pearl Bloom offered the Wilsons.

To Helene it felt odd to be celebrating the adoption of a grown man when her brother had just lost his infant son.

The afternoon of the party, it occurred to her that Mrs. Evans looked healthier than usual, and when she commented on it, Mrs. Evans admitted, "I've just come back from an appointment with Dr. Miles. I always wear makeup when I go to the doctor. So he will take one glance at me and tell me there's nothing wrong with me."

"You're not fooling him." Her husband turned to Mr. Braddock. "Arthritis. She has arthritis and she pretends she has no troubles."

"Stop fussing, Henry."

"Someone has to fuss over you."

"Henry doesn't trust doctors who're younger than he is," she explained to Mr. Braddock.

Miss Garland pulled Helene aside. "A tragedy. It's a tragedy. Now that Mrs. Wilson finally gets Danny, he's too old to need a mother."

Irene Wilson was dashing about, serving and cleaning all at once with her customary urgency to get things done the instant she became aware of them—a curse and a blessing, she'd once confessed to Helene—and though she would eventually get everything finished, she'd feel overwhelmed because she couldn't do it all at once. It left her forever dissatisfied with what she accomplished, impatient with her husband who couldn't do anything quickly enough for her.

"Let me see if she needs help," Helene said.

"I just remembered something about Sara Blau," Miss Garland started, trying to entice Helene to stay with her, but she excused herself and headed toward Mrs. Wilson. Miss Garland shook her head. Ever since Robert had been born, the third Mrs. Blau had not been very curious about her husband's first two wives.

A few steps from her a group of tenants was asking the old lawyer about the adoption, and Miss Garland joined them.

"Yes, but do you think it's legal?" Nate Bloom was asking.

"That's what I want to know," Mrs. Clarke said.

"I checked it out before I drew up their adoption papers," Mr. Bell told them.

"I bet that makes him the oldest person ever to be adopted," Miss Garland speculated.

"I found a case of a thirty-four-year-old woman in Oregon."

"Let me guess," Pearl Bloom said. "Adopted by a thirty-five-year-old man."

Her husband raised his eyebrows at her. Usually a comment like that would make him laugh, but he was angry at her for dropping his old soap slivers down the incinerator chute. She shrugged. Walked toward the tables.

"No, a lady adopted her," she could hear Mr. Bell explain. "Not even a relative. A neighbor lady."

Pearl sat down next to Mrs. Braddock and Fanny. "How are you, Sweetie?" she asked the girl.

"Sweetie . . . ," Fanny laughed, milk dribbling from her mouth. "Sweetie sweetie sweetie—"

"That's enough now." Her mother wiped Fanny's chin.

"Sweetie swee—"

"Sshhh . . . ," Pearl whispered softly. "Sshhh . . . my pretty girl."

"You're her favorite," Mrs. Braddock said.

"I need to be someone's favorite today." Pearl glanced toward Nate who was standing with his back to her. Ever since she'd married him, she'd been after him to stop saving those worn bits of soap that he kept in a jar by the bathroom sink.

As soon as the Wilsons' adoption party was over, Nate followed her to the elevator and started back at her again. "You had no right, no right at all to throw something of mine out."

"That old soap looked like bones, and it smelled like—"

"If it bothers your nose that much, you should keep your nose out of it."

"Can we wait till we get inside our apartment?"

He rode with her in silence, unlocked their door.

"Look around you." She motioned to their furniture. "Everything we have is of good quality . . . but those pieces of soap were disgusting."

"They were mine."

"I'll go and buy you a hundred pieces of new soap."

"I don't want new soap. I want my old soap back."

"Well, it's too late. And I can't believe that with all your generosity and your money you—"

"That's why I have money."

"Because of that dirty old soap?"

"Because I save little things."

"Please." She took off one shoe, gave three quick raps to the pipes that led up to the Blaus' apartment, and half an hour later met Helene at the locked door that blocked off the stairs to the roof.

"I got Birdie to stay with the children for a while," she said.

Both in warm jackets and hats, they unfolded their canvas chairs and settled in them as they had many other evenings. Only a thin border of sun was left on the upper parts of the mountains, while the lower slopes already looked dark.

"That man. He spends tons on entertaining but thinks I'm wasteful for throwing out his soap."

Helene opened a thermos of hot, sweet tea and poured it into two cups. "Here." She passed one to Pearl.

"Thanks. You know what he called me? Irresponsible. You want to know what I call irresponsible? Having a son and not telling anyone."

"Nate with a son?"

"I've only known a few weeks, and he asked me not to mention it to anyone, but hell . . . keeping secrets takes effort, and I'm in no mood to make one single effort for that man. The kid's name is Ira."

"How old—"

"Well, he isn't really a kid anymore. He's in high school already, lives with his mother in Boston. When I asked Nate why he hadn't told me about his son before, he said he just doesn't think about him very often. It makes me furious that he would be so indifferent toward his son. Doesn't visit him more than once or twice a year." She looked up at the clouds, gray and streaked, thinning out where they touched the tips of the mountains in wispy smears.

As dusk enveloped them, they talked about Nate and his son. About how different Helene's brother was with his child.

"Yes, but he's doing too much," Helene said, "feeding and cleaning Trudi as well as his wife . . . running the pay-library. Always the one to be giving."

"Isn't that the way in every marriage?"

"I hope not."

"Maybe as long as the giver doesn't mind."

"I wish I could visit Leo. Help if I can."

"Then go."

"Stefan wouldn't leave the restaurant for that long. Especially now."

"Then go without him. Just take Robert."

"But Greta and Tobias—"

"Can stay with me. Maybe some of the time with their grandparents. You've never had any time all alone with your son."

"I haven't."

"Just take him with you."

Here on the roof, both women often made decisions as each heard herself talk to her friend and, listening to her own words, found out what she wanted. With Pearl, Helene had come to expect that their conversations would go right to where things mattered, that she would feel upheld—in big and small matters alike—and that she was capable of doing the same for Pearl. With Stefan there was usually more kept back than revealed.

"*Mein Lenchen,*" he liked to call her when he saw her attending to the children. "*Mein Lenchen.*" Other than that, his rare words of tenderness were for his children. He would have felt stunned had he guessed at the accumulation of loving words Helene had held back over the years. Anyone listening to him and Helene talk about their days would have assumed a partnership rather than marriage because their duties were so clearly divided: while he operated the restaurant and supervised repairs, she took care of the children and the apartment. A woman of strong and few attachments, she'd come to know her limitations—that she could only love very few people and then with an intensity that kept her breath high and shallow in her throat. Robert was one of those few. So was Pearl. Stefan had been once, but her love had lived for too long in a place where it hadn't been nourished, and she'd survived by becoming immune to that passion until it had faded.

As she tried to explain this to Pearl, her friend smiled. "Passion," she murmured, "can be restored."

Helene leaned back in her chair and smiled, suddenly feeling glamorous. It sometimes was like that when she was with Pearl, talking with such ease, and she would take that image with her and, for hours afterwards, feel glamorous and confident. "And how do you know so much?" she asked.

"I just know about people." Pearl got up to sit on the brick ledge.

"I get vertigo just looking at you," Helene protested. Extending one hand, she pulled Pearl back.

"I see you and Stefan . . . ," Pearl said, "and it is still there."

A few months after Horst's death, Gertrud died in the sanatorium. When Helene tried to make travel arrangements to be with Leo and Trudi, she found that quite a few ocean liners had either been confiscated or were not ready for passage so soon after the war, and it wasn't until September that she was able to book a cabin for Robert and herself on a freighter.

Though she felt selfish not taking the other children, Stefan urged her to leave them with Pearl. "It'll be more affordable . . . and I'll see them every day."

Robert hadn't known the earth was big enough for anyone to travel this long. From the German coast, he and his mother took trains to Burgdorf, and the closer they got, the more excited she became despite her sadness, pointing through the rain-streaked windows to show him the country where she'd grown up. It warmed her to hear familiar sounds, to be surrounded by the language she'd grown up with.

Although Leo had written to her about his knee injury, she was startled to see him limp toward her from the pay-library as if the loss of his wife and son had manifested themselves in his movements. He'd always been thin, but now he was gaunt. Unhealthy. It seemed that he had to remind himself to smile. Except when he played with his daughter. Then he was joyful, patient. It moved Helene to see her brother in the role of father, the kind of father she wished Stefan could be.

She had felt afraid of meeting Trudi, afraid of feeling repulsed, yet all that vanished the instant she held the little girl who, indeed, was hard to look at. When Trudi brought her short arms around Helene's neck and kissed her on the cheek, Helene felt choked with love and guilt at having sacrificed her for Robert. Still, it was better to have both children alive than to have lost Robert—even if it meant that Trudi would not grow like others.

Except for her large head and short limbs, she looked a lot like Robert, and that's what the children seemed to think too because over the five weeks of the visit they kept going to the mirror, strong chins forward as they faced their images. Sometimes they'd laugh, Robert's laugh slow but lasting, Trudi's sudden and high. Until she'd remember about her mother and grow solemn.

One afternoon, when he stood with his fingers linked behind his back, Trudi tried to copy that posture, but her arms wouldn't go that far. She stamped her feet, furious that she couldn't do something that simple.

Robert was watching her in the mirror when her eyes trapped him there.

"You do it." She turned. Stuck her left arm back toward him. "Hold this."

He grasped her square little hand while she swung her other arm back.

"Put them together now."

He tried. But her fingers barely reached beyond her torso.

She craned her neck to check in the mirror what was happening behind her. "Make them touch," she ordered.

Afraid of hurting her, he tugged at her hands.

"Now? Are they touching now?"

He shook his head.

"Make them." She curved her chest forward, threw her shoulders back. "Now?"

"Not yet."

"Now?"

He hesitated. And then he lied for the first time in his life. "Yes."

She let out a long breath. Snatched her hands from his. Cupped them against her chest to stop the hurting in her fingers and shoulders. "Tomorrow I'll do it *allein*—alone."

He followed her into the living room where she hoisted herself onto the piano bench and, standing, jabbed at the keys, making horrid noises.

"Sshhh." Robert climbed next to her. "Let me. I have a piano teacher."

"I want a piano teacher."

"He's in America. His name is Mr. Howard." Robert waited for her to stop before he raised himself on his knees and played for her.

When Helene came in and stood behind the children, they didn't notice her.

"I have a brother," Trudi was telling Robert. "He is in a box."

"I have a brother. A sister too."

"Are they in a box?"

"No, in America."

"My *Mutti* went to the box. To fetch my brother. She'll come back. When I'm tall. And won't steal sugar."

All at once Helene was angry at Gertrud for dying and leaving her child with such confusion. To distract her, she said, "Look at that, Trudi," and picked up a clay pot with the curled, brown remnants of a fern. "All dried out. Shall we give it some water?"

Trudi slid from the bench while Robert kept playing.

"Any other plants? You can show me."

With a tin milk can full of water, she followed Trudi as the girl pointed out flowerpots, most of them dry. Trudi's legs couldn't move as fast as her energy was propelling her forward, and Helene felt a deep pity for the little body in struggle with itself. When Trudi opened the door to her father's bedroom, Helene froze. Photos of the dead Gertrud hung on the walls—everything in white: the candles and flowers and pale dead skin. Quickly she placed herself between Trudi and the photos.

But the girl slipped right past her, and as she stood facing the pictures of her mother, it was obvious that she'd seen them before. "My *Mutti* is coming back real soon," she said.

That evening, when both children were asleep, Helene implored Leo to take those photos down. "Not only because of Trudi. But it isn't good for you either . . . looking at Gertrud like that."

But he was reluctant. "I keep thinking of everything I was not for her."

"And I keep thinking of all you were to her."

He shook his head.

"You brought her happiness, Leo."

"How can you know that?"

She recalled how he'd once spoken of Gertrud as his sister. *A second sister.* "More happiness," Helene said resolutely, ignoring her uneasiness, "than Gertrud could have had on her own. Everyone could see that."

But he did not look convinced. The brown wallpaper behind him made the room feel darker.

"Gertrud's oddness," she reminded him, "was in her long before you married her. But I'm sure she would not have wanted you to have those pictures around you. No woman would. It isn't . . . proper."

"I didn't think about them that way. I just wasn't ready yet to let her go."

"I know. But it isn't right for Trudi to be reminded of her mother's death so constantly."

"I'll do it then . . . take them down."

"I'll help. If you want me to. Did you know that Trudi talks about a box and about Gertrud bringing Horst back?"

"At the funeral—" His eyes grew bright with tears. "At the funeral, Frau Weiler tried to console Trudi by saying her *Mutti* was with her little brother now."

"What a stupid thing to tell her."

"She meant well. It's what people say at funerals."

"Meaning well is not enough."

"Still, it has to count. . . . Did you know that you have an accent?"

"Of course. People in America tell me—"

"No, here. In German."

She was stunned.

"Not much of an accent," he hastened to tell her. "It's like a different melody almost that runs beneath the language."

"A different melody. . . . That means I have an accent in both languages now."

"Does it bother you?"

Slowly, she nodded. "It marks me. Instead of feeling connected to both countries, I belong to neither one."

"A foreigner?"

"That's what it felt like over there at first. And it still does—not as often though."

"For me feeling foreign goes deeper than language . . . into values . . . customs. Being an exile in the world. It was like that when I came back from the war. For other men too. Michel, for him it was worse because he'd been away longer. You come back and everything is changed. Even if it still looks the same."

"Yes. Yes, that's how it is for me."

"People, too, they've changed. Those who stayed. They don't understand that when you come back, you're not the same. And neither are they. It's like that with grieving . . . you enter a foreign country. And sometimes you don't come back."

"Unless you want to?"

"Oh, but wanting to come back is just a small part of it, Helene."

They stayed up late, talking at the kitchen table, and whenever Leo spoke of Gertrud, he sounded far more passionate in missing her than he had been in loving her when she'd still been alive, and Helene thought how deadly a kind man could be if his kindness were to take the place of passion.

All at once she felt an urgency to do something significant for Trudi, and it was that urgency—born of guilt and compassion—that compelled her to offer, "I could bring Trudi up."

"What do you mean?"

"Take her back to America with me," she said, thinking *this is crazy. What am I doing? The three I have are already too much for me.*

Leo looked stunned. "I'll make us some tea," he said.

She kept silent as she watched him prepare his favorite Russian tea, brewing its essence in a small pot, and boiling water in a larger pot, so that they could each choose at what strength they liked it. He served it in paper-thin porcelain cups.

"Gertrud's?" Helene asked.

"Part of her great-grandmother's dowry." He closed the white kitchen cabinet and sat across from Helene.

"What I mean is that I would raise her along with Robert. And with Stefan's other children. Of course you could always visit . . . ," she added. *What am I doing? Three already.* "I like Trudi," she said quickly. "I like her fierceness, even her bossiness with Robert. Because it gives me such hope for her. And I see so much of you in her, Leo. That sageness and—"

Leo squinted at her. Shook his head.

"I already feel closer to her than to Stefan's children."

"I am . . . grateful. Of course I am grateful. How could I not be? But she is my daughter."

"I'm sorry. It's just that I want to do something."

"But you are doing something. You are here."

∞

Every day she visited the Blaus next door, answering their hungry questions about Stefan, watching their delight in Robert while she told them about life in America. She didn't object when her mother-in-law insisted she pack her telescope and star charts for Stefan. With her, as with others of that generation, Helene found that she slipped right back into that politeness of her childhood, where with Americans she felt equality regardless of age.

Whenever Margret came over, she and Helene would be right back to where they'd left off, eight years bridged in moments as they talked about their childhood and about their children. But not about Helene's offer to raise Trudi. She was too embarrassed to tell Margret how she'd trespassed with that offer. And yet there were times when she could picture Trudi in the *Wasserburg* growing up with Robert and the other children.

The small girl would snuggle up to her, listening closely when she and Margret talked about the people in town, like Axel Lambert who had not been right ever since he'd come home from the war, the one survivor of his battalion.

One afternoon, when Margret was whispering to Helene, Trudi leaned closer, and though she didn't know what an affair was, she understood it was something bad between the lady from the bakery and the man who sold asparagus.

"Ottilia is pregnant again. In her last month," Margret said, "and confined to bed."

"I loved being pregnant." Helene stroked Trudi's hair.

"Seven daughters so far. Bettina is their youngest . . . the same age as Robert and Trudi."

Margret's parents watched the children while Helene and Margret went for long walks along the Rhein. One morning at the cemetery they planted yellow chrysanthemums on the graves of both families and said prayers for Helene's parents, as well as for Leo's wife and son.

"I worry about Leo," Helene said as she set a plant into the earth. "He doesn't look healthy."

"Sadness," Margret said. "I think it's sadness, mostly. My mother goes over there at least once a day. Others too. Like Ilse Abramowitz. And Emil Hesping, of course."

The way she said Emil's name made Helene glance at her.

"Have you seen him yet?"

"A few times. He usually stops by the pay-library for a quick game of chess."

"Your brother likes slow games better." Margret's eyes followed the black shape of a widow on her bicycle. On one handlebar dangled a shopping net with gardening tools, on the other a watering can. "People talk about Emil."

"They always have."

"Only more so now. Because he stayed out of the war. Some say he . . . loves your brother."

"And I'm sure Leo loves him too."

"They're not talking about that kind of love, Helene."

"Their friendship was always passionate in spirit. Just because Leo isn't very . . . physical with women doesn't mean he looks for that with men. It's just never been all that important for him."

"And that was painful for Gertrud. It distracted her. Embarrassed her. Some say Emil courted her to—"

"Emil flirts with almost every woman."

"Not like that. I think he courted her to get her away from Leo. So he could have Leo for himself."

"Wait." Helene sat back on her heels. "I don't understand the logic. Sleeping with a woman to get the man?"

"My mother saw her on the back of his motorcycle when Leo was away in the war."

"Maybe Emil just—"

"His reputation is a lot worse now than when you used to live here."

"I never really believed in his terrible reputation. Beneath all that, he's a decent man." Helene pulled a candle from her handbag. "For Gertrud," she said and rummaged for matches. "I forgot matches."

As she searched on other graves for a lantern with a burning candle to light hers from, she was devastated by the many new names on gravestones, young men who'd died as soldiers. Most of them she'd known. A few had even been her students. *Children.*

With the lit candle she returned to the Montag grave; but it was too long to fit into the lantern. Suddenly she found herself sobbing.

"It's just a candle." Margret smoothed the earth around a chrysanthemum she'd just planted.

But Helene cried. Cried for all who had died in the war. Cried for the waste of death and the waste of war. Cried for her parents and for Leo's wife and son. And all along—while a woman with a baby carriage and two widows walked past her family's grave—she kept holding on to that burning candle.

"Let me," Margret offered.

"It's the wrong size."

"The wrong size for the lantern. That's all."

Helene only sobbed harder.

"It'll fit the candle holder on my table. Let me keep it for you. Please?" Gently, Margret placed one palm between her friend's shoulder blades and rubbed it up and down. "You've been away a long time."

❧

Although Helene had heard about Axel Lambert, she was not prepared for the change in him when she saw him in the street outside Immers' butcher shop, where she stood waiting in line with Robert and Trudi to buy *Weisswurst*—white sausage—for their *Mittagessen*—lunch.

A secretive smile on his lips, Axel was circulating both hands in a strange and repetitive pattern between his face and his chest. Devastated by the recognition of what the war had done to him, Helene left the line and stepped up to him. His smile got wide as though he were glad to see her, but his eyes looked through her.

"Axel? It's me. Helene. Helene Montag."

He dropped both arms, then raised them, one toward his nose, the other toward his chest, touching briefly with his forefingers, then dropping his arms again.

"Axel?" A half-forgotten fondness for him rushed in on her. "Don't you remember me? Helene Blau. It used to be Montag. This is my son. Robert. And I'm sure you know Trudi. Leo's daughter."

Up came Axel Lambert's arms again, graceful, purposeful. Unstoppable.

Ilse Abramowitz came walking toward them in a beige linen dress with deep pleats on one side. "He doesn't understand."

"What is he doing?" Helene whispered.

"Touching his heart? Who knows . . . But that's what people call him now, the man-who-touches-his-heart."

"Who looks after him?"

"This month his sister. Then he'll live with his cousin for a month. His parents take him in after that. Then back to his sister."

"But he's never liked being around his family much."

"Well, he's lucky he has them now."

"He always preferred his time alone."

"Not as much as he enjoyed being with you."

"He was a very shy man."

"Not like your Stefan."

"Not like Stefan at all . . . Listen—" Impulsively, Helene laid her hand on Ilse's arm and took her aside, making sure the children couldn't hear her. "Something's been bothering me. I said something foolish to Leo when I first arrived here. I offered to take Trudi back with me to America."

Ilse winced.

"I wanted to help."

"Of course you did."

Axel Lambert brought his left hand to his chest, the right to his face.

"Still—" Ilse hesitated. "It must have been hard for Leo to hear."

"I told him how I admired all he did for her, even mentioned what a good cook he has become—have you ever tasted his *Eierkuchen* with onions?—but he's been guarded with me as if waiting for what I'll propose next."

Ilse glanced toward Trudi, who was sitting with Robert on the front steps of the butcher shop. "I've watched out for Leo's girl ever since she was born. Maybe you won't worry quite this much about her if you know that I'll keep doing that as long as I live."

Because she's Leo's. But Helene didn't say that, though Ilse looked at her as if she knew exactly what Helene was thinking. And didn't mind. Delicate embroidery on her linen collar emphasized her smooth neck. How Leo used to adore that neck. That beautiful skin. "I'm sorry," Helene said. "I'm staring at you."

"Leo knows that I'm here for Trudi."

"Thank you. It's important for me to know."

Down again and up went Axel Lambert's hands. This time the right to his chest, the left to his nose.

Helene stepped in front of him. "Come," she said. "Come home with us. I'll go to the butcher shop later. We still have *Linsensuppe*— lentil soup—from yesterday." To Ilse, she said, "Where should I take him afterwards?"

"He knows how to get to his sister's apartment from your house."

Axel Lambert's reflection in the glass panel of the front door stopped him for a moment, but then he followed Trudi into her house without hesitation. While the children ran into the pay-library to visit Leo, Helene heated a bowl of *Linsensuppe* for Axel. What would have happened if Axel had come for her that day of the wedding instead of staying away? She knew he couldn't have stopped her from marrying Stefan, and yet, as she watched Axel eat—his table manners oddly controlled as if his childhood training were taking over at the table—she pictured herself as the wife of this man, a good teacher not too long ago, who had returned broken from the war, making her an almost-widow, one of many almost-widows in Burgdorf because there were other men like Axel, men who—though still alive—had left pieces of themselves in the war. *The life I would have led had I stayed . . . and always with that longing for Stefan.*

Grateful that Leo had survived with only a knee injury, she wanted to tell Axel that, if she still lived in Burgdorf, he could stay with her and Leo for a month each year. *Two months even. He lives in the sewing room. She steadies his hands, curves his fingers around a pencil, helps him with words that get him back into writing crossword puzzles for the paper—*

But I won't be here.

And she was leery of her noble offers. What good could it do to give Axel a picture to hold in his mind for a moment—if that was possible for him at all—a picture of something he would never have? It would be cruel. All at once she felt more aware of what it meant to have left her hometown, aware of all she could not be part of: she could not give Axel promises that might make her feel better and leave him with yet another loss; she could not be a mother to Trudi; could not give Trudi as much as Ilse could; not even as much as any woman in Burgdorf who might take Trudi home one afternoon each month. And as she came up against the loss of not being able to do this for Leo's daughter, Helene mourned not only what she had left behind, but also what she had missed in the eight years since she'd left here, and what she would miss in the years to come.

Once, she had tried to talk with Stefan about the lives they would have lived had they both stayed in Burgdorf, and he hadn't been able to imagine himself as a man in their hometown, maybe because he'd been so much younger than she when he'd left and—even while still living there—had been so focused on getting away. Helene didn't think they would have married, simply because there would have been other women for him to choose from—younger women, prettier women—and he would have never come to know her through their letters. What she regretted was that parts of her had been asleep while she had waited for him to come for her. Quite likely she had made a mistake in marrying Stefan. And yet she would have married him had she known how it was to be between them, because she had believed—and still believed—that she could win him over.

It would be difficult to leave Burgdorf. But the instant she thought of postponing her return, she saw the familiar view of Lake Winnipesaukee, saw herself talking with Pearl, and understood it would always be like this: that the place where she was *not* would superimpose itself on the place where she was. It had been like that when she'd first come to America, when images of her hometown had shifted themselves between her and the landscape that surrounded her. It had to do with having a home in both countries. With having an accent in both languages. As Axel Lambert spooned the brown *Linsensuppe* into his mouth, she saw herself in the *Wasserburg, stepping toward the silver bud vase that Stefan has given her for her last birthday, and as the vase reflects her shape, fuzzy and long, moving and always moving*—Helene Montag felt herself arrive in America although she still stood in her brother's kitchen, felt herself arrive more completely than she had in the years she'd lived there. Astonished by how much she felt linked to her adopted country, she already understood that she would be able to return there now, no longer feeling that she belonged to neither country, but with a deeper sense of her connection to *both*.

Axel Lambert had finished eating. His hands resumed their journey, and as he rose as if pulled upward by their momentum, Helene caught them on their way up and held them between her own where they fluttered, trembled, and curled inward. As she leaned forward to kiss his cheek, he stood as if stunned, and Helene recalled what Lelia Flynn had told her: "... *they're the men we remember when we're old because their fascination with us will forever stay the same. You see ... it was never tested. Never had a chance to fade in marriage.*" But already Axel's hands were breaking her clasp in a flight even she couldn't halt, his right to his chest, his left to his face, keeping her from coming closer, then his right to his face and his left to his chest as though he were touching his heart for her.

CHAPTER SIX

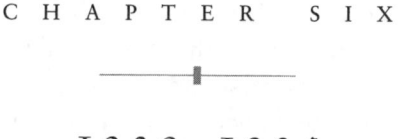

1 9 2 0 – 1 9 2 4

Though he wasn't five yet, Robert could already read the names of
the dead mothers on the tall granite headstone:

ELIZABETH BLAU 1883–1906

SARA BLAU 1888–1910

While his *Mutti* pulled weeds and watered the bush with the
prickly roses, Robert stood with his hands linked behind his back,
staring at the grave. *Dead people turn into rice.* He knew that from
Miss Garland, who made peanut brittle for him. *Inside the grave is
space for* Mutti *too.* Fear as black as beneath-earth filled his belly—
don't think that, no, not Mutti—and he rummaged in his pocket
for a lemon drop, closed his eyes as the sweet-sour puckered the insides of his cheeks and melted that fear till all he knew and felt was
the lemon taste in his mouth. He swiveled his head away from the
grave: all around him, everything was green—lichen and moss and
leaves—so very green; and the light coming through the leaves from
above was turning their undersides pale green, much paler than the
pines that circled the cemetery like a fence.

He sat down on a fallen log, pulpy beneath its new growth of
tiny trees and plants. With one heel, he kicked a line of half-moons
into the raked sawdust that covered the ground all around him, left

over from the brush that the townspeople cleared early every summer to keep the forest out of the cemetery. Birdie Robichaud had said it would take the forest only one year to grow all across the graves and stones if it were left to its will. *The will of the forest . . .*

It made Robert wonder what the forest would want to do to one boy alone. Branches crisscrossed the sky like spiderwebs, and the moss that hung from the branches was a different kind of green altogether, the kind of green that had brown and yellow mixed into it. Some of the moss was low enough to touch when he stood up. As he pulled off one long strand and wound it around his hand, it felt stiffer than it had looked while still moving with the wind. And even after he slipped it from his hand, it kept that circle shape, so stiff and strong that he could imagine tying something with it, something that needed to be fastened. Like maybe the altar gate at St. Paul's. Or the cross that tilted sideways at the cat grave, the smallest grave of all. Birdie Robichaud had told him about the boy who'd climbed up here one night to dig a grave for his cat. When the priest had ordered his parents to get the cat out from the sacred earth, the neighbors had written letters to the bishop, who'd finally allowed the cat to stay.

But only this cat. No other animals. Robert liked animals. His father said they were messy, and he wouldn't let him keep any in the apartment. But once he was grown up, Robert knew, he would have four dogs and four cats. Maybe five dogs and five cats. And they'd never die. He swallowed, searching for the lemon taste, but it was gone, and the old stubborn fear was tumbling right back. *If my* Mutti *gets another baby, she'll die. Then* Vati's *next wife will bring me and Greta and Tobias here to plant flowers on the grave.* HELENE BLAU *will be the third name on the headstone, right beneath* ELIZABETH BLAU *and* SARA BLAU. *That's what happens to mothers. They die. First they have babies. Then they turn into rice. Both Greta and Tobias killed their mothers when they were born. Babies can kill mothers.* He popped another lemon drop into his mouth, fuzzy from being inside his pocket, and curled his tongue around it—*babies can kill mothers . . . babies all powerful, all frail*—and swallowed the tangy saliva. Mutti *knows I don't*

*want to kill her. She's smart. Mrs. Wilson is smart too. She gave her
baby back to God before the baby could kill her. Trudi's Mutti also
gave her baby back to God. But not soon enough.*

Babies can kill mothers.

‰

Miss Garland was peering through the ornate brass screen in her
door when she saw him by the mailboxes with a basket to pick up
his parents' mail as usual. "Robert dear," she called, "why don't
you come in for a little treat?"

His round face swiveled toward her voice, and he smiled. She liked
him better than his brother and sister, this thoughtful boy who had
inherited his father's short frame, his mother's large bone structure,
and a craving for sweets that made him look as though he were about
to rip his seams. Even new clothes soon pinched him.

"Come in. Come in." She opened her door.

He loved Miss Garland's flutter of kisses against his forehead.
Though Greta said Miss Garland's apartment smelled fussy—"of
old lady's corsets and false teeth"—Robert visited her every day.
Sitting across from her at the lace-covered table, he'd color pictures
of castles and kings in the coloring books she bought for him and
saved inside an old shoe box. He'd hum to himself with the pleasure of chewing, while she'd fill him with peanut brittle and stories
of gala balls, of her father's mansion, of six handsome and wealthy
admirers from whom she had chosen the kindest for marriage.

"The ring, Robert, you should have seen my engagement
ring. . . ." She raised her left hand and stroked her bare ring finger.
"A flawless diamond set in a circle of sapphires." When the young
fiancé had died two days before the wedding—"of causes so tragic
that even to speak of them would break the heart of anyone who
were to listen"—she had buried him with her ring. "He wore my
engagement ring on a bracelet, Robert dear. I braided that bracelet
from my very own hair and slipped it on his left wrist before they
closed his coffin."

He looked at her hair—as silky and white as her crinkled skin—
and saw a bracelet of her white hair on a man's wrist, a wrist like
his father's, saw it as clearly as the castle and horses he was color-

ing, the trees that were shaped like huge mushrooms; and as he listened to Miss Garland with a devout expression—his usual response to unlimited sweets—the details of her stories became so true to her that, once again, she ached with the loss of that fiancé, a sorrow so genuine that it would become part of her memories and embellish the embroidery of her life.

All at once she felt deeply tired. She pulled out a handkerchief, dabbed at her lips. "On your way home, Robert dear . . . would you drop off those flyers for me?"

He hesitated before he nodded. Mrs. Wilson always scowled at him when he delivered those flyers. Captain, she called Miss Garland, Miss Captain, and some of the tenants had picked up on that name.

"The role of a messenger has always been one of great value. And responsibility." Miss Garland walked to her desk where a typewriter with silver-rimmed keys stood among boxes of stationery and carbon paper. There, she always composed her long lists, titled: *Helpful Suggestions from Miss Garland, President, Tenants' Society.* When she had first approached Helene Blau with the suggestion of forming a tenants' society—"A little community," she'd said, "where people will get together at each other's apartments once a week for dinner or a slice of cake"—Helene had told her she was too busy, but she had come to regret that she hadn't discouraged Miss Garland from the idea.

Although the tenants' society collapsed after one meeting at Miss Garland's apartment where only six people appeared and left early, mumbling excuses when she asked who would like to host the next gathering, Miss Garland kept writing new lists. Living in the *Wasserburg* was the best thing she had ever made happen for herself, and she was so devoted to the house that she thought about it constantly and annoyed nearly everyone who lived there with her ideas to make it better yet. She didn't mind the work of typing everything six times, one original and five carbons, making a total of thirty-six flyers that she'd either leave in people's mailboxes or send with Robert who'd deliver them door to door. In addition to these flyers, she posted hand-printed reminders in the appropriate places that Mrs. Wilson took down with decreasing patience: *Please, close door of incinerator room! Please, shake your umbrellas before bringing them into the building! Please, don't leave laundry in the drying room longer than necessary because others want to use the rods too! Please, don't drag sand into the lobby from the beach!*

The only tenant who valued her notes was Yates Hedge, a widowed geologist who'd recently moved into the apartment next to her with his forty-year-old son, Buddy, an accountant who'd never married. Since Buddy was sensitive to bright sun, he worked nights in the office of the Winnipesaukee School.

"Without you," Yates Hedge liked to tell Miss Garland, "we wouldn't know half of what's happening."

When Robert knocked at the Hedges' door, Buddy led him into the living room where all windows were boarded up to keep the light out. The only picture in the apartment was of his mother, a huge oil portrait that hung in one of the shut windows and showed Mrs. Hedge in a gravy-colored suit and matching hat.

"May I please look at your Christmas closet?" Robert asked.

Buddy rubbed the top of his bald head. "Oh, sure..." He shrugged. "You'd like that, wouldn't you?" He headed for the coat closet to pull out the decorated Christmas tree that he took out every December or whenever one of the children in the building asked to see it. Like this boy who asked for it at least once a month. Or the Braddock girl who liked to sit on the floor next to it, all quiet with that loopy smile of hers.

Reverently, Robert touched the stiff silver branches, the glossy red balls, the strands of tinsel. Accustomed to his *Mutti* taking an entire day to decorate the family's Christmas tree with ornaments and real candles that she never lit because their father wouldn't permit it—*too dangerous; fire can kill*—he was fascinated by a tree that was ready any day of the year.

"Visit is over," Buddy said. "Make sure to tell Miss Garland thank you from us."

But Mrs. Wilson did not say thank you when Robert arrived with peanut breath and yet another dispatch from the tenants' society. "So involved with such trivia," she muttered. As usual, she tossed Miss Garland's latest ideas into the trash can. "Acts like she's the self-appointed captain of the building."

"You know why Miss Captain mixes into everyone's business?" Mr. Wilson asked Robert, and when the boy shook his head, Mr. Wilson leaned down and whispered, "It's because she never had sex."

"What are you telling that boy, Homer?"

"That she's one lonely old broad." He winked at Robert and scratched the long creases on his forehead.

Though Robert didn't know what having sex meant, he suspected from Mr. Wilson's tone that *not* having sex had to be one of the worst things that could happen to anyone.

"There's work to be done, Homer," Mrs. Wilson said. "Danny needs help in the garage."

"On my way." Homer Wilson shuffled off. Ever since the adoption party, his wife had seemed lost without that goal of making Danny her son, and she looked disappointed when she spoke of him. She'd also been getting upset at Homer for taking Danny to the dog track and for complaining about how cold it was in New Hampshire. Homer wished he still lived in Florida. Alone. He'd been saving some. Not a lot. But a few dollars now and then that he kept in an old tire beneath the workbench in the garage. Where he was heading now.

While his wife's voice followed him. "Also . . . the Braddocks' sink is stopped up again, and—"

He didn't turn. "I've been on my way for the last twenty years," he said, thinking about Florida.

∽

As Helene's adopted language wove itself into her dreams, it became easier to speak it. At times she even found herself thinking in English; it eliminated that slow process of translating everything inside her head before she spoke, and it gave her more confidence to express herself. Gradually she began to recognize American accents. Tourists from Boston spoke differently than tourists from New York; and her husband, who had sounded so American to her when she'd arrived, definitely had a German accent that set him apart from the people of Winnipesaukee.

But what set Stefan even more apart—not just him but his entire family—was the fact that he came from the country America had been at war with; and now that the war was over and several young men from Winnipesaukee lay buried overseas, he could feel that separateness even more than during the years of war. Coming to America had been so easy, like arriving in a place that had already been in his blood, his real home that freed him to become who he was, a home with a far stronger hold on him than his first home. But now it felt as though he were starting all over again in territory more foreign than any he knew, living among people who resented him—not because of anything he had done, but because forty years ago he'd been born in Germany.

It made him draw closer to his family, limit his time with Americans.

On the tenth anniversary of his wedding to Helene, he prepared a veal roast with raspberry sauce for his family, and when they sat down at the dinner table, he presented Helene with an emerald necklace. She tried to fasten it around her neck, but the clasp was too complicated. As he stood up to secure it for her, he suddenly wanted to kiss the curve of her strong neck, but since he figured it would embarrass her in front of the children, he only touched her shoulders before he returned to his seat. On the roof directly above them, the claws of the squirrels were like harsh whispers.

Helene looked at the American children eating, their small hands maneuvering the silverware with the graceful German table manners she'd taught them, and her throat constricted with a startling rage as if the necklace had shrunk: these children had hindered her chance of having a normal marriage with Stefan, a marriage in which their father wouldn't fear giving her his seed and his devotion, a marriage in which all children were his and hers. As she brought her fingers between her skin and the necklace, she found enough space, and yet the tightness remained. From across the table she felt Greta's calm gaze as if she knew and—even more so—understood and pitied her, and in that moment Helene resolved to herself that she would never permit herself that rage again.

But it was as if something unfinished had settled itself between her and Greta, who was touchy and rebellious while getting dressed the next morning, complaining about the shoes that Helene was finally able to order from Germany again.

"They're clunky," she wailed.

"They're first-rate quality."

"But they look third rate."

Third rate. Third wife. She didn't let Greta see how much those words cut. Patiently she told her that she had to wear the shoes because they gave good support to her arches. "It's important during those years when your feet are growing."

"I don't care about my arches."

"But I care about them."

"They are my arches." Greta stalked off to her room.

She can certainly be dramatic, Helene thought. Usually it was easier than this to be around Greta, even if the girl often fussed too much around her, trying to help with chores or watching her as if concerned she might be lonely. To distract her, Helene would ask her to play with Robert, who liked to follow Greta around though she was nearly nine years older than he. They'd read stories together or swim in the lake, diving and leaping from the dock, Robert more nimble in water than on land.

When Helene would go into the water with them, she'd float on a rubber raft while Robert and Greta would bob around her, pulling her this way and that as if competing for her. Afterwards she'd sit on the dock, watching those two play ball or dig channels from the water to the sand, making it flow into the moats that surrounded their sand castles.

But Tobias usually kept to himself. Helene wished he had something he was good at, the way Robert was at the piano, but all Tobias did was build tiny animals from matches, and he didn't like it when she asked if she could touch them. He was secretive, that boy, when it came to what he loved. Noisy when it came to what he didn't like.

∽

Sometimes though he'd let Greta coax him into running with her and Robert through the house, visiting tenants. One Sunday in October, when it was too wet and cold to be outdoors, the three of them rode the elevator up and down. When they knocked at the Hedges' door and Buddy Hedge opened it, they asked at the same moment—just as they'd practiced—if they could look at his Christmas closet.

Next they tried to visit Mr. Bell who wouldn't let them in because he didn't want their father to find out that he was still cooking on his hot plate. Since it was cheaper than using a stove, he'd set up the hot plate in his bedroom. By now, he'd moved entirely into his bedroom and only used the kitchen counters to store his old law books.

After Mrs. Clarke gave the Blau children bread with butter and sugar, they ran down the stairs to the cellar and into the long room, where all the tenants had storage bins that were divided by wooden slats and secured with padlocks. When Tobias stuck his arms through those slats, Greta and Robert helped him move the tenants' belongings around in the hope that it would confuse them. Then they rummaged through the wooden trunks that their father had pushed against the back wall of their family's storage bin and hauled armfuls of clothes to the sixth floor.

By the full-length mirror on their parents' closet door, they tried on hats that sank to their noses and garments that pooled around their feet: the deep-green loden coat that Helene had bought after her wedding, a velvet jacket with piping that had belonged to Elizabeth, the shiny black pants Stefan had worn the day he'd arrived in New York, a blue skirt Sara had sewn for herself, the lace blouse Helene had worn when she was pregnant.

Beneath the light of the wall sconces, Stefan Blau's children pranced in his outdated suits and the clothes of his wives. Generous in sharing and trading, they laughed and screamed with delight, sounds that would not reach other apartments because the walls their father had built were far too thick to allow for noise or fire to pass through. When Stefan stopped by before the evening rush in his restaurant and came upon Tobias in the Persian lamb coat that used to belong to Elizabeth, Robert in a tweed jacket that Sara had worn on their walks, and Greta in a brocade dress that Helene had bought for one of Pearl's parties, he was drawn into a moment of utter disorientation and could no longer sort out which woman had given birth to which child, implying a terrible oversight on his part, and in this fusing of images—wives buried and children born and wives married—the Hungarian came to him once again, one more person he had not been able to keep alive, and he heard the Hungarian's voice along with the voices of the other men in the kitchen and the voices of his mother and of his children, all in different languages until he no longer knew which was his own language.

Dazed, he shook his head. Stepped toward the window. And was calmed by the silent and eternal language of the stars. But then Tobias yelled something—"Give me that," he yelled and grabbed a scarf from Robert—and as Stefan turned toward the voice, it was clear to him that this was Sara's son, and from there he knew of course—*how could I have forgotten even for one instant?*—that Greta had issued from Elizabeth, and Robert from Helene. Seized by a deep regret that his work had kept him from knowing his children better, he promised himself to start teaching them about the stars. Tomorrow, he thought. Or Sunday. Yet it would not be his children, but his granddaughter, Emma, who would listen to his stories about the stars and about his mother who had taught him about the millions of galaxies and billions of stars, the distances between them so vast that Emma would feel lost, overwhelmed. If earth was small compared to the stars—then how could she matter? It was as though she didn't exist. But when she would cry and tell Stefan, he would take her by the shoulders, his palms curving to hold her in, to keep her from flying off into a million bright specks. "For me you exist," he would say, and she'd be safe.

His children hadn't seen him yet. *Butter. I need to order butter. Inventory the spices.* Already he saw himself, wooden spoon to his lips, rolling his eyes upward as if in prayer as he tasted his brandy sauce. Prohibition was making it difficult to get the liquor he needed for his restaurant, but not impossible. He could buy home brew from one of the French Canadians in town or from Mr. Heflin who, officially, had added a very young wife and a post office to his general store while, unofficially, he operated a still in the storage area beneath his store. *Capers. Get capers and cloves. Cream.*

When Tobias noticed his father, he got all quiet and shy. Then Robert.

"You look . . . good, all of you," Stefan said, bothered that the only one glad to see him was Greta. *They don't know me. They don't know me at all.* "Keep doing what you've been doing."

But his sons only stood stiffly.

All at once he felt angry at them. "I need to get back to work."

After his father had left, Tobias made Greta and Robert sit on the floor and got ready to do the one-armed man for them. It was one of his favorites because he could play the one-armed man and the policeman and the woman with the green necklace all by changing costumes and voice. His stepmother had taught him how to make up plays from things that happened and things he imagined, the way she had as a girl in Germany. But Tobias couldn't imagine her as a girl: she'd been big and old forever. Since he hadn't met his Uncle Leo, it was easy to imagine him as the boy who'd watched the play while sitting on a crate, thumb in his mouth. He was the uncle who was always supposed to visit but never arrived.

Although Tobias let his sister or brothers play an occasional part, he liked it best when they watched. *The one-armed man comes to the woman's house. Tries to sell her shoelaces. Sometimes lipstick. Or tonic for headaches. When the woman doesn't want to buy anything, he tears off the necklace that her husband has given her for their anniversary. Runs away. The woman calls for help. A policeman comes, chases the one-armed man. But he doesn't catch him.* Tobias always liked the chase best. He'd seen a one-armed man once. At his grandfather's bakery. Buying an ugly. That's what his grandfather called the pastries he baked from leftover dough. Uglies were his specialty: twice as large as regular pastries, they were different each day because he clumped them together from leftover dough, chocolate and white, and added lots of glaze and whatever he had most of, coconut flakes or ribbons of cinnamon or chocolate sprinkles.

His grandmother had whispered it wasn't polite to stare. When the one-armed man reached for his wallet, he angled his one elbow sideways and pulled the wallet from the back pocket on his other side with two fingers. Tobias had practiced that in the garage with

Danny, that and the way the one-armed man walked . . . as if stepping across new ice on the lake. "What would it feel like to just have one arm?" he'd asked Danny, who'd thought about an answer while his thumb flicked across his thin throat. "Cumbersome. Cumbersome, I believe." Some days Danny was too busy to talk to Tobias because he was working for Tobias' father now, helping the Wilsons take care of the building. Or because he was playing pool or cards with Stewart Robichaud, Birdie's cousin, who was a waiter at the restaurant.

In the pile of clothes, Tobias found an indigo skirt that the one-armed man could wear as a cape. It gave off sparks when he dragged it across the carpets and swished it around. "Look at this." He twirled. "Look."

"It used to belong to your mother," Greta told him.

Tobias bunched the material against his face and became very still. "If you like, I'll have Mrs. Teichman sew you a shirt from it." His stepmother had come up behind him.

Tobias yanked the skirt away from her. "Don't cut it."

"It was only a suggestion. The fabric is still good."

"I remember her wearing it one afternoon." Greta reached for his fingers and stroked both their hands across the creased fabric until his grip eased. "Feel how soft it is." Her neck felt cold, and the air that came into her was thin, pale, because she could feel Tobias' sadness at not having his own memories of his mother, felt his loneliness extending into those years when they both would be far older than their mothers had ever been. "It was windy, that afternoon, and she was walking with me and *Vati* along Weirs Beach. She pointed to the ground and said, 'There's a buried treasure somewhere beneath our feet.' "

Tobias watched her without speaking, possessive of the treasure because it was his mother who'd known about it.

Greta leaned toward him, offering him her memories. "Your mother told us about the man who used to run the Old Red Store a hundred years ago. His name was William Wilcomb. He did all kinds of work." Her glasses had slipped, and she pushed them back. "He was a weather forecaster. And a postmaster. And a banker like my grandfather. One evening he was robbed. After that, he hid gold in his cellar. But it was never found. . . ."

"Maybe we can go look for that treasure."

"There are different kinds of treasures," his stepmother said. "Like the stories your mother knew."

When Tobias took the skirt into his room, he folded it and hid it inside his closet, feeling set apart from Greta and Robert, even more so than he usually felt set apart from other children in his class who didn't like him because he could find facts and spell faster than any of them. That night, Stefan found him sleeping on the Persian rug in the living room, fully dressed, with the skirt draped around him like a cape, and when he carried him back to his bed, Tobias was mumbling, and Stefan touched his lips against the damp temple and drew in the child-scent of sweat and sleep.

But in the morning Tobias had no recollection of having walked in his sleep. As soon as he got up, he asked Greta questions about his mother, and she recalled for him an afternoon on the mail boat.

"We saw the Dolly Islands, and your mother told us the legend of Aunt Dolly Nichols after whom the islands were named."

"Where was I?"

"You weren't born yet."

Tobias couldn't picture his mother. Couldn't picture himself. Only Aunt Dolly, brown and wrinkled the way his mother had described her to Greta, *maneuvering her hand-propelled ferry between Meredith Neck and Bear Island. Fishermen buy rum and hard cider from her. She rows to Weirs for a barrel of rum . . . carries it on her shoulders to the boat . . . lifts it above her head while rowing whenever she gets thirsty. . . .*

From Greta he found out that he and his mother had only lived together for seven days, that she'd recovered briefly after his birth, but then—as if she'd found him wanting—had died one week after his birth. Even after Greta told him all the legends his mother had written into her notebook, he waited to hear them again so that he could watch the people in those stories inside his head, waiting for the day when he'd be able to see his mother as clearly as he saw them. And then one day it happened: images of Dolly filled in the void, and he could see his mother, *brown and wrinkled and strong, drinking rum from barrels.*

That's how he would describe his mother to Danny Wilson. "My mother was stronger than most men," he would tell him that winter when Danny would take him ice fishing in the bobhouse he'd built on the frozen bay with Stewart Robichaud and one of the other waiters. The two of them would sit on stools around the hole that Danny and the others had hacked into the three-foot-thick ice with axes and ice chisels. Live shiners on their hooks, they'd pull the slippery bodies of cusk and brown bullheads and yellow perch from the blue-white glow that would come from beneath them.

༄

Miss Garland felt certain there had to be a community in the house, people who got together and entertained one another; yet, except for the Blaus' annual tenants' parties—Christmas and summer solstice—she was never invited. It had to be an oversight—she was sure of that. The other tenants always seemed glad to see her. Always. By the mailboxes. In the drying room. On the dock . . . When she went about finding out where the parties were held, Robert became her best source since his parents, of course, were usually invited.

Wearing her good navy suit with the fancy buttons or the silk poplin suit—both from Gimbel's catalog; both perfect with her shadow lace blouse—Miss Garland began to appear at people's doors, extending a plate or cake tin with peanut brittle that, even Homer Wilson conceded, was delicious. "I got up early this morning to make this for you," she'd say, smiling with the certainty of being welcomed as she walked in, the bloom of excitement high in her cheeks. Invariably she would stay, the last to leave. Her visit would be followed by a gracious letter, thanking her reluctant hosts for including her and praising the sense of community in the *Wasserburg.*

Whenever Stefan saw her coming toward him, he evaded her, uneasy because she was the one person who cherished his house as much as he did; but Pearl, who gave most of the parties, was amused by Miss Garland's persistence.

"She keeps stopping by unannounced," she told Helene one evening as they sat on the roof. From up here, the flowering lilac bushes looked like bouquets. "And she brings you a gift. Those sticky peanut things. Flowers she's picked herself. Or a note thanking you for the last wonderful talk you had. And—"

"And you start each conversation out by thanking her, already in her debt." Helene laughed and leaned back.

Above, there was nothing between her and the gray bellies of clouds, paler in their recesses as if hoarding light for tomorrow. The hills were pale green. Lately more cottages had begun to appear in that green as if carved out of the hills; and where the narrow road hugged the shoreline, it separated the boathouses from the cottages that were set high behind retaining walls built of fieldstones, steps leading up to their front doors. Two more hotels had opened, providing jobs for some of the wives and daughters in town who cleaned the rooms. Quite a few of their husbands and brothers already were earning their livelihood from tourists: fishermen used their boats to ferry them to the islands, and farmers harnessed their horses to cabs that transported them from the train station to hotels or cottages. Though the townspeople welcomed the income, they didn't welcome the hordes of strangers who crowded their town come summer to swim or boat. Some even returned in the fall when they could watch the leaves turn to brilliant shades of red and yellow, while others preferred Winnipesaukee in the winter when they could hike in the deep snow with skis or snowshoes.

"Right." Pearl tapped the end of a cigarette against her wrist, lit it. "Then you sit there, listening to Miss Garland's confidences. She always starts gossiping by swearing you to secrecy."

"The things I've found out from her about our tenants . . . I have to admit that I like her gossip."

"It's extraordinary what she can tell just by watching what the mailman drops into people's boxes, by the size of an envelope, an official-looking airmail letter, black-rimmed death notices. . . ."

"She has come up in the elevator to tell me I have a letter from Germany."

"You know what she told me about Mrs. Evans? That she's white trash. Lived in a one-room shack in the South."

"Alabama. She told me too."

"Made me feel real good knowing that, considering how uppity Mrs. Evans is with me."

"You're lucky Mrs. Evans doesn't like you. Otherwise she would give you those awful sweet pralines and remind you that you liked them the first time she gave them to you years ago."

"I would have pretended to choke that day."

"I've learned so much from you."

Pearl glanced at her from the side, raised her eyebrows.

"It's true. Unfortunately, I hadn't met you at the time."

Light freed itself from the clouds, slanted across the lake the way dust will when floating in a room while sun moves through it. Against that sudden brightness, the birds looked black.

"I can't stand that prissy little dog of theirs," Pearl said.

Two months earlier, Mr. and Mrs. Evans had bought a poodle. Melody, they called her and fought over her, competing for the dog's attention. They kept track of her age by days. Took turns holding her as if she were an infant.

"They're more focused on that dog than on each other," Helene said. "I heard from Miss Garland that Mr. Evans has been blaming his wife for stealing the dog's affection."

"Yes, but then last week it was sick, and *she* accused *him* of feeding it poison. Supposedly because he was envious that the dog loved her better." Pearl lit another cigarette. "Beware of childless people with little dogs . . . If I ever get a little dog, Helene, will you remind me of this conversation?"

"Absolutely. You know what Stefan said? He wanted to know who'll get the dog if they divorce."

∞

When Tobias was in fifth grade, he entered a stage of pranks. Excited by people's outraged reactions, he'd ring doorbells or throw acorns against windows and then run away. He'd hide around the corner from the elevator and leap out with frightful screams that caused people to drop shopping bags or briefcases. Robert was the ideal target: slow-moving and gullible. It was almost too easy to hide his food, or to make him cry by snatching the toy lamb their cousin had given him in Germany. It wore diapers made of handkerchiefs, and its fleece was matted and smelly because Robert was such a baby and slept with it. He would have even carried the lamb to school if their father hadn't stopped him.

Whenever his stepmother found out about a prank, she'd punish Tobias by giving him chores that he performed without protest before returning to the high-wire feeling that came from pranks. The risk of getting caught only sharpened that delight. But all that changed one Saturday afternoon when his father left the restaurant just long enough to be home as Mr. Braddock arrived, furious because Tobias had lit a paper bag filled with shit outside his apartment. Fanny, upon answering the bell, had tried to stomp out the fire, of course, and ended up with shit all over her shoes.

"He did it to Buddy Hedge. And to Miss Garland." Mr. Braddock's chin trembled. "Our Fanny has a difficult enough life without this. At least she was wearing shoes. What if she hadn't? Your boy could have burned her feet."

Stefan felt stunned. Then terrified. "You could have burned the entire house . . . everyone in it."

Tobias looked at his father's face. It was red, a purple kind of red. He wanted to tell him that he liked Fanny Braddock—Fanny with the loopy smile and the skinny legs; Fanny with the scrambled brain but a heart so clear you could see through it—and that he was sorry because he would have never left the bag outside their door if he'd known Fanny would be the one to step on it. "I'm sorry," he started, but his father was yelling at him.

"You don't even go to the toilet like normal people? You have to shit in a bag?"

". . . dogs."

"What? Speak up."

"It's not mine. It's from dogs. From the sidewalk."

Stefan grabbed Tobias' arm, leaving marks that would turn blue and ocher in the days to come, and marched him into his room. "Do you understand that you could have burned everything?" His eyes settled on the flimsy animals the boy had glued together from matches. *Matches of all things. Lighting bags of shit and keeping enough matches in his room to burn a town.* "Take those down," he ordered. "Put them on the floor."

Tobias stood absolutely still, tall and severe with that deep black hair and defiant stare.

"You do it. And you do it now. Since you don't respect the danger of matches, you can't have them at all."

Silently, the boy obeyed. Took each pair of miniature animals he'd built so patiently over the years—eagles and cows and panthers and snakes and pigs and giraffes—and set them on the polished floor, careful to keep them together the way they belonged. *Two of one kind . . . each of them half of one.* Goats and turkeys and foxes and cats and elephants and sparrows. *Half of me. Of myself. Agnes. Our own ark. Yours and mine.* Tigers and antelopes and kangaroos. Monkeys. Four kinds of monkeys.

"I don't expect you to understand the justice in what I'm going to make you do," his father said.

Justice. But what does that have to do with justice? And with my animals— All at once he felt chilled because he remembered another time his father had talked about justice, remembered it though he'd only been four years old. It had to do with the schoolteacher who used to live next door, Miss Perkins, who'd planted her flowers too early and then let them wilt, hadn't pruned her hedges, and had left the brick walk to her door half finished. "You can't trust people like that because they're negligent about other things too," his father had said. "I have a right to have my property look good, to not let it appear run down because of a lax neighbor." He offered advice to Miss Perkins, chided her, even sent a carpenter over to fix a torn screen door. But Miss Perkins sent the carpenter right back. That winter, the three-day storm tore the roof from the teacher's house. "Justice," his father said. And he said it once again when Miss Perkins couldn't afford the repairs and moved into an apartment across from the school after selling her house to the Marshall family who knew how to take care of property.

Justice.

"Some day," his father said, "you will know that I'm teaching you about the potential of destruction."

Tobias' head jerked up. His nostrils widened.

"Step on those things."

The taste of copper in his mouth. *No—*

"On all of them. Now."

A cold rage in his chest kept Tobias from betraying himself and Agnes with tears—*I don't care I don't care don't care*—as his intricate animals splintered under his shoes—foxes and snakes and ducks and monkeys and nightingales and panthers and horses and falcons and Agnes—

No, Stefan wanted to say, knowing he was making a mistake with his son—

—and elephants and swallows and tigers *together the way they belonged. Two of one kind . . . each of them half of one. Half of me. Of myself. And Agnes—*

No— "You have to learn how dangerous fire is," Stefan said desperately.

—and lions and turkeys and dogs and kangaroos and cows . . . splintered without resistance except for a brittle crunch as if someone had stepped on the ribs of newborn mice, and in the sound of that, in its unerring finality, Tobias understood that his father was trying to force him to kill Agnes too. But he could feel his sister digging herself deeper into his soul, and he held her there, hid her there from his father because he was all at once sure that his father had killed her already once as a baby, and that his father would kill him too if he could. He knew it because the calf's head from his dream had become his father's and he didn't even have to sleep to see it—*bloody with its fringe of lacerated neck, tongue bulging—*

"If I even see you touching a match—" Stefan didn't know how to finish his threat.

Tobias crouched to clean the fragments of wood from his floor, tiny sharp edges that he yearned to pound into his father's head. *Into your severed head. Your bloody head. And I won't come to your funeral.*

"Do you understand?" As Stefan looked down at the slight neck bent over the splinters, at the curved and knobby back, he felt embarrassed for the boy. *I would have fought. I would have never let anyone make me break what belongs to me.* But there was no resistance in his son. No anger. Just that meek compliance. And yet, he wanted the boy to look at him, to understand why he'd had to punish him. Wanted to feel like a father, a decent father as he did with Greta. "You only think things out to a certain point," he lectured the boy as he walked toward the door. "And then your mother and I are left with the consequences."

Another place to live, Agnes says. Tobias heard the door close as he scooped the broken matches into his pockets, dazed at the small pile of debris that had taken up so much more space when it used to be animals. *And now all in my pockets. They fit. Into. My pockets.* From his windowsill he picked up his two flesh-eating plants, glanced around for a place to hide them from his father if he were to return, and decided to take them with him once everyone was asleep. *Another place to live.*

∽

Helene was stunned when Stefan told her how he had punished Tobias. "It's cruel. Extreme."

"A pansy already, the boy, and you're spoiling him more." He stormed out. "I have work to do in the restaurant."

"Do your work then."

To calm herself, she spooned vanilla pudding into a glass bowl—"No, not for you Robert. You stay here with Greta"—decorated it with canned cherries and took it into Tobias' room.

Face to the wall, he was lying on his bed.

"Tobias?" She sat on the edge of his bed, though he refused to answer or turn toward her. One hand on his back, she tried to reach through his silence. "Are you asleep?" she whispered, only too aware that whatever she was to him, was not what he wanted.

He kept his eyelids closed. His breathing steady.

She saw his empty shelves and felt ashamed for not defending him against her husband. How often had she abandoned him to Stefan's judgment, though she considered it wrong? That old habit of obedience, of loyalty. She railed against it, railed against knowing something was wrong and yet not doing anything about it. It made her angry at herself, angry at her husband. "I'm sorry," she said.

Tobias turned on his back, his eyes at her, probing. "Why?"

"Because . . . I didn't protect you. I'm sorry for that."

"I won't come to his funeral."

"Hush," she said quickly. "No one is dying."

"I won't."

"You don't have to," she said gently. "But don't wish him dead, Tobias."

When Stefan found her waiting for him late that night in the living room, he was startled. "What time is it? What happened?"

"Tobias is not the only one who ever played pranks."

"I'm very tired."

Her voice rose. "You did plenty yourself when you were his age."

"Nothing that dangerous."

"When the priest caught you, it got dangerous enough for you."

He had to smile as he recalled the chocolate-brown paint he'd sneaked into church. "That was different."

But his wife did not smile back. "Of course. What you do is always different."

"Lenchen, listen, it's late, I'm tired . . . and it's not that I don't understand wanting to play pranks."

"He loved those little animals."

Used to be that he could justify what he did—if not to Helene, then at least to himself—but he was no longer certain that his punishment had been right. Still, he insisted, "I won't tolerate destruction."

"And that's why you make him demolish something he worked on for years?" Her eyes burned into him.

"I worked on this house for years."

"Your house still stands. What Tobias built is broken."

"Matches for matches."

She shook her head, unwilling to let him justify what he'd done.

"You have punished him before," he challenged her.

"Never like that."

"Well, he is *my* son."

Suddenly furious, she squared her wide shoulders. "And he became a son to me when I married you. Don't try to push me from him now by saying he's only yours. Don't ever try that."

"I didn't mean to. But that boy does not think—"

"That boy has a name."

"—does not think beyond the immediate pleasure of those pranks. Does not think that the odor of dog shit will stay in the carpet."

"There are worse offenses than the odor of dog shit, Stefan. Like what you did to *our* son today."

∞

In the morning, when they discovered that Tobias was not in his room, Stefan tried to shrug away his fear by saying he'd be back once he was hungry. But Helene could tell he was as worried as she.

He tried not to think of terrible things that could happen to children. *The boy's eleven. Tall and fast. Eleven and a half. Too tall and too fast to be carried off by someone crazy and evil. Old enough to feed himself and keep warm. At least it isn't winter.* But nights in April were still cold. He hoped that Tobias had spent the night in his room. Hoped that he had waited until early morning. Hoped that he'd made himself breakfast—a warm breakfast—before slipping away. But had he taken enough clothes? A blanket?

As Helene witnessed his concern, she felt a softening toward him. Still, she was too angry at him to show it.

"He'll be back once he's hungry," he told her as they searched through Tobias' room. Two blankets were missing. A pillow and winter coat. Even those creepy plants that ate bugs. "What if—" Stefan swallowed hard before he could say the thing he didn't want to say aloud. "What if he hurts himself?"

She brought her forehead against his, closed her eyes. "I don't believe so," she finally whispered. "He chose to take things that will keep him comfortable."

But his fear only increased while he and Helene helped the police search the building. He thought of his parents waking up and finding him gone one morning nearly three decades ago, and he knew if he'd understood their terror and loss back then, he could have never left Germany.

None of the tenants had seen Tobias. Danny Wilson checked the garage and every room in the cellar, even the large storage closet where his uncle kept the still. Though he went into the drying room where the air was thick and fuzzy with steam that rose from damp sheets and towels that lay draped across the heating rods, Danny did not look behind the shelves by the back wall where Tobias crouched. As tenants came in to fold their dry laundry into wicker baskets or hang up other things, Tobias got to listen to the story of his disappearance again and again. For a while, it was exciting to hear them speculate about the mystery of his escape. He found out that his father had not opened the restaurant—the first time ever, as far back as Tobias could remember.

He overheard Mrs. Braddock tell Mrs. Wilson that her husband wished he'd never mentioned the matter of the burning paper bag to Mr. Blau.

"He probably got rough with the boy."

"He does have a temper."

"Actually . . . that's where he and the boy are alike."

As long as Tobias heard their voices, he didn't feel alone; but that night the steam took on the coldness of the floor and walls, wrapping him into a damp, heavy chill that seeped between his socks and ankles, wound itself around his neck. So used was he to being warm in this room where towels and sheets dried quickly, that now the cold felt foreign to him. Even his breath. He was a ghost walker inside his own tomb. He shivered. Crouched low. And finally slept. But just for a few hours. Each time he woke up, it was to the picture of himself crushing his miniatures. And as he felt them beneath his feet, he wished he could will himself to die, lie still and end those thoughts forever. Go to sleep and never wake up. Old Eskimos died like that: when their families moved on to new camps, they stayed behind, and death became theirs by wanting it. When his teacher had read them the story of an old Eskimo, abandoned on the ice without food or a coat while his daughter and her family moved on, Tobias had felt furious at the daughter, ready to go after her and ask how she could leave her father and say he was worn out and useless. But now it came to him that the old man had chosen death and that his choice shouldn't have anything to do with age.

Stop it, Agnes says. Stop it now. His two blankets weighed on him—cold and heavy like wet snow—but when he kicked at them to free himself, they only got tangled around his legs. How long would it take to starve himself? *Maybe I'll be dead in a week if I stop eating. Stop it, she says,* and all at once he was hungry. He raised his face. Imagined *leaving the drying room and walking up the stairs to the apartment. He stands in the kitchen, feet cold on the tiles, and makes himself a jam sandwich.* No, two. *One with strawberry jam, the other with grape jelly. Saliva pools on his tongue as he cuts the bread into triangles the way he likes them. As he eats—* No, starving would take too long. Because whenever you ate something, you'd have to start all over with the starving. *Maybe I'll freeze to death. . . . A train—I could throw myself in front of a train.* He'd seen that in a movie once, a woman in a railroad station, face pale, coat black. She stood immobile on the platform, arms along her sides, hands empty, while others rushed past her with bags and suitcases. As the train sped closer, she let herself fall forward in slow motion, hands calm and white against her coat. *Or I'll drown myself in the lake.* It certainly was deep enough. But he was too good a swimmer for that. His body would keep coming back up. *At least until I get too tired to swim. My body is never found. They bury an empty coffin. My father stands at the open grave site in his black coat, snow on his shoulders, tears on his face. "If only I had known . . ." He's crying, my father who is also the father of Agnes. Agnes whom I saved from my father, hid from my father, stronger with me tonight than any other time ever before. Crying, my father, he is crying. "Tobias, my son . . . I am so sorry."*

"And I am not," Tobias said aloud. "I am not sorry. And I won't come to your funeral."

It soothed him, saying it aloud. Soothed him because already he sensed that this was much worse than saying, "I wish you dead," worse because it presumed that wish and reached beyond its deadly summons by knowing this about his father's funeral: that he would not be there. And taking power from that promise to himself. Power for daring to do the worst possible—obliterating his father beyond death.

And he said it once again. Louder. "I won't come to your funeral."

Toward dawn of his second night in the drying room, Tobias packed up his plants and his blankets and his pillow, took the elevator to the sixth floor, went into the kitchen, and ate so quietly that his parents, who had not slept since they'd found him missing, did not know he was back until his stepmother found a cutting board and knife on the kitchen table, along with an open jar of strawberry jam, half a loaf of bread, three apple cores, and the rind from a large chunk of cheese. She rushed into Tobias' room but did not wake him. When he emerged from his bed late that afternoon, his father was waiting for him in the living room with several pieces of wood—cherry and ash and maple—two kinds of glue, and a set of small tools for building whatever a man's son might desire to build. Tobias thanked him. Politely. The way he'd been taught. But left his gifts on the bench by the tile stove. For that entire week, every morning he woke up, he felt dead—*Your severed head. Your bloody head*—until he latched on to the rage deep inside himself.

It happened one morning when he saw his stepmother read to his little brother who looked so satisfied as he prattled about, that Tobias suddenly felt his rage at his own mother for not even staying alive long enough to read him some stupid story. He glared at Robert who was holding the silly lamb he'd gotten in Germany where Tobias had not been allowed to go. His father would have never made Robert destroy the lamb.

When his stepmother left for a few minutes to stir the lentil soup, he snatched the lamb and ran from the apartment, followed by Robert who chased him down the steps and into the fourth-floor utility room. Identical to the utility rooms on each floor, it had a trap door in the wall for throwing garbage down. Holding the toy out of Robert's reach, Tobias climbed on top of the trash can and from there on the sink, his breath coming in and out through his mouth. As Robert kept leaping for his lamb, the small room magnified his screams.

"Give it to me," he wailed.

"Catch!" Tobias tossed the lamb into the air and caught it himself. The fleece was almost entirely worn off its head, and its stuffing was lumpy. "Catch!" But on his third toss, the lamb fell past his outstretched hands and landed on the floor where Robert threw himself across it, defending it with his body.

Tobias leapt from the sink and stood above his brother. "Give it back."

Robert scrambled up and scooted against the wall, the lamb between his chest and the wall.

"Give it back, you!"

"But it's mine."

Tobias jabbed his fingertips into the soft flesh of his brother's back, wanting to hurt, to decimate—*your severed bloody head.* "Ticklish . . ." He whooped with laughter. Grabbed hold of the lamb's front legs. "You're ticklish. I know you are."

To protect his lamb, Robert yanked the trapdoor open. But the instant he thrust the lamb inside, a look of terror settled on his face. Shoving Tobias aside, he darted from the utility room, past two alcoves with fire extinguishers, and into the elevator where Tobias caught up with him, as intent on retrieving the lamb before it got burned as on keeping Robert from telling on him.

"We can save it," Tobias shouted, "we can save it."

But Robert didn't answer. A wildness in his eyes that Tobias had never seen, he stared at the brass arrow that traced their descent in a semicircle, ready to pounce from the elevator door.

In the furnace room, the lamb had dropped into the Dumpster with the refuse that Mr. Wilson shoveled into the trash burner every day, and as additional trash tumbled from the chute above, the lamb settled amidst chicken bones and coffee grounds, peach pits and stained butcher paper.

Robert tried to shinny up the side of the dumpster. "Boost me up," he yelled.

But Tobias had stayed on top of the six stone steps that led into the cavernous furnace room, and when Robert called out to him again, he slid out and slammed the door. It was not that he meant to lock his brother in when he turned the key—he only did it to have time. Time to think. While his heart pounded with the thrill of taking revenge. On his fat little brother. His father. Punishing him through Robert, who was racing up the stairs, hurling himself against the door.

But his weight didn't force it open. At the far end of the room, beyond the trash burner, dim light filtered down an air shaft through the grated opening above. He tried not to cry as he inched down the steps. In front of him loomed the immense boiler, its round door latched tightly. On its back he found several red-and-white cards, each with the *Wasserburg*'s address, a date, and a signature: *Stan Erkins, Boiler Inspector, City of Winnipesaukee.*

The big water tank rested high against the side of the boiler. Eighteen feet above him floated the ceiling and pipes, countless pipes that crisscrossed the ceiling and walls like the veins on the leaves of his brother's hungry plants. Any moment now they would close around him, trap him, swallow him the way he'd seen them swallow the spiders and mosquitos that Tobias caught for them. Tobias who'd locked him in here. His steps, they sounded hollow. And his feet—his feet were right on the large metal lid that was set into the cement floor. He knew what was beneath there. One day when Mr. Wilson had removed the cover, he'd seen the sheen of filthy water far below. All at once he was afraid he might want to lift the lid and let himself fall. Just as he'd dropped his lamb through the chute. Only deeper. To the center of the earth. Already he could taste the putrid water, cold and slimy, and then the taste of rice. *Dead people turn into rice, Robert dear.* Trudi—she wouldn't be afraid. Trudi wasn't afraid of anyone, not even of the big boys in school who laughed at her and imitated how she walked. With her father's last letter, she'd sent him a picture she'd drawn of herself and her friend, Eva, playing with her new dog, who was black and gray, not white like his lamb who reminded him of Trudi with its pale hair and short legs.

If he had a dog, he'd teach it to listen only to him, and then he'd tell it to bite Tobias. Carefully he straightened. As he backed away from the lid, something stiff prodded his shoulder. Screaming, he whirled around. Stared at the shrouded figure that leaned against the wall by the boiler. Though he was used to seeing the leftover Virgin Mary from the nativity whenever he came here with Mr. Wilson, it was different to be locked up with her and her bashed-in face. The hand that had touched him was extended in a blessing. Wrinkles of grime blurred the folds of her gown, and dust clotted the injury on her face as if her blood had dried around it. The baby Jesus, wrapped in the statue's arms like a small mummy, had a dirty hole where his nose had been.

Robert was his own echo as he flew up the stairs, tears blotching his sight. They didn't sound like his, those howls that rose from his chest and brought Homer Wilson running from the back corner of the garage, where he'd been washing Nate Bloom's silver Model T.

"Hold it . . . hold it there." He swooped Robert up into his wet arms. "How'd you get in here?"

But Robert only pointed toward the statue.

"It's just that goddamn BVM. . . . Look, there's nothing to her."

Robert covered his face with his fingers.

"Pal . . . little pal." Homer Wilson pried Robert's hands loose and carried him down the steps. "Look at it. Just a statue. At least this one's keeping herself decent. The ones I can't bear are the flashers . . . them who pull their gowns apart and flaunt their bloody hearts. That's what they are—flashers—most of the BVMs."

Robert dared a quick glance.

"If I have to look at a flasher," Homer Wilson said, "I'd much rather see a set of tits."

Tits. Robert knew what tits were. His mother had them underneath her dress, but Mrs. Wilson sure didn't. Mrs. Wilson was flat. Like a picture. And she yelled at Mr. Wilson whenever no one else was around. Except Robert, as if he were invisible. Lazy, she called Mr. Wilson. Drunkard. Bum. Gambler. While Mr. Wilson simply stood there and nodded. But in front of Robert's parents or the tenants, Mrs. Wilson was always friendly to Mr. Wilson and praised him whenever she mentioned his name, saying he knew how to repair anything.

"What were you doing in here by yourself?" Mr. Wilson asked.

"My lamb. It's in the bin. It—" He thought of his brother, tall and angry. "It fell," he said. "From upstairs."

And of course Mr. Wilson was able to retrieve the lamb, just as he was able to fix sinks that were stopped up and doors that squeaked. He shook it till its fur was almost clean, sniffed it, and passed it to Robert with a grimace. "Your pal needs himself a bath."

Robert clutched the lamb against his chest, mumbling sounds of assurance to it while Mr. Wilson took him by the shoulder and walked him out of the furnace room, through the hallway with its black-and-green diamond-shaped tiles, and to the elevator. There, Mr. Wilson pulled aside the gate that opened like an accordion and pushed the sixth-floor button.

"What happened to your face?" his mother asked. "It's all messy." She was sitting with Tobias and Greta on the corner bench in the kitchen, lunch and a vase with tulips on the table.

Robert hid the lamb behind his back and glanced toward his brother, who was crushing his thumb into the firm bread of his *Frikadelle*—meatball sandwich. "I was playing," Robert said.

"Your manners, Tobias," his mother said. "Don't mash your food."

Robert slid on the bench close to her.

She shook her head. "Mr. Howard has been waiting. You don't have time to eat before your lesson. Wash your hands."

He peered at the *Bratkartoffeln*—fried potatoes—and *Frikadellen* she'd prepared, and he knew exactly what they would taste like and how much better they would make him feel. His stomach cramped in protest as he headed toward the sink to wash his hands and his lamb. In the living room, Mr. Howard sat on one edge of the piano bench, his back very straight as he waited, prepared to listen. Quickly, Robert stuck his lamb behind the sofa.

Once his fingers rode the ivory keys, his hunger shrank to a cold point deep inside, and soon, the familiar solace flowed down his neck, his shoulders, and into his fingers.

That afternoon, when Robert sat on the swing, rocking himself with one foot on the ground, Tobias sauntered toward him, black hair sticking up like a brush around his thin face, one arm hidden behind his back. *A knife?* Robert was sure it was a knife. But it was too late to jump from the swing and run. The fast pulse of panic in his throat, he tried to push himself high on the swing, away from his brother.

But Tobias' free hand grabbed his knee.

Robert kicked. Kicked hard.

"Idiot." Tobias let go of him, but his hidden hand swung forward. Shoved something at Robert. "Here."

A knife a gun a saber—

Not a knife.

A chocolate bar.

A chocolate bar? Robert hesitated, fearing another prank. *Dog shit pressed into an empty chocolate wrapper.* But the silver foil was new, uncreased. Still . . .

"Because you didn't tell," Tobias said.

Carefully, Robert unwrapped the foil. The chocolate had almonds in it. He took one small bite, hummed softly as he pressed it with his tongue into the high curve of his mouth to make it last. It was so good that he wanted to go there, all of him, to that sweetness at the roof of his mouth, melt there—*prayer is like that, high and arched and holy*—but then he thought of his brother and broke off a piece for him. They chewed, slowly, and there was just the sound of Robert's humming till they were finished with the chocolate, till his brother stepped behind him to give the swing an easy push, then another, and Robert pumped his legs till he was flying alone, far above the stone bench where his brother sat down, long skinny ankles stretched in front of him.

∞

Though Tobias never built with matches again—*not safe to do so in my father's house*—he assembled a secret compartment in his top drawer in case he ever wanted to hide something. At the lumberyard across from school, he had a sheet of thin wood cut to size, and he glued four of his old scuffed alphabet blocks into the corners of the drawer, the M and the I and the N and the E—*spelling MINE*—to support the wood, creating a three-inch space only he knew about. When he stacked his underwear on top, even he couldn't tell that the drawer had a false bottom. Yet, once it was finished, he couldn't think of anything worth hiding there. He let his flesh-eating plants die. Promised himself that he would never again own anything he couldn't bear to destroy.

Instead of remaining Robert's tormentor, he elected himself his protector, launching into speeches of defense, especially when his father scolded Robert for leaving his shoes untied or walking too slowly; and as he honed his strength in these daily battles against his father, Stefan saw a side in his oldest son he'd never seen before. It made him feel a certain pride, made him wonder if, perhaps, having the boy step on those flimsy little fabrications of his had been good after all for his spine. Still, he would have liked to reverse what he'd made Tobias do.

One Sunday at breakfast, he felt the blaze of the boy's eyes on him and glanced up, only to catch him turning away. He pointed to his son's plate. "Eat your eggs, Tobias. They're getting cold."

The boy glowered at him. Asked what he'd already asked him several times lately. "Could you please pronounce my name the American way? *To-buy-as. Not To-bee-as.*"

"Eat your eggs then, *To-buy-as.*" Stefan tried to joke. "They're still getting cold."

But the boy didn't even smile.

Maybe, Stefan speculated, he's embarrassed to have a father who speaks with an accent. Recently, he'd been feeling clumsy and un-polished whenever he talked to the boy, who made him self-conscious about an accent he usually didn't hear. The awareness of his son's distrust, hate even, would shift itself into Stefan's thoughts while he was at his restaurant, cooking or greeting his guests. He was used to making happen what he wanted, but with Tobias that didn't work. With others the boy was talkative, always philoso-phizing, persuading; but with him he was evasive. Except when he was flying at him with words to defend Robert.

As Stefan finished his coffee, it occurred to him that he was not well suited to be a father. And here he was with three children, but without the skill or habit of asking forgiveness. All at once he desperately wanted to reach Tobias. "Let's go rowing, you and I," he said.

When Helene frowned at him, he realized his words had sounded like an order. She'd been distant with him ever since the boy had run off, watchful, taking the children's side against him.

"You'll enjoy being in the boat, Tobias," he said, and when the boy squinted at the window and the gray sky as if to question his decision, Stefan insisted.

He obeyed, of course, the boy. But for the two hours that they were on the lake—switching seats to take turns at the oars whenever Stefan suggested—Tobias only answered in short syllables and kept his eyes on the water as if he didn't feel welcome in any space where his father was. As Stefan thought of Sara and what she would say if she knew her son didn't feel welcome with him, he felt ashamed. Angry too that Tobias was not responding to his efforts. And yet, to be honest with himself, he had to remember how often he had pushed the boy aside because he was too busy.

The clouds were getting denser, darkening their reflections on the water, and in the blunt light, the boy's jaw and cheekbones were even more angular than usual. He has his mother's *Schlafzimmer-augen*—bedroom eyes—Stefan thought.

Aloud, he said, "Are you eating enough?"

Tobias nodded. *I won't come to your funeral. What if he's drowning? I won't save him. What if a train is coming right at him? No. What if—*

"Because you're awfully thin." He had gone into Tobias' room one day when the children had been at school and Helene at the store, and he'd found nothing built from the wood he'd given him, nothing made from matchsticks. The room had been so bare that he'd felt a deep failure at having a son who lived in his house as if he were a guest. He had checked beneath the boy's bed, inside his closet, feeling odd and yet unable to stop himself as he'd opened his closet and drawers; but other than clothes, he'd found nothing personal. Nothing. He'd been seized by a piercing and inexplicable homesickness, and it wasn't until now, in the boat, that he knew the homesickness had to do with the distance from this son whom he hadn't tried to know. And that something had been wrong between him and the boy for much longer than these last few weeks since he'd made him break his toy animals.

Suddenly he wanted to fill Tobias with the best nourishment he could provide for him, build a wall of safety between his son and death by cooking for him, him alone, as extravagantly as for an entire wedding party: cream of leek soup; liver pâté; ratatouille; omelets stuffed with the *tapenade* he made from garlic and capers and ground hazelnuts; roasted vegetables brushed with olive oil; *frangipani—hazelnuts. Put hazelnuts on the list. Cream.* "You really should eat more," Stefan said hoarsely.

Even my body. Even that is not right for him. What if a tree falls on him? No. What if he asks for me while dying? No.

"If you weren't so thin, you'd look a lot like my father. . . . You know what he used to tell me?"

Don't, Tobias thought, but here it was already, the old embarrassing story about the hair, about Blau men being hairier than other men. . . .

" 'You can recognize a Blau by his back,' that's what my father told me. 'Pelts,' he would say, 'regular pelts. . . .' And that he could pick out a Blau man, just by his back, from a hundred men." Stefan reached across to touch his son's shoulder.

But Tobias flinched.

Stefan's hand fell away. "Let me have the oars," he said hoarsely and motioned to pinpricks of rain on the surface of the lake. "I want to get you home."

Tobias hadn't noticed the drops till he saw their indentations on the water, but when his father turned the boat around, he felt them cold on his wrists, his forehead. Curving his shoulders, he tucked his fingers beneath his armpits and watched his father's house draw near, immense beyond the dock and the stripe of pale sand. On the gray water, its reflection was even more immense, spreading toward the rowboat like spilled ink, darker than the clouds; and as the rain came at him, harder, the house seemed to be boiling around him and his father.

∽

After that, Tobias became aware how much he disliked to be touched—not just by his father, but by anyone. It could be a teacher resting a hand on his shoulder, boys brushing against him in the hallway or sitting so close to him in class that Tobias would feel their elbows against his, making him feel hot and jumpy. Though he ignored girls, they were always going dreamy over him: they'd follow him on his way to classes, ask Greta and Robert questions about him, stroll past the *Wasserburg* hoping to see him. Even Fanny Braddock chased after him, affectionate like a three-year-old though they both were twelve.

"You have a nice, nice body," she'd say and get on her toes to kiss him on the cheek.

Usually he'd dodge her, though, with her, he didn't mind touch because he'd known her all his life, her oddness, her weakness, her sweetness. Warm days she'd sit on the front steps of the building, sucking at her knuckles while watching the weather and waiting for him to come home from school. For a while, her parents had tried to keep her in school, but since she'd distracted other students or simply wandered off, the principal had suggested keeping her home.

"She isn't capable of learning," he'd said, infuriating Pearl Bloom who started to read to Fanny every morning for an hour. Though Fanny got fidgety when Pearl tried to get her to look at a book, she liked to touch newspapers, those large soft sheets of paper that smudged when she rubbed her palms across the letters. And she'd listen with fascination to any article or report that had to do with weather. Because weather she knew. Weather she could see and smell and taste every minute of every day. Weather she felt behind her eyes before it happened. That's why she liked it whenever the weather report in the paper was wrong.

Elated when she'd see Tobias turn the corner, Fanny would leap up from the steps, run toward him, and then skip alongside him all the way into the elevator, telling him about rain or sun or a storm that was coming. It was easy for him to be kind to Fanny because she couldn't do anything to him. The same with Robert who was hesitant, gentle. Who was not at all like their father. Who brought their father as much disappointment as Tobias did.

Although Robert was at first suspicious of his brother's sudden attention, he came to count on Tobias over the next years when he was teased about being fat. Other boys would leave him alone when Tobias appeared, sullen and intense as if searching for a reason to fight. Helene was glad that Robert and Tobias were getting along, even if it meant an increase in pranks because Robert was turning into his brother's willing and accomplished apprentice. Those pranks were harmless, she told herself, maybe even good for Robert, because they took him out of his shyness. Pranks like tearing down Miss Garland's signs about shaking out umbrellas or not dragging sand into the lobby. Nuisance signs that no one missed.

What she didn't know was that Tobias was teaching Robert the sharp-sweet taste of danger by standing on the edge of the railroad platform and leaning into the breath of fast approaching trains. She did get complaints however from school where, to the teachers' dismay, Robert tried to be as noisy as Tobias. Even at the Royal where the two liked to see Sunday matinees and whistle whenever people kissed on the screen. They wanted to be as wicked as John Barrymore in *Dr. Jekyll and Mr. Hyde,* and although they made fun of Gloria Swanson in *Male and Female,* they both cried over the death of Lillian Gish in *Broken Blossoms.* They pretended to be John Barrymore when they dropped soap into the fountain that bubbled in the lobby of the theater or when they ran up and down the royal-blue carpeted stairs while the ticket matron chased behind them.

The evening of Tobias' fourteenth birthday, they figured out a way to mess with the floating fire escape. If they climbed down the metal stairs to the second floor where it hung suspended on a pulley, their combined weight caused it to drop. Although their father knew that heavy snowfalls brought the metal structure down, he couldn't figure out why this was suddenly happening without snow and only on the side of the house that he couldn't see from the restaurant. But Homer Wilson noticed that Robert became unusually furtive on days when the fire escape came down—*no talent for deception, that one*—and he began to watch the boy and caught him and his brother early one morning bouncing on the metal landing while the steps descended to the sidewalk.

They accepted his offer of silence eagerly in return for stopping this nonsense, as he called it, and he reported to Stefan that the problem was solved.

"Just needed some tightening," he muttered.

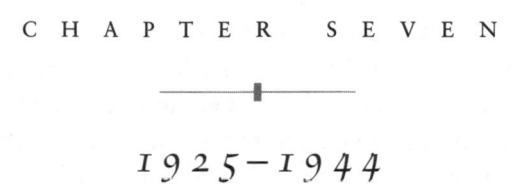

CHAPTER SEVEN

It was nearly impossible to get an apartment in the *Wasserburg*. People would place their names on the Blaus' waiting list and take whatever apartment became available, even if it was smaller or larger than what they needed. To live in the *Wasserburg* meant an increase not only in comfort but also in status—and for that it was worth it to make sacrifices. Whenever someone moved out, Stefan gave his current tenants first claim to the vacant apartment before he offered it to the next person on his waiting list. Moves within the building were handled by Homer and Danny Wilson, who padded the walls of the elevator to protect furniture against scratches. Some tenants had lived in as many as five different apartments since the house's completion fourteen years earlier.

Stefan preferred keeping old tenants because new tenants usually needed educating to the way things were done in his building—like the Perellis who promptly installed a wash line between their fourth-floor kitchen and bathroom windows and hung their personal laundry out there for everyone to see. Over the past years, while Louis Perelli and Rosalie Nussbaum had both been married to other people, they had watched how the Blaus had improved the town just by the example of their *Wasserburg;* and now that Louis was divorced and Rosalie widowed, they'd married, though they were over forty. For the walls of their apartment they'd chosen fern-green paint. While Rosalie had brought her French rococo furniture and a trunk full of expensive men's boots into the marriage, her new husband had arrived with the stuffed animals he'd shot on safaris.

The first time Robert saw those animals, he was playing in the courtyard of the *Wasserburg,* floating paper hats in the fountain. When the movers carried those huge, lifeless beasts past him and up the front steps of the building, they were the saddest creatures he'd ever seen, and he longed to restore their lives to them, longed for it so strongly that he knew all at once he would become a veterinarian, keeping animals alive. In the past, grownups had asked him occasionally what he wanted to be once he was grown up, and he'd felt dumb not knowing. But now he knew. Already he could see himself telling Miss Garland and Mr. Evans. *"I want to become a veterinarian."*

But when he tried to tell Tobias about becoming a veterinarian, his brother only asked, "Are the Perellis' animals bigger than our father?"

"Much bigger."

Tobias nodded to himself as if he already knew. "So they're coming back into the house. Did you see any that are two of one kind?"

"No."

"Still . . . They're coming back into the house."

Even after a full month of marriage, the second Mrs. Perelli would still get startled when coming around a corner and seeing a leopard or a wild boar poised forever to charge at her. But she was pleased that her new husband wore the boots of her dead husband whose clothes she'd given to the Temple a week after his heart failure. His boots, though, she'd kept because they were of excellent quality, and then—as if by miracle—Louis Perelli had turned out to have the same shoe size, certainly a sign that she was meant to marry him.

She did not like it at all when Stefan Blau came to her door to complain about her laundry hanging in the fresh air. "We have a drying room in the cellar. Mrs. Wilson will be glad to show you how it works."

"But I like the smell of wind on my laundry," Rosalie Perelli insisted, small eyes glinting.

He took in the rouge on her cheeks, the carefree hair piled atop her head. "It cheapens the appearance of my building to have laundry hanging from the windows."

Twice more he came to her door to remind her. After that, he kept checking automatically for a wash line fastened between her windows, and he felt satisfied when he didn't see one, unaware that Rosalie Perelli still dried her laundry outside every Thursday night, and that she was stubborn enough to stay up late until he'd closed his restaurant, and that she got up early to reel her line in before dawn.

Another tenant who made him uncomfortable was the Braddock girl whose parents let her roam the building and who had a way of smiling at people that just wasn't right—the kind of smile little girls will give you before their mothers teach them that it's not proper or safe to smile at men like that. Sometimes Fanny Braddock would saunter into his restaurant, grab a sponge in the kitchen, and start cleaning his counters, going after every speck and glancing up from the side, wanting him to notice how well she was doing. If he wasn't busy, he would let her. But usually he'd have to send her home. Other times she'd be in the lobby of the *Wasserburg* and slip with him into the elevator, smiling that smile of hers. Ever since he'd heard that she'd kissed old Mr. Evans in the elevator, he'd stayed far away from her. If you didn't stop her, she'd ride the elevator all day. Up and down. Some days when he had to wait for the elevator, sure enough there'd be Fanny Braddock, greeting him when the door finally folded open on his floor. It was wasteful.

He already had enough other worries about expenses. Despite high rents, the building swallowed most of its revenues in maintenance and improvements. Profits from his restaurant took care of his family's living expenses. By now he'd set aside enough money to pay Lelia Flynn once she demanded the return of her loan, but she never reminded him, and he wondered if it was out of generosity or because her memory was failing. There certainly were signs of decline: she was forgetting names, appointments. Fortunately Father Albin and Dr. Miles would call him whenever Lelia didn't arrive for a scheduled visit. He'd drive to her house, and if she didn't open her door—her hearing was weak—he'd wait outside for a few minutes before he let himself in with the key she kept under a flowerpot on her porch. He made sure she had enough food in the house, and if he was too busy, he sent Greta or one of his waiters with a covered tray.

One Thursday afternoon Lelia didn't hear him until he walked into her dining room where she sat at her bare table—no dishes, no food, no tablecloth—stroking her fingers as if struggling to pull off tight gloves.

"I have an idea," he said. "How would you like to move into the *Wasserburg?*"

"I wouldn't know how to live with so many other people. . . ." She shook her head. "No. Oh no."

"You'll have your own apartment," he encouraged her.

"It's not for me, Stefan." Her gray eyelashes flickered. "No. Thank you."

"You would only need to talk when you'd feel like it. And you'd be right there with your granddaughter."

Again, she said, "It's not for me." But then she peered at him in a strange, probing way as though waiting for him to say something else.

"What is it?" he asked, though he knew that it had to be about the loan, that she wanted him to bring it up. Instantly, he felt offended. She should trust by now that—regardless how much longer she lived—the money he owed her would ultimately belong to Greta. He was simply preserving it for his daughter. Far better than Lelia could. And if occasionally he had to withdraw from that fund to repair the furnace, say, or modernize the loading platform in back of the garage, that too was ultimately for Greta's benefit since, one day, after both he and Helene were gone, his children would inherit everything he owned. Things like that were understood without words.

∞

The first Sunday of May 1925, Father Albin climbed the stairs to his pulpit, but instead of preaching, he announced that his urine was bloody and asked his congregation to pray for his kidney stones to dissolve. Embarrassed by a public prayer of such personal detail, the people of Winnipesaukee averted their eyes; yet, the priest raised his voice as if forcing them and God to look upon him.

"Lord, I stand here before you with these good people who ask your mercy for me. Lord, my urine is red as the sea you parted for Moses."

Several women rushed their children from the pews and toward the door.

But the priest's voice followed them. "Lord, I don't sleep well, and last night, when I lay on the floor and passed those wretched stones you have cursed me with, I cursed you as they traveled down my malehood."

Others stood up. Stalked from the church.

Those who stayed whispered. About how they'd seen Father grip his crotch in the almost dark confessional. How the bishop had suggested an operation. How Father had said he didn't want Dr. Miles or any other quack to cut on him there. When people speculated about his odd behavior—crazy, some called it—Lelia Flynn defended the priest, though even she had to concede that he'd made too many inappropriate comments. It wasn't clear who informed on Father Albin—Helene heard from Miss Garland that the bishop had found out about the prayer from nine different parishioners—but the following week the bishop admitted Father Albin to a Catholic convalescent home in Concord that had one entire wing just for crazy priests.

His temporary replacement was a young priest from Boston, Noah Creed, whose name—so the people in town said—sounded as though he'd been intended for priesthood since birth, and they were not surprised when he told the altar boys that his mother had chosen that name for him in the hope that he would become a priest.

The Sunday Helene invited him for lunch, Lelia sat next to him at the oval mahogany table where she used to sit with Father Albin, and as she watched him eat the *Schweinebraten*—pork roast—in tidy and precise bites, she knew he was the kind of man she would have liked for her Elizabeth. He appeared well taken care of. By the church and before that by his family. It was the kind of bearing Lelia Flynn knew well because she had it herself. The kind that comes from a history of others looking after you—parents and maids and tutors—instilling in you a generosity that grows from appreciating the certainty that there'll always be others who'll consider it a privilege to anticipate your needs.

With a man like that, my Elizabeth would still be alive.

Suddenly she felt disloyal to Stefan who sat at the head of the table, eating hurriedly as he usually did when he wanted to get back to the restaurant. A bad example for Robert, who was eating just as quickly. Sometimes it made Lelia queasy, watching him go at his food like that. She looked at Helene, wondering if she ought to speak to her about the boy's manners and size. But how to do that without offending her? It was obvious that feeding the boy was Helene's way of loving him better than the other children. She liked to talk about how he liked to eat. Once, she'd confided to Lelia how it pleased her that Robert preferred her solid meals—roasts and *Apfelstrudel* and herring salad with beets—to his father's delicacies. As far as Lelia had noticed, the boy ate anything. In huge quantities. Except for rice—the one food he refused eating. Odd, Lelia thought.

"Can I get you anything?" Helene asked.

Lelia realized that she'd been staring at her.

Helene smiled. "Can I get you anything?" she asked again.

"Oh no," Lelia said and turned to Father Creed, reminding herself that he was a priest. Not available for Elizabeth even if she were alive. And he did look like a priest. Attentive. And tall. And abstinent. You could tell about abstinence by a man's lips. Actually he was more like a priest than Father Albin—though, once more, she felt disloyal to even think this—whose pink skin grew pinker each year as if his thickening body were laboring to turn itself inside out.

Not that Father Creed was handsome. Still, his face—quite homely with its long ears and soft chin—became expressive when he talked. And he was skilled at conversing: questions to Stefan about the architecture of the town; observations to her about the church; compliments to Helene about her cooking; even compliments about her view.

"How fortunate you are to live by the lake, Mrs. Blau."

"Thank you." With one foot, Helene pressed the button beneath the table to call a maid. "The lake seems different every day. That's what I love most about it, how it can turn from brown to green to blue within minutes. I can always look down at the water and know what the sky will be like."

"Is that your rowboat?"

"Yes."

"Oh, but it was my daughter," Lelia corrected her, "who gave this boat to her husband when she was pregnant with Greta and—"

"Grandma—" Greta touched her wrist, lightly. "We think of the boat as belonging to the whole family."

"That's right." Tobias' voice was curt. "It belongs to this family. Not yours," he said though he hadn't touched the boat in three years, not since his father had made him row with him.

"Rudeness," Mrs. Flynn said, "does not become you, Tobias."

Robert ate faster. Coated his uneasiness with gravy. Swallowed it all.

Tobias felt his stepmother's gaze on him. *Grateful.* "I don't believe Tobias intended to be rude," she was saying.

I didn't do it for you. Still, he'd rather think of her as family than his father's first wife, the rich wife whose old mother came here as often as she pleased because it was her money that had started it all. *Family.* Tobias didn't even like the word. And he didn't like those family dinners on Sundays when his stepmother got out her German china and lace, and they all had to sit here in their church clothes, pretending to enjoy roasts and dumplings that were slippery with gravy.

"But he sounded rude," Lelia Flynn said.

When the priest glanced from her to Helene and saw their eyes fused in a moment of open strife, he offered them a different direction. "I used to row as a boy," he exclaimed as if that revelation were sure to fascinate them both. And, indeed, they both followed him, asking where and when, listening as he described a pond near his parents' house in Vermont.

Tobias rolled his eyes at Greta, and they both stood up and carried stacks of plates toward the kitchen.

"May I help you with those?" the priest asked.

"We have maids for that kind of work." Lelia Flynn laid her thin fingers on his black sleeve, keeping him there at the table. "Greta will be honored to take you out on the lake."

From the window, Tobias watched as Greta rowed the lanky priest far into the lake. There was something about the way she leaned forward with the oars—her red hair almost touching the priest's chest before she would lean back and, along with her twin reflection on the surface of the lake, pull the oars through the water again until her arms would circle forward, once more, hair following on their path toward the priest—that made Tobias support himself with one palm on the windowsill because his skin had become heavy and warm, his underwear tight, making him languid and restless all at once. Robert was calling his name, but he couldn't bear to leave the window that was filled with the back-and-forth circling of Greta's red hair, and it was only when the boat had grown small and distant that he finally loosened his hand from the windowsill, leaving behind the damp print of his palm.

His skin felt heaviest across his belly and groin. Maybe if he walked that heaviness would dissolve. But even when he ran down six flights instead of waiting for the elevator, the motion of Greta's hair swaying toward the priest stayed with him, making him feel oddly unsteady as he walked down to the edge of the dock, and then back to the house and around it to the garage, where he found Danny Wilson sorting through the shelves above the workbench that stored spare lightbulbs and copper pipes, coiled wires and bicycle tires, boxes of nails and bolts all sorted by size.

Danny glanced up when he heard the steps. "Hey . . . What are you doing here, Tobias?"

Tobias walked up to him and—without letting himself think or reconsider—placed his right palm against Danny's chest and closed his eyes. Leaned his face against the back of his hand. Felt Greta's hair swinging against the priest's black-clad chest. Swinging red. And smelled his own familiar scent and something else—tobacco . . . sweat . . . the black grease you find on tools—*Danny's scent*. Smelled it along with his own. Felt Danny's heart against his palm.

And heard Danny say, "Hey now, Tobias. Tobias?" Dark hair

sprang in a cowlick from his forehead, curled up and back in a bulge.

Tobias did not move. Only felt that heavy warm skin, felt it expand as he breathed Danny into his own scent.

But then Danny's fingers—bony, resolute—settled on Tobias' shoulders, guiding him. Away from Danny. *Away?* Moving cool air into the space between them where, before, there had only been their smell. And Tobias felt the way you do when waking from half-sleep, when you feel half-blind and half-warm and burrow yourself back in, finding without seeing yet knowing by scent the place where you were all-warm before. *The exact place.* Only now there was Danny's warmth, gone, and Tobias wanted back to that.

"What's this all about?" One rough-skinned thumb flicked against his cheek. "An eyelash. You lost an eyelash, Mr. Tobias Blau. Open your eyes."

He did. His eyelash lay on Danny's thumb, black and curved and insignificant. *No longer mine.*

"Blow it away and make a wish, Mr. Tobias Blau."

He did. Made a wish. Then took hold of Danny's thumb. Pulled Danny's hand to his heart. And felt a fluttering in his chest to the right of his heart.

Danny blinked. Glanced past Tobias. "No," he said.

Tobias felt cold where Danny's hand no longer was.

"If your father—"

"You said to make a wish."

"If you still want your wish when you're older, I'll be here."

"How much older?"

"When you're as old as I am."

"Ten years from now?"

"It's the time we have between us. That's why I understand we have to wait." Danny crossed his arms as if to protect himself from Tobias and leaned against the workbench that was set up like a desk with its many drawers and an opening for legs so that you could sit down to repair a curtain rod, say, or open the vise that was fastened to the left side of the workbench.

"Swear you'll be there."

"All right."

Tobias shook his head.

"What is it now?"

"You'll have a wife by then. Debts. Kids. False teeth."

Danny grinned. "I doubt either one of us is headed in that direction, Tobias. Still, if I am, I'll just have to wait with the family life and what comes with it. Because this is something I don't want to miss. Now hop hop. I got work to do."

Dazed, Tobias sauntered from the garage, and as he came around the house, Greta and the young priest were standing in the boat that tilted as they switched positions, their reflections elongated as if stretching toward unknown and dangerous depths, and in that instant, Tobias felt Greta linked to himself as never before, knew what she felt and wanted, though his own wanting was secret while hers was public, there for any fool with eyes or binoculars to witness.

Finally, Greta was settled in the boat, and the priest lowered himself, took hold of the oars, and rowed them back toward shore. Stripes of sun shivered across the surface of the lake, and where the water became shallow, it took on the color of the sand beneath. The priest tied down the boat and climbed on the dock, extending one hand to help Greta. His touch felt like church to her, only sweeter; and when he slipped, she was the one to help him up and felt it again. And knew he felt it too as he left a smear of blood on her hand.

"Let me." She bent across the deep scrape that split the fleshy ball of his thumb. Instinctively, she pressed her fingers against it.

Though the bleeding stopped almost immediately, she kept her fingers there and led him to sit on one of the boulders next to the beach. The following Sunday at mass, when he raised his hand to place the communion wafer on her tongue, the scrape had healed without leaving a scab.

During his three months in Winnipesaukee—until a permanent replacement for Father Albin arrived—Noah Creed often talked with Greta after mass and continued those conversations during afternoon walks or in the rowboat. Being with him, Greta found, was almost as good as being alone, sometimes even better because he didn't disturb her aloneness, just placed his own aloneness next to hers.

∞

Too much space around herself. That's what she had where before he used to be when he returned to his diocese in Boston. And though he wrote to her, his letters only emphasized that he no longer lived near her. It confused her that being alone was not as complete as it had been before; and she felt restless in that empty space around her, a space that grew wider yet that November when her grandmother died.

Stefan was in his restaurant when he found out that Lelia had named the bank as trustee for Greta. Heat burst into his hands, and he excused himself, walked through the kitchen and out of the side door. *Haven't I always provided for Greta? Looked out for Greta?* How could Lelia have betrayed him like this? As Greta's father, he was the logical person to be trusted with her inheritance. *Three million.* Wind rose from the lake, cooled his burning hands. *Three million.* In comparison, the old loan was paltry. Insignificant.

So insignificant that it wouldn't even show in the papers that Greta received from her grandmother's lawyer several weeks later. Some time during all those years, Stefan figured, Lelia must have lost the document. With Greta that well provided for, he saw no reason to mention the loan. The bank might request immediate payment on Greta's behalf with the result that her brothers, in comparison, would have even less. Knowing Greta, Stefan felt certain she would agree with him. And eventually she would benefit, really, because he would use those funds to make the *Wasserburg* more magnificent. For her and her brothers.

In the meantime, though, he was left with his own copy of the loan document. If he ripped it up and dropped it down the incinerator chute, it might end up with Homer Wilson. Flushing it down the toilet could result in plumbing problems. Late one night, when he got ready to burn it in his restaurant, he heard the Hungarian's voice—*nothing good can come from fire*—but still he set his match to the paper, though his fingers were shaking—*nothing good nothing good nothing good from fire*—and as he felt his rage rise with the flames, he felt justified because of Lelia's betrayal. But the Hungarian was not about to be silent. *When did you really begin to treat the Flynns' money as your own?*

In January, Greta moved into a small apartment on the first floor. It troubled Stefan that she was choosing to live away from him, but Helene pointed out to him that many young women of Greta's age went to universities, farther away from their families than a different floor in the same building. Still, Greta was his only child who'd often made him feel like a worthy father, and by leaving, she was shaking that image he would have liked to have of himself. He never knew what to say to his sons. With Tobias—either sullen or quick to cut him with clever words—even small incidents, like reprimanding him for passing notes in class, caused injured silences. And the other boy was so cautious. Spoiled soft by his mother. Almost ten but young for his age. Except when he played the piano.

∽

The first reported healing happened by chance.

Miss Perkins, the teacher who used to live next door to the Blaus and whose hands had been deformed with arthritis for nearly ten years now, dropped her umbrella outside Heflins', and Greta—on her way to mail a letter to Father Creed—bent to pick it up. Though Greta only touched the teacher's hands for an instant, Miss Perkins felt a warmth throughout her fingers and palms, a warmth that stayed with her and made it possible to uncurl her fingers that evening. By morning the stiffness had seeped from her hands as though Greta had released something within her, and within a week her fingers were restored to the agility they'd had when she was in her forties and used to plant flowers at the first hint of spring in her garden by the lake, shoulders warmed by the sun while her knees burrowed into the earth, dislodging the last skin of winter.

After tales of her recovery spun through town, people recalled other incidents they'd mistaken for coincidences—Mr. Small's headache disappearing moments after Greta Blau had brushed against his arm in the library; that pain in Betty Simms' knee easing up when Greta Blau had helped her up the church steps; a wart vanishing from the right thumb of Mrs. Teichman after she'd sewn a winter coat for Greta Blau. While Stefan was skeptical, Helene believed in Greta's uncommon talent for healing. Every time she looked at Robert, she knew that—without Greta—her son would have bled from her that long-ago morning.

The people of Winnipesaukee took to coming to the *Wasserburg* at all hours to wait outside Greta's apartment, and Stefan would find them leaning against the carved railing that led up from his lobby or sitting on the mahogany chairs. When he protested to everyone in the family, except Greta, that his lobby looked like a doctor's waiting room, Helene suggested he simply talk to Greta. But he found it impossible to question his daughter on anything. *Because of the loan. Even though I did what's right. For everyone.*

Though Greta did not encourage the townspeople, she didn't turn them away when they appeared at the *Wasserburg*. That gift of touching—she had known since childhood that it passed through her to others, but she'd used it rarely and without thinking about it much. And until now she'd never been asked to reach for someone in pain.

Sight-seers, Mr. Wilson called the people because, while they waited to meet with Greta, they stared at the light-filled lobby with its rich paneling, the marble tiles and the peacock carpets that were still lush and colorful. Most had only seen the house from the outside, and they'd come to love it—or rather an image of it that was shaped by their own dreams of opulence and by what others had told them about the house. They were more absorbed with what happened in the *Wasserburg* than in their neighborhoods, and when they entered the vestibule and stepped through the French doors, they gazed up at the crescents of multicolored glass that signified their passage into a place unlike any they'd known before.

While Miss Garland complained, "Most of them couldn't afford an apartment here," Mr. Wilson soon became accustomed to chatting with them, snatching minutes of gossip while acting busy in case his wife were to see him and remind him of his unfinished chores.

And so they continued to come and sit outside Greta's door, the people of Winnipesaukee, tearing through her reluctance with the power of their belief in her abilities. Yet, when she called them into her living room, they felt disappointed because it was so plain: wooden floors without a carpet, books stacked against the walls, a table with neither lace nor linen, narrow chairs without pillows. Puzzled why she didn't make her apartment as splendid as the rest of her father's house, they speculated what they would do if they inherited three million dollars. Certainly not stay in one place like Greta who hadn't even gone away to college, who'd chosen the only apartment in the building that was as small as Miss Garland's. It mystified them why she would spend most of her hours by herself, the banker's red-haired granddaughter, the one they had to convince to tap into her gift, a gift she would have sheltered in the silence of her rooms if the town hadn't pressed her into dispersing it as though extracting dues.

This gift had nothing to do with the house and, yet, made up for the house in an odd way as if she were reinstating something her father had taken from the town, though no one could have said precisely what it was, because the *Wasserburg* had become the finest accomplishment the town could pride itself on. It had stood here on the shore of the great lake that the Indians had named Smile of the Great Spirit, had stood here long enough for many people to find it difficult to remember what their town had been like before it was built, while for the children it had always been part of their lives.

With tumors and arthritis the townspeople came to Greta.

With headaches and broken bones.

Some brought their bad dreams.

Their secret fears.

And she'd feel the suffering that belonged to their bodies, now and again even their deaths, though she never told them. That knowledge came to her in pictures—some bright and sudden, most gradually as if strained through a screen of dust. They wanted her to touch them, and she didn't mind doing that, touch them, lightly, on the shoulder, say, or on the knee or forehead, and after they'd leave, they'd report to others a tingling that expanded to heat their entire bodies and made them capable of doing what they hadn't done before. Like the Heflins' little daughter, Betty, ill with polio since she was one year old, who'd never walked till Greta ran her fingers along the thin, pale legs; and even though Betty would never walk quite right, she'd manage to propel herself forward from one foot to the other, refining that movement into an oddly elegant limp by the time she'd go away to teacher's college.

When Greta was alone, she often drew in her sketchbooks, drew in fast and fluid lines the way she had as a child when premonitions had appeared in the pictures she'd drawn on the butcher paper Sara had given her, showing her things she didn't know yet. Sometimes she felt depleted by the hopes of the people who came to her.

"What I want for myself," she wrote to the young priest, "is to learn how to touch without fusing, without bleeding away."

When Noah Creed replied, he suggested she make a list of what she liked. "And then provide those things for yourself."

Oranges.

Solitude.

Trousers instead of skirts.

Chocolate.

Books.

Walks along the lake.

Being with my family—though not as much as being alone.

Noah Creed.

She sent him her list except for the last item on it. She'd never missed anyone before, but Noah Creed had been walking through her dreams since that afternoon she'd rowed him out on the lake. *Much easier to provide chocolate for myself.* Still, his suggestion to provide for herself what she liked gave her the idea to volunteer for errands her family or even the tenants had in Boston. She would take the train and stay at the Blanchard Hotel in a room overlooking the Charles River. And if she had no reason to travel there, she would invent one, because to admit to a two-hundred-mile round trip just to meet Father Creed for dinner would have been risky because he would have felt forced to stop seeing her.

She brought back a set of French pans for her father's restaurant.

Silk roses for Pearl Bloom.

A blue terrycloth robe for her stepmother.

Sunglasses for Buddy Hedge.

Silk dresses and high-heeled shoes for herself as if visiting a priest required a different sort of attire than the loose, pleated trousers and blouses without starch that she normally wore. Yet, along with her familiar clothes, she also left behind some of her stillness, so that the priest came to know her as excitable and rather strained, her ease lost to her in those formal and ill-fitting clothes.

Deeply committed to his vows, Noah Creed made sure to remind her of the church whenever he became uncomfortable with her devotion. Still, he was not willing to do without that devotion—as long as he could hold it in check with references to his priesthood.

As Greta prepared for those overnight trips, she'd ask her stepmother's opinion on which clothes to take, evoking for Helene the faceless priest of her fantasies. It amused Helene, made her wonder if by imagining a priest for herself decades ago, she had somehow manifested Noah Creed for her stepdaughter. Ironic. At least Greta knew her priest's features. *"Priests can be great lovers,"* she imagined herself telling Greta. *"Mine was often faceless."*

Instead she limited herself to advice on which colors looked best on Greta. And when her husband got intrigued by his idea that his daughter was trying to snatch a priest from God, Helene made him promise not to tease Greta. He liked to say Greta should snatch at least two priests to even out what God had robbed him of. "Greta's visiting her priest," he'd hum when he'd step from the elevator to find the lobby empty—*no one waiting today to be healed, hallelujah*—and when Greta returned on the train, he'd be there for her at the station, searching beyond her embrace for the black-clad figure of a priest emerging from the train; but she would always be by herself, quieter than usual, and as soon as she'd settle in his car, she'd slip off her tight shoes.

She bought transparent gel to fortify her delicate fingernails.

A backpack and suitcase for Tobias when he left for Connecticut a month before his freshman year at Yale started.

Six chocolate bars for Robert that he ate without stopping though he loathed that part of himself he thought of as Fatboy and would have liked to obliterate. Fatboy had been born fully grown one morning during gym. While playing volleyball, Robert had felt Fatboy inside himself, *settling to stay, reminding him: One more hour till lunch.* Robert hated gym, hated the way his legs jiggled when he ran, the way his stomach bounced. On Dr. Miles' scale he weighed 187 pounds. The most ever. Al and Matthew on the other side of the net, skinny-fast, whispered something. Laughed. Robert knew they were making fun of him. He was hungry. *A Bratwurst sandwich today, Fatboy reminds him. And a pear. Tomorrow will be better: pork cutlets from tonight's dinner, plum cake for dessert.* The ball came toward him, and he rushed forward, bounced it off the inside of his wrists. "Good shot," somebody shouted. And it was a good shot. But everyone was staring. Some were laughing. At him. His wrist stung. The elastic of his shorts cut into his waist. His thighs were chafed where they rubbed together.

Greta bought smaller tablecloths for her stepmother now that she'd taken the leaves out of her mahogany table.

Cosmetics and magazines and gloves for Pearl who always had a list for her. But after the crash in the fall of 1929, the Blooms had a lot less money and many more arguments. Nate even brought up the old argument that she wasted soap.

"How could those slivers of dried-up soap have helped you?" Pearl challenged him.

"It's the principle of saving."

"You haven't saved on anything else for as long as I've known you."

"It's different now."

And it was. For the Blooms as well as for others in the building, the town, the country who'd bought stocks on margin during the Hoover bull market, often for less than five percent down, borrowing the rest from their brokers. While Nate still had Liberty Bonds and land and gold, the Clarkes lost everything and moved out of the *Wasserburg.* Already business at Stefan's restaurant was declining, and he had to let go of one cook and two of his waiters.

But through all those changes, Greta kept returning to Boston at least once a month. Several times she bought sheet music for Robert who'd felt restless ever since Tobias had left, and who would immerse himself even more in his music until he, too, would go to college, Ohio State, to study veterinary medicine.

Sometimes, sitting in a compartment, Greta would catch a glance into other trains as they passed, and be left with momentary images of people as smoke billowed between her and those people who were not constant in her life. Despite that fleetingness—or perhaps because of that fleetingness—she'd feel connected to them in an odd way.

As the priest's hair receded and his limber body grew more solid, he began to worry that Greta might encounter a man who might be available to her every day. To keep her from slipping from him, he would plan their next meeting while she was still with him in Boston and write her thoughtful letters, advising her in her selection of the books she read and the charities she supported: two hospitals, an animal shelter, an education program for deaf children. He liked to make a fuss over her birthdays, taking her out to dinner and then to the opera.

~

On her twenty-eighth birthday, they saw *La Traviata,* but she found it impossible to enjoy the opera because she was thinking about the troubles in Germany. Recently, the newspapers had been full of Adolf Hitler. His meeting with Mussolini. His execution of several officers who were suspected of trying to overthrow him.

Her parents were worried about everything having to do with Germany. Hitler's increasing power. Their families. Even about their accents that had worn smooth in their years of living in America, but were still noticeable enough to remind others that they had come from Germany. Only last week, her stepmother had said, "What reassurance can we offer them here that we are not dangerous to them? The way they believe every German in Germany is."

As Greta and Noah Creed walked down the steps of the opera house, she wondered how she would feel if she'd been born in Germany and had an accent. But since her mother had been American, the townspeople considered her one of their own.

"You seem sad tonight," Noah said.

All at once she didn't want to think about Germany. She tried to smile at Noah. "Maybe it's because of these operas you take me to—they all end with people dying of broken hearts."

"I never thought of them that way."

"And they all need something else to help death along . . . consumption in *La Traviata,* poison in *Romeo and Juliette,* a pistol in *Werther* . . . but basically they die of broken hearts."

He gave a theatrical sigh and covered his heart with one palm. "They die for love."

"After suffering great agony."

"Yes, but they have a moment of bliss together just before they die. Romeo . . . Werther—"

"But it's only for a moment. So . . ."

"What is it? Why are you grinning like that?"

"So Catholic."

"Catholic? Wait till we see *Madam Butterfly.*"

"She dies for love too?"

"Commits hari-kari."

"For love."

"For love."

"Foolish people."

"You think so?"

She felt his eyes as strongly as she would have felt his hands had he brought them to her skin, and as he kept her there in his gaze, his left arm rose toward her as if to touch her chin. Though he dropped his arm quickly, it was the kind of gesture Greta would replay in her mind in the weeks to come and file away with hundreds like it, magnifying its significance, letting it comfort her through the nights.

∽

When Danny looked up, Tobias was standing in the opening of the garage door, wearing a gray suit. Behind him the sky was equally gray as if all the world had suddenly gone black and white, no color at all, and Danny thought that this was good. Very good.

"Ten years," Tobias said.

In those years since that other day here in the garage, Tobias had been friendly but distant with Danny, and Danny had thought he'd forgotten, although he himself had thought of it often—not in the way of expecting Tobias to come to him like this exactly ten years afterwards, but rather remembering the pale scalp beneath Tobias' short hair . . . the knobs on the back of Tobias' neck . . . and Tobias' hand against his chest as if reaching inside for his heart. Remembering. And imagining more. Fifteen years old Tobias had been, and what had stayed with Danny most was the courage it must have taken Tobias to come toward him like that. *Like a sleepwalker almost. And the will it took me to push him away.*

"You're back," Danny said, remembering Tobias' eyelash on his thumb. "Blow it away and make a wish, Mr. Tobias Blau," he'd told him, and Tobias had made a wish, had extracted a promise: "When you're as old as I am." To Yale he'd gone, the brightest of the Blau children, and Danny hadn't seen much of him except for brief visits during the summer and Christmas vacations—never the entire vacation because Tobias had school friends in New York and Boston who invited him.

"Yes. I'm back." With sudden and weightless grace, Tobias hoisted himself up to sit on the workbench between the vise and a bucket, no longer all-gray because he was framed by the wooden shelves behind him, by pliers and wrenches that hung from hooks beneath those shelves.

"You'll get oil on your good suit." Immediately, Danny wished he hadn't said that. It sounded fussy. Like the fussy bachelor he'd become.

Tobias' fingers curved around Danny's upper arms.

All at once Danny felt incredibly shy. "No false teeth yet," he said, trying to joke himself free of a shyness more awkward than the first time with Stewart Robichaud and with other men.

"That's a relief."

"And no family."

"I didn't think so."

And then Danny was standing between Tobias' knees, his hands on Tobias, swifter than their words had taken them, noticing how Tobias' jaw had widened with the years, changing the shape of his face from heart-shaped to oval. But how he still had that straight line of freckles across the bridge of his nose. And remembering his Aunt Irene trying to wipe off that line with spit and Tobias breaking free from her. *Why am I thinking about my aunt now? Now.* He'd never been able to call her *Mother,* hadn't been able to be the son she'd imagined, the son who would prefer her to his first mother, the son who would marry and give her the grandchildren she waited for with the same urgency she'd waited for his adoption.

Five months ago, without any prior word to him, she and his uncle had told him they were getting their marriage annulled. His uncle had retired to Florida, though he wasn't sixty yet; and his aunt had gone where no man could follow, had joined a group of rebel nuns who were fighting to be recognized by the church, women who'd left marriages and were working at getting them annulled. After praying to find the best possible name for their order, they'd followed his aunt's suggestion: Sisters of the Angel of Mercy. Two of them were wealthy, and they'd bought a three-story brick house right next to the Catholic church in Concord where, to the mortification of the priest, they'd established their convent and attended daily mass, wearing severe black habits. Danny had visited her twice, meeting with her on a bench in the churchyard, and as she'd told him about the sisters' feud with the bishop, he'd felt affectionate toward her now that he was no longer the focus of her disappointment. *Stop thinking about her.*

But he was still thinking about her as he and Tobias moved toward each other once more, slower now, seeing her with Mrs. Teichman and hearing the seamstress telling his aunt that she'd no longer sew for the Blaus because they were German. *Why am I thinking of this now? Because Tobias is too. His Germanness.*

"We could go to my apartment." Danny steadied himself against Tobias. "Someone might come in."

"But your workbench—it's part of it. Do you know that every fantasy I've had of you always included that workbench?"

"I'm flattered . . . I think."

"Sometimes I didn't even need to think of you."

"That story of yours—does it allow that I might have a life away from your workbench?"

"Now you sound pissed."

"That doesn't fit your story either?"

"Don't be pissed, okay? It's just that all I needed was to think of that workbench." Tobias decided not to tell Danny that in some of those fantasies his father had entered the garage, had found him loving Danny, and that Tobias had ignored him, had continued with Danny. Like now.

"My workbench, huh?" Danny took Tobias by the shoulders. "No wonder you put your ass right on it."

"Priorities . . . I mean, don't you get a hard-on thinking about pipes and wires and tiles and screws—"

"Don't forget pliers."

"—and grease and nails and . . ." Tobias leaned back his head and inhaled deeply. "Bliss."

"Bliss?"

"Being here—"

"On the workbench?"

"No, no, with you. So . . ."

"So what?"

"Am I still invited to your apartment then?"

Although they would never make plans to be together in the years to come, Danny knew enough about the Blaus' family patterns to predict Tobias' returns from Hartford where he'd become the manager of a bookstore. Never for his father's birthdays, but usually for his stepmother's and Greta's, always for Robert's. Sometimes he visited in February if the ice on the bay was thick enough for skating and ice fishing—except of course for those years when Tobias would be stationed in England and Danny could only imagine being with him.

∽

While some of the Jewish tenants began to treat the Blaus differently—with uncomfortable silences or even hostility—Nate and Pearl Bloom continued their friendship with them. Nate and Stefan never discussed Germany, but Helene and Pearl were able to talk about the newspaper accounts that reported the persecution of countless Jews. Pearl knew how conflicted Helene felt about being German, how she worried about the Jews in her hometown, the Abramowitzes and the Rosens and Frau Simon.

Every month she sent packages with food and money concealed in the hollow cores of spools to her brother and his daughter and

Stefan's family, who wrote fearful letters about what was happening in their town. But in 1941 mail from Germany stopped, and all Helene knew came from American newspapers that wrote about Germany as a monster with many arms, a Germany she no longer understood because it was not at all like the town she knew so well, a town no larger than the town of Winnipesaukee.

The few times she tried to explain to people in Winnipesaukee about the ordinary people back home in Burgdorf, like her brother and Margret, they looked at her as though she were defending the enemy. And it was not that. Only that she could not take the newspapers' descriptions of Germans as evil and apply them to everyone over there. Because if she had stayed in Germany, the Americans would see her as evil too. Mrs. Teichman already did. And others in town regarded Helene with a different awareness of her Germanness, considered her punctuality and efficiency German traits, where before they would have thought of them as part of her personality. It made her want to miss appointments, slop food on her dress. Made her want to say, "It's not what Germans are like."

And yet to say that felt dangerous. Suspect. Even to herself. Because what was stronger than her pain at being eased out was her horror at the violence committed against the Jews and the unavoidable certainty that there had to be people—ordinary people, too—who were making this happen. How could they live with that knowledge? But in trying to understand, she always kept coming back to her own family in Burgdorf, to people she loved over there. How to connect them with those reports? And yet, what felt terribly familiar in all this was that attitude of superiority she knew from having grown up there, from seeing it bloom so quickly against anyone who was considered to be different. Still—how could it have turned into something so monumental?

When Germany had declared war on Poland, she'd been terrified, and her consolation had been that at least Leo was too old to fight, and that Leo's child was a daughter, not a son. Because it was Trudi's generation that was fighting the war. The Weilers' son. The Hansens' son. Both Weskopp sons. To imagine sending a son off to war. It had to be worse than seeing a husband go.

And then it had happened to her.

First Tobias.

Then Robert.

How to sleep through a night when your sons were in a war? How to not think of soldiers buried or returning broken like Axel Lambert?

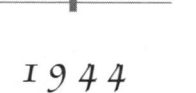

Robert, who fought in North Africa, would be the first to return in February of 1944, a bullet in his left thigh. The month after he had surgery and moved back in with his parents, he opened a one-room veterinary clinic next to the hardware store. Though he didn't have much time for his music, Pearl coaxed him until he agreed to play the piano at Nate Bloom's seventieth birthday that spring, an elegant event to which she'd invited friends from Boston, the town, and the building. The guest of honor was Nate's son, who had never visited his father before.

After weeks of bartering and buying on the black market, Pearl managed to pull together the kind of abundant celebration she used to give before the war.

When Robert arrived late after examining the Morrells' lame horse in the north end of town, Miss Garland was the first to greet him by the Blooms' door. "It's lovely to see you, Robert dear." Her delicate fingers grasped the edge of his hand.

"You too, Miss Garland," he replied, "you too," feeling flustered and obligated to say something else that would take the hunger from her eyes. Ever since high school when he'd stopped visiting her, she'd looked at him as though she carried a balance sheet of things she had done for him and things he had failed to do for her. He wished he hadn't agreed to be here, that he had lingered with the horse. He felt dirty. Tired. And above all heavy. On the way home he'd stopped at the bakery, and he could still taste the uglies, those wonderful clumps of multicolored dough, their glaze milky and half-transparent with a hint of vanilla.

Miss Garland was nodding at him while thin coils of hair bounced around her face. "You should see all the food she's serving. Roasts and fish and ham. Four kinds of cake. And the wines . . ."

"I'll take a look." Awkwardly, he freed himself from her and walked into the music room that was filled with people. The velour hangings that had draped these walls when he was a boy had been replaced several times over the years with different materials, the latest of them a green satin, and against that deep green stood his brother, alone, eyes amused while he observed everyone, face flushed as if he'd been out in the wind.

Robert pulled him into a big, clumsy hug. "When did you get back?"

"Just a few hours ago."

"How long can you stay?"

"I don't know yet. Couple of days . . . maybe. I'm on my way to Officer Training School"

"I'm so glad you're here. Did you get all settled upstairs?"

"Downstairs, actually. Danny's putting me up."

Robert blushed. "Your old room's still ready and— Why am I doing this? It's just that I want to get you away from everyone else, find out what's been happening to you. But I sound like my mother, trying to convince you to stay with us."

"At least you don't try to pretend that some day I'll bring home a nice girl and start making grandchildren."

"God, no."

"Which leaves the burden of procreation to you since Greta's never going to get her priest away from the church. Carrying on the family name and all that."

Another blush. "Don't even start on that. There's no one . . ."

"You got any time for me tomorrow?"

"Breakfast?"

"Sure. How early do I have to get up?"

"Seven?"

"Good." Tobias stroked his chin, still tender from the stubble on

Danny's face. Already he was thinking about getting away from the
party and to Danny's apartment. When he'd come back to the
States, he'd taken the first train to Winnipesaukee and had found
Danny in the garage as though he'd been there all along, waiting.
They hadn't touched until they were inside Danny's bedroom,
where the windows were set so high into the foundation wall that
the light that came through them only skimmed the air above their
bodies. When Danny got a cramp in his left leg, Tobias leaned forward and took hold of Danny's big toe. With his other hand, he
massaged Danny's calf for him until the cramp subsided.

"Usually I just hop around until it stops by itself," Danny said,
hands linked behind his head as he watched Tobias' dark, intense
face.

"This is a better way. Try it. Sit up and grab your big toe—just
do it, try it, come on—and pull it toward you . . . like this, right.
And then hold on till the cramp goes away."

"Where'd you learn that?"

"My stepmother. I guess her father used to get cramps like that."

"One of those old German customs?"

Abruptly, Tobias let go of Danny's leg. He looked tired as though
all energy had drained from him, leaving him empty.

"I didn't mean anything by German. I meant custom. One of
those old customs. I could have said French. Or Italian."

"Okay."

"I'll get us some food."

"Okay." Tobias propped a pillow behind his back and sat
against the solid white headboard. Every piece of furniture in the
room was painted white, making the room look larger and brighter
than when Danny's aunt and uncle used to live here. Their religious
clutter had been replaced by pictures of greyhounds in white
frames, a long mirror without a frame, and several plain white
lamps to make up for the lack of daylight.

From the kitchen, Danny carried a large tray with sliced apples
and cheese and bread. He opened two beers. "Grab a beer," he
joked. "Pull it toward you and hold on till it's empty."

Tobias had to laugh. "Very good. Just pretend you're reaching
for a beer the next time you have a cramp."

"Unless you're here. Then you can massage it."

"You can always show one of your other . . . friends how to do it."

"Open your mouth." Danny fed him a slice of cheese. "There's more." A slice of apple. A piece of bread.

"I can't eat that quickly."

"Not if you keep talking."

"Don't you see others? Didn't you and Stewart Robichaud—"

"What do you want me to do? Wait around till you show up?"

"I mean—"

"Hey." Danny raised one hand to stop him.

But Tobias took hold of what courage he could find and said it. Said: "What I mean is that I don't feel like looking for anyone else." And saw Danny flinch. Though he closed his eyes, Tobias could still hear him.

"Don't push at me to do the same, Mr. Tobias Blau."

∞

"Look, the birthday boy wants us to come over," Robert said, and they headed toward Nate Bloom, who sat propped in his wheel-chair, dressed in a tuxedo, a mohair shawl across his emaciated legs.

"Congratulations." Robert bent to shake Nate's hand.

Nate asked the usual: "Still healing cows?"

And Robert replied with his usual: "Cows and alligators."

"Promise to keep both away from me." Nate winked and introduced Robert to his son, Ira, a tall man with beautiful, even teeth, who worked as a lawyer in Boston and had brought his fiancée, a woman as tall as he. Her hair was so black, it looked night-blue.

"Yvonne is a window decorator," Pearl said. "For Powell's store in Boston."

Robert nodded and quickly looked down from the woman's eyes, only to notice her silver sandals that showed off her delicate ankles.

Nate and his son were talking with Stanley Poggs, Nate's busi-ness manager, about the renovation of a first-floor apartment, where it would be easier to maneuver his wheelchair. But its com-pletion kept getting delayed because of war shortages. Two years ago, when Nate had lost the use of his legs in a car accident, Stan-

ley Poggs had moved into the Blooms' guest room to care for business matters and accompany Pearl to concerts and other social
events. People in the building gossiped because Stanley was handsome and only in his mid-forties, younger than Pearl, who didn't
seem bothered by the rumors that her husband was grooming Stanley as his replacement.

"In business and in bed," people would whisper.

"Play the piano, Robert. Please," Pearl urged.

When he sat down at her white piano, he heard her say, "He's
such a brilliant musician," and he wished he'd never agreed to this.

As he struck the first notes of Mozart's piano concerto No. 23,
the woman with the night-blue hair took the chair closest to him
and sat erect. She had always been enchanted by music because it
unfolded something within her that was usually closed to everyone—including herself. Music released her from the constant loneliness that waited beneath her polite smile, the kind of loneliness
that tightens your skin until you can no longer sleep. She knew how
to dodge that loneliness for hours, days even, by surrounding herself with people who admired her beauty; but then there were those
other times when she felt careless and had to force herself to do
things slowly, properly, in order to offset that wish to hurl out,
mess up, destroy.

Some days tearing a single piece of paper would do. Would return her to who she really was. Tearing it quickly would infuse her
with lightness; tearing it slowly would make the paper scream. The
slower you tore it, the more resistance you felt. It depended on
what you needed to bring yourself back. Sometimes she had to tear
several pages, some fast, some screamingly slow. But there were
days she needed more, needed to bring that devastation closer to
her skin. Like holding her hand over the flame of a candle, raptur-
ous with that pain of being there in that instant, only, and breathing in the intensity that she looked for in others but found too
seldom, the intensity that she now felt in this man as he leaned
across the piano.

The bulk of Robert's torso strained the material of his tuxedo,
and he rolled his head as if in a trance. He doesn't look like the
kind of man who would wear a tuxedo, the woman thought. Low-

slung pants perhaps and a wrinkled shirt—but not a tuxedo. It only emphasized his massive frame as he hunched over the keyboard, almost crawled across it, crawled into it—a spider, a troll, an angel— as close as any human and piano could possibly get, while his right foot pumped furiously, and his immense bottom lifted in staccato intervals as though he were raising himself up by his fingertips. She gazed at his face, which was all wrong for his body—still the face of a boy—and past him at her own reflection in the mirrored front of the cabinet that displayed Pearl's collection of crystal and, at the same time, Robert's reflection—superimposed on the glass, on her, as if he were meant to envelop her.

She didn't notice Helene who was watching her from across the room, her chest constricted by apprehension at the eager way this woman leaned toward Robert, whose awkwardness had been lifted from him as if in one remarkable act of grace. The woman's features were pronounced—just on the pretty side of being too bony with that narrow nose and flat cheeks—Helene thought, and she wanted her to see Robert the way he was, a shy man, less comfortable with people than with the animals he treated, not this vibrant stranger at the piano who might inspire her to claim him and discard him once he revealed himself to her. A woman like that would not appreciate Robert's ease with animals. He would not fit into her world.

Helene knew only too well what it felt like not to fit in: although she'd spent nearly half her life in her new country—more familiar to her now than Germany—she didn't belong, just as she didn't belong any longer into the country where she had grown up, the country that America had been at war with. Arching her neck, she moved two fingers between her skin and the emerald necklace that she rarely wore. Because it was tight. Because the clasp was complicated. Because of the rage she had felt that first time Stefan had laid it around her neck.

But tonight he had coaxed her into wearing it to Nate's party. "To honor him for his birthday," he'd said.

"I'll wear it for our sons," she'd said. "For returning to us. Without lasting injuries."

It pleased her, that proud tilt to Stefan's chin as he listened to their son, who was mesmerizing everyone with his music. What didn't please her was the attention of the woman from Boston, and she was glad when Nate's son stepped next to the woman and laid his hands on her bare shoulder.

"Yvonne—" he started.

But she raised one finger to silence him.

Nate's son studied Robert who attacked the keyboard like a lumberjack even if he wrested flawless tones from it, whose left foot veered off like the gaze of a cross-eyed child from time to time until he retrieved it.

Easing her shoulder from beneath her fiancé's light grasp, Yvonne kept herself turned toward the pianist, who made her forget the lawyer, the silk gown she planned to design for herself, even the way she looked now, this moment, an awareness that had been with her ever since she was a small girl and others had stared at her, an awareness that provided her with a constant summary of her impact on those around her. And yet, fearing it too, being on display. But he pulled her back, the pianist, gave her shelter in his music. And as he merged with the keyboard in a mating ceremony that, ultimately, would be impossible, she felt dizzied by a warmth that spread low in her belly. Drawn to this grace that flourished from his ugliness, she smiled at the image of him bending over her with that same intensity.

∽

And so she pursued him.

Over the next two months, she battled his shyness and her disgust at watching him eat enormous portions of food and hearing him hum to himself as he chewed. She felt a certain tenderness at his confusion why a woman as beautiful as she would be drawn to him. Three weeks after meeting him, she announced that she loved him, and she was moved by his gratitude but even more so by her own kindness because it proved to her that she was not frivolous— something that Ira Bloom and other men had accused her of. A frivolous woman would never be able to love a man whose body revolted her. No, her love proved to her that she was capable of enormous depth and compassion.

But Robert could not believe it fully—this proclamation of her love—and suspected that what she loved was only the image of him at the piano. And maybe that was enough, he reasoned with himself. Maybe it was even better. Because that was the part of himself he, too, liked best.

"You are extraordinarily gifted," she told him when he visited her in Boston. "You could be a concert pianist if you chose."

"I'm a veterinarian," he reminded her.

Being with Robert made her want to match the passion he had for his music. He made her feel chosen and interesting in the same way she used to feel about herself when she was twelve and still believed she could know everything in the world, believed it enough to try and stay up all night reading novels and books about philosophers, feeling chosen whenever she managed to keep from sleeping.

He thought of her all the time: she was like quicksilver where his mother was serious and deliberate; she was playful and charming; she was the most exquisite woman he had ever met, the kind of woman he would have never dared approach. And yet she wanted him. Had ended her long engagement to Nate's son to be with him.

"Somehow I never really believed I would marry Ira," she'd told him. "It was the kind of engagement that goes on forever because . . . I guess there's no next step. And so we stayed engaged. Until I met you."

And yet it mystified Robert that she would choose him over the tall lawyer. For her he would change, he decided. Become that man at the piano even when he was away from his music. In bed he wanted her to look at him with that desire. But she was disappointed by the consideration he brought to their lovemaking—she yearned for the abandon with which he hurled himself at his music.

Since she liked dancing, he didn't object when she tried to teach him some basic steps, and she made sure to praise him if he remembered a sequence. "With all you know about music," she told him one Sunday evening when they practiced alone in her apartment, "you'll be a wonderful dancer before you know it."

She got him to laugh at mistakes, and they'd try again until he had the steps right. It amazed him how confident she made him feel about his dancing. Sometimes her hands would get cold and turn from pale to blue to purple, outlining her knuckles and the bones of her wrist. Embarrassed, she'd hide them in her pockets or tuck them into her crossed arms. They stirred him, those hands, stirred him in a profound way and made him protective of her one vulnerability.

Regardless how lightly he danced with her in her living room, he felt clumsy the Saturday they stepped on the dance floor in the Weirs Beach pavilion, which was famous because some of the great bands had played here. But not that night. And he was glad for that since he felt heavy and slow.

In the morning, though, he felt faster than she, lighter, when he took her swimming in Lake Winnipesaukee after picking her up from Greta's apartment where she had stayed the night.

"Wait for me," she shouted after him, laughing and splashing as soon as she reached him.

When they walked into the *Wasserburg* afterwards, sun followed them through the stained-glass moons above the French doors and turned the lobby golden-red. Yvonne stopped. Touched the intricate inlay on the desk. "How lucky you are to be living here."

"Would you?"

"Would I what?"

"Live here. You could. I mean—you could marry me and then live here. With me."

She laughed. "Of course it would be with you."

"I shouldn't have asked. I'm sorry. You've only known me five weeks and—"

"Yes."

He stared at her. "Yes that I shouldn't have asked? Or yes that you will . . . I mean, marry me?"

"Which one would you prefer?"

"In my bravest moment?"

"Only in your bravest moment."

"That you said yes to marrying me."

"Does a man have to be brave to marry me?"

"Brave only in believing you could say yes."

"Yes."

"My dear," he said and instantly felt the ancient fear he'd known as a boy—*babies can kill mothers . . . babies all powerful, all frail*—when he'd stood by the grave of the dead mothers. "But you have to promise—"

"Promise what?"

"No children. That you won't have children."

"I don't want stretch marks."

"Promise then."

"That's easy enough." She took his face between her cold hands. "Oh, Robert. Isn't this the moment when you're supposed to kiss me?"

◈

When Nate Bloom heard that Robert was about to marry his son's fiancée two months after meeting her at his birthday party, he told Stefan, "You people want everything that isn't yours." It was a comment that needed no explanation, a comment that cut through years of their friendship and their silence regarding Jews and Germany. *You people.* And he did not come to Robert's wedding, though Stefan tried to act around him as though that comment had never been made. *You people.*

Pearl, however, arrived with Stanley Poggs and two hand-cut crystal vases. "Nate won't stay angry," she told Helene when the two women escaped to the roof during the last hour of the wedding reception that Pearl had helped to set up in the courtyard, arranging for delicacies and cake and even champagne. "Besides, he has always liked your Robert. He even knows him better than he knows his son. It's just now—with everything that's in the paper about the Jews in Germany—I'm sorry. I shouldn't be saying any of this."

"Go on," Helene said. "Really."

"His son is family."

Helene nodded, wishing she could apologize to Pearl for Germany, and yet afraid that she didn't have the right, that it would be arrogant to apologize for the actions of others . . . for their decisions. What if she was only doing it to feel better about herself? To Jews who'd survived, an apology from her certainly would not make a difference. "Even the ones who got away—" She stopped.

"What is it?"

"I often think of how they had to leave behind everything that belonged to them. Start all over again. Noah Creed, he told me about a Jewish doctor who lives on his block. She had her husband and daughter taken from her, and she's been in America over a year. You know what she does? Works at a grocery store because she isn't allowed to practice medicine until she's passed all kinds of medical and language exams. When I think how long it took me to get used to the language . . . And it's not that I'm comparing what happened to me."

"I know you're not."

"She didn't choose to leave Germany. She didn't have a house waiting for her. She lost her family and her work. I mean, her work is all tied in with language. You can be real good at your work, an expert, and then you're taken out of your language and you lose your work too."

"Hey . . . this is Robert's wedding. A day to celebrate."

"I'm not so sure." Helene adjusted the lace collar of her mauve dress. "I wish they had waited. . . . Yvonne doesn't know what he's like."

"They obviously adore each other."

"What I don't understand is why it had to be right away."

"And to consider—" Pearl interrupted herself, laughing.

"Consider what?"

"This conversation between two women who decided within hours to get married."

"I knew Stefan for many years."

"Knowing and marrying are two separate things, Sweetie, unless you mean knowing in a biblical way."

"Unfortunately, it was entirely chaste."

"Well, I could count the time between meeting and marrying Nate in minutes."

"Stefan calls Yvonne a thin wire."

"And what does that mean?"

"The first time I heard him use that expression was about my brother's wife, Gertrud. A certain frailty. Being stretched so tight you'll snap."

"But Yvonne is not weak. She's a powerful woman, just not in the same way you are. Your power comes from doing for yourself. Hers from letting others do for her." Pearl's dainty feet rested on the low edge of the roof as she sipped the wine she'd brought along. "Yvonne reminds me of my Aunt Amy who always had suitors though she was in a wheelchair. Even as an old woman, Aunt Amy had suitors. They competed with each other, couldn't do enough for her because she made them feel so helpful . . . so appreciated."

"I never thought of that as powerful."

"Oh, but it is. I bet my Aunt Amy got more often what she wanted than you do. She once told me she would have been a fool to marry, to limit herself to one of them."

"And where do you fit in with your power?"

"Oh, probably somewhere in between. I can do for myself, but sometimes I choose to appreciate others and let them do for me." Pearl looked out over the town that had grown in the three decades she'd lived here, spreading into the hills and along the shore of the lake, thickening in a half-belt around the *Wasserburg* as if drawn to a mysterious source. Below her, on the lawn that ran from the house to the sand, three children were playing with a red ball. A few of the guests had brought swimsuits and were in the lake or on the dock. "A thin wire . . . ," Pearl mused. "Leave it to Stefan to have an expression for that. Still, I have never seen our Robert this much in love. And don't forget that they're both nearly thirty. Old enough to make those decisions."

"Age doesn't protect you from mistakes."

Pearl glanced at Helene steadily without a comment.

"I must sound like one of those mothers who'll disapprove of anyone their sons might marry."

Pearl didn't even hesitate. "You do."

"I'm trying not to be like that."

Pearl grinned. "You must try harder then."

"I wish I liked Yvonne."

"You're sure? Or do you wish she were different? Not so glamorous and pretty?"

"Maybe . . ."

"Start by finding one positive thing about their marriage."

"Yvonne's belief in Robert . . . that he is a genius."

"You'll get used to her. Wait till you have your first grandchild."

A sudden stinging behind her eyes made Helene press her lids shut. She saw Robert as an infant in his crib, saw him turning over for the first time without her help, saw his sturdy back as he sat atop her German encyclopedia in front of the piano, saw him leaving for his first day of school. . . . Leaving. All those years. Every single day. Leaving. As if rehearsing for this day of his marriage. And of course she had known since the day of his birth, had readied herself for his eventual leaving that seemed so far off in the future, gradually letting him walk by himself, feed himself, clothe himself, letting go more of him with each day, each year. All at once she felt as if those years of his life had passed in just one instant, far too quickly for her, and as she drew in a sharp breath to keep down the panic of losing him forever, it came to her that this was not the end of it all, but that her years with him were still happening now, and that these changes—his marriage and the move into his own apartment—were merely rounding out that picture without taking anything from her.

Suffused with gratitude at the gift of having had him in her life, she wished she could tell him. And because Robert wasn't there, she told Pearl as she had countless times before with other words she'd felt inside herself for her husband or son, words so filled with emotion that she needed to filter them through this friend who loved her, who'd never made her regret these outbursts. Pearl—without speaking—could sift the rawness out of Helene's words by the time she took them to her husband or son. Sometimes, after Pearl had heard the words, Helene would not even need to say them again.

"It was a splendid reception," Pearl said. "Even if the bride's parents are cheap."

"Oh, come now. They couldn't have afforded it. Besides, they offered."

"But they didn't insist. There's a difference between offering and insisting. I ought to know. See, you're smiling. You know exactly what I mean. There is a way of offering to do something in such a way that the offer is refused. A lot of it has to do with just a moment of hesitation. For example—and I've done this to you a million times—"

"Do I want to know about this?"

"Well—" Pearl laughed. "It may keep me more honest in the future. Maybe I'll really return the things I borrow from you, instead of telling you that I'll be glad to replace whatever it is as soon as I've had a chance to go out and get it, while you, of course, assure me that I don't need to do that."

"You *are* good at this."

"Very good. But it won't be fun anymore now that I've confessed."

"You'll find something else to enjoy."

"Always . . ."

"Your crystal vases . . . they were lovely."

"Yvonne said they were the perfect height for roses."

And then the two women were silent in the lush summer night that settled around them and grew denser, shrouding them from the town and erasing the lines on their faces until they looked as they had three decades earlier when they had started coming to this roof together. They took measure of one another with the secret recognition of conspirators who'd conjured themselves back into their youthful bodies, and they stretched their shoulders, their necks, and eased back into their chairs with a half-remembered litheness.

It was Stefan who found them there on the roof after the last guests had left. They heard the whir of the elevator before they saw him approach—an old man from another generation—hair gray, though still curly, the curve of his nose more pronounced now that his face was thinner. In one hand he held a bottle of champagne, in the other three long-stemmed glasses upside down between his splayed fingers. It startled them how far he had outpaced them in time, and they felt almost guilty for not having protected him from that passage, for having let him move ahead of them into old age without warning, without sharing their private knowledge of remaining young with one another.

∽

Yvonne's body fit around the curve of his back, her thighs and knees into the V-shape of his bent legs, her toes against the arches of his feet. Through his pajamas and her nightgown he felt the heat of her body. In the morning, the layers of material were damp with sweat—*mine? hers?*—and his pajama top clung to his back, growing cool as soon as she moved away from him. It was like that every night, on their honeymoon in Rye Beach and once they returned to Winnipesaukee where his mother—with the help of Danny Wilson—had readied the only available apartment in the *Wasserburg* for them, a small unit that was to be theirs temporarily.

Once the Blooms had relocated to the first floor, Robert and Yvonne were to move into their lavish suite of rooms on the fifth floor. But suddenly Nate no longer wanted to move. He had his own war with Stefan, accused him of letting Robert steal Yvonne from his son.

"And now you're stealing my apartment."

"But it was your decision to relocate," Stefan reminded him.

"Relocate . . . That's how it starts."

Stefan tried to calm Nate by taking him in his wheelchair to the first floor and showing him how the expansion of his new apartment was progressing. He'd agreed to let Nate combine two apartments into one that included a suite for Stanley and opened the large kitchen and dining room into a greenhouse that jutted into the courtyard.

"We'll keep the apartment on the fifth floor too," Nate insisted as Stefan wheeled him through the rooms.

"I'll need that for Robert and his wife."

"Well, he can't have it."

"All right. Then Robert will move into this apartment here."

"No. Not after all the planning I've done to get it right."

"You choose which apartment you prefer. And then Robert can take over the other one."

"Relocate . . . Take over . . . I used to think you were a different kind of German, but I was wrong. The same way the fools over there were wrong about their neighbors. Some neighbors . . . I know what you're doing. You're trying to force me out altogether just like—"

"Nate—"

"—just like they're doing to Jews in your country."

"This here is my country, Nate. I came here as a boy."

"Once a Kraut—"

"Don't." Stefan felt sick. Furious. "What have I done to you?"

"You people have done plenty."

"Listen to me. I have lived here half a century. I have only been back to Germany once. For many years I have regarded you as a friend. And I don't think—the hell I don't think—that I deserve any of this." He wheeled Nate from the apartment. Slammed the door on their way out. Pushed the up arrow for the elevator.

"Don't tell me—" Nate started, but stopped when the elevator door opened and Fanny Braddock was standing there in her bright red sweater, one finger on the control panel. Her short hair, gray already, stuck up in tufts.

"Can you move aside a bit, Fanny? Thank you. I need to get Mr. Bloom's chair in here."

"Five?"

"Yes, you can get us to five."

Pleased, she pressed her thumb against the number five button. While the elevator rose, she stared at Stefan as though she knew about his fight with Nate. But when she opened her mouth, she said, "You have a nice body, Mr. Blau."

I don't need this. I don't need any of this. Still, he told her what he'd taught both his sons to say to Fanny when they were boys. "Thank you, Fanny."

She leaned against him, smelling of cheese and lake water. Fit her head beneath his chin.

"Stand up straight, Fanny." He tried to step away from her, but behind him was the wall of the elevator, and next to him Nate's wheelchair.

She sighed with contentment. "Weatherman says sunshine."

"Fanny? Stand up straight."

But she didn't budge.

"They're relocating people like her too," Nate said. "Jews and morons."

Stefan couldn't breathe. It was hot in the elevator. Tight. With Fanny pressing at him with her body, Nate pressing at him with words.

"They throw them all together into camps and—"

"Fanny," Stefan said desperately, "you must stand on your own, Fanny."

She disengaged her head. Peered up at him sideways. Licked the underside of his chin.

"Jesus!" He dried his chin with his sleeve, dreading Nate's laugh or another nasty comment about him and morons and sex.

But Nate looked solemn when he said, "You shouldn't do that, Fanny."

∞

To live in the rooms where she had met Robert seemed romantic and exciting to Yvonne, who immersed herself in a feast of decorating. She hired two women who'd started their own construction company a few years ago, and they tore down Pearl's dark green satin hangings, built shelves, sanded the floors, and painted the walls ivory, emphasizing the graceful arch where the walls merged with the ceiling. Meanwhile, Yvonne sewed ivory lace curtains for the long windows, bought a soft ivory carpet, and dyed white fabrics of different textures in the same hue of ivory, so that she could make slipcovers and pillows for the chairs and sofas she'd brought here from her apartment. It gave her pleasure to tell Robert how she'd managed to find what she needed despite shortages.

Though he couldn't make himself comfortable in their apartment, he told himself that it was important for her to express her decorating talents. After all, she'd given up stimulating work in Boston. Once the apartment was finished, their expenses were sure to go down. But Yvonne had an expensive wardrobe to which she constantly added, and though she sewed most of her clothes, she still chose the best fabrics. Often she'd change outfits three or four times a day. To him she looked good in everything, especially in blue.

"It's your color," he'd say.

She particularly liked evening gowns, chiffons and silks and brocades that she'd wear to restaurants or the theater, moving with such confidence that—even if she was the only woman in a long gown—she never looked overdressed. It was rather that whatever she wore seemed right and made everyone else seem underdressed.

"She makes a lot of things herself," he told his mother one day when she worried about Yvonne's constant spending. "She finds remnants, puts them together in interesting ways."

"I know she sews beautifully. But that carpet she bought was not a remnant. And the mirror she put on your closet door wasn't inexpensive either."

He didn't tell Yvonne about that conversation because she already felt intimidated by his mother's accomplishments in the kitchen, felt ignored because his mother never commented on the style and colors of new clothes. Still, she welcomed his mother's invitation to dinner every evening since it kept her out of the kitchen and made it possible to spend her days decorating the apartment or sewing clothes.

Yvonne was intrigued by what she thought of as Stefan's European ways—how he bowed his head when he held her chair for her, inquired about her day. But when Helene tried to include her in conversations, Yvonne gave brief answers and retreated into strained silences that baffled Helene.

Yvonne liked it when Greta joined them for dinner or invited her along on her daily walks; and she enjoyed visiting Pearl Bloom and sitting with her at the marble table in her greenhouse. That greenhouse allowed Miss Garland a view into the Blooms' life, and she was able to confirm what others in the *Wasserburg* suspected: that Stanley Poggs had indeed become Nate's successor.

"What else did you see?" Mrs. Perelli asked, eyes bright.

"Scandalous," others said.

"What's most scandalous," Miss Garland informed them, "is that Pearl Bloom doesn't even hide their affair from her husband."

"You mean he knows?"

"Approves of it." She'd describe to anyone willing to listen how the three of them would sit at the dinner table, Pearl in the middle, sometimes holding the hands of both men.

"Unnatural," Mrs. Evans told the other tenants.

"Deviant," Mrs. Heflin told her customers when she added up their groceries.

One morning, when Pearl had her first cup of coffee and saw the curtain shifting in Miss Garland's window across the courtyard, she strode into the greenhouse, opened her bathrobe, and pressed her bare breasts against the cool glass. Already, she could picture herself telling Nate how unexpectedly sensuous her breasts felt. High and taut. As though she were twenty years younger. So much of her daily pleasure came from imagining herself talking to him about moments as she experienced them. To him and Helene. She used to save all that up for Helene, but Nate's illness had made him a better listener.

"If the crone has a heart attack," he said, "you can sing at her funeral."

"What a great idea."

To Helene she said, "What does that woman want from me?"

"The same thing she wants from all of us. A piece of our lives."

"Right. Well, this is a part she can't have. Stanley is like a brother to Nate. He takes care of things for all of us. He knows where everything is. It's like—like being with the younger Nate all over again."

"Maybe that's how Nate keeps you."

Pearl nodded gravely. "Maybe he believes that. Except I wouldn't have left him. Not for getting old . . . Or ill."

"I know."

"Stanley and I haven't done anything that Nate hasn't wanted for all of us."

"There are different ways in which people can live together. . . ."

"I adore Nate. How many men would be that understanding? He knew what I needed long before I missed it . . . so he chose someone who is loyal to him."

"What about you?"

"Me?" Pearl smiled. "I have grown awfully fond of Stanley. His mind and his body."

∽

On his way home from work, when Robert stopped to check his mailbox, he glanced toward Miss Garland's door, hoping that she wouldn't come out and detain him. Relieved that her door remained closed, he started toward the elevator when it occurred to him that he hadn't seen her in days. Usually she'd open her door at least a gap when he'd pick up the mail and ask him about his work, his parents, and, lately, about Yvonne in a voice that was both coy and hurt as if he'd betrayed her by marrying.

Just yesterday Pearl Bloom had mentioned that Miss Garland hadn't been watching her in the greenhouse. "Probably because I blinded her with my breasts. I wish I'd thought of it sooner."

Robert hesitated, then knocked on Miss Garland's door. No sound. When he tried the knob, it turned. The door moved a bit before it stopped. "Miss Garland? It's me, Robert. Are you there?" When he leaned against it, it yielded a little further. Whatever blocked it appeared to be soft. That's when he noticed the odor. He gagged at the sudden image of rice, *moist and white and swarming. Dead people turn into rice Robert dear Robert dear—*

He wanted to yank the door shut. Instead he stared at the old woman who'd become slighter with age. Yet he did not see her as she was there on the floor, but as she had been, alone in that apartment, feet in embroidered slippers, head tilted toward any sound that might come from the hallway. *She arranges chewy bars of peanut brittle on a flowered plate. Makes maple ice cream by drizzling syrup over a bowl of new snow.* But then he saw her falling. *Crawling toward the door for help.*

How long did she lie there before she died?

Did she call out for me?

When did I last visit her?

Six years, he realized. Six years since she'd sent him that note, asking to meet with him. *For official reasons,* she had written. And when he'd arrived, her eyes had been cloudy with shame, and it had taken her a while to come out with the words.

"I thought I had enough saved, but— It's almost gone, my rent money."

"No one needs to know," he'd assured her.

"I never expected to live to eighty. And look at me now. Ninety-two, Robert dear."

"I'll talk to my parents. I'm sure they'll want you to stay."

"I can't imagine why . . ." She faltered. ". . . why I keep surviving people much younger than me." She raised her face toward him, her skin the texture of dry bread, and fidgeted with the top button of her blouse. "It's against all laws of speculation."

And because he no longer had any of his childhood love for her, he knew he had failed her. Failed her terribly with that absence of love. "I don't want you to worry. Will you promise me that?"

Without telling his parents, he had instructed his bank to make monthly transfers to her account, buying his freedom from further visits. But those contributions—easy enough before his marriage— had become a strain now that he had a wife. So far he'd postponed telling Yvonne because he had figured Miss Garland wouldn't live much longer. What if he'd brought on her death with that thought?

When the morticians arrived to claim the body, her rigid form— covered with a white sheet on the stretcher—looked solid, heavy, as if resisting her final evacuation from the house that had inspired her stories of gala balls, of dashing beaus and of a young fiancé who had preceded her into death, wearing her diamond ring on a bracelet she'd braided from her hair. Robert stood aside to let the stretcher pass him. When he stepped into the apartment and turned on the light, he felt shifted into an earlier time: her living room was unchanged except for a fading of colors as though she had managed to do here what she could not accomplish with her body— preserve it the way it had been. *Dead people turn into rice, Robert dear.* What Greta had called the fussy old lady smell still hung about. That, and the smell of rotting flesh.

Since he'd never been invited into Miss Garland's bedroom, he felt as if he were betraying her as he entered. Shabbiness furnished the room: the thin mattress, the scratched chair by the window, the dresser where she had placed a framed picture of him, tilting him right back to the spring morning his father had taken that photo on the dock. *Seven? I must have been seven.* Waking early to find his father in the hallway about to leave with the camera his mother gave him for Christmas. Asking: "Where are you going, *Vati?*"

"Out on the dock. To take some pictures of the house."

"Can I come?" Asking yet expecting his father to say no and rush from him toward whatever his father was usually rushing toward.

But his father nodded. "If you can get dressed in five minutes."

Near the dock, skeleton branches stuck from the water, black-shiny beneath the surface, silver above. Pockets of mist. Leaves floating close to shore.

"Are you warm enough, Robert?"

Nodding, though chilled. Feeling closer to his father than usual. Because he had asked. *"Are you warm enough, Robert?"* And then his father pointing toward the paling sky, toward the faint echoes of stars. Naming them quickly. And already the panic of not remembering if his father were to ask him tomorrow. The panic of not being enough for his father. *But it didn't show in my photo, that panic. Because I was already figuring out my own ways of being a man. Different from him.*

On Miss Garland's windowsill stood an ivy plant, still healthy, though dry, next to a shoe box filled with the pictures Robert had colored for her as a boy, old tenants' society newsletters: *Please, don't drag sand into the lobby from the beach! Please, shake your umbrellas before bringing them into the building! Please . . . Please . . . Please . . .* Tucked beneath the newsletters was a yellowed envelope, ROBERT BLAU printed on it, containing funeral instructions and the money for her burial, the one responsibility she must have rated higher than rent.

As he closed the box, Robert wondered if the ghosts of her invented past would stay in her apartment, confined to this space, and he suddenly found himself smiling as he concluded that they might as well. After all, they were no more peculiar than the people who already lived in the *Wasserburg,* starting with his sister who healed others; Pearl Bloom who lived with both a husband and a lover; Buddy Hedge who could pull Christmas from his closet any day of the year; Fanny Braddock who rubbed herself against men in the elevator; even he who was married to a woman so beautiful that just looking at her filled him with dread that she was about to leave him.

∽

It was evident that Pearl took pride in the powers of her bare breasts, and she liked to retell that story of Miss Garland staring at her from across the courtyard. With each telling, the interval between the flashing of her breasts and the old woman's death decreased until, finally, it shrank into one incident—Miss Garland

clutching at her throat, falling, while Pearl pulled her robe closed—
and the gossip in the *Wasserburg* would carry that story beyond its
walls until it became yet another one of the town's stories about
Stefan Blau's house that the children of Winnipesaukee would grow
up with, the story about the ancient woman who was struck dead
by the sight of the hussy's breasts.

Now that Pearl lived on the first floor, Helene missed the mes-
sage system they had established via pipes and dumbwaiter; but she
realized soon that her daughter-in-law was quite helpless when it
came to matters of the kitchen, and she encouraged her to borrow
whatever she needed. Soon the dumbwaiter was in operation
again—*one knock: open the dumbwaiter; two knocks: come to the
window*—transporting sugar and apples and sponges and soap and
whatever else Yvonne forgot to buy. Like Pearl, Yvonne never returned anything.

"Must have something to do with the apartment beneath us
swallowing things up," Stefan joked.

"At least Pearl meant to return things."

"Yes, for over thirty years."

"She has given so many gifts to the children. And to us."

"But never what she borrowed."

"More than she ever borrowed. While Yvonne doesn't recipro-
cate."

Yet, if others talked about her daughter-in-law, Helene defended
her. Because of Robert. One afternoon she saw Yvonne pour fresh
milk into a bowl, dip a dustcloth into it, and wipe the leaves of a
rubber plant until they glowed. To squander food on a plant—even
only a few pennies' worth—struck Helene as excessive and embodied everything she distrusted in her daughter-in-law.

Yet, when she mentioned it, Yvonne struck back. "Stuffing food
into people is more of a waste than rubbing it on plants."

Both women felt something so volatile beneath their first clash
that they retreated quickly, alarmed where this could have taken
them. From then on, Helene tried not to notice Yvonne's wastefulness. But how could anyone miss it? Before Robert's marriage,
they'd never had any water problems in the *Wasserburg*. But
Yvonne used too much soap, too much water, causing Mrs. Perelli's

kitchen sink in the apartment below to fill with foam that bubbled up from the drain.

When Danny Wilson explained to both women that an older house with two-inch drains and half-inch water pipes wasn't set up for that kind of water use, Yvonne asked why they didn't change over to larger pipes.

"Why don't you suggest that to your father-in-law?" Mrs. Perelli told her.

Yvonne turned to Danny. "Not if it's an ignorant question. Is it?"

"Yes."

"Tell me why."

When Danny wrote to Tobias, he told him he liked Yvonne's directness. "At least with her you know she won't ask the same stupid question twice. She listened closely when I explained to her about the plumbing and what it would take to redo a house that size. Mrs. Perelli, though, she'd love to blame Yvonne for anything."

Rosalie Perelli continued to be suspicious of Yvonne, and for good reason, it turned out, because Yvonne Blau dyed a bath mat to match her yellow towels and hung it out one night right above the Perellis' wash line. Nothing had ever happened to their laundry, but that morning Rosalie Perelli discovered yellow drips in four of her bloomers.

"Like pee stains," Mrs. Perelli complained when she appeared at Yvonne's door with her bloomers, eyes furious in her lined face. "I insist that you replace these."

Yvonne frowned. "How do I know they are not pee stains?"

"They probably were," Robert said when he heard about it, and they laughed together. He adored her quick wit, her straight way of delivering outrageous lines. With her, you didn't always know if she intended to be funny because she could say things like that with the most serious expression.

One morning, she got him to dance the tango with her while still in his socks by telling him it was part of New Hampshire marriage law. "Really. If one of us wants to dance, the other one has to."

"You're so good at making things up."

"In other countries it's not dancing but something else, like herding goats or making cheese."

He spun her around, her face at the same height with his, and she drew him to the bed, pressed her forehead against his.

"Stay home with me," she said.

∽

Soon, she longed for clear soups.

For paper-thin slices of meat without gravy.

For salads and raw vegetables.

For white bread instead of the solid *Graubrot* that her mother-in-law baked.

Most of all she longed for small portions. For herself. Even more so for her husband. But his mother kept urging seconds on everyone, and he eagerly accepted, while Yvonne could barely swallow as she watched him distend his body even more. As soon as she'd get him back to their own apartment, she'd throw out the leftovers that his mother invariably wrapped for his lunch.

One evening, when she slammed the lid back on the trash can, words finally burst from her: "She'll stuff you with that German food until you're too heavy to move, until no one else wants you." His eyes were so frightened that she stopped herself. "I'm sorry," she whispered.

But his mother's food made her think of everything she'd heard and read about Germans. Weighty. Humorless. Orderly. And not just the food. But also that German way of getting things done right away. And in only one certain way. As her mother-in-law did. Suddenly she felt ashamed thinking about her mother-in-law that way. Hadn't she always formed her opinions based on what people did as individuals?

"I'm sorry," she said again.

"We can eat here, at home," Robert said. "You and I."

"I didn't mean to hurt you. Do you know that?"

He felt hungry. So hungry that his entire belly was aching. "Let's not talk about it right now."

She nodded. "Maybe it would be nice to be alone more . . . together, I mean, you and I."

When Greta made her next trip to Boston, Yvonne asked her to buy cookbooks and a set of pots with copper bottoms. For five weeks she retreated from the pattern of family dinners and labored over meals that refused to turn out the way they looked in the pictures. Though Robert pretended to enjoy the meager rations that were usually dry and bland, he felt ravenous. After Yvonne presented him with his breakfast of oat flakes and sliced fruit, he'd stop at the bakery, get a dozen uglies, devour five or six of them on the way to work, and finish the rest with the salad she'd packed for his lunch. He began to stash food at his clinic, and before returning home for dinner, he'd fix himself a couple of cheese sandwiches.

He thought about food almost constantly. Sometimes, to keep from eating, he'd escape into the tub. After filling it halfway, he'd lower himself into the warm water as it rose to the top of the high rim. In the tub he felt weightless, agile even. He'd add some hot water. Swish it across his body with his hands. Add more. He'd postpone getting out of the tub till the steam had cleared from the hexagonal tiles and the water had turned lukewarm. When he'd climb across the enameled rim, he'd hate the way his flesh moved, the way his stomach got in the way as he bent to dry his legs. Straightening himself with a sigh, he'd reach for the ointment on the shelf and spread a thin coating on the insides of his thighs where they were usually chafed from rubbing against each other. He'd rinse the sulphur smell of the medication from his hands and take his bathrobe from the hook by the door.

But the hunger would be waiting for him. Stalled. But not subdued.

Worried about being hungry after his next meal, Robert would eat far more than he used to, and he'd get so afraid of food that the only thing to stop that fear was to eat even more, leaving him disgusted with *Fatboy who presses himself against his insides, keeps him imprisoned, demands more as he pushes his flesh, his skin outward. Fatboy who has him on his knees in front of the toilet, one finger down his throat.* He had discovered vomiting one evening in college when he'd eaten so much that he had to throw up. Instantly, he'd felt *better. That instant release. A lightness, even.* After that he'd started doing it on purpose, figuring he could eat all he wanted now without gaining weight. Without consequences. Oh, but there were consequences. He knew that now. Knew it with each drop of water that splashed from the bowl into his face.

Many times he had tried to exorcize Fatboy as though he were an evil spirit; but, just like an evil spirit, the image of his fat self kept haunting him, threatening to reclaim him. To ward Fatboy off, he'd gone on fasts and long walks. Anything to keep Fatboy away. Yet, he was constantly aware of Fatboy, waiting for him to fail so he could take his place. Whenever he became self-conscious, he felt Fatboy behind him. He didn't have to turn around to know what Fatboy looked like—he knew: his features, his body, only bigger as in the fat mirror at the fair. *The crowd files past Fatboy who sits on a ridiculously small stool, wearing a sequined shirt and tight-tight trousers. His rolls of flesh quiver with each laborious breath. Laid out in front of him is a display of cakes, fifteen different kinds, baked especially for him every day. Steadily, he eats one after the other, wiping powdered sugar from his lips and chins.*

Always an audience.

Incredulous eyes fasten on Fatboy's bulk with fascination and horror. That's what they're here for: not to see the bearded girl or the beagle with two heads, but to watch Fatboy expand in front of their eyes.

❧

When Yvonne burned hard-boiled eggs and lost two kettles to charred bottoms, Robert tried to laugh with her about the mishaps; but he was relieved when she decided that cooking was tedious and let him talk her into resuming their dinners with his mother and father.

Though he worshiped his wife, even worshiped the sound of saying "my wife" when he introduced her, he tried to prolong those evenings with his parents. To be alone with Yvonne was confusing. Complicated. Sometimes he was afraid to comply with her request to play the piano for her at night—"Just for me, Robert"—but when he did, he became so immersed in the music that he felt surprised, invaded even, when he glanced up and discovered the desire in Yvonne's eyes. But he had already learned to keep himself at the piano, resisting his longing to take her into his arms because he knew her desire would vanish as soon as he held her.

Yvonne felt exhilarated, awed, when he removed himself into regions where she couldn't follow him and—by that act alone—almost made them accessible to her. However, if he raised his hands from the keys to touch her, the reality of his massive body repelled her, and she felt herself go rigid. Ashamed. Because it made her feel like a tease, a bitch. She didn't want to be like that, and when he'd release her, instantly, eyes distant with hurt, she'd feel compelled to cling to him with excessive caresses that would lead to contrite lovemaking, which left both of them bewildered. Their first child, Caleb—long limbed and exquisite like his mother—would be conceived during one of those nights of troubled copulation just three months after their wedding day.

CHAPTER NINE

1945—1953

After her initial shock, Yvonne began to sew elegant maternity clothes. Pregnancy was a reason for an entire new wardrobe—flowing materials that concealed her swelling body and lent a slow harmony to her movements. Every night when she oiled her breasts and belly to prevent stretch marks, Robert watched her, paralyzed by the old fear—*babies kill mothers*. How had his father ever dared to marry again after burying his first wife? His second? In this fear, Robert felt more linked to his father than ever before. Again and again, he apologized to Yvonne for endangering her life, for settling her with stretch marks and with varicose veins that began to branch out on her left leg. It made Yvonne feel generous to reassure him.

Caleb was born with his eyes wide open—tranquil and intuitive, his grandmother thought as she guided his head in her palms. Dr. Miles was letting her help, and her grandson was gazing at her as if he knew her and wanted her to bring him toward her and away from his mother whose body still confined his shoulders.

From the beginning of his life, Caleb would absorb all that happened around him—pictures and sounds and smells and touch and taste—take them all in long before words would define them for him, and spin them further, transform them. He would see his surroundings the way a painter would, understanding instinctively how everything picked up light and color from everything else.

Like the lake where his mother would take him that first summer of his life, prop him up on the dock in a basket with blankets so that his head would be supported, and swim back and forth in front of him so that he could watch her splash and wave. The reflections in the lake would be a mingling of many colors: his mother's skin and hair; the mountains and dock; sky and the houses along the shore. And then there was the color of the water itself. Ever-changing. While the dock and houses and his mother would absorb the light that bounced off the water.

⁓

From the instant her son was born, Yvonne was fascinated by him. No one had told her it would be like this. How it moved her—the softness of his downy head in the hollow between her neck and shoulder, that feather of breath against her skin. With astonishment she watched Caleb's face as he sucked pale strands of milk from her breasts. She was the only one who could do that for him—Helene might bathe him or change his diaper, but she was the one who connected her son to life with an intensity that shut out all else, even those God awful lonely-attacks. Her hair took on a new shimmer, and she smiled when people commented on the softness in her features.

With a child in her arm at her breast, she felt something unfamiliar that she finally defined as joy, a joy that often lasted for hours and spilled onto others because it was too vast for one child to absorb, a joy that made her feel benevolent toward her family, even the town.

With a child in her arm at her breast, she was no longer intimidated by Helene's cooking skills.

With a child in her arm at her breast, it was only natural to request household help.

Though Robert couldn't afford a maid, he was so grateful that Yvonne had survived childbirth, that he didn't mind cleaning the apartment on Sundays. Yet around Caleb he felt clumsy. Odd, how with newborn dogs and cats—tinier than newborn humans—he was capable, skillful, perhaps because his responsibility for their lives lasted only a brief time. This infant, however, was here to stay.

He admired Yvonne's ease as she held and bathed Caleb, admired her tenderness with their son. *If only she would touch me with such joy. But that's jealous. Wrong.*

He noticed how some tenants regarded him with respect as if his son were a miracle, and how his parents, too, were treating him differently now that he had moved on from being a son to being a parent, equal with them since his own son had taken up the role of child. Sometimes he sang to Caleb in a melodious voice that—had the older people of Winnipesaukee heard him—would have reminded them of Stefan Blau's tenor in church before his deal with God had proven worthless.

Gradually, as Robert learned from Yvonne how to bathe and rock his son, he forgave himself for risking her life, and years later during one of her many absences when he'd look back on their marriage, he'd see her holding their son as if she were in a painting—always holding him and always surrounded by light—and he would understand that those early months with their son had been the best part of their marriage.

Caleb brought out the light and kindness in Yvonne that Robert knew she was capable of, but that his parents were unable to see. "My two boys," she'd say to Robert some evenings while nursing their son, raising her hand from Caleb's face to his, and he'd feel glutted with bliss.

Cautiously, he'd move through her ivory rooms that were too bright for him, too likely to be stained. Wishing he could shrink his bulk, he'd end up standing in the kitchen with milk and cookies or, if there were no cookies, bread with butter and sugar until the sugar made him queasy and he'd neutralize it by sprinkling salt on the buttered bread instead. And keep eating.

One morning while getting dressed, he saw Yvonne watching him from the bed. Instantly, he felt Fatboy standing right behind him. He knew if he turned around Fatboy would be gone: he never came face to face with him. That wasn't the way Fatboy waited. But he was there, massively, persistently, studying every movement Robert made, gloating when the scale revealed a gain because it lessened the distance between them. At times he slipped into

Robert's place, fumbling and blushing, larger and more grotesque every minute. While Robert's walk, his movements became awkward.

To stop Yvonne from seeing him like that, he said quickly, "I've been thinking about cutting out sweets."

"What a good idea." She raised herself on her elbows, sounding pleased as he knew she would. "Just think, if you lose one pound each week, you'll be trim in two years."

"That doesn't sound too hard," he lied. How could he ever tell her about Fatboy? About all those times he'd tried to destroy Fatboy by becoming thin? During his sophomore year at Ohio State he'd lost the weight gained in high school. But even then he'd never felt thin enough. One by one the pounds had come back and he had to start all over again.

"One year if you lose two pounds a week." She nodded as though she could already see him trim. "I'll help you. I know how to lose weight. Remember how quickly I lost my pregnancy weight? How I got right back to my size?"

Sometimes she bought suits for him that hid some of his weight, clothes that made people at the clinic ask if he was getting thinner. But thin never felt real. He would have loved to have a twenty-six-inch waist. So he wouldn't have to be afraid to eat. So he could keep Fatboy away. When he felt good about himself, he'd forget about Fatboy for a while, but other times he felt him close by. Fatboy had taken him over in stores, in the apartments of tenants, in his father's restaurant, even in bed with Yvonne. But Fatboy had never claimed him at work, though Robert sometimes felt him waiting outside the clinic. In his work Robert felt safe. There, Fatboy could not get him.

❧

Helene Blau was one of those women who grow beautiful with age, whose features—though never pretty in girlhood—take on a loveliness during the years when many women mourn the passing of their youth. In her sixties, she had finally claimed her body, grown into her shoulders instead of denying their magnificent span. She even moved differently, with a certain harmony and fluidity, comfortable with the space her body took up. At times this new awareness of herself made her feel almost giddy, extravagant.

Ready for further changes, she went with Pearl one afternoon to get her gray hair cut to chin length. Bought lipstick in a deep shade of red. Purple tulips. Filled three short glass vases with water, and trimmed the stems so the blossoms were close together, petals of flame-tipped purple, a surface of colors you looked down into, so different from the way she usually arranged flowers, leaving their stems long, their blossoms falling away from each other.

Stefan noticed her lighter step, that different tilt to her neck as if the grace that had manifested itself in those letters she'd sent him from Germany had now shifted to her body. No longer did she have to endure comparison to his previous wives: they had stayed behind, fading more every year, turning into girls younger than Greta until they had become transparent. What Helene had with him was solid—friendship, esteem. She had learned to balance her love for him with that for her son and grandson; and what was left for Stefan was the right portion, a portion that did not make him uncomfortable.

Still, there were times when he missed the all-consuming passion she used to center on him. One night he watched her calm face on the pillow next to his, and it stirred him beyond language when she turned toward him in her sleep and—in that moment of turning—reached for the back of her neck as she had for so many years to gather and move her mass of hair along with her body in that one motion of turning. And though her neck was bare now and her hand stayed empty, her body completed that motion without waking.

After a while, when the pattern of her breath changed, he reached for her wrist and curled his fingers around its width.

"You can't sleep?" she asked.

"What happened to that early love of yours, Lenchen?" he whispered, half expecting her to say she didn't know what he meant.

But she knew. Oh, she knew. And was far more familiar with the touch of her own hands. Had preferred it ever since she'd understood that Robert would be her one chance at a child of her own. To mate with any passion seemed frivolous after the knowledge that Stefan would not impregnate her again.

"Lenchen?" He rubbed two fingers across the soft base of her thumb.

"You mean the way I used to love you?" she murmured. "Without holding back . . . ?"

In the dark, he felt the blood racing through every vein in his body as though he were in one of those medical textbook pictures with all his insides exposed, and he felt certain that if he let himself think about the intricacy of that network of veins and nerves and bones for too long, his body would stop working.

Next to him, Helene was so still that he wondered if, perhaps, she had dozed off. But she laced her strong fingers through his. "Stefan—"

"Yes?"

The rustling of sheets and pillows. "Would you really want that again?"

Yes, he wanted to say, *yes,* but the truth was that he wasn't certain. To accept a passion that immense carried far too much responsibility. To ask for it was even more risky. He felt her waiting for his answer. Patiently. Insistently. And felt his eyes forced open with sudden tears. *All those years . . . the waste of all those years I wasn't with her fully because I grieved for the other two. Even those years with Sara I was grieving for Elizabeth.*

"Yes," he said.

"I am not sure," he said.

"Forgive me," he said.

∾

One afternoon that fall, when Yvonne's heart felt too generous for her family alone, she offered to help with the packages that Helene sent regularly to her old neighborhood in Germany. Together with Rosalie Perelli and Pearl Bloom, she inserted the leaves in Helene's mahogany table and spread out items that several of the tenants had dropped off: a lace bed jacket and three pairs of hardly worn shoes from Mrs. Evans; two suits with vests from Buddy Hedge who'd retired from the school; four aprons and a flashlight from Mrs. Perelli. Others in the *Wasserburg* had contributed canned food and even money that Helene was rolling up tightly and, as usual, hiding in the cores of wooden spools.

When Yvonne read the thank-you letter that Robert's cousin Trudi had sent back with lists of what was needed most—flour and rice; dried eggs and dried milk; blankets and clothing; cigarettes to use as currency—she realized how hungry the people in Germany were. Cold and hungry. Although she'd read about that in the papers, it wasn't the same as finding out from her husband's German relatives. She began to worry about them, especially Uncle Leo whose knee had gotten worse. Whenever she went to Heflins', she bought a few special things, not just the basics the German relatives asked for, but smoked sausage, hard lemon candies, powdered chocolate to make that dry milk more appetizing.

One evening, when she was helping Helene and Pearl with another package, she volunteered to shop for clothes, to find specific sizes and colors—something Pearl acknowledged she was good at.

But Helene told her, "It's better to send used clothing."

"I think it would be more generous to give them something new."

"It isn't generous if they don't receive it," Helene said. "Trudi wrote that things get stolen on the way. Worn clothes have a better chance of getting there."

"Why don't you wrap the gifts," Pearl encouraged Yvonne. She turned to Helene. "You've seen what Yvonne can do with a piece of leftover wallpaper and some yarn. She makes the most gorgeous gift boxes."

"I can do that," Yvonne said, pleased. "I can also—"

"Anything wrapped like that," Helene interrupted, "will look new."

Yvonne glared at her mother-in-law. *Always adding her gloom. Her German gloom.*

"But you could sew for them," Helene offered.

Yvonne hesitated.

"I'll help," Helene said. "If you show me what to do."

That week, she and Yvonne sewed a cherry-red blouse for the midwife in Burgdorf from the lining of Nate Bloom's old coat; a bathrobe for Stefan's mother cut from the Staneks' blue towels that had frayed around the edges but otherwise were still good; four striped silk ties from one of Mrs. Klein's skirts. At first it felt odd to Yvonne to be teaching her mother-in-law anything, but Helene accepted instruction so willingly that Yvonne enjoyed working with her, patient if a seam needed to be undone, praising her when she completed something.

∞

As Caleb turned from Yvonne's breast and that very first bone-aching need, she lost the fascination that had bonded her to him. It was her yearning for that intensity and for that status of early motherhood—not for another child—that led to her next pregnancy. But Emma, born two years after Caleb, was not the serene child Yvonne had envisioned. A stocky and red-faced infant who'd fight sleep until she was exhausted from crying, she would clutch her mother's hair or breast, trying to force her into merging with her once again, making the journey back to that fusion of blood and flesh.

Though Yvonne would try to soothe her, she'd usually end up pulling herself free from this daughter who tugged at her nipple and depleted her instead of filling her with contentment. Some days she felt so afraid of Emma's fierce needs that she'd yearn to lash out at her. But she'd make herself turn from the red-screaming face because she was not about to hurt her child. *Though I want to. Oh how I want to. Never the boy, though. Never Caleb.* Beating your child bloody-blue did not fit into the way Yvonne saw herself as a mother, did not fit the image of herself *bending over a happily gurgling child, satisfying and calming that child with her presence alone, smiling while her dark blue hair—shining, always shining—emphasizes her pale profile. . . .*

But the child she pictured had no resemblance to Emma, who would tear at your hair if you ever were to let it hang close enough to those greedy fists. To divert that urge of hurting Emma, Yvonne would break a plate or tear a newspaper. Usually that would settle her. And if not, she knew how to stop from harming her daughter by bringing the hurt to her own skin. By spilling hot coffee on herself. Or beating her hands against the tiled wall of the bathroom. Sometimes she stood in front of the stove, watched the wide coils of the right front burner redden, and imagined pressing her palms against that slow glow. But she always stopped there. Because if she did, Robert would notice. And who would bathe Caleb? Change

Emma's diapers? Easier to cut the insides of her upper arms. Move the paring knife through soft, pale flesh till she felt calm. Hidden beneath sleeves in the day. By the dark at night. Robert made love in the dark, ashamed of his body. Believing her body to be so perfect. How little he knew of her.

To make up to Emma for that rush of destruction that Yvonne never let her see but that the child, nonetheless, could feel behind the strained smile, Yvonne would flood her with affection, confusing her. *But at least I've never hurt my babies.* It gave Yvonne some comfort to remind herself that. And brought back the sensation of being *small and flying at her parents' bedroom door as they lock it against her—too late, she's always too late—beating her hands against their door till all she becomes is the wing-beat of her hands, such ugly hands, the slap and flutter that drown all other sounds.*

What terrified her most about being a parent was that you never knew which of your actions would affect your children for life. And because she wanted them to remember her as lighthearted and loving, she would dance with them around the apartment, take them hiking or skiing or swimming, depending on the season. She'd build kites for them from narrow slats of wood and half-transparent paper—green or blue or red—making the tail by tying bows of tissue paper and spacing them five inches apart along the length of twine, enchanting Caleb and Emma with her playfulness so much so that, sometimes, it all would become real.

But never for long. Then she'd pass the children along to Robert. And so Emma and Caleb both switched parents: from their mother during that initial season of need—their need as well as hers—to their father, steady and kind and large, who could lift anything with his strong arms, who made music for them with fast-flying fingers, who always had stories and sweets for them when he'd tuck them in at night, who knew that Caleb liked to fall asleep with the light on, and that Emma needed more blankets in the evening, when her skin felt cold, than in the morning because she'd only throw them off once she had warmed herself with sleep.

Though the Blau children wouldn't be able to explain this to themselves, they'd always feel a searing, wordless link to their mother, a longing that had not been satisfied entirely, though—for a brief time—they both had known the promise of it. And while Caleb would find that link within himself and, eventually, translate it into films that would make audiences feel they were watching something too intimate to witness, Emma would seek that connection in others, chasing a bliss so inflated by memory that she would only be able to match it with her *Opa*—grandfather—who would be alive till she was six, long enough to infuse her with his passion for the *Wasserburg*.

That day of Emma's birth, when Stefan had first held her, he'd felt startled because he'd recognized the whirling child from his long-ago vision. Decades ago, after his own children had been born, he'd stopped searching for that child, but now that she was here, he felt entitled to her because she was his family—more so than anyone before her—giving him an even stronger foothold in America than he'd thought possible. Drawn to Emma's need—the very same need that now repelled Yvonne—he marveled at the grasp of those tiny hands, the force of her wail, and he predicted it would be impossible to wrestle anything from her if she refused to let go, a prediction that Caleb would remember years later.

Stefan's bond to Emma was instant and far stronger than his bond to Helene, to his children, or even to his dead wives. And he was sure Emma understood that, because as soon as she learned to walk, she'd head for him first. He lulled her into the German language, although Robert reminded him that it wasn't wise to speak German in public, and Emma grew to cherish the language so much that, often, she refused to answer her parents when they spoke English with her.

"*Hoppe, hoppe Reiter, wenn er fällt dann schreit er . . .*" was her favorite game. Her *Opa* would bounce her on his knees—" *. . . fällt er in den Graben, fressen ihn die Raben . . .*"—and she would ride across ditches, past ravens to the final tumble into the swamp, "*Plumps,*" squealing with delight as *Opa*'s knees opened and she fell, fell into bottomless adventure and exhilaration while his hands pulled her up again to another "*Plumps,*" her breath snagging with a sound that was as close to laughing as it was to crying when she plummeted again and again, confident her hands were anchored in *Opa*'s. They had other games, of course, but none left Emma as breathless. "More," she would cry each time he'd pull her up, "more."

Whenever they had dinner at *Opa*'s apartment, Emma would claim the chair next to him and sit on top of the old encyclopedias from Germany that used to boost her *Vati* on the piano bench when he was a boy. *Opa* had told her that sitting on those leather-bound books would put the German words right into her blood. While Robert enjoyed it when Emma called him *Vati,* he spoke English with both children. Though Yvonne agreed with him that it was better for the children to not be identified as German, she rather liked it that they were growing up bilingual because she had always wanted to speak more than one language and had admired that ability in Robert, although, considering the times, she would have preferred French or Italian.

It not only astonished everyone in the family but also the tenants how much Stefan Blau, who'd never been one to fuss over children, adored his granddaughter. While Helene was glad that he was capable of such joy in a child, she felt disappointed that his own children had missed out on that. And Yvonne, though relieved whenever Stefan took Emma along, felt jealous because it seemed too easy for Emma to leave her behind. To be the object of Emma's unrestrained devotion—she missed it as much as she had dreaded it.

And now Emma's affection had shifted to her grandfather. Yvonne was reminded of it in a hundred ways. Like one summer afternoon, when the entire family was walking on the path by the lake, and she stretched out her hand for Emma. Who reached for Stefan's hand instead. It was over in a second. And of no significance, Yvonne told herself. No significance, really.

But why then did she feel cut to the bone?

Why then did she hate Stefan as he crouched, circled his arms around Emma's shoulders, and told her, "I want you to hold your *Mutti*'s hand"?

Why then did she have tears in her eyes as she walked away from her daughter and said, "You don't have to"?

❧

Emma learned to dodge the warm milk that her *Oma*—grand-mother—insisted was good for children, but Caleb said the skin was the best part. It made Emma shudder when he slurped it up, flecks of white on his lips.

"Your Uncle Tobias was like you about milk," *Oma* would say to her and shake her head as if everything bad that had ever happened to Uncle Tobias was a result of his refusal to drink warm milk, like always looking so angry, or like living by himself and being lonely.

But Emma didn't think Uncle Tobias was lonely, because she'd seen him dance with Danny Wilson in Danny Wilson's living room one morning. She'd been playing hide-and-seek with Caleb and had crawled behind the shrubs along the back of the house where the windows were wide but not high, so that when you were outside, you saw the ceiling but not the people inside. Not until you looked down, the way you would into a fish tank. And that morning the people down there had been Uncle Tobias and Danny Wilson, dancing on the couch, and as Emma had watched them from above, she'd noticed how smooth Danny Wilson's back was while her uncle's was covered with black hair so thick it looked like fur.

Another reason Uncle Tobias was never lonely was that he had every book in the world. When her father had taken her for a visit to Uncle Tobias' bookstore in Hartford, he'd let her climb up one of his long ladders that rolled along the shelves and had read her a story from a red leather book.

❧

Those times Tobias slept with other men were not because he was drawn to them, but because of Danny—trying to crowd Danny less with his love; wanting to get even with Danny for not loving him as much as he did. But what Tobias was always left with afterwards was disgust with himself and the unease at having used himself as well as someone else, even if that someone else had gotten what he'd wanted. Still, sex without love felt all wrong—not in the sense the church considered it to be wrong, but in a deeper and more personal way.

In a few years he would be forty, and he no longer wanted to be alone; but whenever he talked to Danny about living together, Danny would get skittish. Distant. That's why their days together were better if Tobias didn't mention it. Though Danny would always start out glad to see him, Tobias would soon feel burdened by maintaining that balance of lightness with his silence. Yet, whenever he managed to keep quiet about moving in together, he'd drive back to Hartford anxious about Danny with other men, especially Stewart Robichaud who worked right next door at the restaurant and had been Danny's first lover.

If only he could see Danny struggle with being faithful. But Danny refused to understand any reasons for being faithful, and Tobias was afraid that if he ever made Danny choose between only him and those others, he'd be sent off by Danny with a generous hug and minor regrets.

One weekend in January, when Danny visited him in Hartford, Tobias got impatient with himself for being cautious and offered, "I'd even move back to Winnipesaukee if you wanted to get a place together."

"You'd get cranky being around your family that much. Besides, you have your work here."

"I bet you could find a really good job here."

"That would be convenient, wouldn't it? For you."

"That's not how I meant it."

"I already got a job."

"What I meant was that there are a lot of apartment buildings in the city, and with your experience—"

"My experience is doing just fine where it is."

"But you've worked in the same place since you were a boy, practically. Do you want to retire there?"

Danny didn't answer. Wouldn't answer when Tobias kept at him with questions. And started to pack, though he'd planned to spend the night. While Tobias stayed behind with the heaviness of wanting more, feeling lost in the house he'd furnished over the years with Danny in mind, choosing the upholstery for his sofa and chairs because Danny liked that deep shade of green, the white lamps because they were similar to the ones Danny had.

At the train station he caught up with Danny. "Why don't we just go back to my place?"

Danny rubbed his forehead. "I got some stuff to take care of."

"Like what?"

Danny shrugged.

"Can't it wait?"

"Not really."

"But you were going to stay," Tobias said, hating the whining in his voice.

Danny turned his head toward the direction from where his train was to come.

Resolutely, Tobias added, "Then I'll come along."

"Now?"

"Because this is important to me."

"Well . . . this weekend won't be that good for me. Why don't you visit some other time soon?"

Visit. When Tobias stepped from the railroad station, frozen leaves clogged the gutters. He kicked them, broke them into clumps. Took sharp breaths to rid himself of the sadness in his throat. *Visit.* He drew up his shoulders. Zipped his leather jacket to his chin. Promised himself to ignore Danny for a while. To stay away from him. Maybe for good. But then Danny called, of course, as he usually did after an argument, and when Tobias took the train to New Hampshire a few weeks later, Danny was excited to see him and gave him expensive ice skates he'd bought for him from last summer's dog track money.

That evening, as they skated away from the *Wasserburg* in their long woolen coats, the moon was pale. Snow capped the mountains across the lake, and beyond those mountains, clouds that were lighter than the sky feathered upward, nearly transparent, as weightless as Tobias felt next to Danny while they raced across the ice.

∽

"Higher," Emma shouted and felt *Opa*'s palms against her back as he pushed the swing. Stretching her sturdy legs, she flew. "Higher."

He laughed. "You're a bossy little girl. I like that."

Flying, still flying, she dropped her head back until she saw *Opa* standing upside down, wind blowing his gray suit jacket to one side. "Higher!"

Red and yellow leaves tumbled across the ground and from branches that were almost bare. In one pile of leaves, a squirrel was playing, its movements as noisy as those of a much larger animal, a dog, say, or even a bear. Otherwise, the garden above the garage was empty since Caleb and the other children in the building were at school. Because she was the youngest, Emma had *Opa* all to herself. She liked it best when they were the only ones here, when she could soar above the sandbox and the stone bench like the seagulls that rode the wind above the lake, their wings graceful, their cries shrill.

"Aren't you hungry?" *Opa* shouted as she came flying back toward him. "What do you want *Opa* to cook for you?"

"A hot dog. With mustard."

"So American."

"And chocolate mousse."

"At least you have good taste when it comes to dessert." He walked to the front of the swing, and as he caught the ropes to slow her down, he saw Tobias on this same swing. *Did I ever catch the ropes for him? Hold him steady? Let him soar?* His sadness at his distance from Tobias had grown sharper ever since Emma had positioned herself in his life. Tobias' visits were rare, and though Stefan wished he'd see him more often, he found it hard to be near his son. Because of the anger in his shoulders. An anger that had been there forever, it seemed. Tobias moved like a man who felt wronged in the world and had learned to be cautious because others were sure to misunderstand him. When he walked, he had to turn his entire body to keep the anger contained in his shoulders because, if he didn't, it would surely swell and spill into his arms, his fists.

"Can I have two hot dogs?" Emma asked.

"With mustard, I know. Hold still," Stefan told her. "You're all tangled."

On the way to his restaurant, yellow leaves drifted toward them, and she caught two, dry and light; but when she rubbed them between her fingers, they got sticky and came apart, making her hand smell green. Like cut grass, only stronger. On the path ahead lay a white stone. Leaves rustled beneath her feet as she ran to pick it up. Smooth, it was smooth, the stone, and it fit into her palm.

Opa bent across it, ran one thumb along its surface. "See? It has a line of gold right down the center."

"Real gold?"

"It's a treasure."

"You can keep it."

"Thank you, Emma." He looked so pleased when he dropped it into his pocket, and she knew that, once they got to his restaurant, he'd lay it into the basket on the shelf with the St. Joseph where he kept all the treats—stones and feathers and shells—that she found for him. Whenever she wanted, he let her play with the Joseph statue, but he always put it back on the shelf because it had given him the land for the *Wasserburg* and his restaurant.

Slipping her fingers into *Opa*'s, she noticed how much prettier the stone was than she'd first thought. It often was like that—seeing something with him made it better. Especially when they went through the house together, checking on repairs that needed to be made, visiting tenants who were always glad to see her, climbing the ladder to the platform above the elevator while the breath-song of the house billowed around her, opening *Opa*'s wooden toolbox to see if he'd left one of his treats for her inside—licorice or crayons or a compass on a key ring.

She liked it when he let her help him with his lists. "Will you remind me to get prices for carpeting?" he'd ask. "Will you remind me to have the laundry room painted?" She prided herself on keeping his lists in her mind, ready to recite them for him. "I wouldn't remember half of this without you," he'd say.

He'd laugh when she did somersaults on the peacock carpets in the hallways; sniffed the old linen blueprints; traced the golden flowers and birds on the flocked wallpaper in the lobby; tap-tapped her fingers against the shrouded Mary-and-Jesus statue in the furnace room.

Sometimes she'd get *Opa* to play the hiding game with her. She'd slip away from him and hide inside one of the tenants' delivery cubicles, trying not to giggle while she'd listen to him search for her.

"Now where did Emma go? I just saw her a minute ago. . . ." And when he'd pull her out, he'd look amazed that he'd found her. "Now tell me what you sat on," he'd say. "A pound of butter? A head of lettuce?"

Her *Opa* loved the *Wasserburg*. And Emma knew she was the only person he loved as much as his building. Because he had seen both her and the *Wasserburg* the very same day—long before she was born. First he had built the *Wasserburg*. Then he had waited for her to get born. "Getting what you want," he had taught her, "has to do with holding it in your mind so strongly that you keep returning to it—without thinking—so that you are always linked to it. That's how I built this house. That's how I came to America."

And that's how I came to be here.

That's how.

∞

"Blau-blau-blau-blau . . ." Frankie Morrell was making fish faces at Caleb, lips puffing outward each time he said "Blau."

One of the other boys started doing it too. "Blau-blau—"

"Stop it." Caleb grabbed his jacket from the rack in back of their classroom.

"What kind of name is Blau anyhow?"

"Blau-blau-blau—"

"It means—"

"Quiet, you boys," their first grade teacher, Miss Heflin, called out to them. "Get your coats on. Hurry up or you'll miss recess." Her voice sounded friendly and impatient at the same time, the can-I-help-you-voice she used when she helped her parents in their grocery store after school and found the children gawking at the display of candies. "Hats *and* mittens," she called after them as they ran out into the snow.

"Blau-blau—"

"It means blue."

"No, it doesn't."

"Does so. In German."

"That's Nazi."

Judy Magill laughed.

Nazi? Caleb didn't know what it meant, only felt its ugliness when several of the children jumped around him, chanting, "Hazi tazi we got a Nazi. . . ." When he ran from them, they chased after him, around the granite building and to the edge of the schoolyard, feet crushing the frail ice that had sealed the puddles overnight— "Hazi tazi we got a Nazi hazi tazi . . ."—and they stopped by the dormant hedge of roses, obeying school rules to not leave the grounds until the final bell. "You'll be in trouble," they shouted after Caleb as he kept running, pressing his thighs together while dampness spread hot against his crotch, already cooling, smelly and heavy. *Hazi tazi?*

Too ashamed to run home, he headed toward Weber's Hardware and the lumberyard, past stone walls and the railroad station. On the other side of the tracks the snow was crusted, and upon it lay the shadows of bare birches, thin and black. *Hazi tazi?* He found a boulder, bare on top where the sun had heated it, though its base was still ringed by snow, and as he sat down, he pulled away from himself the way he often did and into a darkened movie theater— dark and warm and blue like the Royal—watching the screen where *this boy sits with his knees against his chest, shivering, this boy who can't figure out what to do next.* All Caleb had to do was watch as the screen changed to a different day filled with sun while he and *Emma leap from the five wide steps that lead up to the front door. Leap again and again. And then swing by their arms from the wrought-iron railings that run up along both sides of the steps to the posts with stained-glass lanterns.* He wished he were fierce like Emma who got him to do things that were forbidden, like shinnying from windows in the lobby or playing on the fire escape. Bossing him as if she were the older one. Looking out for him when tenants gave them candy, making sure he got as much as she did. A good climber, his sister. Not careful like he. Dreamer, his grandfather called him. Caleb didn't mind. Liked knowing he could dream people and houses and clouds onto a movie screen and watch while dreaming, enter his world on the screen and be part of it while he made it up and embellished it. If that's what it meant to be a dreamer, he was glad he was a dreamer.

Once in a while he'd get Emma to dream along with him, pick

out a house and imagine what it looked like inside and what the people who lived there were like. He called it the people game and loved playing it with his sister, but soon she'd be running off again. She was all body. Liked to jump. To touch things. To have things. Keep them and hoard them: feathers and rocks and coins. Caleb didn't care about having things. Only cared about living inside his head and dreaming. *Till dreaming becomes seeing. Becomes the I-can-use-this. Use for what? Saving what he sees as if a camera inside his head were recording what happened outside of him, pulling it inside, making the inside-seeing and the outside-seeing one.* Much of the time the I-can-use-this was his friend, but sometimes he hated not being able to turn it off. Like when his mother watched his father eat. Or when the kids had shouted, "Hazi tazi . . ."

Wind blew through the wet fabric of his trousers, made his legs feel like ice. *The screen.* He brought himself back to the film, to the boy. And to help the boy, he put the boy's father on the screen too, *who takes the boy's hand. And after the father leads the boy home and draws a warm bath for him and promises not to tell anyone about the pee, the boy in the warm tub knows that the boy waiting in the snow is ready to get up from the rock and go home by himself.* But as he approached the *Wasserburg,* it was not his grandmother he encountered, but his mother who'd come looking for him because Miss Heflin had phoned her. When she ran toward him, he started crying, and she lifted him up, carried him into the building without getting angry at his mess and smell. She sat on the edge of the tub while he bathed and told her what had happened. And while he dried himself off, she called his grandmother.

When he came into the living room, his grandmother was already there, angrier than Caleb had ever seen her. "I'll talk to that Miss Heflin tomorrow. She should have stopped those children from calling him that. That woman couldn't even walk with her polio until her parents brought her to Greta."

Caleb's mother surprised him and his grandmother by kneeling in front of him and saying fervently, "You are not a Nazi." Her eyes were close to his, troubled. "Your grandparents have lived in this country since long before the war. Your grandfather was a boy when he came to America at the end of the last century."

Caleb's grandmother was leaning forward, listening gingerly as his mother explained to him how just as there were different kinds of Americans—Democrats and Republicans—there were different kinds of Germans. "And Nazis were one kind of German," she said. "The bad kind. Bad, evil people. But what I want you to understand and remember is that not all Germans are Nazis. And knowing that makes you wiser and smarter than those other children."

"Thank you, Yvonne." Caleb's grandmother was looking at his mother with respect.

"It's what I believe."

"Yes, but because you're American, you can say it aloud. Because I'm from there, I can't. Americans would only assume I'm defending all Germans. I wish they'd understand that talking with a German accent does not mean I supported the terrible things—" She faltered. Cleared her throat. "What the Nazis did to the Jews over there . . . crimes like that, they go against everything I think of as German. Human."

"We know you didn't support any of that," Caleb's mother said.

"Being German is my oldest identity. . . ." Caleb's grandmother ran one hand up her throat. "I didn't know how afraid I've been of that word until now . . . afraid someone would call me Nazi. No one did. . . . I never thought it would happen to one of my grandchildren. Seven years after it all ended. Maybe it never ends." She shivered. "Maybe it will always be there in some form. It was already going on way back, when I was pregnant with Robert. I tried to be as American as my husband. Even in small things. For so long now, being German has been tied in with being careful about German customs, German food."

Caleb blinked. Other than food and stories about Burgdorf—what else was there to being German? It wouldn't be until fifth grade that he'd begin to understand what else there was to being German, understand it as much as an eleven-year-old can in a history lesson; and he would remember being called Nazi on the playground, remember his mother being there for him while explaining

about good Germans and Nazis, remember his parents meeting
with Miss Heflin, remember Miss Heflin's mother giving him a long
strand of red licorice for free and saying he was a decent boy, really; but most of all he would remember how being German had
shifted that winter day into something far more shameful than wetting your pants, although that, too, the wetting, would enter the
film he would make as a man—not his first film, but the one he
would put off as long as he could because he was fearful of looking
that closely at the history he had inherited, put off until he would
be in his sixties and feel driven to finally take all those other moments that had sucked themselves onto that winter day of shame,
snagging him with the potency of their own picture-making that
continued as if independent of him while he slept or hiked or loved,
fusing moments that conjured feeling German although these moments might not have had anything to do with being German,
and—from that fusion—begetting further pictures and fostering all
within the fascia of his imagination.

∞

Greta saw her father's decline nearly two months before he had his
stroke: it assembled itself in sudden images of a half moon lying
cold upon the lake. She wished she could warn him, but ever since
she was three and had felt Sara's death waiting, she'd understood
that she could do nothing to prevent illness or death. The only person she could talk to about the burden of the gift was Noah Creed
when she visited him in Boston. He understood that her gift was
such that she could soothe, heal even.

To caution her father would not help him and only betray that
gift. But what she could do was urge him to have a checkup, persist
when he objected, and accompany him to Dr. Miles, who'd recently
brought his nephew, Justin Miles, from Chicago into his practice
with the intent to have him take it over once he retired.

When both doctors assured her father he had the body of a man
ten years younger, she wanted to haul him back into the examining
room and tell both doctors—one too young, she thought, the other
getting old—to be more thorough with her father, but she pressed
her tongue against the roof of her mouth, barring those words because she knew her father would not go back in there again.

"Satisfied now?" her father asked her as they got into the car.

In the weeks to come, she increased her visits to his apartment. To ward off his loss, she'd touch his shoulder or his arm, casually, the way you would during a conversation. Quite often she'd find Emma sitting on Stefan's knees, twisting the buttons of his suit jacket or patting her fingertips against the loose skin beneath his jaw to make it sway.

"Your grandfather is not strong enough for that," Greta told her one afternoon.

"Not so." Emma shook her head.

Stefan laughed and repeated what Dr. Miles had told him. "Ten years younger than other men my age."

"Don't let her tire you." As Greta reached for her niece, trying to distract her, the robust little legs scissored her waist. She was a bold child, Emma, a child who liked to get her face right against yours and stare into your eyes as she did now while Greta swung her around. White blond hair—so frizzy and fine it lifted at even the slightest movement or draft—floated around Emma's round face as if about to leave her altogether.

As soon as Greta was gone, Emma climbed back onto her *Opa's* knees and got him to sing with her the rhyme his mother had taught him when he was a boy, the one about the little flag—"*Wie das Fähnchen auf dem Turme sich kann drehn bei Wind und Sturme . . .*" They stretched their hands up as high as they could and watched them become flags that turned high on the tower in the wind.

Afterwards they played the finger rhyme: "*Dies ist der Daumen, der schüttelt die Pflaumen . . . ,*" wiggling one finger at a time to the rhyme of the five brothers who went to fetch the plums, starting with the thumb, the big brother, and listing the chores each brother had: shaking the tree, gathering the plums, carrying them home un-til—how could it be otherwise?—the little finger, the youngest brother, ate up all the plums.

∽

That spring Stefan had the first of several small strokes. It was a mild stroke, following a morning when he had seemed confused, unable to understand what Helene was saying to him, so she would report to the young Dr. Miles, who would keep him at the hospital for six days. Although Robert and Yvonne sat by his bedside every evening, Tobias did not visit when Greta called him with news of their father's stroke.

"He's weak," she told him. "Harmless. He will never hurt you again."

"I don't understand you," she said when she called him once more.

The people of Winnipesaukee were convinced the stroke would have been worse had it not been for Greta's intervention, and they envied Stefan Blau a daughter like that—"better than having a doctor in the family"—and gossiped that the most noticeable effect of his stroke was how he'd lost the English language. "As if all his years in America had been taken away," they said. Most didn't mind his German words because he'd become too frail to fit their notion of the enemy.

Tenants who would encounter him in the hallways or garden would greet him loudly, slowly, the way you would speak to a child who was learning to talk, and they'd strain to hear what words—if any at all—he'd use to respond. A few, like Mrs. Klein and Stanley Poggs, even made the effort to learn a few German words and would greet him with "*Guten Tag.*"

When Helene's brother died in Germany, it felt to her like a prelude to her husband's death, a rehearsal. In grieving Leo's loss, she found herself preparing for her life without Stefan, mourning him though he was still alive. She longed to walk through the rooms where Leo had last breathed, plant flowers on his grave, and whisper to him past the kernels of dirt. Certainly, there in the cemetery, she would feel his presence once again, this brother whose kindness had remained in her life even after she'd moved thousands of miles away from him.

On the phone, she told Trudi that she wished she could be with her in Burgdorf, but that Stefan wasn't well enough to travel or leave behind. She didn't dare promise Trudi what she had promised herself—that she would visit Leo's grave after Stefan was gone. It felt wrong to say that to anyone, wrong to even think it, because it could only rush the day of her husband's death.

For the next year and a half, Stefan would live within the language of his childhood, excluding anyone who could not follow him there, even his children, though Greta tried with words she remembered from her early years; but Robert found it difficult to understand enough German.

Stefan didn't need those two. Or the son who didn't come to see him. The son who'd never tried to learn his language at all. He had all he wanted in his granddaughter who followed him with ease as if she'd never spoken English. To have more than one language in the world struck him as unnecessarily complicated. Ludicrous even. A trick people played on themselves and others. He felt as though he'd been scattered for decades across two continents.

As Helene felt a funneling of her world into his, into one language where once there had been two, she chose to join him in that tightening circle, knowing she would not limit herself to this forever. Sometimes she'd see him smiling secretly as if he'd gotten away with something. And he had. Because he'd be off somewhere in his memories, *playing with Michel Abramowitz by the brook behind his house or watching the stars with his mother—not the way she was in the last photo his sister had sent, past the age of ninety— but round-faced and laughing, one arm pointing toward the stars. Summer vacation and they're at the North Sea, digging their heels into the sand as the waves come up and swirl around their ankles. When the water is drawn out again and they step back, his footprints are not as deep as hers.*

"Look," he says as the next wave washes over their prints, wipes them from the sand as though he'd never stood here. "Just think of all the footprints that are gone . . . even thousands of years ago."

"I sometimes feel that way when I study the constellations. How people used to see the same stars and believe they were lamps lighted by the gods."

"But none of the people lasted." He picks up a flat pebble. Skips it across the waves. "Only the stars. And the ocean. Does it—does it make you afraid?"

"Because we won't last?" She skims one hand across his fore-head. "Sometimes, yes. But I also like knowing that the stars will go on, that hundreds of years from now others will enjoy them. . . . Come here." She walks with him toward the brown strip of tangled seaweed by the high-tide line, and they sit in the warm sand. "There may even be another boy who'll stand where you stood before, and for a moment his footprints will exist. If he wants to, he can make other sets of prints or build a sand castle that might stand for days."

"If it's far enough from the water." Leaning against the curve of his mother's arm, he watches the waves run up the shore. They leave puffs of foam that flatten out and vanish into the sand. In a wide band that stretches from the damp sand to the horizon, sun shimmies across the waves in yellow splashes, making the ocean look as though it were exhaling light.

After consulting with Robert and Stefan's American children, He-lene arranged for the sale of the restaurant to two sisters from Maine. When Stefan wanted them to have guidelines for operating the *Cadeau du Lac,* Helene took his words, translated them inside her head into English before she set them down on the lined page, and then gave the words back to him in German, reading aloud, pausing to ask now and again, "Is that what you wanted?" as she transformed them on their passage between the two languages. It pleased him, her careful attention to his wishes. But he was furious when he found out that the new owners had changed the restaurant's name to Homestead, abandoned the French menu to solid American fare, God forbid—pot roasts and steaks and fried chicken—and refurbished the airy porch into a gift shop where you could buy trifles like scented soaps wrapped in gingham, embroidered finger towels, and fancy jams with gingham-bordered labels.

Every afternoon Helene took Stefan for a walk around the block. Since the *Wasserburg* contained all he wanted, he didn't like to go further than that. She'd feel sad for him because as a boy he had loved to roam, had wanted his freedom so much that he'd left a continent; but now he was content to sit with her on the bench at the end of the dock while waves bobbed the planks beneath them. His eyes would travel the magnificent lines of the house he'd built, its long windows with their leaded panes, the blue tiles in the brick facade, the graceful steps leading to the polished oak door. Periodically Helene would notice his brief spans of disorientation. Both doctors had told her these would happen with little strokes.

Stefan was a tender old man, a thoughtful and even funny old man who could be alert but then retreat into memories, into sensations, wanting to be touched, to be held. During these final months, he finally offered Helene the passion she had longed for as a young woman. Nights he would roll on his side, facing her, nestling his head on her shoulder, fondling her nipples, her genitals as well as his own, curious about their bodies as if he'd forgotten all previous experience.

Sometimes she let him. But usually she would distract him.

She liked it whenever they talked till dawn, isolated within their native language from the rest of their adopted country, and as they spoke of their childhood, the lines of immigration shifted once again, a fluid border, spilling the two of them across distance and time to Burgdorf, which kept reasserting itself as home despite the horrors of history, claiming them with memories of a time before the horrors. *The river. The dike. The church tower. The fairgrounds. The pay-library.*

Though Helene had been aware of Stefan since childhood, she was stunned to find how much he had noticed about her: *the candle with the white silk ribbon she carries in her first communion procession; that green dress with the heart-shaped buttons she wears on his sister's eleventh birthday; the attic in her house and watching her act.*

While Stefan would forget things that had happened the day before, details of his childhood would swell into that void, invoking those memories for Helene too. *The wooden barrel for catching rain outside his parents' house. The clear taste of new rain from the dipping cup. And the day when he comes home with manure on his shoes, and his father, angry—as angry as Tobias? Is that where his anger comes from?—dumps Stefan into the rain barrel, dumps him upside down. A fever, that's what he gets, hands hot, so hot, that he cries for the cold water of the barrel, wants to put his hands into that very same cold water. . . .*

And then he'd be lucid again, noticing his surroundings, forming links between the now and before. Like one afternoon when it was too blustery to sit on the dock and she took him inside the restaurant. While they drank hot chocolate, he glared at the decor and the gift shop where his best tables used to be, whispered loudly that the new owners suffered from *Geschmacksverirrung,* a term that carried no direct translation but meant that their taste had gone hopelessly astray.

On the way up to their apartment, he fretted about the elevator. "It doesn't sound right."

"It sounds the way it always does."

He smoothed down his tie where it disappeared into his suit jacket, always neat, wearing a suit even on days he didn't feel well. "People could crash if the elevator fails."

"If you want, we'll have Danny check it."

He got even more agitated when they found wasps in the apartment, five wasps that swirled upward from the kitchen counter and toward the fan above the stove. He grabbed a newspaper, folded it. But as he swung it at the wasps, he stumbled and fell. Ashamed that he couldn't take care of something that simple, he felt the sum of all he hadn't been able to do. *Like keeping Elizabeth alive. Sara.*

"Here." Helene crouched to help him raise himself up.

As he looked at the wide face of his third wife, he felt a sudden fear of death—*hers . . . her death?* But there was something not right about that fear. He yanked himself back into the kitchen where Helene's hands were pulling him up, yanked himself back to what he knew: that this wife was healthy, strong; however, just then, he felt it again, that fear, as though it were a separate person standing there in the kitchen, and he knew his wife felt that fear too, except that she felt it about him—*my death?*—and it was then that Stefan knew he was the one who would die, knew it in the way you touch your own arm in the dark and know it's yours, in the way you know that light flitting over the lake's surface comes from above, not below.

So that's how it is.

But before he was going to die, he had to let his wife know what he wanted to happen with the *Wasserburg*. Heavily, he leaned against her. "Lenchen—"

"Let me get you to a chair. Hold on."

"*Wichtig*—important." From his knees to his feet to the chair.

"What is it?"

"*Halte alles zusammen*—keep everything together."

"*Ich werde das Richtige tun*—I'll do the right thing."

And he knew she would. Knew he didn't have to specify that, eventually, she would leave everything to his children. "Don't sell it, Lenchen."

Again she promised, "*Ich werde das Richtige tun.*"

He nodded, relieved. His wife would do the right thing—just as she had done the right thing in raising the children of Elizabeth and Sara as though they were her own, never preferring Robert over them. Fair, she was, his wife. Fair even in allocating her love.

◦◦

Sterne. Stars. Their patterns and legends. More familiar to him now than in half a century. Because he was approaching them with the words in which he had first learned about them. *My mother's words*. That's why he could teach Emma about the *Sterne*: he did not have to translate them to her. With his own children the *Sterne* had eluded him because of the translation. And therefore had been lost to his children. But now that the *Sterne* had come near him once again, shifting the entire sky closer to earth, he marveled at their fabulous stubbornness, their wisdom, and took delight in revealing them to his granddaughter.

For her he set up the telescope that Helene had brought back from Germany when Robert had been Emma's age. *What happened to all those years in between? Faded.* Even the wanting that used to drive him had faded, had become a recollection. How often had he deluded himself with the wanting that he trusted to get him what he set out for? What had he missed while rushing from one achievement to the next, convinced he was doing the best for his family? Instead it had been much more about the finest satisfaction he knew—the satisfaction that came from effort and success.

Oh, but he could still recognize that wanting in others, even in the son who disappointed him because he was too mild to ask for anything beyond the piano, but who was manifesting his silent wanting in the mass of his body. But there was nothing silent about Emma, his favorite, who'd been born with his furious wanting in her blood, and for now, her wanting was directed toward him and the *Wasserburg.*

Mornings, as soon as she'd wake up, she'd insist on visiting him.

"You're too heavy for *Opa,*" Helene would say when she'd catch Emma climbing on his knees.

"Let her," he'd say. And though it sometimes made him dizzy to play *"Hoppe, hoppe Reiter . . ."* with her, he still did that too. *For her.*

Even if his arms ached after letting her drop and pulling her up again.

Even if Helene fretted that Emma would hurt him. "She'll be the death of you."

But he'd laugh, not knowing that Emma would remember those words and carry them with her after his death. *"She'll be the death of you."* He found he didn't need much—far less than he'd ever thought—as he moved deeper into the German language and took Emma with him, connecting her to all he'd left behind in Burgdorf as a boy. "Someday I'll take you there," he said.

"We'll make a list of things to bring."

"A list . . . *ja.*"

Here she was, six years old, and the spark between them was all that mattered. But it had taken him his entire life to get to her, and all they would ever have together were these brief years where their lives overlapped. *If you knew,* he wondered, *if you knew you'd only get that kind of love once—would you want it at the beginning of your life or the end?* Oh, but he wanted more for Emma. *Still, if six years were all you were given—what would I have chosen for her? The first six years or the last?*

∞

Opa took a lot of short naps in his leather chair—her mother said he had little strokes—and sometimes Emma would watch him sleep and dab her fingertips at the prickly red-and-silver hairs on the backs of his hands, gently, so she wouldn't wake him. When she was with him—even while he was asleep like that—she'd feel quiet and pink inside, and as she'd breathe with him, for him, she'd feel the house all around her, breathing along, helping her to keep him alive. The house was as much a part of *Opa* as his heart, and often her love for both felt undistinguishable.

Some days she'd surprise him by slipping a treat for him into his toolbox—a picture she'd drawn of him or a Christmas ornament she'd snitched from Mr. Hedge's tree—but *Opa* never got well enough to return with her to the elevator housing. Days when *Opa* was too sick to have her visit, she'd take solace in following her brother and telling him *Opa*'s stories of Burgdorf. Caleb would fill in the gaps that surrounded these stories with stories of his own that sometimes had little to do with what had actually happened, stories that Emma would eventually tell the son she would name after her grandfather. That's how *Opa* swimming in the Rhein became the story of how he almost drowned and was saved by his sister, Margret. That's how, at the wedding, every single one of *Oma*'s students, past and present, came to honor her. In Caleb's stories *Opa* played the lead in all the plays in the Montags' attic, and winters in Burgdorf were so harsh and sudden that the ferry would get trapped by slabs of ice in the middle of the Rhein and sit there for months.

With each new story, Caleb would carry a more detailed picture of Burgdorf, part true and part distorted, not unlike the way his grandfather, as a boy, had believed all of America to be occupied by tall buildings and buffaloes. It made Caleb grasp how—if you yearn for a place you've never been to—what you've heard about it will fuse with what you envision, engendering something far more real than you will find if you're ever to come to that place. Then, of course, you will have to adjust how it first resided in your soul.

∽

Half dozing in his leather chair, Stefan watched Emma count her Halloween candy and print the words she'd learned in school that day: D O G, L O G, B O G . . . "Don't forget F O G," he said and heard the voice of the Hungarian, " . . . too much fog out there."

Only Tibor didn't say it right—*but who am I to tell him, an immigrant myself?*—said fock instead of fog while the others in the kitchen were laughing and yelling that they wanted some of that fock if there was too much fock out there for the Hungarian, teasing him even months later that it was very focky outside or asking him, "Hey, Tibor, have you had a good fock lately?"

Stefan tried to laugh, but his face felt numb. *Ghosts. Some burned dead. Along with Tibor who led me to New Hampshire, who still comes to me. The slant of his back as he limps toward a stove. Specks of cinnamon and tobacco in the lining of his pockets* . . . As the numbness spread into Stefan's skull, he was back on the Dutch freighter, bending across the injured seagull, *its frail cry rising from Stefan's own throat, the wound in its back becoming Stefan's, a wound so deep it pierces his chest—now, as one day I too will have to die alone? Now?*—and as the membrane across the seagull's eye dims Stefan's sight of his living room, he feels the flutter of small fingers on his arm, Emma's, as she ties his shadow to his chair.

"*Opa?* There now . . . *Opa?* Wake up? I said wake up!"

He heard Emma breathe—*in out in out in out in*—and suddenly, suffocated by the splendor of the *Wasserburg,* by the costly weight of every single tile and brick and timber pressing down on him, he understood that the vision he'd seen from the rowboat that long-ago day had contaminated something within him. He wanted to warn Emma, but when he raised his eyelids once more—*now? alone? as one day I too*—she was standing by his chair, one hand plucking at the long-burned stubble on his wrist, the other covering her mouth, and as he recalled that she, too, had been part of his vision, he felt terrified for her.

∞

The morning of his funeral she awoke with red imprints of her fingernails on her palms from clutching her sorrow inside her fists all night. *She'll be the death of you. Emma will be the death of you. And still climbing back on his knees.* Once she opened her fists, her sorrow was everywhere, in her father's eyes, in the drinking water, in her *Oma's* steps one floor above her.

Slow, Helene's movements were slow as she dressed. Now and

again she'd find herself stopped altogether and would need to remind herself to do whatever was next: *attach your stockings to
your garters; button the cuffs of your dress; buckle your belt; brush
your hair; put on the emeralds.* She felt tired as she opened her jewelry box, reached for the necklace Stefan had given her on their
tenth anniversary. During the night she'd read some of the letters
she'd written to him but had never mailed, and as she'd looked at
the familiar slant of her writing and tried to recall the passion she'd
felt for him, it was as though she were reading the words of someone she didn't know very well. What surprised her was that he—at
a time not so long ago—had been able to draw words from her that
struck her as far too dramatic now, reminding her of stories she'd
read of bundled love letters discovered in some ancient trunk. But
then she opened the very first letter she'd kept from her husband—
*That love is a hollow ache, a constant part of me that makes it dif-
ficult for me to be near you . . .* —and was right back to the day
she'd written those words, right back to the old sorrow that fused
with her sorrow over his death. Other letters. *You've drawn back
with such a cruelty that confuses me, that contradicts what I believed we would have between us.* It was hard to continue reading.
I fall asleep and wake with the awareness of your indifference. And
yet, as she held the letters, she preferred that old sorrow to the caution that had set in afterwards.

Four decades she had been married to him, though people back
home had predicted she'd be an old maid forever. Even Agathe
Lange who'd been about to become a nun. "I'm so pleased it's your
wedding. I never thought you—"

Silly bride of Christ.

Silly pious bride of Christ.

I did better than you.

Got myself a bridegroom in the flesh—not on the cross.

And I did not hate you that day of my wedding.

Then why now? She wanted to smash Agathe Lange's pious face.
Sister Agathe, pardon me. Smash the silly pious face of the silly pious bride of Christ. Smash Stefan's face for betraying her with his
absence of passion. *Stop it. Make yourself do whatever is next. The*

necklace. Put it on. As she fastened it around her neck, it suddenly stood for everything Stefan had given her—opulent and uncomfortable—and she resolved to wear it from this day forward. To keep Stefan and her rage present for herself, she would continue to dress in black like the widows she had known as a girl in Burgdorf. Against the black of her clothes, those green stones would look so remarkable that within weeks of her husband's funeral, the people of Winnipesaukee would remember her as having always worn that necklace; and they would come to think of her as the Widow Blau who wore her grief in public, who made others speechless with her grief; and they would tell one another she was the most beautiful old woman they had ever seen.

"Like she was always meant to be old," they would say.

1953–1956

Inside St. Paul's church the air was clotted with prayers and incense and flowers that surrounded Stefan's coffin. Father Creed had arrived on the train from Boston to say mass, and nearly everyone in town was there—merchants and teachers; tenants from the *Wasserburg;* people who'd eaten at Stefan's *Cadeau du Lac*. At his grave, Helene stood between Greta and Robert, with Danny Wilson close behind her as if he were prepared to catch her if she fell. As she heard English spoken around her, she felt herself re-entering a wider world she used to be part of before she'd joined Stefan in the language of their childhood.

Tobias' absence was so noticeable that it felt like a presence. When Greta had called him—angry with him for many months now because he hadn't visited their father—she had told him about their father's death as though he had caused it. "He's dead and you were not here."

"I am sorry."

"Is that all?"

He didn't say anything.

"Are you coming to the funeral at least?"

"I can't. It's a promise I made to myself when I was eleven."

"This is not about you, Tobias."

"I know."

"And you're no longer eleven and building matchstick animals."

"Believe me, it's hard for me not to come to his funeral."

"I don't believe that."

"I do want to be there for my family, but I need to do this for myself."

"This is not about you."

This is not about you. But then, ironically, early this morning it had all turned and become about her—about her and Noah—when he'd come to her apartment for breakfast after staying at the rectory overnight. While she told him about her phone call to Tobias, he stood in the middle of her kitchen, shy and stubborn and looking at her so closely that her skin strained toward his. She did not ask him to sit down. Did not offer him coffee. Did not turn on her stove. When she took off her thick glasses, Noah brought both hands to her face and held her in his palms like the most valuable offering he'd made at any altar in his lifetime. Though she didn't care if God sanctioned or condemned them, she felt certain he was their witness, evoked by the priest's loyalty to this God as much as by her respect for the priest's loyalty.

And somehow their witness did not hinder them, but rather filled them with sacred purpose. Their bodies had fought so long to uphold a wall to keep their flesh from touching, but now that they finally lay on her bed with daylight on their skin, touching became more than they had imagined in their loneliness. What was happening between them was totally right and totally wrong, was what it all had come to—those many hours of talking, of writing letters to each other—and God was here with them in this love, the kind of love that should have been celebrated in a church or at least a sacristy.

Her hands followed Noah's bony limbs where they sprung from his body to where they tapered off in fingers and toes, traced the pattern of gray hair around his genitals, weighed his warm testicles in one palm. God was not her rival. God was the high priest who measured the union between them. She kept her eyes open when Noah Creed's hands and mouth found all of her, and though she had known it would be like this, she had not known all of it, had not known how deeply it would resound in her, how her body would demand its own way as it surpassed reason and fantasy. The voice of her body rode her, pressed her back. It taught her to open herself to Noah, to hold nothing from him or herself. Taught her to not feel embarrassed by her soft thighs and belly, by the coarse skin beneath her feet. And then he was ready too and she was whispering, "here, here," though what she meant was now. *Now.*

He expected both of them to be clumsier, less certain, but there was a grace about their coupling as if they had decades of holding and loving. As her hips rose to meet him once again, Noah understood what prayer could be because he became his own messenger to a God who certainly would understand, who had understood all along. Not in spite of God. But with Him. Because of Him this rapture. And praise.

∽

"This is not about you," Greta had told her brother, and at her father's grave site she was still angry at him, unaware that Tobias had started out for the funeral that morning and driven as far as Concord before a ridge of nausea had slammed up in front of him, forcing him to the side of the highway. As he leaned his forehead against the steering wheel, he saw himself as a boy stepping on his miniature animals and knew that if he went to the funeral he would undo the vow that had kept him and Agnes alive. Sane. *Circling through my blood—someone like me; almost like me.* "Through your severed head," he whispered to himself, summoning the steam-filled drying room and the bleeding head of the dream-calf that always instilled in him that odd mix of power and guilt and revenge. And of being damned by this image. "Your bloody head. And I won't come to your funeral."

Robert kept looking for his brother at the cemetery and later in the lobby of the *Wasserburg* where Pearl Bloom and several other women had set up tables and food. When he reached for a piece of chocolate, Yvonne caught his wrist before he could take off the silver foil.

She dropped it back into the glass dish. "Let's have some vegetables and turkey."

"We'll die anyhow." He picked up the piece of chocolate once more, unwrapped it, and slipped it into his mouth.

"I am sorry about your father."

He nodded. Turned from her to help Pearl light the candles.

Yvonne adjusted the belt of her black chiffon dress. "We should sit with your mother and the children."

Eating, he swallowed the loss of his father, swallowed it over and over, and as its sharp edges were smothered, he thought of Miss Garland and how she used to love those dinners. He refilled his plate—corn niblets with butter; chicken and gravy; sliced tomatoes—secured his napkin between the buttons of his new black suit jacket, and listened to the hum of food inside his temples until a sleepy feeling came upon him.

"You're humming," Yvonne whispered.

Startled, he looked up from his plate.

"You were."

"I didn't notice."

"I don't mind," his mother said.

Emma watched him set his fork aside. Take his napkin. Dab his lips. She slipped from her chair and walked toward the front door, trapping her sorrow in a list for *Opa*. *Paint over scuff marks on walls next to elevator. Shampoo the rugs.* A list of things to do in the house, to fix, to tell Danny Wilson about. *Wax the lobby. Polish the mailboxes. Fix the drying racks.* Outside, in the fountain, water was flowing sideways as the wind curled itself beneath. It seized Emma's hair, billowed her black dress. As she let the wind turn her body and raise her arms, it spun her around the fountain. *Oil the door hinges.* Again. Faster. *Rake the leaves. Hose down the sidewalk.* Faster and faster the wind twirled her.

Totally unsuitable, Noah Creed thought when he saw Emma. Totally unsuitable for a day of mourning. "Would you like me to stop her from dancing?" he asked Helene.

"Stop our Emma? My husband would have liked to see her like this," she said, not knowing that Stefan had already witnessed this dance half a century ago and—all his life since then—had been waiting for it to happen again.

When the wind tapered off, Emma stood still and looked around, suddenly aware of the grown-ups. Only one was missing. *Opa*. Her mother said he was gone forever, but Emma knew that wasn't true. He was just away for a while. Soon he'd come looking for her. He always found her when they played their hiding game.

The first place he'd search would be one of the cubicles. But which one? His own? Her parents'? Usually she made her choice so it would be hard for him to find her. But today she wanted it to be as easy as possible. The Braddocks'. That's where she'd hidden the last time he'd found her.

Emma wedged herself inside the cold metal liner that smelled of milk gone sour, of apples gone too ripe. How tight the cubicle was getting. It used to be so spacious. Through the inside door of the cubicle she could hear the radio. Ever since Mr. Braddock had died, Mrs. Braddock had been sick in bed, listening to the radio, waiting for Fanny to bring her food from Mrs. Bloom's apartment. That's where Fanny really liked to be. Getting paid for what she enjoyed—mopping floors and washing counters. Once, Emma had seen Fanny hose off stones she'd brought up from the beach. That's how much she liked to clean. The other thing Fanny liked was calling the weather report, keeping the line tied up for others who tried to call in and were already impatient enough with the weatherman who had a stutter; but that stutter was exactly what Fanny liked. Because the weatherman didn't rush. And if she stayed on the phone at the end of his report, he'd start all over.

Emma tugged her knees close so her body would fit better and waited for *Opa*. All at once it came to her that he was in Germany, that he must have been getting ready these past years to move there altogether by speaking the language and telling her stories about Burgdorf. But now he had gone ahead of her, and she didn't know why. Was it because she'd done something wrong? Or because he had forgotten her? No, *Opa* would never forget her. Any minute now she'd hear his step outside the cubby. *He knocks and calls out, "Emma? Now where did my girl hide this time?"* Safe, she was safe again. She closed her eyes, thinking of moments she knew when the entire world felt safe: watching the stars with *Opa;* following him around the house; turning off her bedside lamp in that first drowsy slide toward sleep. All around her, she could feel the *Wasserburg,* and the cubicle that had been too tight now fit her just right, contained her, made her part of the house. *"Emma? I just saw Emma a minute ago."* And even before he opens the door of the cubby, he's *laughing, they're both laughing. "You're getting too big for this hiding place, young lady." And then light in her eyes as he pulls the door open and—*

∞

Dead people turn into rice, Robert dear.

"Where are you going?" Yvonne asked when he stood up.

"I'll be back." Black as beneath-earth fear spread in his belly, made him dizzy with hunger as he headed for the elevator. His hands shook when he bolted the apartment door behind him. *Rice, moist and white and swarming.* He heated a pan, made a cheese omelet. Four slices of toast with butter and strawberry jam. As he soaked up the last bit of egg with an edge of toast, he suddenly felt his father standing behind him in the kitchen, and though he couldn't possibly be there, Robert was afraid to check, afraid to see the disappointment in his father's eyes as they appraised him—soft in body and will. *The Halloween candy in the children's rooms. No.* He was not about to take candy from them. But it might be good to make sure nothing they'd been given was bad for them. After all, last year he'd found moldy cookies in Caleb's stash. This Halloween they'd each collected half a pillowcase full of sweets from tenants and neighbors.

In Emma's room, he straightened the yellow bedspread, adjusted the stack of library books on her built-in desk. She'd hidden her candy. *A hoarder, this one.* But in Caleb's room the top of his desk was heaped with candy bars and bubble gum, bags of peanuts and those little Drake's coffee cakes topped with crumbs. *Caleb won't mind if I eat just one thing.* As long as he told him and gave him money to buy himself something else. Sitting on Caleb's bed, Robert ate a Snickers. Then a Hershey's bar. *Enough already enough.* Four Drake's coffee cakes. *No good as a father, a husband, a son.*

By the time he had finished the peanuts, he knew he had to get to the store to replace what he'd eaten before anyone found out. Suddenly he had a purpose. Energy. He grabbed his keys, took the elevator to the basement. From there to the garage and into his car. At the Heflins' parking lot, Danny Wilson was pulling out in his truck, his silver hair brushed into meticulous wings over the tops of his ears. Always so vain about his hair. Robert hunched over, hoping Danny wouldn't notice him. Inside the store, he quickly found a Hershey's bar, Snickers, and peanuts, but the only Drake's—easy to spot with the duck on the label—were slices of marbled pound cake with the same brown-and-white pattern. He hesitated but then figured he'd tell Caleb he'd eaten his crumb cakes and bought him pound cake instead. *Jelly beans. Some jelly beans would be good right now. A bag of chocolate chip cookies.* What else? Nauseous with hunger, Robert approached the cash register.

As Mr. Heflin added up the purchases, his wrinkled hands touched each item, turned it, brought it up to his glasses to search for the price. "I'm sorry about your father."

"Thank you." Robert felt conspicuous. Like a drunk in a liquor store. With a small cough he said, "My mother needed a few more things. Primarily for the children. Primarily . . ." He dropped a quarter and felt bulky, awkward as he bent to retrieve it.

Mr. Heflin glanced at him as if embarrassed for him. *The way my father would if he could see me now. Dead people turn into rice, Robert dear.* Inside his car he opened the cookies, careful not to get crumbs on the seat that Yvonne might ask about—*and he was having a feast, the Fatboy, crooning to himself, absorbing the cookies while driving away from town, absorbing the peanuts and jelly beans, the candy bars and slices of pound cake*—just tell Caleb you took a few of his Halloween things and will take him to the store—*making up lies to tell his child.* Only when it was all gone was Fatboy silent. And Robert felt so bloated he could hardly move. As if he weighed at least five hundred pounds. This was the worst in months. While all over the world people were starving. He felt haunted by pictures he'd seen of skeletal children with distended bellies and eyes huge with hunger. It frightened him, having forced food into himself after it became painful. Even if he fasted, he'd be in his biggest clothes for at least a week. He felt useless. Trapped in this moment. In this body he hated.

He still had to get rid of his empty wrappers since Danny Wilson saw all trash that went down the chute to the incinerator. At a gas station Robert cleaned out his car, asked for the key to the men's room, kept the faucet running to muffle the retching. How he loathed himself as he knelt in front of the stained toilet. Loathed himself while drops of water and vomit splashed from the stained bowl into his face. While he soaped his face and neck and hands. While he gargled. Bent to brush dust from his knees. Wiped specks of vomit from his tie with toilet paper.

∞

Light in her eyes—
   Light in her eyes.
   "Opa?"
   "Emma?"
   Tilting her face toward the light, toward—
   "Emma?" It frightened Caleb, finding his sister folded into that cramped and dark space, looking much smaller than she really was. Seized by a sudden and deep urgency to reclaim her, to get her out of there and into the sun to offset that darkness, he felt his own grief for his grandfather, felt it all coming together in one moment that would reverberate in his films—that urgency to move from shadow into light. He pulled both his sister's hands toward him, and after he got her to stand next to him, he closed the cubby door on the smell of long-spoiled food and tears. And then they were sitting on the stone bench in their garden, the cold of stone through their clothes, solid and chilling. Below them on the street Mrs. Perelli—still in the ruffled black dress she'd worn to the cemetery— was coming around the corner, slow on high heels, her left shoulder drawn down by a large shopping bag.
   Caleb glanced at his sister. "What's in her bag?" he asked, trying to cheer her out of her sadness, though that sadness was wedged inside him too.
   She shook her head.
   "She just bought food for her pet," Caleb said.
   Emma watched as Mrs. Perelli climbed up the front steps of the *Wasserburg.*
   "I wonder what kind of a pet it is." Caleb waited for her to move into the people game with him. "I wonder . . . I wonder . . ."
   "A monkey."
   "A monkey? A monkey fits right into the Perellis' apartment.

With the leopard and the baby zebra. . . . Only this monkey is not stuffed. This monkey is alive. That's why Mrs. Perelli carries—"

"Bananas."

"Lots of bananas in her bag. Because that monkey is huge."

Emma nodded. "And very very hungry."

"Mrs. Perelli has to rest after each step. Because that bag is heavy. And she's scared of the monkey."

"Because he throws fits. When she doesn't bring him enough bananas."

Caleb could see the monkey breaking all the dishes and glasses. "He breaks the dishes," he told Emma.

And now she could see the monkey too. Could hear dishes crashing against the wall. The glasses. She said, "And he breaks all the glasses."

"Right. Then he swings from Mrs. Perelli's big plants."

"Like a jungle."

"Birds fly around in Mrs. Perelli's jungle. Green and red birds."

"Yellow too. Don't forget yellow."

"They shriek at Mrs. Perelli. That's why she wants to run away."

"But the monkey only gives her money for groceries. Not for a train ticket."

"A train ticket? To where?"

"Burgdorf," she said without hesitation.

"You can't go to Germany by train."

"Can so," she protested and was right back inside her sorrow. "Once you get off the ship. *Opa* says so."

෨

When Greta visited her stepmother, she noticed how her accent that had smoothed out over the years was becoming more pronounced. What she noticed too was how much closer Caleb and Emma had become. Changes like that were more obvious when you didn't see them every day. The week after her father's funeral she had moved into a suite at the Blanchard Hotel in Boston but came back to her apartment in the *Wasserburg* at least once a month to see her family.

According to Helene, Emma had taken the St. Joseph statue and was hiding it somewhere in her room. Helene had decided not to say anything, but to watch Emma closely. The girl wasn't eating well and was clinging far too much to Caleb. Often he was patient with her; but sometimes he'd disentangle himself, run off and roam the neighborhood in ever widening circles where Emma wouldn't follow him—not only because she was two years younger and therefore restricted in how far she was allowed to go, but also because she missed the *Wasserburg* when she was more than a few blocks away from it. *Opa* had told her that the house spoke a language of its own, and she imagined that language to be much like his. It was only inside the house that she could hear his voice.

One afternoon, when Caleb was playing hide and seek with her, he found her hiding on the second-floor balcony above the front door. To tease her, he locked the window she'd climbed from.

At first it was funny when Emma banged her palms against the glass. "Let me in," she screamed.

He waved to her as if about to leave. Took several steps back.

As she rattled the window, she was suddenly filled with the certainty that she was forever shut out from the house. There was a sense of death in that certainty. Pressing her eyes closed, she could see her bedroom with its white built-in desk and shelves, her *Oma*'s tiled kitchen on the floor above, the peacock rug in the staircase, and as she felt the loss of all that, she cried out, "No. No," and walked through the glass, blindly, head first beyond that initial resistance into the breath of the house, birthing her face—bloody like that of a newborn—into familiar and sacred territory.

"I didn't think you'd do that," Caleb whispered when he saw the blood. "I didn't think you'd do that." Next to his sister—sturdy and screaming—he felt insubstantial. Too light. Too slender. Too pale. Hers was a screaming of rage without tears, face red beneath the blood, and it was with awe that he raised his hands to her cheeks as if to anoint himself with her blood, her strength.

"Go—" A deep voice right behind him. Danny Wilson. "Get Dr. Miles."

"I didn't think you'd do that," Caleb whispered again.

"Go get Dr. Miles. Now. Where is your mother?"

"Reading. On the dock."

The doctor's hands smelled of milk and of medicine as he extricated slivers of glass from Emma's face. She tried not to blink. Everything was red in *Oma*'s kitchen, and she could feel *Oma* holding her on her lap, steadying her with strong arms clasped around her.

"It's not wise to lead with your face." *Oma*'s breath, warm against the side of Emma's neck.

"That's right." Emma's mother, still in her swimsuit, was weeping. "You don't go through things with your head. You just don't."

"Your head is for thinking," Dr. Miles scolded gently, "not for butting through walls."

"I didn't think you'd do that," Caleb said. "I wouldn't have locked you out."

"And it doesn't matter if those walls are made of glass or stone," *Oma* said. "I know what I am talking about. Your grandfather was like that . . . leading with his head . . . always his head."

Emma tried to imagine *Opa* with blood on his face. But she couldn't see him at all. Not even when she tried to put him next to the doctor.

"You have to lead with your heart, Emma," *Oma* said.

The doctor was swabbing something cool against Emma's forehead and eyelids, blotting the red, turning it cool, transparent. "Am I hurting you?"

Emma shook her head. *I'm back inside. At least I'm inside.*

"I don't think we need stitches."

Emma blotted their voices till they too became transparent, a cool, transparent hum, but soon *Oma*'s rose above the hum— "Congratulations on getting married"—pulling other voices right behind her.

"Thank you," the doctor said.

"She's not from New Hampshire, I hear."

"Chicago. Laura and I used to work at the same hospital until my uncle brought me into his practice. Laura is a nurse. We just bought an old Victorian. About four blocks away on Gilman Street. It needs fixing up, but that's all right. What we both love about it is the porch."

"I've always liked that porch. And that great old maple tree right across the street. A girl who used to work here as a maid when first I came from Germany, Heather, she grew up in that house."

"First thing we'll do is paint it. I don't like yellow on a house."

"Emma?" Her brother's hand on her arm. "I'm sorry, really."

Her cheeks hurt when she tried to smile at Caleb, and all at once she wanted to be sitting with him beneath one of the tables in the lobby, surrounded by the legs of the grown-ups while above them voices and laughter mingled with the scent of food, wanted to return to those celebrations she relived so often that they seemed to have happened constantly—not just twice a year—making up her entire childhood . . . *people in festive clothes talking, laughing, . . . everyone there . . . her grandparents and parents, all the tenants, Uncle Tobias, Aunt Greta and Father Creed, Danny Wilson . . . eating the delicacies that Opa always prepares in his restaurant for his summer solstice and Christmas dinners. Her mother in a gay mood and pretty in her new dress, walking among the courtyard tables that are set up with white linen. Emma in her white dress and Caleb wearing his white suit, sitting together beneath the longest of the tables, playing with each other's hands: they link their fingers; stroke thumbs; explore each other's hands as if studying intricate maps. They breathe fog against Pearl Bloom's patent leather shoes, right next there to Stanley Poggs' shoes. A couple they are, Mr. Poggs and Mrs. Bloom. Through the white fringes of the tablecloth, Caleb and Emma see candles on the other tables, people strolling past their table without noticing them, some with wine glasses and cigarettes. Old Buddy Hedge and his even older father hobble past them, heads down, bad backs curved, giving Caleb an idea for the people game. There, beneath the table, he and Emma play Krieg der Greise—war of the old men—the fight Mr. Hedge has been having with Mr. Evans for years now, not speaking though they come to the same parties and rush to the mailboxes every day as soon as the mailman arrives, seeking out occasions when they can ignore one another in public though no one remembers what their feud is about.*

Hands, long hands, cupping Emma's ears. "Look at me. Good." The doctor's eyes, moving up her face golden and smooth and slow like honeybees. "Good. Good." Nodding, he was nodding, saying, "You should never let yourself get that angry, Emma."

"I wasn't angry."

"Then why did you break the glass?" Though he studied her face as if ready to know everything about her, she couldn't give words to the yearning that had made her step through the glass.

"My brave darling." The face of her mother swam next to the doctor's. "But how about scars, Dr. Miles? Will she have scars on her face?"

A few of the slivers would leave tiny scars on Emma's forehead as if proof of her temper, there for anyone to see and be warned: *this is what this girl is capable of.* However, in the weeks following her injury, she had no toughness left in her as she basked in her mother's concern. She'd feel content whenever her mother allowed her to try on her rings or watch her apply makeup, when her mother asked what she thought of a certain color dress, or dabbed medicated lotion on Emma's face and stroked it gently into her skin.

As she discovered her mother piece by piece, even a flaw, like the varicose veins on her mother's left leg, looked like an adornment, a perfect winter tree growing upward from her delicate ankle. Below her knee, one large vein branched into thin lines. It was a pattern you could memorize and trace on a blanket, say, or a tabletop when you were alone.

One morning, when Emma felt irritable because her face itched badly from the many small scabs, her mother took her into the kitchen. "Whenever your skin gets cut," she said, "parts of yourself are left frayed." And as Emma imagined countless red ends just beneath her skin, her mother turned on the faucet and saturated a clean dish towel with cold water. "Then it's up to you to bring those parts back together again. Here." She folded the towel over once and held it against Emma's face until the itching receded as though all her ragged ends were connecting beneath her skin— sleek and smooth and new.

She kept that towel against her face, followed her mother into the big bedroom where children were only allowed when invited, and stood behind her mother as she sat in front of her ornate mirror and her crystal vase with roses. The mirror made it look as if there were two vases. Every Friday her mother had eighteen white roses delivered from the flower shop, and she arranged them in the matching vases Pearl Bloom had given her as a wedding gift, one for the mantle above the fireplace in the living room, the other for her bedroom. "You always place an uneven number of flowers into a vase," she taught Emma. Beyond the reflection of the roses and of her mother swum Emma's own reflection, and beyond that shimmered the open closet with all its dresses and suits and gowns. The clothes of Emma's father used to hang in the far left side of the closet, but gradually they'd been squeezed out of the bedroom entirely and into the guest room. Because it was important to hang up clothes properly. That was something else her mother taught her. "Always with a space between them to keep them from wrinkling."

As her mother's hands drew a brush through her hair, Emma tried not to look at the blue hands, hands so blue and cold that they were almost purple, hands that were clammy and not beautiful like the rest of her mother. Carefully, she took the mother-of-pearl brush from those cold fingers and lifted the dark hair from her mother's neck while drawing the bristles through its many fine strands. They gave off the scent of limes, and as Emma leaned closer to breathe in that scent, she noticed her mother's eyes in the mirror, startled, and then distant, as if she'd expected to see someone else.

The more Emma clutched at her mother, the more Yvonne drew away from this fleeting and mismatched courtship. She'd find excuses to not have Emma follow her around, sent her off to play with her brother, to visit her grandmother. Some evenings Robert took the children to the Royal. They liked *King Kong,* a film he'd seen more than twenty years ago when he was in college. Both were mesmerized by Fay Wray who didn't have all that many lines but got to do lots of screams. She could scream better than anyone the children knew, and they would practice Fay Wray screams, dropping to the floor in a swoon, a faint, getting it right—that languid folding together where you'd bend at your knees and waist at the same moment so that you wouldn't just flop down flat but glide into a decorative heap, or pose rather, the back of one hand, ideally, ending up against your forehead as your last scream faded into a sigh.

Fay Wray. They were Fay Wray in the elevator. In the lobby. On the dock. Some days, on the roof, Emma would test the embrace of the house by playing Fay Wray, balancing on the low walls along its edge, daring the house to hold her if she were to slip and fall. Fearless when it came to the house, she ultimately believed it would always be there for her. *Not like* Opa. *A house cannot be buried like that.*

~

When Robert Blau was still in his twenties and thirties, the people of Winnipesaukee used to tell him he looked younger than he was, and he had come to think of himself as youthful until—just around his fortieth birthday—his age suddenly overcame him, softening his body with additional layers of flesh, tugging his hairline toward the crest of his skull. That same summer his wife began to leave for weekends, even entire weeks, without offering reasons; and because Robert did not dare ask the first time she disappeared, it made it impossible to ask from then on. She would simply be gone when he'd come home from work, and the children would be upstairs with his mother.

Occasionally there'd be a forewarning. "I need to be away for a while," she might say, and if he'd offer to take a trip with her— "Just tell me where you want to go"—she'd say there was no rush to decide. But then she'd be gone again while he'd pretend to his mother and children that she was taking a rest in some seaside hotel along the Maine coast where her family used to vacation when she was a child; and as his words evoked her *strolling along a beach or wading through one of the many tide pools, dress hiked up ever so slightly to keep the hem above the surface,* he'd smell the briny air and dislodge other pictures that pressed at him, pictures called forth by her confessions: *Yvonne dancing with a man slimmer than he, taller too, her face against his shoulder; Yvonne in a train compartment with a man who still has all his hair, her white legs wrapped around him while the train rocks her even further away.*

"*Let her go,*" Helene would have liked to tell him. "*I'll look after the children.*" She didn't believe his stories that became more convoluted, involving some ailing aunt of Yvonne's in Maine, who needed to be taken for medical tests, needed help shopping for a refrigerator, needed Yvonne to pack her summer clothes away for the season. From what Pearl told Helene, tenants who asked Robert about Yvonne didn't believe those reasons either.

Had Robert been able to speak to his mother—*but how can I, about things like that?*—she might have told him that her brother Leo used to be uneasy with closeness too and, therefore, needed to change admirers frequently; that people like Yvonne and Leo were skilled at leaving others behind, settling them with longing, even though Leo had never left the way Yvonne had—at least not with his body.

And Stefan?

Don't think about him like that. His leaving was different. Never for the adoration of others. For him it was always the house. But how about the other wives? No. Not for many years. Odd, how she felt more certain of Stefan in death than she had in life. Although that certainty did not lessen her pain when her body sought out his empty half of the bed, it gave her a greater understanding of Stefan. Because his part of their history had already ended, she could conjure it in its entirety or move back and forth between any moments she chose to illuminate or ponder.

While her son only had uncertainty with his wife. Whenever Yvonne was away, Helene could smell her father's sweat on Robert, the sweat of failure. It was obvious that he missed Caleb and Emma but couldn't bear to have them see him in his dreary sadness. He would come to Helene's apartment to visit his children, eat dinner with them, and stay till he could tuck them in with a good-night story—Caleb in the room that used to be Robert's when he was a boy, Emma in Greta's old room. Since the children had always moved freely between both apartments, they felt at home among their grandmother's carved cabinets and woven tablecloths.

Each time Yvonne left, Robert was more certain that she would not come back; and each time she proved him wrong: after a few days or weeks she'd return rested as if indeed she had spent solitary hours by the sea, doing nothing except watch the waves smooth themselves into the sand. She would unpack gifts—toys and clothes and books—and for days or weeks, usually in direct proportion to how long she'd been away, she would be indulgent and playful with the children, charming to Helene, seductive toward Robert. She bought roller skates for Caleb. A pink bicycle with training wheels for Emma.

Whatever questions Robert asked, Yvonne would answer with such frankness that, soon, he stopped mentioning that she'd been away at all. Certain it was his weight that caused her to seek other men, he found it easier to pretend to himself—and her—that she'd visited this aunt he'd never met.

At least I'm honest with him, Yvonne told herself. In giving him the truth, she was urging him to fight for her; but what she got instead was his understanding. He infuriated her when he became so accommodating. *If he cared about me, he'd keep me from other men.*

Nights when she was gone again, Robert fell into light spans of troubled sleep. Occasionally he'd be fully awake by four in the morning, surrounded by the ghosts of men she had told him about, and he'd flee from his bed to seek solace with his beloved Russians: Rachmaninoff, Tchaikovsky, Prokofiev. Hands consuming the ivory keys, he'd fuse in his union with his piano as he could not with his wife, rendering his heartache with sounds that would have moved her, had she been near enough to hear him.

In the apartment one floor above, Caleb would lie with his eyes far open, soul filled with the passion of his father's music as it swelled beyond the *Wasserburg,* the town, the continent, music that would thread its way into Caleb's dreams and, years later, emerge in his films. What these films would evoke—much more than his mother's absence—would be the quiver of his father's music deep beneath Caleb's skin. People would say Caleb Blau understood the language of longing, that it was there in all his films. He would invoke the *Wasserburg* and his family—the living and the dead as far back as his grandfather's first bride—for audiences that had never been to New Hampshire, and they would come to know it as if they'd grown up there, because what they saw in his films would mesh with their own memories, rendering indiscernible what was theirs and what had come from Caleb Blau, and he would feel honored when people who had been raised in capes, say, or ranches would tell him, "As a child I lived in a house much like yours."

✎

Robert stood at the kitchen counter in his wet raincoat. Eating. *Wurst.* Two pieces of *Streuselkuchen. Schnitzel.* Chocolate with hazelnuts. Cold *Reibekuchen,* no longer crisp. All week he'd begun each day fasting and had allowed himself only two thin slices of rye bread at work. But once he came home to this empty apartment, he couldn't stop feeding himself. Tonight his belly felt sore, stretched—*enough already enough*—and outside it was raining, hard fast drops of April rain, and though he knew he didn't want to eat the marinated herring his mother had sent home with him the night before—*enough already*—his movements were getting faster, that sequence of sending the food on its terrible journey from his hands to his mouth, faster—*enough*—assuaging the hunger he could not slake with music, the hunger that was coming at him like a runaway train, and even though he felt horrified at the thought of his body expanding even further, he could not keep from swallowing. Swallowing.

Until.

Until the familiar shame and ache supplanted that hunger. Supplanted all else. He would have gladly killed Fatboy who closed around him. Countless times he had imagined killing Fatboy, *turning around swiftly, knife in his hand, and slicing Fatboy open—upward from his prick through the enormous belly, between the nipples of the fleshy girl-breasts, right up through his wide jaw and forehead. Fatboy never bleeds but falls back in two identical halves like a pear that's been split, giving space for Robert's true body to rise from its trap. Lithe. Slender.*

On his thumb a smudge of chocolate. As he licked it off, he remembered his mother was expecting him for dinner. *No. Eat again? Impossible.* He rushed to clean the evidence of his desperate feast. Shook off his raincoat on the way to the bathroom. Turned on the shower. And knelt on the mat in front of the toilet. By the time he stepped into the tub, the water was getting lukewarm. This past year he'd begun taking showers, though he still preferred the full heat of a bath to the abrupt needles of water, but it had become too cumbersome to dislodge himself from the tub once he sat down.

Hair still wet, he took the elevator one floor up and—as every evening since Yvonne had left—sat at his mother's lace-covered table with her and his children. He took small helpings, though she reminded him that she'd made the *Rouladen* especially for him.

Patting the stomach he detested, he made himself smile at her. "Not with my reserves, *Mutti*." When he saw the concern in her face, he thought how the two of them had been left to take care of his children, and he felt an immense gratitude.

After dinner, he came upon Caleb in the living room, gazing through a rain-streaked window at the dark sky. There was something so private about him that Robert slowed his breath, not daring to speak as Caleb raised one hand and traced the outline of his profile with his forefinger as though reminding himself who he was. From his forehead, he followed the curve of his short nose, across his parted lips, down his chin. *The Montag chin.* When he touched his collarbone, he stopped as though suddenly aware that he was not alone, and it came to Robert that Caleb reminded him of himself. In a way it amused and hurt him to see a resemblance between the graceful body of his eleven-year-old son and his own body that had grown too large for use and comfort.

He felt tender toward Caleb when he said good night to him.

"A story," Caleb reminded him.

"Once upon a time—" Robert stopped, ashamed he hadn't come here right after work, ashamed he wasn't there more for Caleb and Emma. He wanted to be loving. Attentive. But the eating took him away from his children. The eating and his worries about what he could become if he obeyed his appetite.

"Once upon a time what?"

". . . there lived a woman."

"Where?"

"Portugal."

"Why Portugal?"

"Well, I guess the story could have happened in any country."

Caleb waited as his father shifted his weight on the chair that was too narrow for him. His belly hung over the belt of his gray pants, and his thighs overlapped the seat.

"Do you want me to change it to China or Germany?"

"Portugal is good."

"This woman, she loved with—with such an abandon that it made her float in the air. It was a wonderful feeling—light and free and joyful. . . ." His father squinted upward as if, indeed, he could see the woman high above the ground.

All at once Caleb saw himself *sitting in a darkened movie theater, watching the screen where his father stands on a hard-packed circle of earth among endless meadows, or rather fields of wheat, far below this woman who floats above him—still light and still free and still joyful* . . . and already he saw himself telling Emma about what he saw on the screen.

His father's voice dropped as if he were telling the story to himself. "But as she drifted higher, she saw how far it would be to fall. That very moment she stopped rising. Instead she tightened her wings and fought the air current, holding on to her position way up there in the air till she forgot what it felt like . . . that airy sensation of floating. She felt . . . she felt heavy. Afraid that any moment she could fall."

"And did she?" Caleb raised himself on his elbows. "Did she fall?"

His father sighed. His breath smelled of toothpaste, and his fingers—so confident at the piano—fidgeted with a torn buttonhole on his shirt. Caleb could see how hard it was for him to tell that story. Now if his father were to take those words and tell them through the piano, they would rise on their own and carry his father along. Because at the piano his father was more himself than any other times. It made Caleb wonder if all people had one talent that made them totally themselves. And if so, what would be his? Whenever he saw his father hunch his shoulders around the piano as if taking it into himself, Caleb felt certain his father was almighty. Noble.

"It became painful for the woman to love," his father said slowly. "Painful and uncomfortable. She felt angry at . . . at her husband for not flying with her. For not holding her up there. For not sharing her fear."

"Where was her husband?"

"Away."

It was then that Caleb knew his father was talking about the kind of love he had for his mother, and that he was really speaking of himself even though the story was about a woman, and that—to tell this story at all—his father had to set it in a place far away. And it came to Caleb how in telling a story through someone else, you could get at it closer. And by letting that changed story pass through you, you arrived at a greater truth.

"When she was with her husband," his father continued, "she was afraid to be happy because she didn't know how long he would stay. . . ."

Caleb nodded. He'd seen his parents like that.

"When her husband was away, her days were tinged with sadness and longing. She'd imagine him thinking about her and—"

"But that wasn't enough," Caleb said.

His father hesitated. "It never is," he finally said.

∽

When Robert woke up the next morning, he first felt aware of Yvonne's absence and then, immediately, of the amounts of food he'd eaten the night before. Disgusted with himself, he vowed not to eat any breakfast. He'd lose the new pounds before his wife returned—those and all the other pounds he'd put on since their wedding. The silvery stretch marks on his stomach and thighs would vanish. He'd take Yvonne dancing. She used to enjoy dancing, but she hadn't mentioned it in years because he'd always found excuses. But all that would change. *He leads her to the dance floor, trim in the gray suit he hasn't been able to wear since Emma's first communion. "You look good," Yvonne says. "Real good."*

Dancing would get weight off him. Walking too. Simply moving around. He saw it with horses and dogs: they stored weight when inactive, shed it once they were exercised regularly. To think that he'd known all along. If he could do it for animals, he could do it for himself. Fortified by his conviction, he showered and dressed. During his noon break, he ate his two slices of rye and went for a walk around the block, past the shoe factory where Miss Garland had worked many years before he was born. Moments like this he loved her fiercely. More than he'd dared love his father whose example had felt so unattainable. Who'd usually seemed disappointed in him. While Miss Garland had accepted him as he was. As she would even now at this size. While he'd come to think of her as a nuisance. As a child he'd worshiped her, but she'd been far more loyal in her affection.

Three times he walked around the block.

Three times he passed the shoe factory, his stomach light with hunger.

Definitely on its way to becoming flat.

Yet, after spending the day famished, he could think of nothing but food. Couldn't wait to get back home where, alone in his kitchen, he ate. And ate. Standing by the open refrigerator with tears on his face.

∽

She came back that night. The instant before she switched on her bedside lamp, he awoke, and what he felt—rather than relief at her return—was dread at listening once again to her unburden herself of whatever man she had been with. She seemed to need those confessions before she could be close to him. Through half-closed lids he watched as she took one of her long-sleeved nightgowns from a drawer. Her body felt warm as she lay down next to him and tried to slip her arm beneath his neck as if this were an ordinary night, as if she had not been away. Reluctantly he raised his head. Let her pull him close.

"Tired?" As she kissed his forehead, he could feel her readying herself for her latest confession. "Robert?"

To stop her, he slipped her nightgown from her shoulders, closed his lips around one nipple the way she liked him to.

"Wait—Robert?"

He rubbed his thumb across her other nipple. When it stiffened, he ran his hand over the bunched up material of her nightgown—*always keeps it on while making love*—across the skin below her breasts where her ribs rose and fell. Her breath came faster as he stroked the slight rise of her belly where her nightgown had slipped up, where she was smooth and— *Hands. Other men's hands. Here. Touching her pale belly. Her thighs. Wide joints or slender fingers. Touching her. Here. Smooth hands or hands with hair curling up from the wrists—*

"Why did you stop?" she whispered. "Robert?"

He wanted to break the hands of those men, snap them apart.

"What's wrong?"

"I— I can't fall asleep with you here."

She pulled her nightgown down. Pushed her hair from her cheeks. Her skin was flushed. "Would you like me to get you a glass of water?"

"No." He felt something rise in his chest that, he was sure, would make him dangerous if he let it, and he was suddenly afraid of what he was capable of.

"Please? What's wrong, Robert?"

"I'm just . . . restless." He didn't have any idea what he was doing, only that he had to get away from her. Now. He got up, slipped his bathrobe over his pajamas. "I'll sleep in the guest room." For a moment he stood outside the door of the bedroom, listening for what he didn't know, but he couldn't hear anything beyond the rushing of his blood.

In the guest room, he pulled back the green bedspread. The sheets felt cold. Turning on his side, he drew his knees against his belly. Through the open curtains the full moon cast a whitish square on his floor. It filled the room with a frozen glow that made him shiver. He wished he could fall asleep, but when he finally did, he was awake soon after, heart beating too fast, and it took him a moment to remember where he was. The patch of moonlight had narrowed and shifted to a different section of the floor. When he woke up again, he heard the thumping of the percolator, the refrigerator door closing.

His tongue felt dry as he walked down the hallway in his bathrobe.

"Good morning." Yvonne smiled at him from the stove and held out one arm to pull him in for a hug. The smell of coffee was everywhere as the black liquid shot against the glass bubble of the lid.

"Good morning." His voice sounded hoarse.

"No kiss?"

He didn't know what to do with his hands. Kept them along his sides. Large. Clumsy.

She came toward him. Kissed him on the lips. "You're a grouch this morning, aren't you?" She took a copper pan from a hook above the stove. "Let me make you some eggs."

"No, thank you."

"How about a bacon omelet?"

He stared at her. At best, she was a reluctant cook. Whenever she fixed anything at all, it was low in fat and starch and sugar and taste. And now she was offering him bacon? He almost said yes, just to watch her do it. "I'm not hungry."

"You have to eat something." This from the woman who usually tried to stop him from eating.

"Cereal then."

While she took the milk from the refrigerator, he filled a bowl with corn flakes. She sat down close to him, and he made himself lower his spoon, raise it to his mouth. Though he longed to hide his face against her neck and hear her say that she would not leave him again, he sat stiffly. Silently.

All day at the clinic he was distracted. Several times, he found people waiting for his answer to a question he hadn't listened to. When he got home, Yvonne was playing dominos with Emma and Caleb. The three of them had baked cookies. Flown kites. It seemed so much easier for the children to let her back in. But he couldn't bear the thought of being in bed with her. While she took her bath, he changed into the silk pajamas she'd given him for Christmas. Newspaper in his hands, he sat on the bed in the guest room, flipping pages without absorbing a word.

"Ready to go to sleep?" She stood by the open door, towel wrapped around her, shoulders still damp.

"I— I'm still reading."

"Come on." She extended one hand while the other clasped the towel in a knot above her breasts. "It's getting late."

In their bedroom he tried not to look as she took off the towel;

yet, he couldn't help seeing. Quickly he slipped into bed and lay on his side facing away from her. The beige and white stripes of the wallpaper seemed to narrow toward the base molding, but he knew that wasn't so, that they ran in equally wide stripes from the ceiling to the floor.

The mattress shifted as Yvonne lay down and curved her body around his back. "Sleep tight."

"You too," he mumbled without changing his position. When her arm came around him and her hand rested on his chest, he drew in his belly, ashamed she'd notice how much bigger it was getting.

"Robert?" Her lips touched his neck.

He pressed his eyes shut.

"Robert?"

Though his body strained for her, he didn't dare take on the risk of pleasing her. As her hand burned against his chest, he tried to pretend it was something else, *a stone baked by the sun, a frying pan left on the stove,* but it was still her skin against his, and even after her arm twitched and became heavier, he lay awake, afraid of her confession, afraid of how much he wanted her touch.

For weeks he worried about doing something that would make her leave again. Some nights he would have preferred to sleep in the guest room so he wouldn't have to be so careful. Early one morning, while she still lay asleep next to him, lips open, breath light and even, it occurred to him that it had to do with power—her power to go away, his powerlessness to keep her home. Although their bodies didn't touch, her warmth filled the gap between them, draped itself around his body, and for one moment—the briefest of moments—he wished that she would leave again.

He took to sleeping in the guest room whenever she was away. Less complicated, to lie in a bed made for one. He resolved to spend more time with his children, brought them home with him after they'd eaten dinner upstairs with his mother, sent them to sleep in their own rooms, got up early to make breakfast for them. But then there'd be an evening when he'd arrive home to find Yvonne fixing chicken or pot roast or tuna, while the children watched, delighted with whatever treasures she'd brought them from this trip. There'd be a tie with seashells for Robert. A box made from seashells. A scarf with seashells for his mother who would be called down for dinner. A rarity, that invitation. Equally rare a dinner that wasn't too dry. Chicken with lemon. Tuna with capers. A bit tangy. *Like the sea?* And his mother watching him across the table as if waiting for him to ban his wife from the house forever.

What he did instead was take Yvonne's power away. Reverse it the evening of Emma's tenth birthday after both children were asleep. While Yvonne was still reading in the living room, he undressed in the guest room and got into bed, pulling the blanket to his chest. When he heard her steps, he grabbed a book. Opened it. Tried to hold it steady.

Her steps paused outside his closed door. "Robert?" She knocked.

"Come in."

A pulse beat between the fine bones at the base of her neck. "What's the matter?"

"I'm getting used to this mattress." He bent a page and closed the book, then wished he'd kept it open so he'd have something to look at. "Maybe I should," he said, "you know . . . sleep in here from now on."

She stood silently, neck taut, a frown between her eyebrows.

A corner of the book binding jabbed into his palm, and he grasped it tighter. "My clothes are in here anyhow, and it would be easier."

She raised one hand as if to stop him, but instead she pushed it into the pocket of her bathrobe and started for the door. "Sleep tight, Robert."

"Wait—"

She turned.

What he wanted to say was, *"Wait, I'm coming with you."* But instead, he forced himself to say, "Don't forget to close the door."

In the dark, he lay with his arms crossed beneath his head, listening to the bath water running, to her body lowering itself into the tub. He could picture her in the water, *hair piled on top of her head so it won't get wet, a few black strands clinging to her neck, shoulders submerged, hands soaping her arms, around her breasts, between her legs—*

But this time he'd been the one to send her away.

CHAPTER ELEVEN

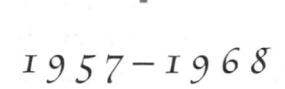

1957–1968

As long as he feared her disappearances, she returned to him as if drawn by his fear; but when he finally knew to expect the pattern of her returns, she didn't come back for two entire months. And four days.

While he was left with dreams in which she walked toward him.

Dreams in which he was slender with hair so full it covered his forehead.

Every morning he drove to his clinic with fantasies of her return: it would happen when he didn't expect it, of that he was sure. *He's vaccinating Mrs. West's basset hound while his receptionist whispers to him that Yvonne is in the waiting room. . . . He comes home to find her on the front steps of the* Wasserburg, *wearing a flared dress he's never seen on her before. . . .*

But this absence of hers, the longest of them all, was to be the last because the day after her return, she felt an ache in her lower back, at first just a flutter not unlike the first time she'd felt her babies stir inside her womb, a flutter certainly not troublesome enough to lie down for, as Robert suggested. But she humored him and stretched out on her pale sofa while he applied compresses, alternating between ice packs and damp heat the way he would treat a horse, and she turned herself over to these knowing hands as if indeed she were an animal, all instinct, all body.

By the following morning a stiffness had settled in her back that made it uncomfortable to stand or sit. When it seeped into other parts of her body, Robert postponed his appointments and stayed with her until Caleb and Emma got home from school and could look after her. His mother brought dinner, four bowls wrapped into dishtowels that she'd knotted on top so that she was able to carry those bundles at once. Colorless, Yvonne thought when she saw the chicken and potatoes, the peas and string beans with all the green boiled out of them. But it moved her, made her feel grateful how Robert and the children and even his mother sat around her bed to eat dinner. *Family.* That feeling of gratitude seized her once more in the morning when Robert prepared her breakfast before leaving for the clinic.

It was like that the next day. And the day that followed. After several weeks had passed, Robert noticed something odd: by feeding Yvonne, he required less nourishment himself. Gradually, his body took on a different shape. What helped, of course, was that if he ate a large meal, he knew how to get rid of it. It was simple. Close the bathroom door and keep the water running so that no one would hear.

Yvonne stopped going anywhere alone, waiting for him to accompany her, one of his arms steadying her waist. He moved back into their bedroom, made sure she had her water and medicine before he went to sleep. Torn between keeping her home and wanting her to get better, he took her to a neurologist, an orthopedic surgeon, a chiropractor, and when they couldn't find anything wrong, he drove her to the lingerie shop where she bought seven lace-trimmed peignoir sets as though she'd accepted that her bed had become her habitat and wanted to reside there with the appropriate wardrobe.

At least now she can't leave me.

She began to subscribe to the local paper, became interested in charitable causes, and wrote out generous checks for a newborn needing a lifesaving operation, a family destitute after the father died from cancer. She made a planning book of decorating ideas she cut from catalogs. Items arrived by mail: clothing; towels; massage oils; records; dishes.

Whenever Robert resented their shrinking finances and his increased duties, he'd remind himself that she was not well, and he'd try to be more compassionate. He'd offer to rub her back even though her skin would release the knowledge of other men into his hands; and when she'd sigh and close her eyes, he'd feel certain she was retreating into those memories.

Emma and Caleb quickly adapted to the pattern of their mother's illness—far more predictable than the pattern of her absences. When they came home from school, Emma would pour her mother a glass of white grape juice and tiptoe into the big bedroom where Caleb already sat on the edge of their mother's bed. She'd drink her juice while listening to them tell her about school. Though always pleased when they came to her, she'd soon be ready for them to run upstairs to their grandmother.

While Emma found her solace within the *Wasserburg*, Caleb liked to roam, taking images of the house with him. He'd stroll through town, hike to the cemetery, or head to the Royal Theater where the matron used to chase his father and Uncle Tobias decades ago, where kids still poured soap into the lobby fountain, and where he'd sit spellbound and watch stories unfold on the screen. Later, he'd retell those stories to Emma. *Invasion of the Body Snatchers. Blackboard Jungle. Seven Brides for Seven Brothers.* Sometimes the two of them would sit on the dock, taking turns with the I-am game that Caleb made up as they talked. *I am a cup, a wave, a tree.* Becoming. Being. *I am a cup: A while ago I was full of tea, warm, but now I'm half empty, cooled down, a brown ring left inside.* While sun warmed them from above. *I am a wave: I curl myself up, run onto the sand as far as I can, retreat before the sand can pull me down.* While the breeze that rose through the wooden slats cooled them. *I am moss hanging from the trees in the cemetery. . . .*

What Emma didn't tell her brother about was the game she played without him, the game that took her into stores where she got presents for *Opa*. The first time had been in Magill's one day after school when she'd stepped inside from the cold rain, blinking at the lights. At least it was warm in here. Dry. A woman with a baby stroller came toward her, and as Emma stepped aside to let her pass, her arm banged against a counter with a display of ties. One had a geometric pattern in the golden browns *Opa* liked. Testing the softness of the tie—*silk, is it silk?*—between her thumb and forefinger, Emma glanced around: an elderly couple passed through the aisle behind her; a clerk, tall with skin stretched over sharp features, was fitting a suit jacket on a customer; two women stood talking by the jewelry counter. No one looked in her direction. Breath quick and light in her throat, she slipped the tie into the pocket of her raincoat, and though she felt like running from the store, she made herself walk slowly toward the exit, even stopped in the luggage department where she opened and closed the zipper on a leather suitcase as if she were interested in buying it. *"For when I go to Germany,"* she planned to say if anyone were to ask her. As she saw herself moving toward the mirror by the door— taller somehow and older—she adjusted her ponytail and turned up her collar.

It became her game alone. Choosing the perfect moment, the perfect treat for *Opa*. Thoughts on nothing but what she was about to do, she'd walk through brightly lit aisles, prolonging the minutes before she'd take something, turning them into white-hot time that burned through all longing, all pain. One fist in her pocket around the treat, she would walk home. After sneaking the key to the roof from *Oma*'s china cabinet, she'd scale the ladder to the dusty wooden platform above the elevator, hide the treat inside *Opa*'s old wooden toolbox, and sit down on it, leaning into the hazy-warm breath of the house. And if she was patient and lucky, she'd hear *Opa*'s voice below the familiar hum and whisper-flick of bolts and wires and chains, below the wheeze of the elevator.

∽

That winter, as Yvonne's backache became a part of her—dull and constant—it was the awareness of it that troubled her more than the pain itself, an awareness that this pain, quite likely, would always be there and keep her home. In an odd way, the pain got between her and the urgency to burn or cut herself. She didn't have to because her body was doing it for her, giving her the release that pain offered—and without leaving scars.

But it was obvious that the tenants didn't think she was ill: she could tell by their questions about her health that they saw her as a spoiled woman, a useless woman. Just because her suffering did not disfigure her, they assumed she was pretending. They'd probably picked up that attitude from her mother-in-law. Not that Helene ever said anything like that—no, she was helpful, showing off her hard work just to make Yvonne feel useless.

But Robert understood. Yvonne was sure because she could feel it in his hands when he massaged her back. Now, that pain had freed her from excuses for not having sex with him, she felt eased by his caresses and could be tender without worrying that he might want more of her.

Robert found that once she had something to look forward to— holidays and family vacations—her back would get stronger for a while. The summer the children were thirteen and eleven, he suggested renting a cabin in Rye Beach where he and Yvonne had spent their honeymoon.

"I'll be glad to come along to take care of the children and the cooking," his mother offered.

"That would be wonderful," he said.

Yvonne was too angry to say anything until she was alone with him. "I'm tired of German cooking. Tired of that old German woman running my life." And yet, even as she was saying this, she was thinking how her children were half German, and how she always felt she had to protect them because of that very Germanness, and how odd it felt that they had come from her body, though she wasn't German while part of them was.

Robert looked dazed. "But my mother's been helping us so much."

"That's just it."

"The children, they liked the idea too. And without her—I don't know how we'd manage."

"It's hard enough that we have to accept her help the rest of the year, but our vacation is so short that I want to enjoy it with my own family."

"She *is* our family."

"I'm talking about my husband. My son. My daughter."

By now, Yvonne was feeling so ashamed that she refused to talk about it anymore. But it took her till the following evening to admit to Robert that she was sorry for what she'd said about his mother. "She's so generous with her help. And I do appreciate her. You know that. And if it's important to you that she comes along, it's all right with me too."

"I already said no to her."

"I'm sorry. I really am."

"So am I." He told her he'd phoned his mother from the clinic because he didn't know how to look at her face once he told her. "Of course," his mother had said, "families belong together." And when he'd apologized, she'd interrupted him. "Do you have any idea how many times I used to wish it were just you and me and your father? I never got that." He'd felt a sudden and deeper comprehension of her distance from Greta and Tobias, and how—by loving him better—she had kept them separate from herself. From him too. More than once, while sitting on her knees, he'd sensed Tobias' jealousy, Greta's sadness, but above all, his mother's resentment of those two. "I wish I'd had Yvonne's courage back then," she'd said to him. "Enjoy being with your family. That's how it should be."

℮

Though Robert ended up with the cooking and laundry, the vacation was the best he'd had with Yvonne and his children. Their cottage was right on the beach. The first day, his children gathered pocketfuls of shells, and when Yvonne suggested they keep only the perfect ones, Emma still hoarded everything she collected, while Caleb only held on to eleven shells that he lined up on the windowsills in the cottage. The others he threw back into the ocean, picturing the waves carrying them ashore further down the beach where a girl would find them. *A girl with long, bare legs. And as she touches them, she knows they're mine and comes searching for me.* While Caleb waited for this girl, he returned his best shells to the sea for her. Emma cried when he tossed his largest shell into the waters. Its outside was crusted, while inside it shimmered pink and white like a mother-of-pearl hairbrush.

Mornings their mother would sun herself on the beach, her yellow swimsuit like sun against her skin, while their father kept himself covered up with baggy shorts and a T-shirt to hide his white belly, even when he went swimming. Caleb liked to swim with him because, in the water, his father was fast and agile; but he didn't like going for walks with him. It was embarrassing, the way his father's body jiggled. And it was even more embarrassing to hear him cough after dinner in the bathroom. On Caleb's last birthday, when he'd been about to go searching for his father after they'd eaten cake, Pearl Bloom had taken him by the arm. "It's best to leave your father alone right now," she'd whispered.

The last day in Rye Beach, Caleb got up at dawn to swim before the beach became crowded. When the sun was half above the line that split water from sky, his mother walked from the cabin and brought him the green kite they'd built together. She held the flat piece of wood with the string wound around it, letting it out as Caleb walked with the kite toward the jetty, where the rocks were smooth and sunbaked beneath his bare feet.

"Now!" she shouted when he reached the largest boulder.

He tossed the kite up, and she ran along the beach, hair flying around her shoulders as she glanced back toward the kite. Jerkily, it rose, then straightened, and she let out more line till it soared, a green diamond in the sun. She handed the string to Caleb, and he walked backwards with it, eyes on the kite. When the line slackened, he ran, pulling it tighter. A wave snagged his mother's feet, and as she laughed, Caleb wished she could be like that every day. While the kite wavered, she hurried toward where it was about to topple down. Caleb wound up the string, and she held the kite until he was done. Then she tossed it into the air, and he ran with the kite until, once again, it stood high above them, tail fluttering in the wind.

When Robert stepped from the cottage and saw his wife's body moving with an ease it hadn't shown in years, he was seized by the dread that, once again, she would leave him behind, and all at once he wondered if she'd ever really had lovers. What if she'd told him her fantasies as if they were real? After all, she liked to flirt, not have sex. *No.* Those other men had been real, so real he'd felt them in bed with him and Yvonne. Still, he wished she would tell him it had never come to anything, that she had merely traveled with someone for a week, say, or a few days.

Even more so, he wished he could take that for the truth.

∽

When they arrived back home the following afternoon, he urged her to rest while he and the children unloaded the car.

"I am more exhausted than I realized," she said when he helped her into bed and brought her a glass of grape juice.

By morning he was glad he'd taken that precaution, because she mentioned a tightness in her back, and within a few days she spent most of her hours in bed once again, lovely in one of her peignoir sets.

The closest Yvonne could come to admitting her regret for excluding Helene from the vacation was to ask her if she could teach her some German recipes. Some afternoons Helene would invite her upstairs where she'd position her on the corner bench with pillows that supported her back, and let her watch while she prepared *Kalbsrouladen* and *Apfelmus, Schnitzel* and *Rotkohl.* Though Yvonne took notes and asked questions, she never made those recipes. Still, she knew it pleased Robert that she was trying to learn from his mother.

One morning, as he sliced a Bosc pear into paper-thin rounds and arranged them in a fan on a white plate for her, he felt certain that he had brought on her illness by wanting her home with him. Instantly he felt ashamed. And yet he knew that he would choose illness for her again if it were to stop her from leaving. Between them, now, there was not much room for anyone else: so focused were they both on this illness that Yvonne had given birth to as if it were their third child—coddling it, conferring over it—that they would only half-listen to Caleb and Emma. While Caleb was content to spin dream pictures inside his head, Emma withdrew into the old sorrow: *Opa.* The familiar sorrow that every new loss evoked for her: *Opa.* But at least she'd learned how to calm herself by moving deeper into the house *Opa* had built—*for me he built it, for me alone*—by breathing its many scents, by retreating into the warm boiler room, or looking from a window at the familiar landscape.

∞

They all came together for the celebration of Helene's eightieth birthday: Greta and Noah Creed on the train as usual, though—according to Mrs. Perelli—they could have afforded a limousine from Boston; Tobias driving up from Hartford in his white convertible; Robert taking the elevator one floor up with his children and Yvonne, whose strapless chiffon gown with its glitter of sequins was too elegant for the occasion.

Dr. Miles brought his wife, Laura, and their little daughter who was just learning to walk; and Pearl Bloom was followed by Fanny Braddock who'd been living with her ever since her mother had died. For years before that, Fanny had kept house for Pearl, and she liked living there now every day because Pearl didn't get angry at her the way her mother used to when she smiled at men.

While Pearl and Greta helped Helene to finish the elaborate meal she'd been cooking, Yvonne rested with her back against the warm tiles of the *Kachelofen*. She felt shut out by the three women, felt disappointed that Helene had thanked her without enthusiasm for the cashmere shawl she had chosen so carefully for her. Emerald to match Helene's necklace, the only color she wore to offset her black clothes. Three different catalogs Yvonne had checked, and she'd sent the first two shawls back because the green had not been the right shade.

"Can I try it?" Pearl had asked while Helene was still opening the beautifully wrapped package, and Helene had nodded and said, "Of course," without trying it on herself. Rude, Yvonne thought. Both of them. Rude. Worse yet that Pearl—who'd started wearing blonde wigs when Stanley Poggs had moved out on her—still had the shawl around her shoulders. She'd probably forget to take it off. Get food stains on it. And, just as with everything else she borrowed, forget that the shawl wasn't hers.

She heard Robert in the living room, opening the piano, and she closed her eyes, willed herself to move into the solace that he always found in his music, and soon she was with him, closer than if he'd sat by her side.

Tobias lifted the lid from a pot of *Gulasch*. "This smells so good."

But Helene didn't acknowledge him. "Pearl?" she said. "Will you taste that gravy for me?"

"Why don't you let Tobias?" Pearl glanced at Tobias who stood by the stove, shoulders wide and bony beneath his starched shirt, eyes alert, injured. "He's got excellent taste," she said, though she knew that Helene wouldn't want his help. It was like that between them when he visited. Still, what Pearl admired was that he always tried to approach Helene, though she'd been distant with him ever since his father's funeral six years ago.

"Let me know if the *Gulasch* needs any more *Paprika,*" Helene told her.

"We all trust your tasting skills, Aunt Pearl," Tobias said. But his eyes stayed on his stepmother, who had never spoken to him about the funeral. At the time it had felt too soon to burden her with his reasons for not coming to his father's bedside or to the cemetery. Still, he'd felt certain she would understand once he told her how that promise to himself had come about. *I won't come to your funeral.* Yet some days he still wondered if he should have broken that promise. To stay away had been more of a struggle than he'd expected. For months afterwards he'd felt edgy whenever he'd thought about approaching his stepmother, and he'd stalled, convincing himself it was too soon. While all along the chill between them had grown. Until too much time had passed to bring it up. With her or with Greta and Robert. Even with Danny, though sometimes he wanted to ask him what it had been like at his father's funeral.

"Let's use the larger bowls, Pearl," his stepmother was saying. She never refused his visits when he came to her on his trips to see Danny, and she'd even told him she'd let him know if she found the old notebook with the legends his mother had written down.

"Can you pour the water off those *Knödel,* Greta?"

He wished he were in the garage with Danny. Soon, he thought. *Soon.*

Steam rose into Greta's face as she drained the *Knödel.* But despite the steam, she felt cold. *Breathe,* she told herself. *Breathe slowly.* The air felt flimsy as though she were standing at a high altitude. For the past week she hadn't slept well, dreams darkened by images of a quarter moon too dim to sustain its reflection, and she'd awakened each morning with the dread that something was about to happen to Helene. When she'd told Noah, he'd said to expect death at her stepmother's age was natural; but what Greta sensed was more complicated than death, something that was to affect the entire family, and she observed Helene closely for any sign of illness, although she moved through the preparations for her birthday dinner with her usual ease.

After Noah and Robert inserted both leaves in the mahogany table and they all sat down to eat, Helene felt a sense of strangeness and belonging all at once. *Stefan should be here. They're his. Especially Emma.* She looked across the table at her granddaughter. There was something about her that Helene felt in herself too, the kind of solidity that held things together—families; houses; one's soul. Emma would not turn into a thin wire like her mother.

As Emma felt her *Oma* watching her so gravely, she smiled, and when *Oma* smiled back, Emma felt all grown up. And she was. Twelve, she was twelve, and she liked sitting at the table between Aunt Greta and Uncle Noah. Even after they'd married, Uncle Noah had refused to stop being a priest. Some said he wasn't a real priest—because how could he, a married man?—but he liked to talk about how being married only made him a better priest. "It gives me more compassion," he'd say. But the bishop didn't agree. He'd taken away Uncle Noah's parish and vestments. And he didn't like it one bit that Uncle Noah held mass at his own house. Emma liked visiting there because sleeping at Uncle Noah's house was like sleeping in church without getting into trouble. He and Aunt Greta had turned the largest of their five bedrooms—right next to the little room where Emma usually got to sleep—into a chapel with a plain wooden altar, lots of candles, and chairs much softer than church benches.

They ate the German delicacies Helene had enjoyed cooking and baking for weeks, and they toasted to her health and many more years, not knowing that in the early morning hours she would let go of all breath. Gently, they teased her with stories that were older than some of the people around her table but had been told and re-told so many times that they had shifted, losing some details while gathering others: how Helene had mistaken those little boys play-ing football for hunchbacks and had called the hospital; how she'd thanked the Evanses for their awful, sweet chocolates, and they'd brought her a box every year from that day on; how she'd lit real wax candles on her first American Christmas tree and had set the curtains ablaze; and how she'd married her husband within two hours of his proposal. . . .

"It was not quite like that," she'd protest now and again, but she'd be laughing.

Robert was humming, forgetting himself within the pleasures of taste, but Yvonne frowned as he pressed one thumb against the crumbs on the tablecloth, licked it off while his eyes followed a slice of *Sauerbraten* on the way to his brother's plate. When he leaned forward to help himself to another serving of the sour-sweet beef, he glanced at Tobias' plate, measuring the size of their serv-ings against each other.

"Are you going to finish your *Knödel*, Yvonne?"

Embarrassed by his appetite, she snapped, "Take it."

"Thank you." He ate her *Knödel*, raised his napkin to his lips, and then reached for both her hands—blue and cold as they often were—to warm them between his own.

It moved and saddened her, his tender acceptance of those hands she hated. Moved and saddened her because she could not do the same for him, could not shed her disgust at his size. Though he wasn't quite as huge as he used to be, she had her suspicions though she'd rather not think about him in the bathroom with the water running, about the red in his eyes when he came back out, the sour breath beneath the smell of toothpaste. She felt certain he lied to her about food, that he ate far more than he let her see, that he kept snacks hidden at the office. Why couldn't he just stop after one sandwich? One piece of cake? How often had she seen him fluctuate between fasting and eating? Once he had one bite, it was as though a dam had split open.

"What is it?" he asked.

"Nothing."

"You're looking at me."

"That's why I married you." She nestled her fingers in his, *warm now, warm.* "So I can look at you. So I won't have to go to your mother and ask her permission to look at her son."

He laughed. "I see."

"Part of New Hampshire marriage law. That you can look at your spouse for six hours every day."

"Six hours?"

"Seven if you apply for an extension. The same goes for dancing, as you well know."

"And where do we go to apply?"

As Helene followed the light banter between them, she felt glad for Robert. *At least they have that between them. That and Robert's music.* She also felt tired. *Probably from all the cooking. The talking. Getting a room ready for Tobias.*

A hand on her arm. Pearl's. "Lie down for a while."

She hesitated.

"I'll make sure we keep celebrating. Go."

When Helene lay down on her bed, she left her black shoes on, and as she gazed at the sturdy leather far away there at the end of her legs, at the shoelaces winding into five sets of holes, at the tiny perforations forming the shape of a bow, she thought of the shoes Yvonne liked to wear—airy straps and thin heels—and wished she'd owned some herself. *I would have broken both legs in them. Not if I'd learned early. Still . . . Greta would have been happier as a girl wearing those.* All at once she felt a terrible sadness that she hadn't bought Greta shoes like that. Tears dripped from her cheeks into her ears as she thought of Greta rebelling against those solid shoes she had ordered from Germany. It hadn't been all that important to make the children obey. If she could do it again, she would let up on that. Just let up. If only she had been kinder. Less strict with Tobias. Suddenly it all seemed to be about shoes, the way things with her stepchildren had gone. She saw Greta *at twelve in Yvonne's silver sandals, running up the steps to the front door of the* Wasserburg, *laughing. And I'm following her. Surefooted on red heels that are even higher*—but the picture wouldn't hold for

long. Wobbled. Helene laughed. *Because I'm the sensible shoe type.
Tobias—* Stop it. *Still, there he is, prancing around on four-inch
heels—that kind of man, though how can I know for sure?—prancing and clicking his fingers as if summoning her. And there's Leo,
applauding while Margret plays Manfred and I play Lieselotte,
stalking around on high heels and whisking the pregnancy pillow
from beneath my dress for Leo to catch and return to me for yet
another pregnancy that Manfred discovers with great dismay.
"Lieselotte?!" While I raise my veil to confess,* "Ja, Manfred."
Dozens of pregnancies. Hundreds of pregnancies, all counted.

While I've only had the one. Robert—

Robert. Knocking at her door and coming in without asking.
Bringing Emma and the lanky doctor who sat right down on the
edge of her bed as though he were Manfred and she Lieselotte.

She giggled as he reached for her wrist. "*Ja,* Manfred."

"I beg your pardon?"

"That's something I'm not, for sure. Not even with a pillow. I've
only had the one."

"Your son—"

"He's all Stefan would let me have."

"Your son thought—"

"Why are you here?"

Sweet pipe tobacco on his breath. "Your son thought it would be
good if I checked in on you. All this excitement today . . ."

"I've handled worse in eighty years." She patted the other edge
of her bed, motioned for Emma to sit there.

"Congratulations." Fingers still on her wrist, the doctor tilted
his head as if listening to her pulse beat from far away. Chin with a
pinprick dimple. Hands narrower than mine. Doesn't take much
for that.

"*Ja,* Manfred."

He turned to Robert. "I want your mother to rest tomorrow. At
her age, it's sometimes good to spend an entire day in bed."

"Wait," Helene said.

But he didn't hear because he was asking Robert questions about
her health as though she were too feeble to answer him.

"You—" She pushed herself up on her elbows. "You are here because of me."

"Mother?" Robert sounded uncomfortable. "Dr. Miles didn't mean—"

"My body—when you talk about my body, you must talk to me."

"Your mother is absolutely right," the doctor said to Robert.

"*To* me. You're still not talking *to* me."

Emma leaned toward her *Oma*, fascinated and proud. *I want to be like that.*

"I apologize. I really do. I won't let that happen again."

"Where I grew up, the old were honored. Not in this country. Especially old women—they become so transparent that you don't even see their windpipes."

"Windpipes?"

"Windpipes and hearts."

"You *are* honored here," Robert said urgently. "With us."

"You need rest." The doctor looked straight at her. Black eyebrows a shade darker than his hair. "If today were not such an important day for you, I'd ask you to stay in bed. But given the cause for celebration, I know you'd get up anyhow to be with your guests."

"You don't know."

He turned to Robert. "I wish all my patients had your mother's independence. Actually—" He covered his mouth. "I did it again."

"You did." Emma nodded.

"Mrs. Blau, I wish all my patients had your independence."

"I have independence too," Emma said. "And I'm one of your patients. So you have at least two patients who have independence, my *Oma* and me."

"Dr. Miles probably wants to get back to his family," her father said.

"You don't know what he wants."

"Emma—"

But Dr. Miles laughed. "In fact, I'm enjoying the view from this room. I didn't know there was a view like that anywhere in this town."

"It's even better from the roof," Emma said. "I'll take you there."

When he wavered, Helene could tell he was the kind of man who didn't know how to say no, the kind of man who'd then extract himself through passivity. She could have rescued him from Emma, but it seemed only just to leave him to her.

"Do you want to see our best view?" Emma persisted.

That wonderful stubbornness. Helene smiled to herself.

"If your grandma and dad don't mind."

"As long as she doesn't go close to the edge," Robert said.

"Careful," Helene said, and it seemed that before she had finished that one word she was alone once again. *Where are they? From tears to laughter to rage. No dividers between all those feelings. Spilling across.* She wanted to reach down and take off her shoes, but it seemed like too much of an effort: they would be too heavy, too cumbersome to put back on. Just the thought of unlacing and then lacing them once again . . . *Too much.* She thought of the years when taking care of her stepchildren had often been too much for her, when there had never been enough left for Robert. *Or for myself.* As well as she could, she had loved these children who were not hers. And still loved them now. Even Tobias. She had done what she could for them. *No more.* She saw *Dr. Miles following Emma to the china cabinet, saw Emma reaching behind the old pewter cups for the key to the roof. They walk down the hallway, unlock the metal door to the roof and the cool housing of the elevator, voices echoing as they climb the steps into the scents of stone and dust and oil where Emma has gone so often with Stefan.*

Stefan? Helene felt exhausted as if she had climbed those stairs to the roof along with Stefan and Emma; yet, it was the kind of tiredness that allowed for only one kind of encounter with sleep—struggle. As soon as she won that struggle and felt herself drifting toward warm and familiar forgetfulness, she got scared because she felt too far from the place where she had started out as a child. What would her life in America have been like if she'd arrived from a country she wouldn't feel ashamed to name as the place she'd come from? She closed her eyes; tried to fight her way back into sleep; but was distracted by the sound of squirrels scampering across the roof. All at once she felt pushed. Greta pushing at her to make an appointment to get a physical; Tobias pushing at her to search for his mother's notebook, pushing at her just by being here today with his soul full of resentment, with that sharpness in his features. *Like the great vultures of the earth.* Pushing at her to do it now, whatever it was they wanted. *Now.*

No more, she thought. *No more.* And was right back to all those times when she had resented the American children, when she would have liked to be only with her husband and child, when she had still assumed that she would have more children. *But you only allowed me the one.* She felt it again then, that pain of Stefan's betrayal, as devastating as it had been the night she had first understood that he'd married her for the sake of his children, the night she had forced him to relinquish his seed. *Relinquish the child I had to steal from you.* With more children of her own she would have been a gentler mother to his American children. She could still feel it, her failure of not having been enough for them. And she hadn't even been able to look after all of Robert's needs because one or the other of them had always wanted her. *But now I can. Can take care of my son.*

It was long after midnight when she got up and took her white stationery from the rosewood desk, and as she wrote her will, leaving everything to Robert, she felt the presence of the biter—*so let it be then, let it*—smelled the sweet-sour scent of *Sauerbraten,* and was drawn into an afternoon more than four decades earlier when she'd sunk to the kitchen floor, terrified that the one child who would ever inhabit her womb was about to bleed from her. She recalled Greta crouching by her side, recalled the touch of her small hands, and felt ill knowing how close she had come that day to losing Robert. She wanted to give Greta something of equal worth, but because that was impossible, and because she could not bear to give her anything that would deprive Robert, she wrote down that Greta's apartment would be rent-free for as long as she was alive. Not that she used it that often now that she was married to her priest. Just when she visited. But it was hers. The one who really deserved something from her was the girl whose life she'd offered up for that of her son. *The necklace.* Not that it would ever undo what she'd taken from Trudi. But she wrote it down: *my emerald necklace to my brother's daughter, Trudi Montag.*

It was almost three when she rang the bell to Pearl's apartment and, without explaining herself, asked Pearl to witness her signature.

"A hard night to sleep," Pearl said as she let her in. "For me too," she added, watching her friend closely.

"Wait till you're eighty."

"Let me turn seventy first. Please." Without the wig, Pearl's head was small, childlike almost with her residue of gray hair and stringy neck. She motioned to the cashmere shawl she'd wrapped around the shoulders of her nightgown. "Do you want this? Are you cold?"

"No."

"I used to think I was so different from others in the building, so much younger, more adventurous. . . . And now look at me. What I am is one of many old people who live in this house."

"A child." Helene smiled. "You're just a child."

"Quite often I feel all of twelve."

"Quite often you act all of twelve."

"Thank you. And it doesn't even take effort."

They sat down at the marble-top table in Pearl's dining room, shadowed by the greenhouse plants and the night beyond the glass.

"How about you?" Pearl asked. "Your real age . . . inside of you."

"I have always been old."

"No, you're not."

"I like being old. It's easier. Besides, it's what people say about me. Some days though . . . on my best days . . ."

"Yes?"

". . . I'm thirty-five, the age I was when Robert was born. It was my best year, Pearl."

"You were beautiful."

"I had what I wanted."

Two raps—come to the window; one rap—open the dumb-waiter. It came like a chant to Pearl. Moved her to tears that she'd ever had that kind of friendship. *Two raps—to the window; one—to the dumbwaiter.* All at once she felt afraid. She tried to laugh it away. "Remember how we used to bang against the steam pipes to send messages to each other?"

"You made this place home to me. Pearl—"

"Yes?"

"About me coming from Germany and—"

"You didn't live there when any of it was happening."

"Still. It's where I come from. Sometimes I wonder what I would have done if I'd stayed over there."

"I never thought about you that way."

"Nate did. I wish I had told him how sorry I am. It's just that I didn't know how to say it, or if I even had the right to say it."

Pearl leaned forward. "Why now?"

"Can we do this?" Helene smoothed the pages of the will that was to make up for every harsh word she'd spoken to Robert when she'd felt drained by the older children, make up for the brothers and sisters she'd deprived him of because her husband had believed he'd fathered enough children. *His American children—* "His American children," she said aloud.

"If you like, we can wait till morning."

"No." Helene seized the fountain pen. "Keep this safe for me," she said and set her signature in blue ink to the paper that left everything—except her necklace—to the son who had issued from that one night's sweet struggle. *Let it be yours, Robert. It's only right.* And as she watched Pearl sign her name beneath hers, she was overtaken by relief and exhaustion.

∽

"She was calm," Pearl would tell Helene's family the next day and, again, three days later at her funeral. "She was calm."

Standing by the wide grave that also contained her *Opa,* Emma looked at his name, last for now on the gravestone:

STEFAN BLAU 1881–1953

Above him on the granite was the name of his daughter, Agnes, who had died in 1910 after living only one year and one month; and above Agnes were the names of *Opa*'s other wives. Emma felt outraged that they had to lie beneath the ground, outraged that her *Oma* was about to be placed there in the dark with them. But at least she hadn't killed *Oma* with her weight. "She'll be the death of you," *Oma* had told *Opa,* but he'd only laughed and bounced Emma on his knees.

She'll be the death of you.

From nearby came the sound of the Brook-that-finishes-grieving—a sound like that of a very strong wind—and as Emma raised her head, she noticed how the mountains across the gray lake had a sense of stability about them, of eternity that was in odd contrast to the lives of all who had walked up here for *Oma*'s funeral, all so fragile. And yet, seeing these mountains made it seem almost possible that humans, too, could be forever. And perhaps they were, once they lay buried and became part of this hillside where she stood, became part of the undergrowth that had sprung from the pulpy trunks of fallen trees and gave off scents of decay and recent growth.

When Dr. Miles and his wife came to the *Wasserburg* for the funeral lunch, they stood with her by a window and watched as darkening clouds raced across the hazy sun, watched as a swarm of birds was blown sideways against the sky. Instead of scattering, the birds moved into a tighter formation that looked like a dirty sail. Then, all at once, filaments of water linked the lake to the sky. Emma hoped that, once it cleared, the doctor would climb on the roof with her again and let her show him around as he had a few days earlier on *Oma*'s birthday; but it was still raining when he and his wife got their coats.

"Our daughter Amy gets scared of storms," Mrs. Miles told Emma's father. "She's staying with our neighbor."

Late that afternoon, when only Helene's family was left, Pearl Bloom brought out the copy she had made of Helene's will and read it aloud.

Emma could see that her father was stunned. "I didn't know," he kept saying. "I truly didn't."

"Your mother cheated Greta and me," Uncle Tobias said.

"I'm sure she didn't intend anything like that."

"I agree with Robert," Aunt Greta said.

"Helene gave a lot to you," Pearl Bloom reminded Uncle Tobias.

But he shook his head. "And now she's taking a lot from us. That house should belong to all of us."

All of us? Does that mean me? Emma wanted to ask, but when she glanced at her brother who stood by the window with her, he tapped one finger against her lips to stay quiet so that the grown-ups wouldn't tell them to run along and find something to do.

"I'm not ready to even think about a will," her father said.

"Why should you?" Uncle Tobias said. "Given that she's left it all to you."

"That's not why."

"Everything I ever got, I got from strangers."

Emma frowned at Caleb. What had Uncle Tobias gotten from strangers?

"Give me time," her father was saying.

Aunt Greta nodded. "Maybe what you can do in the meantime is share the income from the rent. Until you sell the house."

"But that would be against my mother's wishes."

"It was built *before* your mother stepped off the boat," Uncle Tobias reminded him. "Built with money from Greta's grandparents. With hard work from my mother. I'm going to check this out with a lawyer."

"Give me time to think," Emma's father said. "Please."

"One solution," Aunt Greta said, "would be to give equal shares of the building to us. We'd each own one third."

Equal shares of three. Emma thought it was the kind of idea *Opa* would have liked—one third to each of his children: Aunt Greta, Uncle Tobias, and her father. That's how she would divide the house. And then they'd all live here. It was what she and Caleb whispered about by the window, promising each other that they'd never fight about the house the way their father and Uncle Tobias and Aunt Greta were fighting about it.

"But then what if you or Tobias decide to sell?" their father was asking Aunt Greta.

Emma stared at Caleb. "Can they? Are they allowed to sell the house?"

"It's supposed to stay together," their father said as if he'd heard them, though he was still talking to Aunt Greta.

"Keeping the house together will destroy it and drive this family apart," Uncle Tobias warned.

"It sounds like you're putting a curse on it," Emma's father protested.

"It was cursed before I was born. You tell him, Greta. Tell him about your grandparents' money."

She looked uneasy. "He borrowed from them. For the house. Without paying any of it back."

"Tell him what your Grandma Flynn said."

Greta hesitated. "Not to trust him in matters of money."

"But I never asked my mother to give it all to me," Emma's father said.

"Of course you didn't," Pearl Bloom said quickly.

Uncle Tobias turned to her. "But it does not take away the responsibility of what Robert needs to do with it now, and he—"

Emma's mother interrupted him. "Don't push him like that, Tobias."

"All we're asking," Aunt Greta said gently, "is that you rectify it."

"I will."

"Good." She stood up, took her handbag from the top of the piano, and wrote out a check. "In the meantime I'll give you my rent for this month. Here."

"But it says in the will that your apartment is free."

"I can't have an advantage over Tobias."

"I want to work something out. Something that respects my mother's wishes."

"Oh please," Uncle Tobias said. "Don't hide behind her the way you did when you were three."

"I'll find a way to make things just."

That night, Yvonne opened her arms to Robert, but he didn't want her solace: he wanted to be alone so he could eat. When, finally, she was sleeping, he got up and ate till there was only the shame and, afterwards, the release of it all in the downward swirl of water. In his grieving for his mother, he withdrew from Tobias and Greta. He didn't understand how they could think of money so soon after his mother's death, and he felt hurt when Tobias told him the will was invalid because it required three witnesses, not just one. But when Tobias checked with a lawyer about contesting the will on that basis, he was told that when a widow dies without a valid will, her property goes to the widow's children—not her stepchildren.

Soon, Robert believed, he would figure out how to deal with the will. To appease his siblings, Yvonne suggested he send them expensive presents—a leather briefcase for Tobias, a weekend on Nantucket for Greta and Noah; but his brother returned the package unopened, while his sister never mentioned his gift.

"They're not trying," Yvonne said. "They're not even trying."

Whenever Robert let himself think about the will, it was with confusion and anger that his mother had saddled him with his father's request to keep the house together. With one more chance to disappoint his father. The few times he felt content were when he sat down at the piano; but that didn't happen often enough because his days would fold on each other so quickly that he always felt he was losing something. After a full day at the clinic, it felt selfish to play the piano when there was so much work to do on the house. Some day soon, he told himself, he would find a way to divide the inheritance without having to sell the house. Meanwhile, he didn't deposit the rent checks Greta insisted on sending him.

Since he couldn't bear to sort out his mother's belongings, her apartment stayed vacant for two years, though he could have used the rental income, not just for his family, but also to maintain the building since Danny Wilson was always at him with an everlengthening list of repairs. Robert kept her keys in a kitchen drawer with all the other keys for the building, unaware that—quite often—Emma would let herself into her *Oma*'s apartment, compelled to search, to touch her *Oma*'s belongings until she was right back in her *Opa*'s life.

Some evenings Yvonne would urge Robert to play the piano, and he'd do it for her. Invariably then, as his hands proved to him that the music would always be there for him if he let it, he felt himself yielding to its current—sometimes turbulent; sometimes calming—as it spilled him back into himself.

Once, after he raised his fingers from the keys, it seemed possible that, with the right words, he would be able to reach Tobias and Greta. "We'll work this out," he wrote to both. "Just be patient with me. Please."

"I know your intentions are good," Greta told him on the phone. "But it's not enough."

"Write to me once you have facts," was Tobias' answer. "Right now, I give no weight to your words."

From Danny, Tobias knew that his brother was making foolish deals with tenants, letting them break through walls, enlarging some apartments by robbing another room or two from adjoining apartments, making those difficult to rent.

Ever since Tobias had stopped coming to Winnipesaukee, Danny had made the trip to Hartford. "Your brother cares more about animals," Danny told him one Sunday morning, "than he cares about the house. If you add his lack of business sense to his generosity, you've got a mess."

"It's too much for him. Working at his clinic all day and then trying to maintain the house."

"The ones I feel sorry for are the kids because they don't get much from either parent. Emma, she likes to sneak into her grandma's apartment. Stays there for hours."

The day before each of Danny's visits, Tobias would shop for fresh fruits and seafood, for beeswax candles and imported wines, for the long, skinny chocolate wafers Danny enjoyed. Sometimes, when he'd look at Danny next to him in bed, he not only saw his graceful neck and sinewy body, but also the reflection of Greta's hair red on the water, her palm on the chest of the priest, and marveled that both he and Greta had ended up with the men they had first touched that very same day.

He had tried to say that to her once when he'd visited her and Noah in their brownstone in Boston. But she'd shaken her head. "I had no idea how I felt about Noah until much later."

"I did."

"You were a boy."

"I saw you there with him on the lake, and I knew."

∽

During one of her raids, Emma found a red cake tin with folded letters behind her *Oma*'s shoes. When she wrapped it into her cardigan, and smuggled it into her room, she felt calmer than she had in a long time. It was as though something had settled inside her. She didn't tell Caleb about the letters she kept hidden beneath her bed. At first she honored her grandparents' privacy by not reading them. All she would let herself do was run her fingers along the handwritten lines; but eventually that only made her so restless that she read them all.

Lieber Stefan . . . they started. Or *Mein Lieber Stefan* . . .

Emma still knew enough German to figure out many of the words *Oma* had written, words that revealed a passion in her practical *Oma* that amazed Emma. As she imagined *Opa* reading, she was moved by the longing in those letters, something she had believed you could only feel for someone who was not with you, rather than someone who lived with you day after day. Like the way she still missed *Opa*. Had missed him at age six and age eight and age twelve. And would continue to miss him. Obviously, he had kept *Oma*'s letters and read them many times. And obviously, *Oma* had retrieved them for herself after his death. But where then were the letters he had written in return?

Periodically, Emma would search for them in her grandparents' apartment. After it was rented to a dentist and his family, she searched in the basement storage area next to the Perellis', where a moth-eaten thing that might have been a large goat at one time, or a zebra, was wedged atop two steamer trunks behind the wooden slats and kept its mournful gaze on her.

Though she didn't find any letters written by her *Opa*, she felt certain they had to be hidden somewhere in the *Wasserburg*, and as she filled the silences between her *Oma*'s letters with her *Opa*'s words, she imagined the letters he must have written, and she fabricated a story of the love between her grandparents that was based on assumptions and scant evidence, a story that would shape and distort what she was to believe about love.

She was still filling in details of that story for herself by the time Caleb left for film school in Los Angeles, and she took the letters with her two years later when she moved into a dorm at the University of New Hampshire. Though it was just an hour's drive away and close enough to commute, her mother insisted it was important she learn to live away from home.

Her major was German, the comforting sounds that had come to her in childhood along with English sounds as if they were two branches of the same language. Though it frustrated her that she was far ahead of the other students, their struggle at entering German made her appreciate how hard it must have been for her grandparents to approach English from the other direction when they'd first come into the country. Both had told her about the pleasure they'd felt when, finally, they had learned enough to read without a dictionary.

Though she liked her classes, she looked forward to her drive home every weekend, especially to that last stretch along the shoreline once she reached the winding road at the southern point of the lake in Alton. From there, she could always feel the *Wasserburg* pull her back: first she would see it in her mind—built of bricks and higher than any other house in Winnipesaukee—and as she'd turn off toward the lake, she'd first spot the roofline with the ornate tiles, then the courtyard, the fountain, the French doors to the lobby. From that distance, it was impossible to see the peeling paint around the tall windows, the untended garden, the gradual rot that had been taking hold in the years since her grandmother's death.

It disappointed her that Caleb's visits were so sporadic: he'd either arrive from Los Angeles without warning or cancel plans he'd made months before. And when he was home, he'd usually want to get away to Boston or at least Concord because he didn't like the films playing at the Royal. Song-and-dance movies, he called them. Even those that didn't have any music in them. One weekend he took Emma along to Boston, where they stayed with Aunt Greta; but they only saw her and Uncle Noah for breakfast because Caleb dragged Emma from one theater to another. They saw *Persona* and *Stolen Kisses,* and *Rosemary's Baby* and *Viva Maria, Hour of the Wolf* and *Rachel, Rachel.* On the train home, Emma was too exhausted to talk with him about the films. She was thinking about something Aunt Greta had said to her—that her father had a certain blindness when it came to the house. Emma knew he was still trying to convince Uncle Tobias and Aunt Greta that he didn't think of the house as his alone. And Emma could tell that he really believed it, though no one else did. Uncle Tobias hadn't spoken to him at all after accusing him of having lied all along about sharing the inheritance.

It all had become so complicated.

Her father often fretted about Uncle Tobias and Aunt Greta on Sunday evenings when Emma had dinner with her parents at *Opa's* old restaurant before she drove back to school. She usually carried at least half a dozen German novels in her backpack. Occasionally she read German travel books, picturing herself in the open window of a narrow hotel near the Rhein, feeding bread to silver-breasted pigeons or counting the barges go by as her *Opa* had as a boy. Perhaps she would even spend her honeymoon in Burgdorf. Not that she had anyone in mind. By the end of her junior year she'd only had two boyfriends: the first a studious and shy student much like herself who scared himself the first time he touched her breasts; the second a graduate assistant in her language lab with whom she had sex every day for one entire semester.

Since she did not miss them when she was away from them, she didn't know how to define what she felt for them, except that it seemed insignificant compared to the love in her *Oma's* letters. She had read them so many times that not a single German word remained unfamiliar. One of her professors, Franz Haufstolz, a Swiss native, praised her for speaking without an accent and encouraged her to consider teaching German. He told her she had a gift for moving right inside a language, and when he recommended the University of Wisconsin for graduate work, it was the only school Emma applied to. However, when she was accepted, she did not tell Professor Haufstolz because she felt unsettled at the thought of living that far away from the *Wasserburg*.

———————————|———————————

1 9 6 9 – 1 9 8 0

Three weeks before Emma was to graduate from the University of New Hampshire, the secretary of the German department came to the door of her classroom and motioned for her to come out. It was raining when she ran to her car, and what she'd recall afterwards would be fragments of the drive—leaves and wind and rain and the hope that the secretary had misunderstood about her father—but when she reached home, he had already been taken away, and her mother was sitting with Aunt Greta on the sofa, hands on her lap. Blue hands. Still hands.

"He choked," she said. "After he finished his breakfast, he choked, Emma. Not at the table. Afterwards, you know . . . in the bathroom."

Emma looked away. Saw the carpet and her aunt's shoes and the walls and was drawn back to her mother's face. *You used him up. That's why he died so young.*

Her aunt took off her thick glasses. Stood up and folded Emma into her arms. "I am so very sorry." Her eyes were puffy.

"I heard him cough in there," her mother was saying. "Then— Then he fell, Emma. I heard him fall . . ."

Over her aunt's shoulders, Emma could see the roses on the mantle, white blossoms, long stems, encased by crystal.

". . . first he was coughing, and then there was nothing for a while, and then he fell, and I—"

They didn't say what they all knew but never spoke of: that he'd made himself sick on purpose. To keep from getting bigger. *The faucet running. Coughing. Eyes red and moist when he'd come out of the bathroom.* It embarrassed them almost as much as it used to mortify him.

"Caleb—" Emma started.

"On his way." Aunt Greta sat back down. "He's flying into Boston. Noah is picking him up."

"But he was only fifty-three," Emma said.

"Did you know that he was playing the piano the first time I ever saw him?" her mother asked. "Did you know that, Emma?"

Emma saw herself opening her father's closet in the guest room, folding his huge suits and giving them away. But to whom? *Such a waste. Don't think about his clothes. Don't. But it's such a waste to just throw them away.* For years now, he'd been the heaviest man in town, his movements restricted as though he lived in a cage. *The cage of his weight. Of his own making. And the shame of dying because of that.*

"We're all glad he had his music," Greta said. She leaned her head against the backrest of the sofa, feeling very tired. Early this morning, before she had known about Robert, she'd made love to Noah, and they'd both slept afterwards for a brief while. When they'd woken up, they'd turned toward one another and when they'd found the bliss once more, she'd wanted to cry at the waste of all those years they had not been together, although she knew instinctively that in their chaste love those early years had been as significant as the years of closeness between them.

"His music was always there for your father," Yvonne was telling Emma. "For me too. That's what I keep thinking about . . . your father playing the piano. I could always breathe deeper when he played. He lived his best hours inside his music. Did you know that?"

But all Emma could think of was the piano bench at the *Cadeau du Lac.* During their last visit to the restaurant, the chair at the table had been too narrow for her father. Still, he had tried to squeeze in, and then, face flushed with humiliation, he'd waddled to the piano bench below the shelf in the lobby where the St. Joseph statue used to stand. Though Emma had wanted to follow her father and help him carry that bench across the dining room to their table, she'd sat without moving, angry at him for being such an embarrassment to her. They had not gone back since.

In the days between her father's death and his funeral, they found food hidden away: at the bottom of his hamper eight chocolate bars; beneath his summer hat a block of cheddar cheese; in his car four huge, stone-hard pastries in a mess of nuts and glaze and black-and-white dough. Among his papers was the deed to the *Wasserburg,* owned by him and Yvonne with right of survivorship.

Emma tried to talk about the deed with Caleb when they were at Heflins' buying groceries for the reception that was to follow the burial. "It doesn't make sense. After going through all that grief with Uncle Tobias and Aunt Greta, he wouldn't have made the same mistake *Opa* made."

"I always hoped he'd find some way of settling with them."

"Maybe he was angry at those two the day he wrote it over to Mother. He never said anything about it."

"Who knows what his reasons were."

"You think he did it to avoid probate?"

"Let's not. Okay?"

"If he'd known he'd die so young, he would have never put just Mother's name on the deed."

Caleb pushed the grocery cart faster to get away from her.

"For her to get it all is not fair." Emma knew it was too soon to talk about any of this, and she tried to stop herself, but she couldn't. "You know she isn't capable of looking after the house."

"Then she'll get help."

"From whom? And how is she going to pay for it?" When he didn't answer, she said, "I'm sorry. I know I'm not doing this right." As they added cucumbers and pears to their cart, she asked him about grad school. About his films.

Still, beneath those questions, he felt her tunneling back to the deed. "A big chunk of cheese," he told old man Heflin's widow.

"How about a quarter of that wheel over there? And a large salami."

"I wish you would let me see some of your films, Caleb."

"I've only made two so far. Short films . . . study projects, really."

"Do you show them to other students?"

"Well, yes, but that's different. It's seen as something in progress. To learn from. But nothing really finished."

"What are they about?"

"My films?" He stalled, reluctant to summarize for her what he'd spun from memories and imagination, those films that he infused with the intensity of vision his grandfather had experienced from the boat, with details from the stories his grandfather had told him. Like about the fire in the restaurant and the dreams he used to have of America. For Caleb, those two belonged together because the dreams had caused his grandfather to come to America, while the fire had caused him to leave New York and build the *Wasserburg.* Caleb always felt closer to the people he used for material, a merging of sorts, a loving that was coupled with guilt at having taken from them. Ever since he'd heard about his father's death, he'd thought that his next film might be about the woman his father had told him about, the woman who fell from love to earth. Though Caleb didn't know enough about her yet, he had found that, usually, when he envisioned one element, other images that had been evolving separately would suck onto it, become one with it; and what he could already feel coming together with the woman falling were images of a boy born inside a piano with his eyes far open, images of two children playing the people game, of monkeys and songbirds free inside those children's house. Whenever Caleb took fragments from his own life and made them magical, he felt magical himself. He'd always loved that story of coming into the world eyes open, and he would give that detail to the boy who would live inside the piano even as a man, playing his music from within.

"Yes, your films." Emma reached for six loaves of bread. "Can you at least tell me what they are about?"

"It's hard to explain. I guess . . . if I tried to sum them up, they'd fall apart. Look at it this way: if I could say something in a few words, I wouldn't have to make an entire film."

She was listening closely, nodding.

"I need to figure out what they are about before I feel comfortable letting you see them."

"I'll wait till you're ready then."

"Thank you. When I have a film worthy of an audience, I'll bring it home."

"Caleb—" Already she was right back where she knew she shouldn't go. But if she didn't, what would happen to the house? "If Mother dies too . . . and I hate to even think about it—"

"Then don't. We already have one parent to bury."

For a while they added groceries to their cart without speaking.

"But if," she finally said, feeling ashamed and yet continuing, choosing her words with caution. "What would you want to do with the house?"

"It's too soon to talk about that, Emma."

"I know. But I think we should."

"Why?"

"Just so we don't have to worry about it."

"I'm not worried about it."

"Because you don't live here."

"Listen," he said, fed up with her urgency to know, to solve it all this moment. "Dad just died. That really is the one thing on my mind. We haven't even buried him yet." *A huge coffin sinking toward the center of the earth.* He tried to shut off the I-can-use-this voice. Usually he was grateful for the way it collected material, was accustomed to its process of recording just about everything he experienced. And even though he could never use all of it, everything he had ever brought to film had started with that impulse, had played and replayed itself for him as if it were already on screen. *But not my father's death. I don't want to use my father's death.*

"Please—"

"What now, Emma?"

"Don't snap at me like that. Please, can't we talk about it just once?"

Arms crossed, he leaned against the dairy case, feeling a cold draft against his back, thinking how he used to like Heflins' much better before it had been refurbished. "Talk then."

"It would be best to keep the house in the family."

"It's not ours to decide. I can't worry about what may or may not belong to me some day. And I feel goddamn creepy discussing this."

"If she deeded it to us, I'd make sure you and I would own it equally. I'd follow through. You know I would."

That he knew about her. That she followed through. While he now and then forgot to do what he'd promised. He also knew that she was a saver. Careful with what was hers. Right back to her first bicycle that she'd only ridden on the sidewalk to keep the tires clean and new. Imagine. Why bother having a bike if you don't ride it? How devastated she'd been when he'd taken it on the road after a rain. *That's me. Impulsive and messy.* At least that's what every one of his lovers had told him so far.

"I would send you rent money every month. You could focus on your films. Let me ask you something. Do you believe that I want what's good for you too?"

"I don't know how to answer that one, Emma."

"But you do believe that *Opa* wanted to keep the house in the family."

Caleb laughed. "That house, Emma . . . that house has not been in the family for ages. Just think of that whole miserable situation that split Dad from his brother and sister. Remember that afternoon Grandma's will was read, when you and I both knew in our bones that the house belonged to all three of them? Don't you think it's ironic that Mom owns all of it now even though she is not even Grandpa's blood relative?"

"She owns it, yes, but I'm the one who'll end up taking care of it. And of her. So she doesn't just spend it all on roses and . . . and fluff."

"Great with peanut butter and strawberry jam."

"What are you talking about?"

"Fluff. Marshmallow fluff."

She had to laugh.

He grasped her shoulders. "Don't take it on, Emma. Don't do it."

"I couldn't bear doing all this work and then having you sell it." Already she could see buyers inspecting the house. Strangers. She felt stateless, homeless. And because of that, her words came out sharper than she intended. "I deserve to know what you'll do once the house is ours."

"You need to stop this. Right now." He rubbed his arms. "It's cold in here. Let's go."

As they got into the car, he already dreaded the variations of that same conversation that they'd have over the years to come, conversations about ownership and care of the house that would divide them and bring them back together again. And always, always it would be Emma who'd start it with her insistence to know what was to become of the house, but who'd then pull him back with phone calls and letters while—all around her—the house would be crumbling. She would want him to go to a lawyer with her. To draw up something simple. While he'd continue to fight her.

But now, on the day before their father's funeral, Emma was eager to draw away from those questions, to seek solace in what was familiar, comfortable. The idea for the people game came to her the instant they entered the state liquor store and saw a slight man with a bow tie waiting on two women.

She nudged Caleb, motioned toward the man who was holding a bottle close to his rimless glasses. "People game?"

"This would definitely be the superior choice," the clerk was telling the women. "It's full-bodied, yet unobtrusive—what I would call an intelligent wine. You get a subtle taste of the grape." His yellow shirt barely contrasted the color of his skin. "I simply can't stand wine if I can't get at least a taste of the grape . . ."

Caleb's eyes flickered. Emma motioned him toward a shelf with red wine, and they watched as the clerk gently lowered the bottle into a paper bag. As he bent over it, his pale fingers folded its top, creasing the edges meticulously.

Caleb whispered, "Can you imagine him putting his socks on in the morning?"

Emma muffled a laugh. Still, beneath all of it she felt the loss of her father, felt a grief so cold and steady that she was afraid of letting it sink deeper. "Socks . . . oh yes, his socks would be ironed."

The clerk glanced up, briefly. His pink scalp showed through strands of blond.

"Socks folded in pairs instead of rolled up," Caleb whispered.

"I can just see him. He takes at least ten minutes to pull them over his toes."

"The care he must take in brushing his teeth . . ."

"And tying his shoelaces. Bending over each polished shoe."

"Adjusting the laces so the ends are the same length."

"Always. And then the ritual of forming a perfect bow."

The clerk reached for the tape dispenser, slowly detached a piece of tape, smoothed it over a creased edge of paper. He looked like the kind of man, Caleb thought, who'd use fastidious manners and pompous words to cover his loneliness. Who'd live alone—*not because he chooses to, but because he's afraid he's too colorless and passionless to approach anyone. But there used to be someone. A wife who left. Marcia.* Yes. Marcia was a good name for her. Caleb could feel what it would be like to be that man. *To come home to a small, dark house where he's lived for twenty years, the house he and Marcia saved for. He unlocks the front door, turns on the light to a room filled with things Marcia picked out: furniture, dishes, blankets, pictures, lamps . . . The double bed they bought on layaway before they got married, too large and cold for him alone. Framed photos of his son who now lives with his mother: the boy laughing on the swing set in the backyard; in his Sunday suit; in his mother's arms as an infant. In the kitchen he makes himself a pot of tea, unfolds his newspaper and—*

"Four loops." Emma grinned at him.

"What?"

"Two shoes. Two loops in each bow. That makes four."

"Don't rush me." Caleb picked up a bottle of cabernet. Held it against the light. Pretended to study its deep red glow. "I'm still on the first shoe."

"Which shoe?"

He grimaced at her, no longer wanting to play the game, and yet continuing because it was easing the tension between him and Emma.

"Hurry up then. I already got both of them tied. You're even slower than he. Christ—" She coughed to cover another laugh. "I just thought of something."

"Tell me."

"Can you picture him having sex?"

"We just got his shoes on him."

"So? Take them off."

"There are limits, Emma."

"May I assist you with something?" the clerk asked Caleb as the two women walked out with the creased bag.

"We're looking for four reds and four whites." When Caleb glanced at Emma, her eyes were bright, urging him to be outrageous. "Something light, yet full-bodied. Not too obtrusive, though," he added, feeling as though he were betraying this man in whose house he'd been, whose loneliness he'd probed.

"You're wicked," Emma gasped as soon as they were outside the store with their bottles. "Wonderfully wicked." She wiped her eyes.

"Well, I wanted to make sure you'd get a wine with at least a taste of the grape."

But as they approached Emma's car, the reality of their father's death settled on them a sorrowfulness that stayed with them through the afternoon and night, through the morning of his funeral and beyond when Emma would still have dreams about the size of his casket and the circle of mourners around his grave site—her mother and brother, Aunt Greta and her priest who said prayers over her father's grave, several townspeople who used to bring their animals to her father's clinic, and just a few of the tenants—a circle much smaller than at her *Oma*'s funeral ten years before.

∾

Though Emma was prepared to look after her mother, Yvonne only crumpled for a few days and then arose as if the weight of her husband's concern had kept her confined.

"Don't do too much at once," Emma warned her.

But Yvonne had been resting up for decades and felt buoyant with long-stored energy; she went for walks by herself, declined dinner invitations from Pearl Bloom and Rosalie Perelli; decreased her pain medication; called cabs to take her to her favorite stores; talked about studying for a driver's license; and dyed her hair the blue-black it used to be. Still, her newfound strength had little to do with matters of the house: there, she relied on Emma who nested herself back into the fifth-floor apartment, though Yvonne urged her to go back to school. But Emma arranged with her professors to finish her last assignments by mail, and the day her classmates walked across the stage at UNH to receive their degrees, she sat at the built-in desk in her old room, making a list of repairs the way *Opa* used to. Except his lists had been shorter since he'd never let anything get run down. He used to have workmen to call on. Homer and Irene Wilson. Danny. While all Emma had left was Danny.

Since her Uncle Tobias worried about Danny's health, he called her at least once a week to make sure Danny was eating enough and not working too hard. It meant a lot to her to be getting closer to this uncle who'd been so aloof with her entire family ever since her father had inherited the *Wasserburg*. But he was no longer like that with her. Because she'd found his mother's old notebook in the storage bin. When she'd given it to him, she'd apologized because it smelled musty, but he'd said, "Oh no, that's all part of it, of her and that time," and he'd slowly turned the stained, buckled pages, reading to her about fights between the Chocoruas and the Aquadoctans, about the peace between the tribes that came when an Aquadoctan princess married a Chocoruan prince.

"It should be that easy for all of us," he'd said and closed his mother's notebook.

On the phone, Emma would assure him that Danny was pacing himself, that she reminded him about taking his vitamins and arthritis pills. Most days she felt that all she inherited were Danny and her mother. Except it was easier to talk with Danny about expenses.

Her mother would only wave Emma's concerns away and claim

there'd always been enough money to care for the house. She'd want to hear what Emma thought of her new linen coat, say, or if she should get a pink or peach scarf to wear with it. The things her mother bought were useless and expensive, like long mirrors on each floor next to the elevator. "So you can take one more look at yourself before you leave the building."

At almost seventy, Danny was still able to fix almost everything, though he had become quite slow. Yet, about his appearance he was as conscientious as ever: his clothes were stylish, and he brushed his thick hair frequently, often half-crouched as he admired himself in the side mirrors of cars in the garage. Once a month he took an overnight trip. To see family, he said. Family, Emma knew, meant Uncle Tobias who wanted Danny to retire and live with him in Hartford. But Danny was stubborn: he liked to go to the dog races in Belmont; fish from the dock; walk to the diner on Main for breakfast before starting his workday.

It didn't take the tenants long to bring their complaints to Emma. Though Yvonne was charming when they called her, she'd forget their problems, just as she'd forget to deposit their rent checks and let them accumulate in her kitchen along with unopened bills and scraps of paper with phone numbers but no names. When Emma finally took the checks to the bank, her mother didn't let her deposit the ones from Aunt Greta that arrived from Boston every month.

"She obviously wants to pay for her apartment," Emma said. "And it's no hardship for her. She has millions."

"Your father always honored Greta's rent-free arrangement."

"But it's wasteful. She hardly uses the apartment. Still, we keep it available for her. We should either accept her checks or—"

"I'm not taking rent money from Greta."

"Then let's rent her apartment. We need the income." She kept talking while her mother shook her head. "And the few times she and Uncle Noah are here, they can stay with us."

The end of August, Emma decided to postpone her acceptance to graduate school at the University of Wisconsin.

"You don't need to do that," her mother told her.

"I want to help you with the house. It's too much for you alone."

The pattern of Emma's days was alike. After breakfast with her mother, she'd inspect apartments, hallways, and storage areas, scheduling repairs and maintenance. Evenings she cleaned her mother's apartment or washed both their clothes. In her memory every day with her *Opa* had been distinctly different, but now her days of labor bled into each other as she tried to find tenants for empty apartments, helped Danny paint the lobby, brought in a plumber to take care of leaks, an electrician to replace the broken light fixtures in the elevator.

During those years when her father had managed the building without enough foresight and energy, he'd never minded that people moved out without returning the keys to their apartments or to the outside door. As a result, a lot of keys were missing, and some tenants had to keep their doors unlocked in order to get back inside. Since the records he'd kept were incomplete and impossible to balance against bank statements, Emma started a new set of books.

None of the rents had been raised since *Oma*'s death. When she sent out notices, announcing a ten percent increase, and added up all income and expenses she expected for the following year, she felt encouraged that, gradually, she would be able to restore the *Wasserburg*. She painted the rooms in the basement where the maids used to live, bought secondhand beds and dressers, hung a plastic shower curtain in the shared bathroom, and sent another round of notices, announcing that each room would be available for five dollars a night to the tenants' visiting relatives.

"Now she's running a motel in my basement," Danny complained to Tobias one Saturday evening while they were washing dishes. "Makes them bring their own sheets and towels. And if she thinks that it'll bring in another buck, she'll have me serving them coffee and eggs in bed."

"I'll serve you coffee and eggs in bed."

"Bare-assed in a white apron?"

"For you . . . sure. I'll start tomorrow morning. I'll even iron your shirts for you. Cut your toenails."

"Please. You'll turn me into a kept man."

"It's called retirement, Danny. And you're five years overdue for that. My house has space for both of us."

"You don't have enough stuff on your walls."

"That way you can hang up your greyhound pictures and anything else you want."

"What I like about my job is having the entire basement to myself."

"Emma is changing that, isn't she? Soon she'll want your spare bedroom for guests and—"

"Don't even think that."

"You have to be realistic. Since you have a kitchen, Emma will figure anytime now that she can charge the guests for using that. You'll wake up and—"

"Don't."

"—and there'll be four, five people in your kitchen, making pot roasts or pies. . . ."

Danny grinned, shaking his head. "Even as a kid, you were a pain." He rinsed out a bowl, set it in the drying rack for Tobias.

"You can have my basement."

"All of it?"

"Plus half of this bed."

"We're so . . . different, Tobias."

"Not really."

"I think so."

"You mean things like education?"

"That too. Mostly the way we love. You're more like your father that way."

Tobias stopped drying the silverware. "My father?"

"Don't get so upset."

"I don't make people destroy what's important to them."

"I was talking about wanting more than you already have. Keeping at it the way he used to."

"I'm not like my father."

"Okay."

"You don't want more than you have?"

"Mostly I'm content with what I already have."

"And I'd be content to just have you."

"You're so smart with words."

"That's me. Smart with words."

"And angry with me."

"Because I am nothing like my father."

"I'm sorry."

"All right. Sometimes . . ."

"What?"

"Sometimes I still wonder if I should have gone to his funeral. If I would think of him less often then."

"I went there for you."

"What are you saying?"

"Well . . . that I went to his funeral in your place."

Tobias crossed his arms. "I don't understand."

"Not because I thought you should be there—I probably would have stayed away too if anyone had done that to me. But I went just in case you ever doubted . . . or regretted. I went for both of us, really—and I thought about it a lot before I did—because if you ever said to me that I had no right to go there for you—"

"I wouldn't say that to you."

"Maybe not now, but ten or fifteen years ago you would have. And I wanted to be able to tell you in all honesty that I went for myself too."

"What was it like? For Robert and Greta? For my stepmother?"

As Danny talked, Tobias closed his eyes and let Danny take him to the cemetery—not too fast, though—*up the path that is rutted, muddy. Wet tufts of grass. Ferns and lichen. Small trees taking hold in the washout along the side where the long twisted roots of old pines hang exposed, smearing out like the bottom of clouds. Branches so full they block the lake. Except you know the lake is there because you see the mountains on its far side, bluish gray, and above it the backdrop of shadowy sky. The sound of the fast brook comes toward you like an increase in wind when you reach the plateau. You walk toward the open grave. Stand behind your step-*

mother and your brother and sister while your father's coffin is lowered into the ground.

And you step forward to toss grains of earth onto the burnished lid.

∞

When the next bank statement arrived, Emma was sure there had to be a mistake. Over ten thousand dollars had been withdrawn.

"We had to pay the bill for your father's burial," her mother reminded her.

"No, we paid for that a while ago."

"We also had the black clothes I got for you and me."

The following month the balance was nearly five thousand dollars lower than Emma had expected, and when she showed the statement to her mother, Yvonne said, "If the statements cause you such anguish, I'll do them."

"No, no," Emma said quickly. "It's just that I need to estimate expenses. When they are higher than I planned, it throws everything else off."

"Your father always totaled things up after the expenses."

"Too much money goes out that way. I wouldn't know what we can afford next. Besides, I have to schedule repairmen in advance."

"In advance . . ." As her mother waved one slender hand through the air, the sleeve of her silk blouse fell back, exposing the pearl white skin of her arm. Quickly, she pulled it back down. "It doesn't work that way."

"Maybe if both of us cut down on expenses . . ."

"That's a good idea. A real good idea."

But the following Friday her mother had her roses delivered as every week, smiling to herself as she arranged them in her crystal vases. All day Emma tried to ignore them but that evening at dinner, she felt the panic of losing the house. These roses stood for her mother's wastefulness. For drinking bottled water instead of water from the tap. For half a dozen subscriptions to magazines. *Don't say anything. Don't.*

But Yvonne could feel her daughter pushing at her with eyes of reproach. It made her remember Emma as a newborn, grasping, always grasping. And the presence of this daughter still was every-where: first she had inhabited her womb, and now she was suffo-cating her with her busywork.

"I've been thinking," Yvonne said, "about you living in one of the empty apartments."

"But I want to stay right here with you. In my old room."

Yvonne gathered into her voice whatever firmness she could find in herself. "I would like for you to have your own place. You're old enough to live alone."

That firmness also made it into her voice when Emma asked her if she'd taken her medication, or when she had breakfast ready for her as soon as she got up. Very quickly it became clear to Emma that her mother preferred to be alone. To console herself, she chose several pieces of her grandparents' furniture from the storage bin, among them their bed and corner bench, the roll-top desk and pi-ano, *Oma*'s china cabinet, and the massive lion chairs her grand-parents had brought from Germany. With the help of Danny Wilson she cleaned them up and hauled them into the smallest of the empty apartments right off the lobby. From her father and Mrs. Bloom she'd heard stories about the old woman who'd lived there for over three decades.

"That Miss Garland made the best soup," Danny Wilson told her while they set up the bed. "My Aunt Irene didn't like her much. Too nosy, she said. But Miss Garland was all right. Know what she did a few days after my mother died? Called me inside her apart-ment and asked what I'd eaten the last couple of days. When I couldn't remember, she made me sit down and cooked white soup for me. Best soup I ever had."

"What kind was it?"

"I don't know. Thick and white and smooth."

Emma unrolled a six-foot section of peacock runner, left over from when *Opa* had replaced the carpets in the hallways, and placed it next to her bed. "My father told me she made peanut brit-tle for him. He loved that when he was a boy."

"Not just as a boy." Danny adjusted a bolt on the birch head-board. "Miss Garland, she was crazy in love with your grandpa."

Emma looked up. "Really?"

"I don't think he ever figured it out. He was too bothered by how much she loved this house. Made him act jealous. Like he was worried his house would love Miss Garland right back." He straightened himself carefully. "And maybe it did, you know?"

All her life, Emma had lived on the top floor, and her first night alone in Miss Garland's apartment, she could feel the sum of the *Wasserburg*'s history on the floors above her. As she listened to the trees by the lake braid their leaves into the wind, it occurred to her that she might like living in these rooms. Though Miss Garland had died three years before Emma's birth and nearly a dozen different tenants had lived in her apartment since then, it was Miss Garland's essence that Emma still felt here.

While Miss Garland's furniture had been too sparse to obstruct the light, Emma crowded her rooms with so much furniture that light had difficulty passing through. Still, it settled something within her to be living in these rooms. From her window she had a view of Mrs. Bloom's greenhouse jutting into the courtyard, and from her door she could see the elevator and brass mailboxes. Some days she didn't leave the building at all, and the outside would seem of a different texture, gauzy.

She still insisted on doing her mother's laundry, and once a week she vacuumed both apartments, scrubbed the kitchen floors and bathrooms. Living alone made her turn more toward Caleb with phone calls, letters, and he too called at least once a week. What linked them was not only the closeness they'd felt as children, but also the fear of losing that closeness. For the next few years neither mentioned the deed. All Emma was able to do over these years was arrest the decay that had settled in the cracked plaster of the walls, a decay that persisted in the underlying smell that sifted through the staircase and rose beneath your step from the tweed carpet runners. But a house could not die the way *Opa* had, the way her father had. She would not let that happen. And that's what kept her working. That, and seeing the house through the eyes of her *Opa*—splendid and graceful.

Still, each repair would only show off all she hadn't done yet;

and she'd feel overwhelmed by the responsibility, knowing no one else would restore the house if she didn't. She'd remind herself that her apartment was clean, that whatever chaos might be in the rest of the house could not come into her own rooms; yet, that ring of order would not always hold, and she'd feel as if her apartment were about to be overrun like the clearing in the cemetery when growth and underbrush pressed in.

Yet, now and again the house made her feel competent. Joyful. Like when she sanded and stained the arched trim around the front door of the building; and when the tiles came loose in two bathrooms, and she learned to affix them with grout and sealer.

The afternoon the Clarkes' kitchen ceiling got damaged from water that leaked through from the apartment above, Emma thought she'd have to hire someone to plaster it since Danny Wilson already had too many other chores on his list; but then she decided to try fixing the ceiling herself. At Weber's hardware store she saw Dr. Miles with his three daughters, his oldest the size Emma had been the day of *Oma*'s last birthday, his youngest still a toddler, though the doctor was old enough to be a grandfather.

He was buying a large screwdriver. "Mine got all rusty," he told Emma. "I forgot it outside." Though he didn't look like *Opa*, he reminded her of him in the way he listened closely to his children's questions.

When she told him about the water damage, he asked details, nodded, but just when she expected him to tell her how to repair it, he said, "We've had two ceilings like that in our house for over a year now. Let's ask one of the men here. They're very knowledgeable." He followed her to the information counter, where one of the Weber sons recommended Emma scrape the ceiling and patch it with spackle.

"Not as messy as plaster. And it has a longer setup time. You paint right over it."

"See?" Dr. Miles smiled at her. "You'll have to let me know how that worked. Maybe that will motivate me to take care of ours."

When Emma came home, she rang her mother's bell. Waited a moment and then called, "Mother? Are you there?" She knocked.

Opened the cubicle. Empty. Some days, when her mother didn't want to see her, she'd leave a note or whatever Emma had asked for in the cubicle. *Too convenient for her.* Crouching in front of the open cubicle, Emma called out, "I'll be in the Clarkes' apartment, Mother." But there was no answer.

She was scraping the Clarkes' ceiling, brown specks drifting down around her, when all at once she felt the same yearning her *Oma* had written about in her letters. Except that it was directed toward Dr. Miles. It puzzled her, and she tried to scrape it away with the debris; but it persisted as though it had been there since that day he'd pulled fragments of glass from her neck, her lips, her forehead. And perhaps it had grown when she'd taken him to the roof of the *Wasserburg,* and with each visit to his office for ear-aches, coughs, a sprained wrist. As her memory of the doctor's careful hands on her face fused with her *Oma*'s letters, she spack-led the nicks, sanded the ceiling till it was smooth, and coated it with white paint. It looked quite good—not perfect, but good enough—and knowing she'd done it by herself exhilarated her. Because if she could do this in one room, she could do it for the entire house.

∾

All of that same afternoon, Yvonne had been feeling cold, missing Robert. It didn't happen every day that she missed her husband, but that morning, soon after waking, she'd found herself humming a few notes of Chopin and had been reminded of Robert because he would have known the exact name of the piece. Suddenly she felt she could not possibly go on without him, even though, in the three years without him, she'd often noticed how it was more satisfying to love him in death. Purer. Because she didn't have to cope with his body. *Robert the artist. Robert the gentle husband. A wonderful man. How fortunate I've been. And how—*

The doorbell. Then Emma's voice: "Mother? Are you there?" Knocking. Fussing with the outer door of the cubicle. *Thank God she's too big to climb in through there.* "I'll be in the Clarkes' apartment, Mother." *Always in my way. Wanting more than I can give her. Always.* Yvonne held her breath, waited till her daughter was gone and she was alone with the old lure of knives and red coils, a lure she'd rarely felt during the years her back had troubled her. But lately, it had come back, though not as urgent as it used to be. She could decide—and it was that easy most days, a matter of deciding—to get out of the house instead. And she did. Called a cab and met it by the side of the building so that Emma wouldn't see her waiting by the front steps and tell her to be careful with what she spent.

In Magill's, while trying on a white cardigan, Yvonne suddenly remembered another cardigan she'd owned fifteen years ago, turquoise, its hood trimmed with a knitted border of orange and white, and as she recalled its softness against her skin, she was suffused with yearning for that cardigan and the time in her life she had worn it: *She lifts Emma into her arms, smiles at Caleb. They're on the dock and Robert, not too heavy yet, steadies the rowboat so that his family—his young family—can climb into it.* All at once the cardigan stood for those early years when her husband had adored her, when her children had still been small, and when—to anyone who might have passed by that moment and glimpsed her on the dock—she would have seemed the most tender of mothers, the most loving of wives. And yet, seized by desire for that time gone by—*though still not lost . . . still mine*—she understood that her marriage had never been as fulfilling as this memory wanted to trick her into believing. And it wasn't even that she wanted to go back to those early years of raising small children. Just to the youth that had been hers then. *Not that I have changed much.* She was constantly amazed by how smooth her skin had stayed. *Posture. That's so important. Same size waist I had at seventeen.*

"It's lovely on you, Mrs. Blau."

"Same size waist I had at seventeen."

"Do you know how many of our customers would love to be able to say that?"

As she watched the saleswoman fold her new cardigan into tissue paper, she wondered how she would remember buying this white cardigan in years to come, and if her memories would be gentle on her. If only she could get along better with Emma, talk without tension the way she could with Caleb. *A present. I'll get her a present.*

"A present for my daughter." She glanced around. "It's so hard shopping for Emma. She keeps wearing the same clothes. But I'll surprise her with something lovely."

"How about this?" The saleswoman held up an ivory silk blouse. "It goes with Emma's hair."

Yvonne nodded. She could see Emma wearing it, her light hair done up in a French twist—*I'll do it for her; so much more becoming than hanging into her face*—but when she got home, she found Emma in the Clarkes' apartment with white dust and paint in her hair and on her overalls, the floor around her littered with plaster and brown dust and squares of sandpaper. Emma didn't even offer to wash up to try on the blouse. Instead she asked what it had cost—*vulgar, so vulgar to ask the price of a gift*—and then fretted over the expense.

∞

Instead of marrying some day and spending her honeymoon in Burgdorf as she had imagined, Emma Blau gave birth to a child fathered by Dr. Miles. She was twenty-seven when she lay in a labor room on the second floor of the Winnipesaukee Hospital.

"Stay," she would say, "please, Justin," whenever he'd turn to leave her once again, and he—face slick with perspiration—would promise to be back after he had checked on another patient. What Emma did not know, and what the nurses were too kind to tell her, was that this other patient was the doctor's wife, Laura, who lay in a narrow bed identical to Emma's across the hall, in labor with her fourth child, while outside her window—black with night—branches slick with frost swayed in the wind and scratched the glass, making Laura wish she were home with her daughters. While the two younger ones were not afraid of storms, Amy, though sixteen, still grew frightened and would hide beneath her bed, palms pressed against her ears.

Earlier that evening, while the doctor had rushed his wife to the hospital, Emma's water had broken, and the two women had ended up in rooms on the same floor, separated only by a corridor and by the nurses who moved between them, monitoring both labors and the path of the doctor who traveled between his wife and his lover, a startled expression on his face. Laura's contractions had started one month early, while Emma was five days overdue. Once, as moaning came at him from both rooms, he felt so torn that he stood immobilized in the corridor, incapable of moving in either direction because he wanted to be there for both women. He felt certain that those sounds of agony were his punishment, and then instantly embarrassed that he would even consider his torment to be as painful as giving birth.

Finally, a nurse took him by the wrist in a grasp that conveyed the opinion of the entire nursing staff, and led him toward the room of the woman who was legally bound to him; and when he obeyed the nurse, she suddenly felt exasperated with him and all those kind and patient men who found it so difficult to say no to their wives, their nurses, their children, their lovers.

While Laura's experienced hands supported her own belly, guiding it through each heave, Emma tossed from side to side, strands of sweaty hair on her lips. Her tongue felt dry, bloated—even more so than the center of her body—as if she also had to give birth to the secret of who her child's father was. Once it was born, she was certain Justin would make it known that it was his. Of course the townspeople had been speculating after watching him enter the *Wasserburg* so many times. . . . But speculating was not the same as knowing.

"Where is Dr. Miles?" she asked the nurse.

"Another child . . . getting ready to be born," the nurse said, feeling sorry for the Blau woman because hers would be a life of waiting. Taking Emma's hand into hers, she sat on the chair by her bed. "I'll stay with you."

Strong, thin hands. To hold on to. But they weren't Justin's. Emma wanted him here with her and felt bewildered by the same longing that had unfurled between them last August when she'd come to his office, arm swollen from a wasp bite she'd gotten while clearing a nest of wasps from the fan in her mother's kitchen. He had cradled her arm in his hands—*so different from the hands of this nurse*—had cradled it long after he could have sent her home as if he believed his touch alone would bring the swelling down; and oddly, there in his office with the sun cutting stripes into the floating layers of dust, Emma had suddenly felt a waning of that grieving for her *Opa* and—for the first time since his death, it seemed—had been able to take a full breath. Stripes of light grazed her arm, grazed the doctor's hands, as they leaned toward one another.

Ever since then, they'd come together Wednesdays at three after he closed his office, and they'd gone for hikes or for swims on the far side of Lake Winnipesaukee where no one knew them and where tourists had blanketed the earth between the edge of the water and the hilltops with row after row of boxy cottages. Though Emma could see that Justin savored every minute with her, she couldn't do the same because she'd get snagged by the sadness that, soon, he would no longer be with her. They wouldn't return to her apartment till it was dark, and there—after they'd make love, after he'd set her alarm for one A.M. and turn on his side away from her, after she'd adjust her body to fit against his bare back in one smooth motion—she would not sleep at all but lie with her forehead pressed against his spine, willing the sky to conserve its darkness.

After he'd leave, she'd open her windows and air out his smell of pipe tobacco. It would take her days to recover from his visit, days before she'd feel separate from him once more. She'd immerse herself in the house and all its work, and when Justin would return the following Wednesday, she'd feel a resistance in her body when he'd touch her as if, in reclaiming herself, she'd gone too far.

Yet, by the time they'd go to bed, that resistance would have worn through once again. Lying next to him after he was asleep, she'd feel a loneliness greater than the loneliness that would feed on her throughout the week. Now and again—though she tried not to—she would think of his wife, four blocks away in the yellow house with the wide porch and the brick chimney and at least two waterlogged ceilings. Perhaps that very instant Laura was wondering where her husband was or planning tomorrow's meals, while

Emma never had the luxury of planning the next day with him. Perhaps Laura was marking their next tennis game on their calendar. The two of them were on the town's tennis team and played mixed doubles twice a week. "One of the few things we do together," he had told Emma. Other than that, he didn't discuss his other life with her, crossing a definite border as he moved between his house and her apartment.

She longed for him almost constantly. It disturbed her work. Her sleep. And yet felt utterly familiar because she had read about that kind of love in *Oma*'s letters. And *Opa* obviously had been a man worth longing for. Certain that his letters, too, had to be somewhere in the house—*What did you write to her? How did you respond to those letters of hers?*—Emma would periodically search for them in the storage area, the garage, the elevator room, certain that in revealing the flip side of that longing, these letters would make known not only her *Opa*'s feelings, but also Justin's. And as she continued to invent her own version of her grandparents' relationship, their letters—written and unwritten—continued to shape all she believed about love.

She enjoyed buying gifts for Justin—shirts and sweaters and ties—generous while she was frugal in every other area of her life. Even when he was not with her, he inhabited her rooms with these gifts that he couldn't take into his other life; and it came to be so that Emma found comfort in having these gifts around, touching them, telling herself that at least she had that one evening a week when he would hold her lightly in his arms while they'd talk in the darkness of her bedroom. His skin was always warmer than hers in the evening.

"But mine gets warm by morning," she told him once.

"Just the opposite for me. Mornings I feel cold."

"If we woke up together in the morning—"

"Don't make yourself unhappy with that."

"If we woke up together in the morning," she persisted, "I'd keep you warm. Between us we have the perfect way to keep each other warm. Such a waste . . ."

"I'll warm you now."

At the grocery store Emma had heard about Laura's pregnancy one entire month before she had figured out for herself that she, too, was pregnant. During that month she stopped seeing Justin altogether, hurt because she had believed he and his wife no longer made love, angry at herself for being so naive. Not that he had never said so precisely—it was rather what she had taken from his silences.

But after that month without him, when she called him to tell him she was pregnant and he came to her apartment right away, though it wasn't a Wednesday, she could no longer dismiss his wife because Laura's shadow image had been cast around hers, there for the entire town to see. And see they would. And disapprove they would.

Still, Justin never showed her any doubt about wanting this child. He said he was sure it was a boy from the way Emma carried the new weight—in her hips, her legs, her face—and after three daughters, he looked forward to having a son. Though his enthusiasm cut through some of Emma's uncertainties, it bothered her that he wasn't worried about his reputation. *Her* reputation. And that he didn't seem to understand how troubled she was by his wife's pregnancy. Yet, all that fit in with him not planning beyond the following Wednesday. With letting his tools rust outside. With managing problems the way he covered the peeling paint on his house—occasional brush strokes of yellow that didn't match the background.

He still hadn't painted his entire house, though Emma remembered him talking about changing its color when she was still a girl. "I don't like yellow on a house," he'd said. *Opa* used to believe you couldn't trust people who didn't care for their property—"They're lax about other things too"—and it astonished Emma that she could love Justin despite his carelessness.

She didn't tell her brother she was pregnant, because Caleb hadn't liked Justin ever since she'd confided to him on the phone that he was her lover.

"Dump him." His reaction had been swift. "One, he's married.

Two, he must be twice your age. And three, you must not settle for this."

"I'm not settling for anything. And don't give me that attitude about marriage. Not after two divorces."

"At least I never dated someone who was married."

"They were married women by the time you had your second date with them."

"Come now . . . I knew Alison an entire month before I proposed."

"Most people date, Caleb; you get married."

"Dating . . . What an extraordinary idea. You're sure that's legal?"

"Try it. You know what? Being with Justin is good for me. Really good. Some people are worth waiting for."

"Not while they're married."

"I wish you could be glad for me."

"So do I."

"The one thing that bothers me—"

"Only one?"

"I'm not going to tell you. You'll just add it to everything else you already hate about him."

"Try me."

"Well . . . it bothers me that he leaves at one in the morning to return to his own bed."

"And to the wife who lies waiting in that bed for him."

"Thank you."

"I don't want you to forget that."

"I wish I could forget. When I told him how much that bothers me, we had a fight and he said I was corralling him."

"Corralling?"

"I didn't know what to say to him. I was too hurt to—"

"You used to have a mouth on you, Emma."

"I still do."

"Sure, with me. With Mom. But not with him. You're turning into a mouse with that man."

"That's not true."

"Going to that man for love is like going to Radio Shack for bread."

"I don't get it."

"You already know Radio Shack is not where you buy bread. Still, you keep going back, believing this time it'll be different."

"Your wisdom, Caleb . . . I'm forever astonished by it."

"Corralled . . . I'm still thinking about that word, Emma. Jesus, why didn't you tell him you'll get a cattle prod for him?"

"I'll use it if he ever says that again."

"Use it anyhow. The cattle prod, I mean."

∽

Justin's fourth child, Oliver, would emerge from Laura's womb seven hours before Emma's son, Stefan, would fling his arms open to daylight. The children would sit in the same first-grade class, both with the dark eyebrows and with the deep pinprick dimple in the chin that would make others notice their resemblance, though no one would openly comment on it.

From the day of Stefan's birth, Emma watched and fussed over him with an anxious and distracted love, eager to do the best she could. Whenever she was surprised by pure flashes of joy, she'd try to hold on to them, afraid something terrible might happen to Stefan if she didn't. Her worried questions she brought to Justin who owned all the advice, and when he dispersed it with his usual thoughtfulness and kindness, she felt safe having a doctor as her child's father, a doctor who could certainly keep Stefan alive even though he hadn't acknowledged him yet openly as his son.

She took the baby along when she worked on the house, propping him up in his carriage or a small playpen, talking to him while she scraped or painted or cleaned. When she absolutely had to, she'd ask her mother or one of the tenants to watch him for a few hours. Some evenings she carried Stefan up to the roof and tried to find contentment in this high place where she had watched her *Oma* and Mrs. Bloom recline in their chairs with tall drinks as if they were at a resort. But the feelings she'd expect wouldn't always come. Instead she'd notice the cracks in the rooftop, the dirt, the air that was too hot or too cold. And always, she'd remain just who she was: a woman harried by too much to do; a woman already counting everything she was failing to complete; a woman with a child but without a man of her own.

After Stefan's birth, she had waited for her mother and the tenants to ask questions about her child's father, but they never had as though it were totally normal that Emma had given birth to a fatherless child who resembled the town's doctor. It was not that easy with the rest of the town. There were glances, whispers that were hard to bear because they made her afraid that her son would grow up to feel shame. Still—she knew she would not have undone one single hour of having him in her life.

Actually, he was a lot like her *Opa*—not just in name but in willfulness, though it was a quieter willfulness. He too was drawn to the stars and their stories. *They would have liked each other, the old Stefan and the young Stefan.* She felt a link between those two whenever she told her son about his great-grandfather who had built the *Wasserburg*.

"He was a handsome man. Bright like you. He died before you were born. But I'm sure he would have been very proud of you."

From family photos that hung in the hallway, the boy knew what his great-grandfather looked like, and he grew up admiring him, so aware of him that it was as though the old man lived with him and his mother, the three of them moving within a triangle that only changed shape once a week when the other man arrived with surprises: wooden tongue depressors; rubber gloves he'd blow up into cow-udder balloons. They'd have a treasure hunt: the man would hide his surprises in the apartment, and Stefan would search behind drapes and wastebaskets, beneath chairs and beds. "Cold," the man would say, "Warmer . . . Hot . . ." until Stefan found everything. Then the man would swoop him high into the air, laughing, while the skin around his eyes scrunched up all funny.

From the time he was very young, Stefan understood that he was to call this man Father inside the apartment and Doctor everywhere else; and since he had nothing to compare this arrangement to, he considered it normal, just as he considered it normal that it was only on Wednesdays that he was part of what his mother called "our family." Wednesdays his father looked at the pictures Stefan had drawn in nursery school. Wednesdays his father reminded Stefan to keep his elbows off the table while he ate.

"Our son," his mother would say on Wednesdays and smile as she tasted the words. *Our son.*

"Listen to the new words our son learned in school . . ."

"Do you think it is time for our son to go to bed?"

Stefan learned that his mother was sad after the man left. Learned that he could take care of her sadness by climbing on her knees and linking his arms around her neck; by holding doors open for her when they went to stores; by helping her rub lemon oil on the furniture until it gleamed. Learned that even if her face felt all wet against his, he could make her smile. Still—he loved her best when he didn't have to worry about keeping the sadness from her. Loved her best when he had her all to himself and could fall asleep to the sound of her voice telling him stories about the stars and the constellations and about how they got their names. His favorite was Orion, the warrior. He had a sword and a shield and more bright stars than the other constellations.

∾

Stefan was five, had been five for half a year of waiting for an evening warm enough to watch the stars from the dock, but this winter the snow was lasting into May. Finally, it began to melt on the streets and on the slopes of the mountains, though their crests were still white.

The last evening of May, though, the air was mild and the sky clear. Lying beneath the stars on the dock with his mother was much better than watching them through a telescope from his living room window as he had all through the winter and spring.

"Can you see Pegasus?" His mother pointed up toward the sky. "The winged horse that carried Perseus and Andromeda to safety."

"Tell me again."

"You know the story better than I." As Emma began, she could hear *Opa*'s voice beneath her own, telling her the same story in German here on this dock during a night much like this night. "*Andromeda war eine schöne Prinzessin . . .*"—"Andromeda was a beautiful princess . . . and the sea nymphs were jealous of her. They complained to Neptune, who tried to destroy the kingdom of Andromeda's father, King Cepheus, by sending—"

"He sent a big whale," her son interrupted. "A monster whale."

"Right."

"And the whale was so big that nobody could kill him. He swallowed everybody in the kingdom."

"Well, not everybody, but many people. Some of the people who got away from the whale chained Andromeda to a rock by the ocean." Her voice was soft and came to Stefan from as far away as the Milky Way that floated above him like a river of stars.

Below them, the lake slapped against the wooden pilings, sending shivers of air through the gaps between the boards, making Stefan think of the waves around Andromeda's feet, of the chains cutting into her white gown. "Andromeda was very, very afraid."

"That's right. You see, her father believed that sacrificing her to the whale would stop him from killing others. But just as the whale swam up to her, opening his monstrous mouth to swallow her—" Emma paused, waiting for him to tell his favorite part of the story.

"Perseus saved her." Stefan clapped his hands. "He killed the whale. The next day he married Andromeda."

Emma laughed. "I'm not sure it was the next day."

"And they flew away on Pegasus."

"Can you see Cassiopeia, her mother?"

"Up there." He pointed. "In between Andromeda and Cepheus."

"Very good." As his arm came down, Emma followed its descent until it grazed the lake and the rowboat where *Opa* had lain with his first wife on pillows, night surrounding them, looking toward the land where his *Wasserburg* stood high above the bank. *But it wasn't built then. Not yet. Still,* Opa *had seen it.*

"Mom?"

One night. Linking all nights into that one night. Across the water, the wind picked up, carrying the scents of fish and new leaves in its moist wake.

The boy shivered, and for a moment there he was Andromeda,

staring at the gray mass of water as it swelled up and fell from the sleek bulk of the whale. "Mom—"

"I'm here." In the half dark, her strong, pale chin moved toward him. Her blonde eyebrows. Her hand on his hair.

Raising himself on his elbows, he asked, "Was Cepheus going to let the whale kill his daughter?"

"It's a myth." She kissed his forehead.

"I don't think he liked her."

"He believed he had to sacrifice her."

"I would never feed you to a whale."

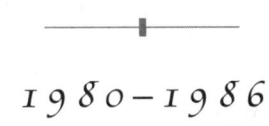

CHAPTER THIRTEEN

1 9 8 0 – 1 9 8 6

The moving men were bigger than Uncle Danny. They wore gray overalls and smelled of sweat when they came into Stefan's room and took the boxes with his toys and books, his clothes and the star charts his mother had drawn with him. But those charts weren't as good as the charts of his German great-great-grandmother that were drawn on linen like the blueprints of the *Wasserburg*. When Stefan had asked if he could hang them up in his room, his mother had said that he was too young.

"You might damage them without realizing," she'd said.

While she checked on the moving men to make sure that they, too, didn't damage anything, Stefan hid in his closet. He always did during moves. But today it was too hot in there, and he followed the men into the elevator and pushed the button to the second floor where he and his mother would live until she would renovate that apartment too and rent it out.

So far, Stefan had lived on every floor of the *Wasserburg*. He wished he lived in a small house where he'd always have the same bedroom and the same kitchen and the same living room. His first move, so his mother had told him, had happened soon after his birth when she'd shown five vacant apartments to Miss Fitzpatrick who worked at one of the resorts. Miss Fitzpatrick hadn't liked any, except the one where Stefan and his mother already lived. "It's yours if you want it," his mother had said and moved everything to the third floor. From then on they'd lived in apartments that were difficult to rent, and once his mother had fixed those up, they'd moved again.

Beneath the moving men's arms were dark stains. Stefan missed Uncle Danny who didn't smell of sweat. But Uncle Danny was no longer strong enough to carry furniture. That's why he lived in Connecticut now. Great-uncle Tobias had arrived to pick him up in his convertible, and Uncle Danny had sent his furniture along in a moving truck. But before leaving, the two of them had gone into the garage and leaned against one another by the workbench. For an instant Stefan had been afraid that Uncle Danny was keeling over. Because that's what he'd done twice now, keeled over with a face whiter than white, and Stefan's mother had sat on the floor with him, holding his head on her lap till the ambulance arrived.

But in the garage Uncle Danny's face was pink and not white, and he was smiling. "Just one more where it all started," he was saying.

"What started?" Stefan asked from behind Miss Fitzpatrick's red Chevy.

"Hey now, Mr. Stefan Blau." Uncle Danny laughed.

But Great-uncle Tobias did not laugh. "What are you doing there?"

"Playing."

"Let the boy—" Uncle Danny said. "This garage has always been the best place to play, Tobias. Don't forget that."

"Where is your mother?"

"Upstairs."

"Then go to her."

Though his voice was grumpy, Stefan wasn't scared of him. He used to be when he was little. But then Great-uncle Tobias had come into his room one day and pointed to the dresser with the green knobs. "Do you know that this piece of furniture will guard your secrets?" He'd shown Stefan how the floor of one drawer rested on alphabet blocks and lifted out to reveal an empty space. "I made that when I was a boy. When I didn't know yet that all I ever needed to hide was already inside me. Still . . . maybe you can use it if you ever need to hide something."

"Go now, boy," Great-uncle Tobias said.

As Stefan turned to leave, he told Uncle Danny, "Don't keel over. Okay?"

"Not today."

"How do you know?"

"I just do."

Stefan hesitated. "If Uncle Danny keels over," he instructed his great-uncle, "you yell for me, and I'll call the ambulance. And if he gets cramps in his legs—"

"Cramps?" No longer Great-uncle Tobias. But the taller of the moving men. Here with him in the elevator. Asking, "Who's getting cramps?" Saying to the other man, "What's the kid mumbling about?"

"Leave him alone, Pete."

"What's your name, kid?"

"Stefan."

Just then the elevator stopped on the second floor, and the man said, "All right, Stefan, will you hold that door open for us?"

"Okay."

The men wheezed as they carried furniture into the hallway. When the elevator was empty, Stefan rode it by himself. Up and down and up and down. A big box of his own where no one could see him. This morning, when the moving men had carried his mother's bed from her room, Stefan had found the broken stem from one of his father's pipes under the edge of the peacock rug. It was dusty, worn down at the end with tooth marks, and he'd slipped it into his pocket. The elevator was humming, and Stefan looked at the ceiling and the light with its dark specks behind the glass. *They look like dead bugs. How did they get in there? Why didn't they find their way out? Are the other bugs in their families still searching for them?* He wished his father would come over to play bear with him. But his father only visited on Wednesdays. When he played bear with Stefan, he'd crawl through the apartment, shaking Stefan off if he tried to climb on his long back. But Stefan always got on, though it took a lot of holding on; and then his father would growl and laugh and ask him if he wasn't getting too old for this.

The gray smell of sweat rode with Stefan, wound its way into his nose, his mouth, and he pumped the number four button. When the elevator stopped and the door opened, he ran from it, taking a deep breath. Most of the furniture was already gone from this apartment: both beds and dressers, the china cabinet, the desk, and the lion chairs. In the hallway, the walls were bare. By tomorrow his mother would have hung the framed photos in the hallway of the next apartment. It always was one of the first things she did. But now she was scrubbing the kitchen counter for the new tenant, a pail with soapy water and a bottle of disinfectant next to her.

She glanced up when his shoes clicked against the black-and-white floor tiles. "Getting bored?" Her face was flushed, and her hands smelled of detergent when she hugged him.

"No."

"Then why are you so gloomy?" She opened a box of animal crackers. One arm around his shoulders, she sat next to him on the corner bench that the movers hadn't taken yet.

The stem of his father's pipe pressed against his thigh. His mother was always repairing things that were broken, and if she found out about the pipe, she'd make him give it to her so that she could fix that too. But he was good at keeping secrets from her. He'd learned that from his grandma.

"Promise not to tell your mother," she'd say when she took him along shopping. He loved to go to stores with his grandma because afterwards he'd get to help her hide the new clothes inside her apartment so that his mother wouldn't make her take them back for a refund.

"Still hungry?" His mother's hand brushed crumbs from his shirt.

He shook his head.

"You know what I could use? One of your drawings to hang on the refrigerator in our new apartment."

While she covered the shelves in the cabinets with flowered paper from a roll, Stefan drew a picture of a boy in an elevator that went way up to the sky. He colored the boy's pants brown like his own, his shirt yellow. His favorite color was white, and he wished he could use that for the boy's shirt, but it wouldn't show up against the paper. He was careful to stay within the lines. His mother always said he was good at coloring inside the lines. But his letters never came out the way he wanted them to: they leaned together or dropped apart in ugly squiggles. Coloring was easy. He drew the door to the elevator closed so nobody could get in, but the roof was open and the boy could see the stars. Stefan drew the Big Dipper for the boy and, to the right of it, Polaris, the only star that always stayed in the same place.

∞

Six months after the move, when Emma had restored this apartment too, she suggested to her mother, "We could rent out your apartment. It's too big for one person anyhow."

But Yvonne refused.

"You'd be more comfortable in a smaller place."

"I don't want to piece together my life the way you do."

"What do you mean?"

"Nothing. I'm sorry. I didn't mean to hurt you." How could she tell Emma that she felt sad for her to be clawing for love from a man who didn't adore her? If she could wish for one thing she could have passed on to Emma—her looks or being adored by every man who met her—it would have been that adoration. Certainly not that persistence of Emma's that was so tedious.

"Do you ever think how much easier it would be for you," Emma asked, "to not have the responsibility for the house?"

"No."

"See, if you deeded it over to me, I could take care of all the bills and all the repairs then, and you'd—" Emma tried to stop herself. It wasn't decent, pushing at her mother like that.

"No, Emma."

"To me and Caleb, I mean."

Yvonne braced herself against her daughter's urgency. "No."

"You wouldn't have anything to worry about."

"And nothing to live on."

"Your apartment would be free."

"My apartment is free now."

"I'd give you a generous amount every month to live on."

"I write checks for what I need."

"But the money won't last. Don't you see? Soon there'll be nothing."

"We never had those problems when your father was alive."

"Because you had his income from the clinic. And all the apartments were rented then."

When Emma told Justin Miles about her mother's refusal to deed the house to her, he held her, stroked her shoulders. "I bet on some level your mother is grateful for all you're doing."

"I hate wastefulness. It drives me mad. And we don't have enough for the repairs. I wish she'd let me do it right. And for that, I need her to deed the house to my brother and me."

"You know what just occurred to me?"

"What?"

"Who your real lover is."

She frowned at him.

"The house. Your real lover is this house. I'll never be as important to you."

She didn't know how to contradict him because—though true in a way—it was not that simple. And she felt irritated that he would try to manipulate her into accepting that his attachment to her, too, was not as strong as that to his family. Abruptly, she got up. "I know we have separate lives. You don't need to remind me of that."

"Don't be like that."

She poured herself a glass of water. "You know what I wish? Do you? I wish you'd bring our son real gifts. Not the things you stuff into your pockets before leaving your office."

"I can do that."

She walked to the window. Laid her forehead against the glass. All she ever had was hope. Hope that eventually he would leave his wife. Why did she always have to want what belonged to others? The *Wasserburg*. This man. Who doled himself out so carefully. What mattered most to her in the world could not be hers unless she took it away from someone. She didn't want to be in that position. With the house or with Justin. But no one looked out for her. No one made sure that she and Stefan had what they needed. If she didn't do it, no one else would.

"Emma?"

"Does your wife ever ask you where you sleep Wednesday nights?" she surprised herself by asking.

He didn't answer. Just watched her from the sofa in that benevolent manner of his. Usually she tried to avoid thinking too much about Laura, who had him every day, while her own weeks were only bordered by his visits. Once he left, all she had was her expectation of the following Wednesday, which—if she settled for it with the patience to which he had become accustomed with his wife—could form a succession of Wednesdays that stretched to the end of their lives like posts, supporting and marking off unshaped barriers of time. While he seemed content to be with her that one afternoon and evening each week. And he would continue to be there. For her and for Stefan. As long as they could arrange the significant events of their lives on Wednesdays. *Guest appearances.* Suddenly, angry that he expected this patience from both her and his wife, she felt a bond to Laura. Felt pity too. Because there was always the possibility that he would leave his wife. *In time.* That's why Emma had settled in for a wait that had seemed manageable at first and was only frightening if she let herself look back at the years she had already spent waiting for him.

∞

The spring of 1983, the people of Winnipesaukee noticed Emma Blau—followed by the son she had named after her grandfather—checking out vacant apartments in buildings throughout town. They knew why: the *Wasserburg* was only two thirds full, and she was trying to find out what new renters might be looking for.

They could have told her that renters wanted garden apartments with individual entrances to the outside. Renters wanted dishwashers. Air conditioners. Garbage disposals. And with those old, narrow pipes in the *Wasserburg,* the townspeople knew, dishwashers were not practical even if Emma Blau had been able to afford them.

But then she surprised them by working an agreement with the owner of Weber's Hardware for a dozen air conditioners, installed, in return for one year's rent on a large apartment for the owner's son, Hank Weber III, who was getting married to Sybil Baxter, whose great-grandmother had lived in the *Wasserburg* as a young woman—not in any of the fancy apartments, for sure, but in the basement with the other maids. Robichaud, her maiden name had been, Birdie Robichaud, and she used to come home with tales of how magnificent the *Wasserburg* was. But once Sybil and Hank lived there, they could only complain about it and plot their move to a modern building as soon as their year was up.

When the air conditioners were in place, Emma Blau placed ads in the newspaper, although—so the townspeople agreed—old Stefan Blau would have never approved of the boxy way in which they protruded from the windows. But one thing they had to admire about Emma Blau was that she did not give up, not even as the house was crumbling around her. And while they did not approve of her holding on to a married woman's husband and having a child with him, they felt sorry for her because nothing came easy to her as it had to her grandfather. Still—what he'd had in luck, Emma had in perseverance. Not that Stefan Blau hadn't shown perseverance too, but with him it had been linked with luck.

Even those too young to have met Stefan Blau had heard stories about that luck. About a certain glamour that had carried over to his house. While he'd always had a waiting list of people dreaming to live in his house, word had it that Emma Blau's tenants were grumbling—those who had lived in the *Wasserburg* a while, and who could blame them, really?—that the first air conditioners should have gone to them. Three families threatened to move out unless she'd let them switch to apartments with air conditioners; and to keep from renting them freshly painted rooms and having to restore theirs again, Emma was then of course forced to get air conditioners for all apartments.

The townspeople didn't envy her the struggle to keep her mother from spending funds she needed to keep the building alive. Recently, Yvonne had taken out an additional mortgage without telling Emma, who finally had to find out from the bank. Yvonne's spending habits that might have been merely flamboyant before her husband had swallowed himself into his grave, had become embarrassing to witness. Even to just go to the store, she'd dress as if she were attending a formal reception.

To her hairdresser she complained that Emma kept at her to deed the house to her, and several women in the beauty parlor agreed with her that it was tacky to pressure your parent for your inheritance. "It's not Emma's to decide over," they'd tell her. Yet later, amongst themselves, they'd decide it was equally tacky of Yvonne Blau to try and rent anyone at the beauty parlor one of the maids' rooms—"If you have visitors, let me know and I'll get you a key, but don't tell my daughter"—for seven dollars a night, cash only. The women could just imagine Emma Blau finding Vera Larch's mother-in-law, say, in the bathtub and demanding to know who'd let her in. They couldn't really fault Emma Blau for watching her mother so closely, reminding her to take her pills, scolding her about money. It wasn't pleasant to watch but understandable because every month she had less to put back into the house. And it was obvious to the people of Winnipesaukee that a different sort of renters were moving in—people who were late with their checks, whose dented cars left dark stains on the ground, who let their children run about without wiping their noses.

And to think that the *Wasserburg* used to be the place to live.

The older ones among them would reminisce how Stefan Blau's house—through its magnificent example—had changed their town and had emboldened all of them to aspire beyond what they'd believed they could do and have. Yet, in its decline, the house had become something to not emulate, a warning of what might happen if they were not vigilant because—much like a marriage that may still appear intact after all warmth has left—it had not deteriorated all at once. After judging the worth of their achievements against the *Wasserburg* for so long, the people of Winnipesaukee found it unsettling to separate themselves from its allure, even more unsettling to determine their own measures and desires. Because how could they ever match something as visible as the *Wasserburg?* Visible in its splendor. Visible in its decay that brought them up against regrets of their own, regrets about times they'd let themselves down, times when something had gotten away from them. Like a dream. A lover. A child.

❧

Though both women were intensely aware of each other, they had not been in the same room since the day of Helene Blau's funeral when Emma was still a girl. But during the fourth-grade Christmas play when Emma's son played a shepherd and Laura's son the angel who announces Christ's birth to the shepherds, Emma sat five rows behind Laura and Justin. She tensed up along with Laura when the angel Oliver missed a line and the shepherd Stefan had to whisper it to him. By the end of the play, she knew the gray and auburn hairs that straggled from Laura Miles' topknot better than she knew the back of her own head.

When all the children, still in their costumes, scrambled down from the stage, Emma saw Stefan heading toward his father as if he'd forgotten that they were not at home. Quickly she moved forward to catch her son's arm and walk him to the other end of the room, where a table with red punch and trays of Christmas cookies had been set up.

"You must be thirsty," she said, wanting to protect him. Protect him from the knowledge of not belonging. *But you're mine. Not enough, is it? No.* As she handed him the paper cup filled with red punch—*I wish I could do so much more for you*—she felt herself being watched. Justin's wife. Gazing at her from across the room in her old jeans and baggy sweater that were too casual, yet made Emma feel overdressed.

Tilting her face to Justin, Laura whispered something that made him smile.

What if they're talking about me? What has he been telling her about me?

"Mom?" Stefan's voice.

The sleeves of Emma's silk blouse felt tight as though her thin arms had suddenly grown heavy. Heavy with shame. With rage.

"Mom?"

"Would you like more punch?"

His mother's hand on his shoulder, Stefan drank the sweet raspberry punch—*too sweet, much too sweet*—and watched his father near the door with Oliver Miles, who was in his class and had the same birthday every year with cupcakes and all the kids singing "Happy Birthday dear Stefan and Oliver. . . ." Sometimes Oliver's name first. Sometimes Stefan's. He still wanted to run over to his father, but it felt wrong to do that. Because of all the other people.

Because of his mother's hand keeping him here. Because of Oliver. Because of an older girl who had the same chin and eyebrows as Oliver. The same chin and eyebrows as his father who stood there with them and with a woman whose hair was piled up on top of her head.

"Don't," his mother said when Stefan raised his hand to wave.

But his father didn't even see him.

Stefan's belly was sour. He drank another cup of red punch to make it feel better. Except it didn't. Only made his belly worse. Because there was something about the way his father and Oliver stood with that woman and the girl. Like a—

Like a family.

That's what they looked like. A family. Like he and his father and his mother were on Wednesdays. But only on Wednesdays. And only inside the apartment.

"Let's go home." His mother's face was blotched.

But Stefan wanted to stand with his father and that woman. Wanted to *be* Oliver. His belly was burning, and he would remember that sensation of burning even years later whenever he'd think of the day he'd first understood about his father's two families, understood clearly what deep within he had felt since before words had become attainable: that he existed at the edge of his father's life.

∾

Two days before Christmas, Caleb flew into Boston and rented a car, surprising his mother and sister with his visit. He hadn't been back in two years, and he was stunned at how drawn Emma looked, how wary his mother seemed around Emma. His nephew was a rather quiet boy, observant, but shy.

Caleb tried to keep it light between them as they set up the manger in Emma's apartment. "Most of these decorations are still from Germany," he told Stefan. "Your great-grandmother brought them with her."

The boy nodded, his eyes solemn. "*Oma* Helene. I know."

"Check out this one." Caleb handed him the wax Madonna with the melted face. "Doesn't she look like she's about to rob a bank?"

Stefan poked one finger at the Madonna's flattened features.

"Like she's wearing a stocking over her face. Like . . . like a Madonna-goon."

"A goonie-Madonna."

"What a great name for her."

"Let's just call her goonie from now on."

Once the boy got silly, it was easy for Caleb to keep him going, to get his help in mixing up the manger scene, letting the Madonna boogie with a shepherd instead of watching over little Jesus, positioning the dog so it was sniffing the camel's ass.

"You two are terrible." Yvonne smiled and picked up the king with the red coat.

"We work at it, right Stefan?"

"Right." Stefan laid a sheep into an angel's outstretched arms.

"There." Yvonne placed the red king so close to the tallest shepherds that it looked as though the two were kissing. "How's that?"

Stefan nodded. "Like Uncle Danny and Great-uncle Tobias."

Yvonne coughed and moved the figures apart.

Caleb winked at Emma. "I want to call them, see if I can drive to Hartford the day before my flight leaves."

"They'll be glad to see you. Maybe you can also meet with Aunt Greta and Uncle Noah, at least for an hour or so at the airport." Her eyes were more intense than usual and hard to look at for long. "I want you to promise me something," she said.

"Tell me?"

"That you'll teach Stefan how to shave once he is ready."

Caleb swallowed against the tears that tried to make it up. "I'll hop on a plane the minute he develops his first fuzz."

"You will?"

It occurred to him that it was more than a request, that it might actually be his sister's way of letting him know she was done with her doctor friend. He certainly hoped so. She didn't look healthy. Pared down, somehow. Functional clothes. Functional hair pulled back in a ponytail. Chapped lips. "Absolutely," he said.

"Thank you, Caleb." As she felt him watching her, she saw herself the way he might—a woman in a film, no softness left, just angles—and it made her proud and yet uneasy that he might transform her into something that then became his on the screen.

At times she hated how he tried to see into her. Because it was not for her sake, but for his own, and for what he could then do with it. A year ago he'd finally sent her one of his films, and she'd borrowed Pearl Bloom's VCR, feeling flattered and then gradually invaded—*it wasn't like that, wasn't like that at all*—as she'd watched the film alone. It was about an opera singer who was born with glass splinters in her hands and with the ability to fly, but only above her own house, which was a church with three steeples—not set in the harsh winters of New Hampshire but in a tropical climate, surreal and lush. To Emma it was obvious that the film held parts of her and of the *Wasserburg,* and that Caleb had woven legends of the lake and legends of the stars into their family's story. But it was so different from the way she relived her family's past, feeling responsible to remember and preserve it the way it had been. *The real past.* And though Caleb's film was gorgeous to look at, it unsettled her that he would use what he could, interpret it as he chose to, and then rework it into something others would take for true.

"Uncle Caleb? How old do I have to be before I can shave?" Stefan was plucking at his chin.

"Couple of years . . . Could be soon . . . Your great-grandfather used to say Blau men are a hairy bunch. Let me look at you." Caleb took his nephew's face between his palms, and as he studied it closely for traces of stubble, he wished he'd see him more often than once every few years. At thirty-nine, he doubted he'd ever have children of his own. After those brief marriages in his twenties, he'd promised himself that he wouldn't even think about marriage until he'd been in a relationship for two years. But the longest any had lasted since was a year and ten months.

"Tell you what," he said to Stefan. "I'll teach you. Shaving and whatever else you need me to teach you."

After Yvonne returned to her own apartment and Stefan was asleep, Caleb made a pot of rosehip tea in Emma's kitchen, and they sat in her living room, resting their heads against the jungle embroidery of the chairs.

"You're good with Stefan," she said. "I like seeing him like that."

"He's a sweet boy. A lot like Dad, don't you think?"

"You think so?"

"That gentleness . . ."

"I wish I had more time for him. But with keeping the house up by myself— Let's not talk about the house, Caleb. Not tonight."

"All right. You want to talk about your doctor friend?"

"I wish Stefan could have the kind of Christmas you and I grew up with . . . those wonderful dinners in the lobby and—"

"You used to get stomachaches."

"No, I didn't."

"Stomachaches so bad you'd cry."

"It wasn't like that."

Caleb didn't say anything.

"It wasn't," she said resolutely. "Oh, and about your question . . . about Justin . . . I finally did ask him some of the things you've been telling me to ask for years."

"Good."

"Not so good. We had a fight."

"Good."

"Our first. And I'm not sure he'll ever want to come back."

"You can't mean your first fight ever?"

"We haven't seen each other enough to disagree."

"In over a decade?"

She curved her fingers around the carved backs of the lions, rubbed her thumbs across the intricate manes. "If you were to add up those hours we've actually been together, we don't have more than half a year, I bet. If that much . . ."

As Caleb listened to her tell him about seeing Justin with his wife at the Christmas play, and about their fight a few days afterwards, he was aware of the I-can-use-this voice that was so constant in his life. Pointing out. Collecting. Usually it meant just looking. Looking closely. And then imagining it again. And again. Translating it onto the screen. It could bring him closer to an experience. Give him greater understanding. Or let him distance himself. As he had now and then with Emma. Sometimes, though, a replay wasn't needed because the transformation would happen within the act of witnessing, already changing what he saw while—beneath all that—he'd remain aware of the process.

Emma was talking, and as Caleb held his cup between both hands, warming them, he could see her with her doctor friend, hear the words between them. *It's another Wednesday, of course, and they've just opened presents—ahead of Christmas as always since Justin will be with his family that day. When Emma finally asks him about his wife, asks some of those questions she has tortured herself with over the years, he speaks reluctantly, volunteering nothing beyond short answers.*

Yes, Laura and I stay together because of the children.

No, we sleep in separate beds.

Well . . . except for that night when Oliver was conceived.

Other than that, we haven't been intimate since.

That part of our marriage was never all that important to her.

Because she's just not very . . . affectionate.

We both understand the nature of our relationship.

Understand it enough to not jeopardize our family.

We're both mature people.

No, she never asks me about you or Stefan.

Laura is a very tactful woman.

She doesn't mention that I'm away once a week.

The children assume it's related to my work.

She is an understanding woman.

A patient woman.

Though Emma was silent now, Caleb wasn't finished yet. He was still with Justin's wife *whose patience endures even when her husband moves his lover and her child into his house. Laura Miles greets Emma and Stefan by the door, takes them inside to introduce her to her four children.* "This is Miss Blau and her son. Stefan, you already know Oliver from school." *They sit at the table, eat the excellent meatloaf—no, make that veal cutlets—which the understanding and patient wife has prepared.* "We are all mature people," *she tells Emma.* "Oliver will be glad to share his room with Stefan. And Justin has been looking forward to taking you to his bed. I knit when I can't sleep. Sweaters for my husband. It *keeps my nights meaningful. I'll knit one for you too. If I hurry it'll be finished Christmas Eve. Won't that be lovely? What color would you like?"*

✐

Ironically, Caleb's fantasy of Emma and Stefan moving into the Miles house was not all that absurd. At least not for Stefan. When his father stopped coming to the *Wasserburg*—as if by seeing both families together at the Christmas play he had realized he only needed one—Stefan began to watch Oliver Miles in school, what he brought for lunch, what he said about his father. More than before he could see Oliver's resemblance to himself. *I could be Oliver.* Only that Oliver spoke faster than Stefan and was thinner with brown hair to his shoulders. Silver-rimmed glasses. Bony wrists. Though Oliver wasn't a jock, other boys liked him. He had better aim than any of them when it came to tossing pennies into the open light fixture in their classroom when their teacher wasn't looking, blocking light from seeping through the milky glass until it was like an elevator light with its hundreds of dead bugs, and the janitor had to get the ladder to remove the coins.

Oliver also had a way of spotting and imitating teachers' weaknesses—the wet cough of the gym teacher, or the way the principal's nostrils vibrated when he quoted Shakespeare—that made Stefan laugh. He let Oliver read his comic books, and soon the two of them began to exchange comic books. Once the snow melted, they rode their bikes to school. Though Oliver had a ten-speed Raleigh, he'd stay next to Stefan's balloon-tire bike. Late that summer, when Oliver caught the bottom of his trousers in the chain, Stefan helped him get the fabric out.

Although Oliver was curious about the *Wasserburg,* Stefan never brought him home. They'd wait for each other outside their houses. Still, it was from Oliver that he heard some of the stories that the townspeople still told about the *Wasserburg:* how his grandma had dyed a bath mat and turned Mrs. Perelli's underpants piss-yellow; how his Great-aunt Greta had stolen a priest from the church; and how old Mrs. Bloom had killed an even older lady by flashing her naked breasts at her. Stefan liked old Mrs. Bloom because she used curse words as if they were just like any other words. But his mother got impatient with her and the other card-playing widows, as she called them, who sat in Mrs. Bloom's solarium, on display from the street like plastic mannequins in a store window, playing cards and smoking and drinking peach brandy. Invariably, Mrs. Bloom would take off her wig to get comfortable, while Fanny Braddock would serve them more brandy.

When fifth grade started in the fall, Stefan was glad that Oliver, too, was in Miss Heflin's class. Already he was imitating the peculiar bounce in her polio-walk, the way she held chalk in her long fingers, or rang up purchases when she helped the clerks in the store she'd inherited.

One day Oliver brought cigarettes he'd sneaked from one of his married sisters, and during recess he and Stefan hid behind the gym, smoking and talking about how Oliver wanted to be a doctor.

"Like my father. Some of his patients can't afford to pay, but he takes care of them anyhow."

"Maybe I can be a doctor too."

"Yeah, we'll go to the same university." Stefan inhaled. Coughed. "Roommates."

"We'll celebrate our birthdays together. Like twins almost."

"Twins . . ." Stefan was still coughing. "And we'll take the same classes."

"Parties, we'll stay up late and have parties."

"And when you get sick, I'll let you borrow my notes."

"Like you did when I missed school because of the flu."

Once in a while Stefan would lift out the false floor Great-uncle Tobias had shown him in his dresser, and he'd touch the broken pipe stem he kept hidden there along with a picture he'd cut from the newspaper when his father had given a public lecture about vaccinations. Its creases were smeared from opening and refolding it. And if he set the pipe stem between his lips, trying to fit his teeth into the chafed marks, it would always taste bitter.

∞

There was a word for it—illegitimate. Stefan had heard it before, that word, but he'd never linked it to himself. Not until the end of fifth grade when, during a math test, his right hand and pencil were caught in a streak of sun slanting through the window. He stared at the line on his wrist that separated light and shadow and saw himself, years ago, on his father's lap, moving his hand back and forth through a beam of light, making it leap from his father's arm to his hand.

Illegitimate. But maybe the word was all wrong. Because what if you knew your father? Were you still illegitimate then? Stefan yanked his hand from the light. His mother and his father had done it, the thing that made him the word. And his father had done it with Oliver's mother. But Oliver was not the word. He stared at Oliver who was bent over his test, stared at him till Oliver glanced up and frowned. His glasses were dirty, and his bangs hung over the top of their frames. He tapped against his watch. Motioned to the test. Gripping his pencil, Stefan tried to make out the numbers on the page, but they were blurred. All around him kids were leaning over the test. Pencils rasped against paper.

"What's the matter?" Oliver whispered.

"Stefan Blau. Oliver Miles." Miss Heflin and the hissing of nylon thighs as she limped down the aisle. "You know the rules. No talking during tests."

Stefan wished he could run from the classroom, hide in some dark place.

She was standing next to him. "You better hurry if you want to finish."

He erased a set of numbers, wrote in a four, a seven, a three. Erased those.

"You look flushed." Her palm fit itself against his forehead like white dough.

He flinched.

"Are you feeling sick?"

"No."

"You only have five more minutes." Thighs whispered, hissed beneath her skirt as she walked back to her desk. Her chair scraped the floor.

He felt Oliver watching him. Behind him someone hiccuped. Setting his pencil against the paper, Stefan forced himself to look at the numbers, but when the bell rang and Miss Heflin told them to pass the tests to the front, his page was still half empty, and Oliver had to pull it from under his hand. He stood up. Ran off to the school library, where he searched for the dictionary. One thumb against the leather tab with the *I* and the *J,* he flipped the pages back, scanned the words . . . incessant . . . incendiary . . . incandescent— There it was: illegitimate. Born out of wedlock . . . unlawful . . . incorrect. He could hear his heart beating the rhythm of the word—il-le-gi-ti-mate—and it was as if he were trapped inside a drum while an invisible drummer brought his palms down upon the skin of the drum—il-le-gi-ti-mate-il-le-gi-ti-mate—down, again and again, louder, faster.

He slammed the dictionary shut, and as he wedged it behind a row of other books to keep it from ever opening again to that word, it came to him that his father had made a choice. It was as easy as math, choosing four children over one child who belonged to the second family.

Except it didn't have to be that way.

Not if Stefan crossed over and undid the word.

∞

He began to imagine himself inside his father's house.

Into his father's real family.

Once or twice a day he would walk past the yellow Victorian without looking at it directly, yet taking in every detail of the overgrown garden, the windows without curtains.

Still, the first time Oliver invited him over, Stefan was terrified. "But when?" he asked.

"How about tomorrow?"

When he told his mother at dinner, she said no as he'd known she would. He pushed his green beans to the side of his plate, lined them up like logs, chose the middle one, and pierced it with his fork. Slippery slippery slip—

"It's not a good situation for you."

"But Oliver already asked *his* mother."

"It's not a good situation, Stefan."

"Oliver's mother said yes."

"And this mother says no." She laid her fork aside. Reached for her water glass.

"But I want to go," he whispered.

That familiar sad look came into her eyes, and he almost told her he'd stay home because that would have taken the look away. But he didn't. He finished his dinner, though he was no longer hungry, helped her clear the table. Only when he was scraping the food from their plates into the trash did he realize that his cheeks were aching because he was biting them from inside. In bed, he tried to read one of Oliver's comics, but he forgot to turn pages and kept reading the same bubble of words without understanding it.

Long after midnight he let himself out of the apartment. Legs stiff and cold, he took the stairs down to the lobby and walked out onto the dock. The lake was calm, glassy, without any of the white-caps that had given it texture in the afternoon. Though Stefan had his back toward the *Wasserburg,* he could still feel his mother's sadness, could see her lying on her bed with her eyes open. It didn't feel right, taking care of his mother. It was all twisted around. Not the way it was supposed to be. It had to do with his father living with his other family. Had to do with his mother's sadness. Other reasons, too many of them, tangled like a mess of string. None of them separate like the constellations he could name and find in the night sky. *She didn't even say good night to me.*

Still—he would go to his father's house.

Walk up the steps of that porch.

And open the door.

He knew this. Knew it with the same certainty that he knew the angle at which Orion held his sword.

∽

The sagging porch wrapped itself around three sides of the Victorian. Latticework concealed the dark gap beneath, but since a few of the wooden strips were broken, Stefan could see patches of the old foundation. With a sense of the forbidden—the dangerous even—he followed Oliver up the wooden steps and into the hallway where plastic milk crates were stacked into shelves that overflowed with books and odd baskets. Clothes, tennis rackets, and papers covered tables and chairs in the living room. No curtains. But lots' of hanging plants in the windows. The house smelled different than Stefan's apartment—not of furniture polish and detergent, but of his father's tobacco and of damp shoes and other things Stefan couldn't identify.

From a pile of blankets by the sofa rose a huge black dog, head square, body enormously fat.

"Just let him sniff you," Oliver said. "He's too lazy to bite anyone."

Cautiously Stefan extended one arm. The dog came closer. When he jabbed his nose against the hand, Stefan wanted to dry it against his pants, but he didn't because Oliver might think he didn't like his dog. "What kind of dog is he?"

"A black dog."

Stefan had to laugh. "That I can see."

"Part Newfoundland, part pig. We inherited him. From my sister Kath. When she and her husband moved into a smaller apartment where they don't allow pets."

"What's his name?"

"Ezra. Ever heard of Ezra Pound? The poet. Kath got him from the pound. The dog, not the poet. Get it? Pound and pound?" Oliver stopped his rapid flow of words to stroke the dog's jaw. "Here, Ezra, want to eat? Come on, show Stefan what a pig you are."

On stiff legs, the dog waddled behind Oliver into the kitchen where dirty dishes filled the sink. Two open cabinet doors exposed mismatched cups and plates. A jug with wildflowers sat on the table, and specks of pollen dotted the wooden surface. In the corner stood two small pails, and while Oliver filled one with water, the other with brown pellets, Ezra jumped up and down, all four paws bouncing off the floor in a grotesque dance. As soon as Oliver set the pails down, the dog nudged him aside with his wide head and—hunched over the water pail—began to slurp, beads of water flying from his jowls.

"He was even fatter when we got him." Oliver opened the refrigerator and grabbed a can of Coke and a bunch of celery. Twisting the lid from a peanut butter jar that stood on the counter, he dipped an unwashed stalk of celery into it. "Want some?"

The dog raised his head, and his ears twitched against the flat, ugly skull.

"Not you, pig-out. I'm talking to a certified human."

Stefan wished he could think of something equally funny to say.

"Here." Oliver pushed the jar toward him and pointed to the celery.

"No, thanks. But if you have another Coke—"

"Take a can," Oliver said, chewing with his mouth open.

Stefan tried to figure out what other boys in his class would do if Oliver invited them home . . . Like Ronny Burlito. The most popular kid. *Always cool. Ronny just opens the refrigerator. No big deal. Ronny never thinks of the word illegitimate.* Dumb-ass jock doesn't even know what it means. *Ronny just shrugs and takes a can of Coke. Like that.* Stefan checked inside the refrigerator as though he'd done it millions of times. Yet, he felt he was snooping. At home his mother usually had a snack waiting for him after school. But he was Ronny now, *and Ronny pulls the metal tab from his can and checks around for a glass.*

Oliver was drinking right from his can.

It's vulgar to drink from cans or bottles. Shutting off his mother's voice, Stefan set the can against his lips and tilted his head back. Above him the ceiling was swollen in several places with rust-colored water rings. He'd helped his mother fix ceilings before they got that bad, steadying her ladder, stirring paint, cleaning up afterwards.

"Want to see my room?"

The dog followed them upstairs. Dirty socks and dishes lay amidst half-finished airplane models and pencils with chewed-off erasers. Fingerprints smudged the window. Outside was an overgrown backyard and a bench with flaking green paint.

They sat on the floor and were just finishing their Cokes when a car door slammed in the driveway.

"My dad," Oliver said.

Mine. Stefan's can dented in his fist.

"Company?" Eyes soft brown with yellow specks. Familiar eyes that Stefan hadn't seen in seventeen months and three days. Eyes that cautioned: *You and I know. Oliver doesn't.* "Well . . . hello."

Stefan tried to say, "Hello," and brought out a croak. Cleared his throat and said it again. "Hello."

"I'm very glad you're here. Oliver told me you'd come."

"Thank you—" Stefan hesitated. *What do I call him now? Father? Doctor? Sir?*

"Call me Justin. All right?"

Another name yet. Father Doctor Sir Justin. Stefan swallowed. Ezra rested his square head on his knees, and he busied himself stroking the fur between the dog's ears.

Oliver leaned forward. "Dad—"

A name that's not on my list. Dad. FatherDoctorSirJustinDad.

"We've got to fix that tear in the tent after dinner," Oliver said.

FatherDoctorSirJustinDad groaned. "Tonight?"

"We've got to. If we want to camp this weekend."

"I was looking forward to camping."

"You want me to buy some bait tomorrow?"

A whole life away from me. Fishing. Camping.

"We'll talk about it later, Oliver." A careful glance toward Stefan.

"We're also out of Sterno. And I need to get batteries for the flashlights."

FatherDoctorSirJustinDad drew a black wallet from his back pocket and handed Oliver a twenty. "Are you staying for dinner, Stefan?"

"I—" He couldn't really say *yes* since it was more a question than an invitation.

"Some other time then," *FatherDoctorSirJustinDad* said as if he took it for granted that Stefan would be at his house again.

⌀

Although the Blau boy spooked Laura Miles, she tried to be easy around him. Tried hard because she believed having him in her house would keep her husband here too. But the boy had such a hungry look to him. . . . *The hunger to be part of my family.* He seemed to have resolved to not only claim his father, but her entire family, and it became obvious to Laura that the way he went about it was through Oliver.

Initially he was a thorn to her.

A trade-off for having her husband home.

For a while even her revenge: *My turn to keep what belongs to the Blau woman.* Picturing the Blau woman alone. "Come early on Sunday, Stefan. Spend the day with us."

But gradually she could see that the boys' friendship was not a sham, that Oliver and Stefan genuinely liked each other, and to her amazement, she found that she, too, was fond of the Blau boy. That she appreciated his thoughtfulness. Enjoyed the sudden light of gratitude in his face when she said he could stay for the evening or spend the weekend, even though having him here was a constant reminder of the Blau woman who—so the townspeople said—was hard about money when it came to paying for repairs or talking to tenants who were late with their rent.

But that's not what bothers you about her.

Still, for over a dozen years now it had been safer for Laura to detest the Blau woman based on the reasons of others. That way she didn't need to ferret out reasons of her own. Didn't need to push herself and her husband into a place they might not be able to return from. Especially now that Justin was home every night. Once in a while she was even glad the Blau boy had followed him here, and she missed him on days she didn't see him.

He never called to ask his mother when he was invited to eat dinner at Oliver's house, because she'd only tell him she had already cooked for him. But his mother wouldn't phone him there. He knew she wouldn't. Still, he didn't like thinking of her eating alone, and he made sure to stay home some evenings. He'd coax her into climbing to the roof and watching the stars with him. Or he'd help her clean out storage spaces or get vacant apartments ready for new tenants.

For a while he worried that Oliver's mother would ask him questions about his mother, but she simply did not seem interested. A short woman with a generous laugh and hips wider than his mother's, she wrote part-time for the local paper, covering town meetings and school events. She played a lot of tennis—singles in the town's women's league, mixed doubles with her husband. Though she enjoyed cooking, she wasn't interested in housework and usually waited with doing laundry until everyone was out of clothes. Walking from room to room, she'd scoop up clothes, hunt for stray socks beneath beds, and throw each armful down the steps into the basement, where for several hours the washer would chug, making the floor tremble as it spun out the water.

About once a month she'd attack her house with a mess of cleaning supplies, enlisting the help of Oliver and Patty, the youngest of her daughters, who was a senior in high school. While Oliver would slide dozens of jars and cans from one end of the counter to the other and Patty would give the floors a few distracted sweeps with the vacuum cleaner, Stefan would usually volunteer to wash dishes and scrub sinks.

"You don't have to," Oliver's mother would tell him while strolling through the kitchen, arms full of newspapers that she'd stack in the garage.

"I don't mind." Suds to his elbows, Stefan would feel like a member of his father's real family.

∽

One Saturday morning when he arrived at the yellow Victorian, Stefan found his father at the kitchen table, folders spread around him. He glanced up from a page he'd covered with long letters that slanted to the left. "Stefan," he said, his voice pleased. The open collar of his shirt framed a pale triangle of skin.

It was his first time alone with his father. In all their years of Wednesdays, they had never been alone in those brief hours between his father's arrival and his own bedtime. *Maybe now. Maybe now he'll say something to me.* Stefan didn't know what—just that it would be about him and his father, and that it would be important.

"Oliver went to the library with his mother. You're welcome to stay and wait for him."

Ezra jumped up and down, jabbing his wide nose at Stefan, urging him to rub the creases of furry skin between his ears.

"That dog really likes you," his father said.

Stefan wished his father had said how much *he* liked him. So far, the welcome he got from the dog was more enthusiastic than anything his father had said to him. Whenever he entered the house, Ezra would rise from his blankets and wag his entire body, greeting him with the same eagerness he showed at feedings.

His father reached out to pat the dog. "And you have a new pal, Ezra, don't you?"

"He doesn't look nearly as ugly as the first day I saw him."

His father laughed.

"I didn't mean to insult him."

"Ezra has that effect on people. . . . It's always good to have you here, Stefan."

"Really?" Warm with pleasure, Stefan waited for more. *If only you could be my father every day.*

His father motioned to the chair across from him. "Would you like something to drink?"

"No, thank you." Stefan sat down.

His father refilled his coffee and emptied two packets of sugar into his cup. "So—how's everything going?"

"Good."

"No problems?"

Stefan shook his head. Strange, how he missed his father when he was at home with his mother; yet, now that he finally was alone with him, he didn't know what to say.

"And school?"

"All right."

"You like your teachers?"

Though he felt his father waiting, willing to listen, all he could say was, "Yes." He remembered the last day his father had come to the *Wasserburg*. Remembered that it had been snowing. Remembered waking crying to the sound of the plow the following morning and going outside with his mother to see how deep the snow was—to his knees. They'd built a snowman with a carrot nose, but he'd kept crying and his mother had suggested he take a carrot to school so the other kids would let him help if they made a snowman. All at once, Stefan wondered if it had been hard for his father to stay away. "Why didn't you come back?" he blurted.

His father blinked. Glanced toward the door. "How is your mother?"

"The same." Reaching for an empty sugar packet, Stefan tore it into small pieces. A few leftover grains of sugar stuck to his finger-tips—*Why didn't you come back to us? Why not?*—and he rubbed them against the fleshy pads at the base of his thumbs.

"You're getting tall, Stefan."

"I guess so."

"What do you like to do after school?"

"I read a lot."

"Good. Good. What else?"

"Stars . . . I watch stars. And I make charts."

"Like your mother." His father sounded disappointed.

Stefan lined the shreds of paper along the edge of the table in front of him. "I guess so."

His father pushed another empty sugar packet across the table. "In case you need something else to pluck apart."

Neck hot, Stefan scooped up the scraps of paper.

"I'm sorry. That was unnecessary. I'm always hoping. . . ."

"Hoping?"

"Well, yes . . . that you'll be happier than this to see me."

"Hey." Oliver came running in, his mother behind him with a canvas bag full of books.

"But I am," Stefan wanted to shout. *"I am happy to see you."* Yet when he looked at his father, he could already feel the moment between them lock, feel his father's concern shift to Oliver, protect-ing Oliver from what Stefan knew. All at once he felt old—twice as old as Oliver—with the awareness that his father made him carry the knowledge that protected Oliver.

And who is there to protect me?

What used to feel like such a big thing—he and Oliver born the same day—now made him jealous, made him wonder if Oliver would ever figure it out.

"When did you get here?" Oliver wanted to know.

Stefan couldn't speak. Felt Oliver's mother step behind him and lay one hand against the back of his neck. Felt her breath light against his hair.

"I'm glad Oliver and you have become friends," she said.

"Oliver is my best friend." Thinking: *and my brother.* Knowing Laura Miles was thinking the same. *I want to live with them.* Instantly, he felt disloyal toward his mother. *Maybe I could visit her. But live with my father and Oliver.*

"Stefan got here just a few minutes ago," his father said to Oliver, and Stefan felt left behind, wishing he were the son who could evoke protectiveness in his father.

CHAPTER FOURTEEN

1987–1990

Third day of summer vacation, his father took him and Oliver fishing at Weirs Beach. Though they only caught small fish that they released into the lake, it didn't matter to Stefan because, for a while there, standing on the pier between his father and Oliver, he was able to convince himself that he lived with them. And that was good . . . until he started feeling disloyal to his mother. She never mentioned his father. Or Oliver. Or anyone else in his father's family. Just as his father's family didn't mention his mother. Sometimes Stefan felt he was the only one who remembered that there even were two families, and that—by shuttling between them—he linked them, though they continued to ignore all knowledge of each other. But whenever he thought about that too much, he'd start feeling odd—invisible and powerful at once.

His mother continued cooking for him, kept his dinners warm in the oven, though he wasn't home to eat them. *"What can I do to bring you back?"* she pictured herself asking Stefan. But she couldn't ask. After a while, she began to buy smaller portions and cook only for herself: chicken legs instead of whole chickens; one small pork chop instead of three; individual-size cans of vegetables and soups.

The Monday Stefan turned thirteen, she suggested pizza and a movie to celebrate. He hesitated, then admitted that Oliver's mother had baked two cakes. "For our birthdays together. Oliver's and mine."

"You can pick another evening for pizza and a movie," Emma said, smiling hard to keep him from seeing how close she was to crying.

"It's more important to him . . . really."

"We'll do it another time. Any evening."

"If you want, I'll come to the movies with you tonight."

"Go. Enjoy yourself."

After he was gone, she heated a bowl of clam chowder for herself and carried it into the living room without switching on a lamp. It was raining, and what little light filtered through the windows smudged the walls and blurred the colors left in the length of peacock rug she'd moved in front of the sofa. She set down her bowl. Slipped into her raincoat. Walked through the darkening streets of Winnipesaukee, her hair wet and cold against her neck. It wasn't until she saw the light in the downstairs windows of the yellow Victorian that she realized she was standing in front of Justin's house.

Instinctively, she took a step closer toward her son who was there beyond that window, the left side of his face toward her as he raised a fork to his mouth. What if he looked out and saw her? She didn't want him to feel sorry for her, didn't want to embarrass him. Quickly, she crossed the street and hid behind the maple tree, the bark of its wide trunk familiar against the side of her face. Long splinters of moon fell at her through its bare branches as she watched her son. Birthday candles on the table in front of him. And around that table Justin's other family. *Celebrating the day I gave birth to Stefan. Mine. I want my son back, want him back, now.* All at once, she remembered how closely Justin used to listen to Stefan when he was a small boy, and for that instant she tried to believe that it was good for him to be here with his father. Yet, already, she wanted to caution him that his father would never give him enough of himself. That he was a kind but indifferent man. That to expect any more of him would only bring Stefan pain.

Drawing her coat closer around herself, Emma shivered as she recalled how *not* being with Justin had often given her more pleasure than having him with her. In her longing for him, she had felt lovely and high-breasted. But as soon as he'd arrived, she'd felt rushed, trying to fill their one afternoon with all she wanted to have with him—while he was unhurried as though they had unlimited time together. Already disappointed, though he hadn't left yet, she dreaded his departure; but as soon as she was alone once again, she began looking forward to their next meeting when the possibility of anything would be hers. *Except it never became more than a possibility.*

Some days her love for him had felt impetuous, ready to risk anything, though he hadn't expected risks from her. That last night with him three years ago—the night of their only fight—he had told her he was afraid. "Because I have nailed down everything so securely in my life, Emma. Because you're the one person who could tear it all wide open."

And I still could. Tear it all wide open and walk in there and claim my place at your table. Celebrate the day I gave birth to Stefan. Mine. I want my son back, want him back, now. Her wet hands stiffened into fists, and when she pushed them into her pockets, she felt her knuckles against her thighs. How restricted she had always felt in how much caring she could show Justin. "We have to take this slowly," he had warned her, and when she'd asked, "How slowly can you take anything when you have a child together?" he hadn't answered.

And now their child was spending more time with him than with her.

In the yellow window, Justin's wife leaned toward Stefan. *Let him be—you already have four of your own.* But Stefan let her touch his shoulder, this woman who had let him nudge his way into his father's house where his mother could not go and had never been, into his father's family that was a family every day, not just on Wednesdays. Emma wished she could carry Stefan home and keep him there. Wished she could get rid of Justin inside her head. And of all that belonged to him. Eyes stinging, she started off into a lopsided run and didn't stop until she reached the *Wasserburg.*

Once again, the elevator wasn't working, and she bolted up the stairs to the fourth floor, gathered the clothes she had given Justin—all of them gifts he'd never taken to his house because of his wife—and took them down to *Opa*'s boat. As she rowed out into the black and uneven waves, she tossed Justin's clothes overboard. One by one, they swirled away. It hurt, but not as much as when he'd stopped their Wednesdays together, and as she fed the last of his belongings to the icy water, his white terry-cloth robe ballooned for an instant as though she had conjured him to drown in front of her.

*One late morning in July—humid and red-hot and without wind from the lake—a package arrived for Yvonne. Enjoying the anticipation, she carefully unfolded the tissue paper around two gowns from her favorite catalog store, *Sophisticated Lady*. She took off her blouse and skirt, held the azure gown against herself in front of the full mirror, one hand pressing the hanger to her clavicle, the other gathering the full satin at her waist.

"It's your color, my dear," Robert tells her.

She smiles. "To you, everything is my color."

Stepping to one side, then to the other, she swirled around.

"May I have this dance, lovely lady?" One summer's lover spins her across the dance floor, and she arches her back and leans into his embrace as he dips her. The tango, of course . . .

As she swayed from one foot to the other, the satin in the mirror brought out the night blue in her hair and made her cheeks look smoother. She could easily pass for fifty-eight, maybe even forty-eight. *Soon I'll be seventy— Don't count. Don't think.* Her shoulders rose from the black lace of her slip, slender, *not bony like some women's;* neck still firm, though the horizontal lines that divided it into three sections had grown deeper. She stroked her fingertips upward across those folds, across the soft skin—*too soft?*—below her chin. New fabric against her skin—there was nothing like it. Still, for years now, Yvonne had tried to please Emma by staying away from her favorite catalogs. But Emma always found something to fret about. That's why Yvonne made sure to cross out original prices and write lower amounts on the tags, claiming she'd bought them on sale. Last winter, when she and her grandson had come home from a shopping trip to Concord with two pairs of high-heeled shoes, he'd helped her hide the bone-colored sling backs till Easter when she'd brought them out as though she'd just gotten them on sale. It was Emma's fault, forcing her and Stefan to lie.

For a while Yvonne had bought clothes and makeup for her—bribes so that Emma would let her keep her own purchases—but Emma wouldn't even use lipstick when her lips were chapped, and she'd returned nearly all the clothes.

But now Yvonne had a second gown to try on. *The delight of it. And I always look best when I smile.* From the cardboard box she pulled the other gown—a deep green velour with sleeves. The more the *Wasserburg* deteriorated, the more she craved new clothes, scarves, perfumes. She draped the satin over a chair and held up the velour. An entirely different feeling—not as lavish but more cosmopolitan, the kind of gown she could wear this fall to the theater or to a good restaurant. She shook her hair. Turned. *Dinner at the* Cadeau du Lac . . .

Robert pulls out her chair. "You look wonderful, my dear."
"Mother?"

She spun to the door. Emma—how long had she been standing there? Feeling oddly naked, Yvonne tugged the gown against herself.

In the mirror Emma saw the back of her mother's flimsy slip, the bumpy veins in her legs, and was seized by a sudden and deep compassion. She remembered her mother as a young woman—so playful, so elegant, so charming that Emma had felt privileged watching her. But that enchantment had worn off, and she was left with embarrassment for her mother's wants, embarrassment that her mother had a witness and that she had to be that witness.

Bright red circles of excitement floated high on her mother's cheeks—*face of a clown painted anew each day over the old woman face*—and her black hair, brittle from too many chemicals, lay matted in back as if she only attended to those parts of herself that she could readily see in the mirror.

Emma pointed to the velour gown. "When did you get that?" And noticed on the chair yet another gown, looking new and expensive even though she'd just had to postpone a major plumbing job on the second floor. Suddenly it struck her, the unfairness of it all. Not all that many years ago, the house had been grand, her *Opa* alive, and she had believed it would be like that forever . . . warm nights on the roof, the people game with Caleb.

When had it all begun to come apart?

With her father's indulgence of her mother's wastefulness?

With Uncle Tobias' curse: "Keeping the house together will destroy it and drive this family apart"?

One day last winter she'd felt so discouraged about the *Wasserburg* that she'd driven to Hartford to ask Uncle Tobias to revoke his curse, declare it invalid as only the originator of a curse can do. He'd seemed embarrassed for her, had insisted on cooking lunch for her, and she'd sat with him and Danny Wilson, both wrinkled and tan, eating shrimp with almonds and currants, drinking wine that was more yellow than white.

"A Sicilian wine," her uncle said. "Danny wants to take me to Sicily on our next cruise." At least twice a year the two of them traveled, always to warmer climates from where they sent presents to Stefan. Small pottery drums from Morocco. A woven poncho from Mexico. A set of oil paints from Paris.

After Uncle Tobias made strong coffee in a glass pot and set out a plate with wrapped chocolate wafers, he told her what he'd already said the day of *Oma*'s funeral—that the house had been cursed before he was ever born, and Emma wondered if it had started the night *Opa* had buried St. Joseph head down, wondered if it was reaching into her own life because she was not only losing the house but also her son.

"It's nothing I did," Uncle Tobias added. "Besides, I'm not that powerful."

"None of us are, Emma," Danny said, watching her closely.

∞

"I couldn't resist." Her mother straightened the bodice of the dress and tilted her head. "Look."

It was obviously made for a younger woman, and the low neckline made her mother look strung together with hollow bones and gray skin. Skin that used to be pale yet soaked up light. Skin that now—when it no longer could hold that light—had gone the other side of pale to gray.

Emma kept her voice gentle. "You know we have to send those back."

Her mother brought her face close to the mirror, and in the still, hot air that slowed down all movements, she tugged with two fingers at a fold on her throat as if about to turn her skin inside out. "Oh," she said and then smiled. "You can't mean that."

"I wish we could afford them. But I have to say no."

"One then," her mother whispered.

"We can't." Heavily, Emma sat on the edge of the unmade bed.

"Of course we can," her mother said in her most charming voice. Holding both dresses against herself, she walked toward Emma, hips rippling as if she were a model in a fashion show. "I'll even let you choose." Surely now, Emma would see how unique these dresses were, how wonderful they looked on her.

Deep inside her body Emma felt an immeasurable weariness that might never be dislodged, not even by the longest sleep. By delegating the choice to her, her mother was trying to make it impossible for her to send either one of the dresses back.

"Which one?" Her mother pressed her with an anxious smile. "Admit it—you like them both."

Emma got up and lifted the blue satin dress from her mother's hands. The price tag was over four hundred dollars. Jesus, she'd better take a look at the other tag too. Nearly six hundred. She let out a slow breath. *What can I do before she squanders it all? What do I have to do to save the house from her?*

Her mother was stepping into the blue satin dress. "Will you please close the zipper for me?"

Reluctantly, Emma guided the zipper up. "How about all your other dresses?" She opened the door of her mother's closet and pointed to an entire row of evening gowns: strapless chiffon with sequins down its bodice; white satin with a huge bow above the seat; gray silk with flowing sleeves and a deep V-shaped neckline; black velvet with a matching jacket. . . . "Some of these you haven't even worn."

"But I will. You know how hard it is to find stylish clothes in this town, and when I see something like this in the catalog, I—"

"Where would you wear this?" Emma pulled out a pink silk with a tear-shaped neckline. "To the dentist? To the store?" Not that her mother hadn't worn absurdly formal clothes just to the bakery or beauty parlor.

"Let me see. I have worn this . . . twice already. When your father was still alive. Once to dinner in Manchester. And to the ballet in Boston. The chiffon I wore on your grandmother's last birthday. And this white one here . . . remember, five years ago when Caleb visited." Her chin rose. "Caleb would let me keep these gowns."

"Sure. While the house is falling down around both of you." Sometimes—while washing her mother's laundry or scouring her mother's tub, Emma would get angry at Caleb who was doing what he loved far away on the West Coast. "Let Caleb pay for the gowns then," she said. "Maybe I should just take Stefan and move out. Caleb can look after you and the house."

Her mother looked startled. "He wouldn't come back to New Hampshire."

"Right."

"Don't be like that, Emma."

"We cannot afford dresses like these. And I'm sorry about that. Because I wish we could. Just as I wish we had the money to repair the furnace and the elevator and—"

"Just one dress then. Please . . ."

"They're far too expensive."

"I won't buy anything else for a while."

"I'm sorry."

Slowly, Yvonne straightened her shoulders. "Not that it is your decision to make."

"Mother—"

"I was merely asking your opinion. And since you're being so very stingy, I have decided to keep both."

"Will you let me show you something?"

"What is it?"

"Just come with me. Please?"

In the blue gown, Yvonne followed her daughter into the hallway where the carpets were so drab that you could no longer see the original pattern; through empty apartments where tiles had cracked and water leakage had left yellow-brown blotches on the ceilings; into the basement where pipes were rusting and several light fixtures had burned out.

"This is where we need to spend money," Emma said. "Not on evening gowns."

Yvonne shrank from the musty smell, the peeling walls. Something was wrong. What if Emma was playing a trick on her? She felt a dull ache in her bones because all at once it seemed possible that she could lose the house altogether. Weakly, she tried to protest. "There always was more than enough." She raised one hand to support herself against a streaked wall. It all was much worse than she had expected. So this was what Emma had been talking about. The house was decaying. *Aging. Creases and skin like ash?* She could feel Emma's frustration because she, too, had known it along with the urge to restore. *Restore myself.* Except that this house needed far more than she would ever need, far more than one dress, one scarf, one jar of skin creme. *Where will I go if we lose everything?* Though she wanted to blame Emma, she couldn't because she knew how Emma loved the house—loved it more than she'd ever loved that doctor who had only given her leftover hours and loneliness. *Odd, that a woman like me would produce a daughter so . . . ordinary.* How she missed Caleb and his appreciation for beauty.

"All we have are the rents," Emma was fretting.

Even now. Even now at my age, I feel more alluring than my daughter has ever been.

"We need to budget."

If only she had inherited my beauty.

"Find tenants."

Men would adore her, would want to help her.

"People want to live in new buildings. Mother—"

. . . more alluring than my daughter has ever been.

"Are you listening?"

"I'll spend less. And I'll return the other dress for credit. This one now—" Yvonne motioned to the satin hem that had picked up dust along the way. "You know they won't take it back like that. But I'll get it dry-cleaned and wear it for several occasions." *More alluring than my daughter has ever been.* "Because from now on, I promise, Emma, no more extravagances. Now that I see what you mean—"

"But you don't see." Emma shook her head. "You're looking at it and you still don't see."

"I'll trade you." Yvonne smiled, suddenly feeling very brilliant. Not only would she keep both dresses, but she'd also get Emma to make sure the house wouldn't get worse. "I'll do it. I'll make it yours, the house."

Cautiously, Emma swallowed. Again. *Don't say anything wrong. Don't mess it up now. Listen to her. Listen closely.*

"I'll make it yours." Her mother's face was radiant. "Yours and Caleb's." She sounded like a child who believed that if she was nice, she'd get what she wanted.

So give her what she wants. "Good," Emma said, her heart beating slower. "Yes."

It would be all right. Yvonne could feel it. "But you'll have to let me keep both gowns."

"Both gowns," Emma repeated, though she hated the waste.

"And you'll fix up the house, right?"

"You'll always have a place to stay. Because I'll bring it back to how it used to be. And then Caleb and I will work it out between us." And she would. Restore the house for herself and Caleb.

The last time she'd seen her brother she had tried to talk to him about saving the house from their mother. Emma had been kneeling on the floor of a vacant apartment, cleaning around the recessed buzzer, getting the place ready for the Ketchums, a car mechanic married to a beautician.

"I've met with a lawyer," she had told Caleb. "We've taken the old deed from the registry, and he has drafted a new one. He'll notarize it once Mother is ready to convey the house to us. It would also make her eligible for Medicaid."

When Caleb propped himself on the windowsill, Emma saw herself all at once the way he might show her in a film, cleaning the floor on her knees, and she felt angry as if she were that maid he'd summoned by pressing his foot against the button.

"If you don't let up with this," he said, "I'll warn Mom, tell her to hold on to what belongs to her."

"What belongs to her?" She stopped scrubbing and raised her

face. "There wouldn't be anything left by now if I didn't work constantly."

"Still," he insisted, "it belongs to her."

"Easy for you to give her advice. You have no intention to help with the house, but you want to tell me what to do about it."

"What not to do about it," he had corrected her.

❦

"And I need shoes," Emma's mother was saying as they re-entered her apartment.

"Shoes?" Emma followed her mother into the living room.

"To match both dresses."

"We can buy them this afternoon. On the way back from the lawyer's."

"We don't need a lawyer for this."

"Just to make it all legal. It won't take long. I'll give him a call to make sure he gets it right."

"But—"

"What color were you thinking of for the shoes?"

"But make sure Caleb gets half," her mother said. And she said it again in the car that afternoon: "Make sure Caleb gets half."

"I will. It's important to me too." And it was. Emma wanted Caleb to have half of it. Only not yet. "There'll be plenty of time later," she told her mother, "to figure the details. Until the house is restored, it's best if I'm the only one on the deed."

"You can restore it if it's in both your names."

"Think about it. He could force us into selling next week. The way the house is now, we wouldn't get much for it. You'd lose everything, while he'd take the money to California and invest it in his films. I'd certainly understand it, considering how important his films are to him."

"Caleb wouldn't do that."

Emma felt her mother getting slippery. Evasive. As she had so often in the past. But she was not about to let her. Not now. Reaching across, she grasped her mother's cold hands. "Caleb does not live here," she said urgently. "Owning a house here would be a burden for him. It is very expensive to make films."

Yvonne turned her face from her daughter and toward the car

window—white clapboard houses, the brick bank, the rose hedge by the school—yet above everything that passed lay the reflection of her daughter's face: determined; always present. Always tugging at her. She pulled her hands from Emma's.

"Eventually Caleb will be grateful," Emma said. "But it's best to wait before telling him. In the meantime, I'll write you a check every month for things you need."

Things I need. Silk slips. Good shampoo and pantyhose. Dresses and lotion—

"I was thinking about two thousand."

Roses once a week. Magazines. A new raincoat. Nail polish. New towels for the bathroom and kitchen. Candles. The shoes we're getting today. Yvonne was still thinking about those shoes while they sat in the lawyer's office, and when she laid down the lawyer's ballpoint pen, she felt glad that, finally, she'd been able to please her daughter by giving her what she wanted. She hadn't seen her this joyful in years. Now Emma could not press her for anything else.

Because there isn't anything else I can give her.

∽

Most mornings Emma would awaken with the awareness that the house was hers alone, with a sense of security she hadn't known since before *Opa*'s death. Again and again she'd look at the deed proving her ownership. She fined tenants two dollars for every day their rent was late. Charged them for burned-out lightbulbs in the hallway of the floor they lived on. Plans for making the house whole again filled her with such energy and purpose that—even when her body felt tired—she could not stop working: she replaced the brick walks in the garden; took down the rotting rails that partitioned *Oma*'s flower beds; gutted two empty apartments and repainted them; covered worn floors with carpeting.

In the apartment that used to be the Perellis', the original green paint had bled through in several places, and when it still showed through two coats of white, Stefan offered to help her paint over it again, and they both had white smudges on their faces and clothes when they finished.

"Just look at us," she said as they washed their faces and hands side by side at the bathroom sink.

In the mirror, Stefan noticed that he was as tall as his mother. Prodding her with one elbow, he motioned to their reflection.

"What are you grinning about?" she asked.

He raised himself on his toes, tried to look down on her, and noticed with alarm that from this angle her hair was graying. He tried to joke. "Shortie."

"Oh yeah?" She felt a sudden and wild joy at having Stefan with her.

"Yeah, you're just a shortie."

She got on her toes too, stretched herself to her full height. "Shortie yourself."

They had other moments of lightness between them. When he helped her with her work. Cooked dinner with her. Thanked her for a present she'd left for him on his desk. A book usually. Or a candy bar.

How she wished she could tell her brother about all the changes she was making, but she wanted to enjoy her ownership just a while longer. He wouldn't be able to help with the work anyhow, and she was glad to restore the house for both of them. Though she didn't like carrying that secret between them, it had to be like that for now, so he wouldn't come at her with decisions and jeopardize what she was accomplishing.

Though she believed that every hour of work brought the *Wasserburg* closer to the way it had been, she also felt its weight in her limbs those mornings when she'd awake disoriented as if, all night, she had labored to crawl from beneath its burden. Ownership did not make it easier to pay the bills. She had to take out another mortgage. Reduce rents to attract new tenants. Move herself and Stefan into a smaller apartment on the fourth floor. Though she turned all she could back into the house, something else would break down as soon as she'd finish one repair.

Whenever her brother called, she was quick to get off the phone. But the longer the building was hers, the harder it was to think of the day when she'd deed him his half. She was sure she would— only not yet—and knowing she would was a constant struggle with what she really wanted: to have it be hers alone. But that wouldn't be right. Now if she'd had that kind of struggle with anyone else, she would have called Caleb, asked him what to do. She missed him. One evening, when Stefan was sleeping over at Justin's house, she felt such an urge to hear her brother's voice that she dialed his number in Los Angeles, though she knew she would hang up as soon as he answered.

"Hello," he said, and then, "who is this?"

She couldn't move. Minutes after he had hung up, she still held the receiver hard against her ear, telling herself that, ultimately, he would have to agree with what she was doing. If she hadn't left school to care for the house, it would have fallen into disrepair, or her mother would have squandered it. The house had been her education. Caleb had his films. Meanwhile she was doing what was right, looking after her mother, paying her two thousand dollars every month as promised, far more than she and Stefan had to live on.

∽

Caleb phoned her the summer of 1989 when she had owned the house one full year. "I'm thinking of flying out for a visit next month."

"It's not a good time," she stalled. "A lot of problems with the house."

"Once I'm there, I'll help with whatever you're doing."

"I couldn't ask that of you." She felt queasy. "Listen, I have an appointment in a few minutes. But let me call you back. Soon. We'll figure out what's best with your visit."

Two weeks later he called again.

"I meant to get back to you," she apologized. "But we had trouble with the elevator again and we—"

"I know, Emma."

"We got it working for a few days, and now it's stuck again in the basement."

"I'm not talking about the elevator."

She leaned against the wall by the refrigerator. Pulled the phone cord close and bunched it against her throat. "I did it for both of us, Caleb."

"The house doesn't belong to us."

"Who told you?"

"Certainly not you."

"Aunt Greta? Mother?"

"Why did you?"

"Because otherwise there'd be nothing left. For you or for me."

"I expect you to return the house to Mom."

"Listen, it's her overspending that did it. I've tried to talk to you. But the house was never important to you."

"I'll tell you what's important to me—more important than any house. My relationship to my sister. And I can't stand feeling cheated by—"

"No one cheated you."

He heard the resentment in her voice and recalled his grandfather telling him how Emma's hands had been so strong at birth that he'd known no one would ever be able to take from her what she wasn't willing to part with. And as that memory fused with what Emma was saying to him now, he didn't know yet how it all belonged together, only that it did.

"What I'm doing is preserving it, Caleb, making sure there will be something for you and for me. But I don't see you helping in any way."

"I've tried to imagine why you did it."

"This isn't doing any good."

"I know for you the house stands for something that was good once. But now you're selling me for the house and—"

"Don't, Caleb."

"You've stolen from our mother. And you're lying to yourself."

"You would have nothing if I hadn't stopped her. Nothing."

"Isn't that exactly what I have now? Nothing?"

"What do you know? Ever since *Vati* died, you have not been there for me or for the house. You're never here. And when Stefan was a baby, I had to leave him with Mother or with tenants while I scraped and painted and cleaned and—"

"You could have hired others to do that."

"And who would have paid those so-called others?"

"You're reaching back awfully far to prove how you suffered."

"It happened. It all happened. And I'm still the one who makes sure Mother has a house to live in, the one who does her laundry, who gets the stains out of—"

"There's no need for you to do her laundry. Send it out."

"It's too expensive . . . and impersonal."

"You keep suffering so that you can justify cheating Mom out of the house. And you know what the sad thing about this is, Emma? That I'm not surprised."

She felt furious. Furious that everyone was after what should have been hers. The *Wasserburg.* Justin. Her son. She was not about to let Caleb take the *Wasserburg* from her. The way he'd taken the pink bicycle with the training wheels that her mother had given her. It had never been fully hers, though she'd believed it was, riding it only on sidewalks, so careful to wipe off each speck of dirt while she'd waited for a dry, sunny day to take it on the path by the lake. But Caleb had ridden it without asking, had brought it home wet with dirt and leaves on its fenders and tires, had made it ugly so that she'd never been able to enjoy it again.

"I don't deserve this," she said.

"Emma—"

"No." She slammed down the phone as rage from that long-ago day pitched through her, tilted her back to yet another day when Caleb had locked her out on the balcony with the copper taste of death on her teeth till she'd gouged her way through blood and glass into all that was sacred and safe.

The phone started ringing. She stepped away from it, breath heaving. And in that very instant she understood. Understood that she alone deserved the house. Understood that even though she had taken ownership for Caleb and herself, she was no longer willing to give him half. *Not now.* Not after he'd accused her of cheating him and her mother. Truth was that *Opa's Wasserburg* belonged to her. Had always been meant to be hers. She had stripped her life bare working for it. It was all she had. And it was all she wanted. All she needed.

⁓

Periodically, that day, the phone rang, and she finally picked it up late that evening.

Caleb. Of course. Talking fast as if worried she'd hang up on him again. "I want you to know that I checked with a lawyer about what I can do to make sure the house goes back to Mom."

"Listen, I have a lot of things to do."

"My lawyer said I would have to prove in court that Mom was incompetent when she deeded the house to you."

"You're bluffing."

He didn't answer.

"You are," she said.

"I am planning to check with a lawyer."

"So go and check."

"At least put me on the deed too."

"Now you want it?"

"For her. I would use it to take care of her."

"I'm already taking care of her. Whatever she gets, Caleb, she spends. Faster than you can count it."

"Then let her."

"I can't."

"I thought your grand plan was to divide it all the way *Oma* should have, to Aunt Greta and Uncle Tobias and with Father's share going to Mother."

"I was twelve when *Oma* died."

"But you knew instinctively what would have been right."

"Can you imagine what kind of a legal mess that would turn into?"

"Not really. It's still the best solution."

"Why? You've checked that out too with your lawyer?"

"I'm sure it can be done."

"I have to go."

When she bought an answering machine to screen his calls, he sent her letters she didn't answer.

"You will always be my sister," he wrote.

"I want to believe that someday you'll do what is just," he wrote.

"If there's ever anything I can do for you, I'll be there," he wrote.

It made her miss him, those letters—not the way he was now with his demands, but the joyfulness they used to carry between them. And that was a great loss, especially if she added it to all she had already lost. Some evenings, late, she would dial his number and wait for him to answer, wait till he had hung up before she would set down her phone. Once, right afterwards when she still held the receiver, it rang in her hand, and she dropped it, afraid it would be Caleb. It kept ringing, and when she picked it up—suddenly sure it was her son calling from Justin's house, though he hadn't called her from there before—it indeed was Caleb.

"What is it?" she asked, sure he'd found out she was the one calling him nights and hanging up.

But what he said was, "I miss you."

"Me too," she said without thinking.

"We may never agree about the house, but I ... All I want tonight is to talk with you, Emma. Nothing about the house."

She leaned forward. "Yes."

"I'm still ready to teach Stefan to shave."

"Yes," she said again. "I'm glad," she said. "I think he's started," she said, suddenly worried that Caleb wouldn't be on the phone long enough to hear all of it. "With shaving, I mean. Not here. But at his father's house. He's there a lot. With the boy who was born the same day. Oliver. Stefan has sort of a shadow on his upper lip. The way you used to. And along his jaw. Some days I don't see that shadow and know he must have shaved. But he doesn't talk about his father to me. Or about what he is doing there. And I don't ask. At times I wonder if it's better that way. For him."

"And for you?"

"There's so much I have to do here. . . ."

"And what does that give you?"

She was silent.

"Are you still there?"

"I think . . . he's used to not needing me a whole lot. And that he wants a full family."

"And what's a full family?"

"A family that is together more than once a week."

"Some of his distance from you may have to do with being almost fifteen."

"And with me never being there for him . . . as much as I wanted to."

They talked for over half an hour, mostly about Stefan, but also about Caleb's work, about Uncle Tobias who was on a Mediterranean cruise with Danny Wilson, about Aunt Greta who was volunteering at a hospital in Boston. Neither of them mentioned the *Wasserburg*.

Caleb thought that Emma sounded glad to be talking with him, and he felt good hearing that gladness in her voice; but gradually it began to bother him how she was leaning on him, counting on him as though she hadn't cheated him and their mother. As his familiar anger seeped back—*you can't have it both ways, Emma*—he could no longer trust himself to keep it from her. "I need to be somewhere soon," he said abruptly. "I'm sorry, but I need to get ready."

"Can't we—"

"I really do, Emma."

"Of course," she said, confused by the sudden change in his voice. "Maybe we can . . . you know . . . talk again? Soon?"

But he was already gone.

∽

All she had ever wanted was to have the house back the way it used to be. But now so much of it felt closed to her. As a child she had been a welcome visitor in all the apartments, following her *Opa* who'd been well-liked by his tenants; but now the turnover was swift, and new renters kept to themselves. Some didn't greet her when they saw her, and a few left their trash bags on the floor of the utility room instead of opening the trap door and throwing them down the chute. Carelessness like that made her impatient because it always created extra work for those who had to pick up afterwards.

It seemed that the only way she could get into their lives was through their complaints, through clauses in their leases allowing her the inspection of any apartment, and through the mail she began to take from their boxes. It was easier than taking things from stores used to be, something she'd stopped when she was pregnant. A few of their personal letters she kept in her closet with *Oma*'s letters; but most she sealed and replaced because they were so shallow in comparison. The last week of each month she would raid all mailboxes for bills. Those she didn't need to open, just store until the tenants had paid their rent. It was only right that they should pay for shelter before considering other bills.

At times, when she would let herself wish that the *Wasserburg* were still a community, a family, it felt as though her grandparents' festive dinners—summer solstice in the courtyard and Christmas in the lobby—had happened every Sunday, linking the years of her childhood; and within those memories, lit and embellished by longing, she would see her entire family: *Opa* and *Oma,* her parents, Aunt Greta, Uncle Tobias. . . . And the tenants, how they'd looked forward to the parties. They brought their families, flowers, tables from their apartments that Emma would help *Oma* cover with white linen. Those who played instruments—the guitar or flute or violin—performed while everyone sang along. While music and voices crisscrossed the courtyard, *Oma* moved from table to table with trays of food, wearing the emerald necklace she only wore when *Opa* reminded her. As Emma recalled how the colors of the food were often enough to satisfy her, she felt once again that certainty of belonging.

And that's when she thought of giving a party.

A summer solstice dinner in the courtyard of the *Wasserburg.*

To celebrate her ownership of the house.

To let the tenants see her generous side.

She was lavish in buying what she needed because this dinner would make up for some of her harshness with them, would show them how they all benefited from living in this house that was unlike any other. She bought thick, ivory note cards and a calligraphy pen. After placing her invitations in the tenants' mailboxes, she wished she'd asked for responses to figure how much shopping she had to do. But the few who couldn't come surely would let her know. This year it would be best to rent tables and chairs. Already she could see the tenants: *in their best clothes they pour through the lobby and out into the courtyard where tables with candles are set up. Some carry instruments or bottles of wine. She brings out platters of potato salad with parsley and radish curls, browned chickens with their feet in white paper lace. The tenants talk among*

each other instead of barely nodding to each other in the elevator.
They drink the punch she made just the way Opa *used to: plain for*
the children, spiked for the grown-ups.

People from other buildings walk by and see the lights, hear the
music, wonder what it would be like to live in the Wasserburg. *By*
July the vacancy sign will have disappeared from the front window.
For months after the solstice dinner, when tenants encounter her in
the hallways, they'll thank her instead of giving her their com-
plaints or a mumbled hello. They invite her into their apartments,
and she enters those rooms that have been closed to her for too
many years, sits down—on their best chair, they insist, "For you,
Miss Blau"—and looks from their windows at the views that are so
different from every angle. By next summer the dinner will be a tra-
dition, and the tenants will bring their own chairs and tables, help
with the planning and the preparations.

But this year it would be her gift to them.

Her mother surprised her by wanting to help, and for the two
days before the dinner, they cooked together, both almost giddy in
the mood of getting ready for the party as they sliced fruits and
cubed potatoes, baked strawberry pies and carved radish curls,
sautéed onions and stuffed chickens with wild rice and chestnuts.
They used both ovens and refrigerators. Face flushed, Emma
hummed as she carried trays of food between her mother's apartment and her own. When she came upon tenants on the stairs—
since once again the elevator was broken—she gave them a
mysterious smile that startled some and made others speculate that
Miss Blau was probably about to raise the rents.

She didn't think of what to wear until the evening before the dinner when she couldn't find anything good enough in her closet.
What she came across, though, were the star charts her great-
grandmother had drawn in Germany, and as she held the roll of
linen drawings, Emma thought of how much her son had wanted
them ever since he was a small boy. She hesitated. Stefan was old
enough. And careful with what belonged to him. As she left them
on his desk, she imagined his surprise when he'd return from his
camping trip with Justin and Oliver. This past year it had become
easier to let him be with Justin, and oddly—now, that he didn't

worry about disappointing her each time he turned to his father—Stefan came back to her with greater ease.

When her mother offered to let her choose a dress from her closet, Emma felt embarrassed, recalling that day she'd found her here with two new gowns. "You pick something," she said, aware of the smell of old carpets and upholstery.

Without hesitation, her mother pulled out a gray silk gown and held it in front of Emma.

"This is too elegant for me."

"But it compliments you."

"You think so?" Emma asked, appreciating—for the first time since childhood when she'd loved watching her mother get ready—her interest in clothes. And when she tried on the gown, she was amazed how graceful she looked, how it made her face softer, pinker.

"Let me try something with your hair," Yvonne said.

When her daughter sat down in front of the mirror, Yvonne felt a tug low in her spine and with it the panic that her back was about to give out again; but then she reminded herself that she hadn't had backaches in the twenty years since Robert's death, and instantly the discomfort ceased. *I don't need this. Don't need to hold it.*

Pulling her brush through her daughter's hair, she gathered it, and as she twisted it upward into a coil, she noticed a few tiny, white scars high on Emma's temples. "I thought those scars had healed," she said.

"Not all of them." As Emma felt her mother's eyes, probing, she suddenly knew that her mother was seeing her with greater clarity than she could see herself.

"If you like your hair this way, I'll do it for you tomorrow."

"Thank you," Emma said, oddly consoled. "For the dress too."

When Emma got back to her apartment, Mrs. Ketchum phoned to say her family was driving to Wolfeboro the next evening. In the morning five others called with excuses. Still, there should be enough people to fill the tables in the courtyard. All day Emma cooked, rushed up and down four flights of stairs to carry china and silverware and food to the courtyard. After she bathed and changed into the gray silk, she arranged flowers on the tables. She took a matchbox from her pocket and was just lighting the candles when she glanced up to see her mother descend the front steps in a white gown as if—so the people of Winnipesaukee who passed by the house would tell others later—awaiting applause.

What had seemed possible just the day before—to bring the community of the *Wasserburg* back to how it used to be—had gone wrong even before Emma served the endive salad. Most of the tenants had either forgotten about the party or had simply not bothered to tell her they wouldn't be there; and the few who'd come were the ones she didn't particularly like: Mrs. Ferris with her husband Duke who was a stockbroker and quick with numbers but hard to look at because he picked his ears; Hank and Sybil Weber who at least once a month talked about moving out; Miss Fitzpatrick who'd been engaged four times so far but never married; and the Clarkes with their six children whose apartment needed more repairs than any others in the building.

All the joy Emma had felt while preparing the dinner vanished as she sat in the courtyard, barely able to swallow, sure that the few tenants who sat at these tables readied for nearly a hundred were only here because they didn't have any place else to go. Like those too old to move away. Some tenants, she was certain, were inside the building. Like the Ketchums who supposedly were in Wolfeboro. Although the light was off in their kitchen, Emma glimpsed someone moving through there. And Mr. Willard, who had told her, "I'll have to let you know," had never called back and was probably hiding out in his apartment. Others entered or left the building without even the courtesy of a lie. The expense of it all. She felt ill thinking of it.

But her mother, across from her in white with bare shoulders, obviously enjoyed being all dressed up in the smooth evening air. "They must have made plans to celebrate summer solstice with their own families," she suggested. "Somewhere," she added vaguely, raising one hand and pulling it through the air as if she were fanning it through water. "And they'll stop by on the way home for a glass of punch. Before I married your father, I used to dance at two or three parties every night. . . ."

They could be seen from the sidewalk, Emma Blau and her

mother, both wearing gowns suitable for a coronation, say, or a beauty contest; and to the people of Winnipesaukee who walked by and noticed the empty chairs and countless serving dishes with untouched food, it looked like the end of a party after most guests have left.

∽

After sending her mother to bed, Emma cleaned up alone, face slick with tears. Still in her gown, she carried tray after tray up the stairs to her apartment, washed the few dishes that had been used, packed away what food she could store, all along crying because what she'd wanted to celebrate with her dinner no longer existed. Instead of meeting up with all that had been safe and good in her childhood, she'd met up with the failure of her party, the failure of the house, and was moving into a state of sorrow where tears were the only expression possible for all she felt. And as the shapes of old griefs spread in her soul and pushed outward to claim their hour of tears, she felt terrified. How God awful it was to only want what wasn't yours. To be forced into lying and stealing to get what should have been yours all along.

Around her, the apartment was too quiet. Without its breath-song, the house felt dead. She stood still. Listened closely. *Nothing.* Nothing except her crying. As she brought her hands to her eyes, she grazed wet skin and remembered Caleb touching the cuts on her face like that, saying: "I didn't think you'd do that." She stared at her hands, surprised they were only wet with tears—not blood as her brother's hands had been. Wiping her palms against the sides of her mother's gown, she left her apartment and walked up the stairs to the roof. When she entered the cool housing of the elevator, she shivered. Thick dust sucked up the imprints of her shoes as she climbed the ladder to the rickety wooden platform. She picked up *Opa*'s toolbox, strained to feel the bliss she had known in this place as a child, and did feel it—for one instant—before it passed through her like the memory of an echo after its origin can no longer be determined.

All at once, and against all reason, she knew she would find *Opa*'s letters to *Oma* in his toolbox; but when she opened it, all it contained were the last few things she'd stolen for him as a girl:

two silver-plated cufflinks with onyx; half a dozen white handker-chiefs embroidered with the letter *S*; three woolen scarves; a bottle of men's cologne that was dried out except for amber residue.

She waited for the familiar hum of the house to resume—the hum of a thousand bees and *Opa*'s voice beneath that hum—but the wheels and rods and wires were rusty, motionless. As she kept her breath even and tried to breathe for the *Wasserburg* the way she had for *Opa* that last year of his life, she could finally see the house for what it was—the ghost of a house, the myth of a house. Yet, so much of her life had been formed by it. All around her, the house tightened as if to hoard the adoration it was accustomed to; and as she felt its massive walls and floors constrict, its fire barriers of cement and brick and sand, she was startled by the urge to undo its construction, to take it back nine decades and open the view it had robbed from the houses behind it, take it back to before that day when *Opa*—still a young man—had rowed a boat out on the lake and envisioned the shimmering image of the *Wasserburg*.

With the same conviction that he had wanted to build this house, Emma now wanted to burn it, stop its decay and corruption, erase from the land all evidence of it, all memory of it. But how could she burn it, knowing how well *Opa* had protected it against fire? How could she think of burning it, knowing there were others in the building? *But they'll get out long before the fire spreads to the floors below me.* She sank to the floor. Sat back on her heels. Pulled the matchbox from her dress pocket and quickly closed her fist around it to prevent herself from striking a match as if she were a woman with matches in one of her brother's films. And as she fun-neled her vision through Caleb's, *the woman holds a match against* Opa's *scarves, his monogrammed handkerchiefs. Flames, small and yellow-blue, spin a fast circle, tinge the air with their biting smell. From the town, people watch the house burn, at first lit like a can-dle, only on top, then filling out and down while tenants pour from the wide doors of the lobby as if late for the solstice dinner; while firemen run up the stairs with their hoses because their ladder truck does not extend that far; while a helicopter dips its huge bucket into the lake and empties it upon the roof and the flames that reach high into the night sky.*

All these years *Opa* had prepared for fire. He had taught her how to want. How to seize what she wanted. And yet it was Caleb who had gotten what he wanted, pulling it from within himself. *Opa* had not prepared her for that. Had not prepared her for her own greed and deception. In fearing that someone would be a danger to his house, he had suspected Tobias, had caused him harm that had become impossible to amend.

You never suspected me.

She tightened her fist around the matchbox. *Hears the Hungarian's laugh, sees* Opa *coming at her with his fury, threatening to punish her as he punished Tobias. Coming at her with his fears that burn hotter than any fire because they're fueled by loss and the knowledge of how impossible it is to keep anything safe, knowledge that it can take generations for a curse to come to fruition. And as she leans into the crescendo of flames and rage, she hears the wind sound of a fast fire.* How proud *Opa* had been that the fire inspector considered his house ten times as safe as other buildings. Suddenly she was furious at him for infecting her with his passion for the house. For preventing her from burning his house. *But I don't have to burn it.* She felt herself going limp. *I don't have to burn the house.* It came to her that she could step away from the *Wasserburg*—even though fire would be an easier way to get free of it—step away and yet retain some of what the house had given her.

The edge of *Opa*'s toolbox pressed into her hand as she pulled herself up. When she stepped out on the roof, the air smelled of rain, and a mild wind rose from the lake. Far below her spread the town and the lake. When the lightning started—a brief flicker at first—she searched the bay to make sure no boats were out there. But the water looked empty and instantly black again until a wild and sudden flicker lit up the entire rooftop, the town, so bright that Emma felt transparent. This was where she lived. This was the place she had always returned to.

All at once she had trouble breathing. Her throat felt hot, and she sat down on the low border of stones, her back to the drop beyond and the lake. Eyes blurry, she tilted her face to the sky, but the constellations were hidden by thick clouds. Beneath her fear, she felt something fragile yet vital as if—by envisioning the *Wasserburg* on fire—she had burned layers of herself down to the marrow. She bent her neck back further, bent it against the ache that blossomed into her shoulders till her face was parallel to the sky, and waited for the familiar stars to emerge and come closer, gather her up. But the sky remained dark, and for the first time ever she felt a longing to live in a place she'd never been to. A town far from here. Maybe closer to Caleb. "You will always be my sister," he had written, but she hadn't answered, had shrunk from his belief that she'd do what was just.

Just. It was not that simple. And she didn't know how to go about it. Only that she would. She thought of calling her brother, asking him how, yet—in that instant of considering the question for herself—knew it would take going back much further than the years she had owned the house, knew what she'd known instinctively as a girl: that it would mean dividing the house the way *Opa* surely must have wanted it: equally to his children. Though she felt frightened—*Where will I go? What will happen to Stefan and me?*—she could already feel herself shedding the weight of the house. And with that came the yearning for her brother.

She stood up. In her apartment she unfolded a towel, held it beneath cold water, and as she pressed it against her hot face the way her mother had taught her, every sensation in her body was pulled into her skin—*now; here*—as though countless parts of herself were rushing back into one.

She reached for the phone.

And when her brother answered, she told him who she was.